The Alexandrite

DIONE JONES

CLOUD INK

First published in 2019
Published by Cloud Ink Press Ltd, Auckland
P.O. Box 8988, Symonds Street, Auckland, 1150
www.cloudink.co.nz

ISBN 978-0-473-48330-2

Cover design and typesetting: Craig Violich (www.cvdgraphics.nz)

To those who have gone before and gave us what we have today.

"The past is never where you think you left it." – Katherine Anne Porter

Baronets, as distinct from barons, are neither members of the Peerage nor of the Knightage (whose titles are conferred by the Crown for life only). They constitute an entirely separate dignity of their own, the Baronetage.

As holders of a hereditary dignity, their place in the table of general precedence is below the sons of Lords of Appeal in Ordinary (judges who are always barons) and above Knights of the Garter.

In the past 'Bart' was the favoured abbreviation to follow the name of a baronet on an envelope, or on a list of names, and this may still be used if desired. However, 'Bt' is now more commonly used.

(explanation from www.debretts.com/expertise/essential-guide-to-the-peerage/the-baronetage)

9th Baronet – Sir Frederick Scawton Bt. 1850–1919
m Alice, succeeded on his death by
10th Baronet – Sir William Scawton Bt. 1898–1947
m Lady Henrietta Shefford
11th Baronet – Sir James Scawton Bt. 1922–1964 m Emma
12th Baronet – Sir Charles Scawton Bt. 1946–2012 m Pamela
13th Baronet – Sir Charles Scawton Bt. 1983–

Prologue

As Captain William Scawton looked out towards the jagged mountains of the North-West Frontier, he looked forward to returning to the grasslands and gentler temperatures of England. Already four months had passed since the war had ended in November 1918, and the Somersetshire Light Infantry was still stationed in India. Now at last they could be relieved by Indian regiments returning from Europe.

The evening before departure, a family of Russian émigrés arrived. Most of the fleeing White Russians, as they were called, had escaped through Ukraine or by train to the east, but some groups had arrived at the remote border post after making the arduous journey across Afghanistan. Most spoke some French and, as the duty officer, William was expected to act as translator.

He grimaced at the thought. His French had been learnt at Winchester while staring out the window trying not to listen to Monsieur Dupont. Yet over the past few years he had been surprised how often this schoolboy French had been required. Between the Russian's poor English and William's appalling French, enough of the man's story was told; accompanied by his wife and daughter, the man intended to get to Paris.

The emigré insisted he wasn't rich. He said he was a 'tailleur' by trade, which William assumed was a tailor. The man shook his head – 'tailleur de diamant'. William became confused. A 'bijoutier'? Non, non. Not a jeweller. William realised that he had something to do with the mining industry. He came from Ekaterinburg and had left when the Czar and his family had been brutally murdered there.

William arranged for this family to travel by lorry to Peshawar. From there they could get a train to Calcutta or Bombay. The man seemed incredibly grateful and obviously expected to pay. Previous arrivals had been searched, and the regiment had collected substantial treasures from these émigrés – none of them were penniless. The treasure had all been packed in trunks and sent to Vladivostok, from where the White Russian Army planned the counter-revolution. The man explained that he had used his now worthless Kerensky rubles to pay off Pashtun tribesman on the way but handed William a drawstring bag of stones. The Russian showed him several cut and uncut gems, including a larger partly-cut one, which looked like a small jagged marble. It glinted dark green, paler on the cut side.

William took the stones to the colonel, wondering how much more was secreted away, usually sewn into hems of the women's clothes. The trunks for Vladivostok had long gone. The colonel suggested that William take the bag to Peshawar and hand them in there.

After a frantic few days' travelling to Calcutta and boarding the _Morea_ for England, William was on the high seas before he remembered the jewels. He dug out the bag and opened it. What in heavens should he do now?

Most of the gems were already cut. He picked up the little marble-sized stone. Under the dim electric light of the cabin, the stone gleamed pink. He was sure it had been green before, but then he remembered the Russian had become quite emotional showing it to him, talking about how red and green were the colours of Russia. These rare stones would change colour in different lights. They were mined close to the man's home in Ekaterinburg, he had said. The gem had been named after the late Czar's grandfather.

The stone William was holding was called an alexandrite.

1

England & New Zealand 2013

The two terriers rushed through the back door yapping, but the black and white pointers waited expectantly, looking at Pamela. As soon as she reached for her jacket, they rushed out too.

'It's okay, Godley, I have all the dogs. I won't be long.'

'Very well, Lady Scawton,' came the reply. 'Breakfast will be ready by the time you get back. It's a lovely morning for a walk.'

Pamela zipped up her puffer jacket as she followed the dogs out. Three of them tore on ahead. Pebbles, one of the terriers, walked alongside. The rain had cleared, and the March air had that fresh, crisp smell. There was still an early morning chill though, and she pulled a pair of woollen gloves from her pocket as she walked.

The sun was sending rays of light through the new leaves on the beech trees. The lawns were still covered with dew and both she and the dogs left wet footprints. The snowdrops were still there, and the daffodils were beginning to bloom everywhere; those big Prince Edward ones heralded spring with deep golden-yellow trumpets.

'Pebbles, this is a lovely time of year. It's England at its best,' she told the dog beside her. The terrier looked up at her. 'And yet I feel so down, so miserable. It's more than seven months since CJ died and surely I should be over it by now. After all, CJ was Charles' father but his dying hasn't made much difference to him.' Pebbles ignored the conversation and, giving into her basic instincts, rushed off to explore.

Pamela turned to walk along the path between the beech trees. Perhaps a spell of good weather would lift her spirits. It had seemed such a long winter – a long winter alone after a long marriage. For the first few months she had forced herself to be busy, but the time had dragged. She glanced back towards the imposing house, this side still in shadow as the sun behind just caught the top of the damaged roof. There were times now when she felt very small, trapped in such a large house. Before CJ died, she had never felt like that.

The path that ran through the woods was a dedicated footpath but didn't feature on any tourist maps. Only locals knew about it. There was once an iron fence between the path and the garden but that had fallen down over the years, and now the beech trees and the path were part of the garden.

Bluebells flourished among the trees but, on the edge of the copse where some of the trees had come down in the 1987 storm, it was thick with bracken. Small oak and beech trees were beginning to regenerate but they still had a long way to go. The dogs fossicked in this undergrowth for rabbits and the occasional stoat. Bentley, standing on the path itself, seemed to be on to something. The handsome pointer stood still, his front leg lifted and his tail straight out as he indicated something among the bracken. Was it a bird's nest? Pointers preferred birds to rabbits. His tail moved and he took a step forward and barked. That was unlike him and it attracted the other three dogs. The two Jack Russells rushed up together. The other pointer stood further away, watching. She preferred to wait until the bird took off, and then follow in a mad gallop as though she might catch it. This wasn't a bird – a pheasant would have flown by now. Pamela half expected a hare to jump up instead but nothing stirred. She walked up to where Bentley was standing. The terriers didn't seem to want to go any closer. It wasn't like them at all.

Partly hidden in the bracken, she saw a black sack with waterproof covering. She crept up slowly, in case it moved. Then she saw it was trousered legs sticking out from beneath a dark raincoat. Pamela's heart lurched. It was a man, quite a tall one, not moving. She called the dogs off although they hadn't moved and even the terriers didn't seem to want to go any closer. They looked at her for orders. She approached the prostrate figure, expecting, willing it to move. The raincoat was wet with dew and the cord trousers looked damp. His shoes seemed clean though. Pamela could only see part of an ashen face. The rest was covered by his dark hat, which was askew. She bent down and barely touched his outstretched hand. It was icy cold. She wondered whether she should check his pulse but the part of the face she could see was bloodless. She had last seen that lifeless skin on CJ.

For a second she felt her chest tighten and placed a hand there, staring at the figure but seeing instead a vision of CJ as she had found him, inanimate and cold. She heard her breath rush out, and still half crouched, she stayed frozen for a second. Then, standing slowly upright, she looked around in case someone was there. But no, there was just silence and stillness. She peered again at what she could see of the man's face before taking in a deep breath. Realising that not even the dogs had moved, she turned to hurry back to the house, calling the dogs as she did so. The terriers were reluctant to leave but picked up on the insistence in her voice and turned to follow. She hurried across the lawn and stomped in the back door, without even stopping to close it. She yelled for Godley.

'Godley. Godley. Oh, there you are. I think you'd better phone the police. There's a body in the garden.'

✶ ✶ ✶ ✶ ✶

It was already late afternoon in Villefranche. A siesta had seemed a good idea and Charles was smiling as he left Joanna lying naked on the bed reading the news on her computer tablet. He still couldn't get used to people staring at small screens all day even though he found his mobile phone indispensable. As he started down the marble steps, Joanna called to him.

'Charles, come and see this. Ashly House is where you live isn't it?' He stopped and debated with himself whether to continue fetching a couple of glasses of wine. Perhaps he should return and get dressed. He shouldn't appear in his dressing gown when his friends arrived.

'What's the problem?' he asked, checking the pocket of his dressing gown in vain for a packet of cigarettes.

'Your mother's been finding dead bodies, it says. Or I assume this is your mother.'

'What? Let me see.'

Charles scanned the news on the screen. *Body found in grounds of stately home . . . Ashly . . . unidentified . . . discovered by Lady Scawton herself . . . an early morning walk with her dogs . . . butler called the police . . . checking for missing persons . . .*

Ashly House was hardly a *stately home* and *the butler* made it sound as though there were hundreds of servants. There was only Godley and the cook. Why hadn't his mother rung? He wondered whether he should phone her. He glanced at his watch, 4.30pm here in France, 3.30pm in England; she'd probably be out.

'Frightfully *Downton Abbey*,' Joanna commented from the bathroom door, 'making the butler call the police.'

The article said the body was unidentified.

As though on cue, his phone rang from on top of the chest of drawers. He went over and answered it.

'Mother,' he started, 'I've just this minute read about this body. Are you all right?'

'I have been trying to phone you all day. Gave us a dreadful shock, Charles. The dogs didn't like it at all. Up in the beech trees beyond the flower beds. Only just off the public pathway. Goodness knows where he was going.'

'Had he been dead long? Who was it?'

'They don't know. The police phoned just now. They haven't identified him, but they found a small package on him addressed to you. The detective said they're checking the package, and the letter with it for some clue to his identity. He wants to know when you are going to be here so you can see it.'

'Good God! Surely it's not someone I know! In the woods! What did the man look like?'

'Darling, I don't know. Godley helped the police and said it was no one he recognised. An older man. There was no blood or anything. Godley thought he looked a bit of a tramp at first but he was clean-shaven with a raincoat and good shoes. The police have been around the woods all day stringing up that tape stuff. They seemed worried I'm in the house by myself at night.'

'You could stay with the Williamses or something, I suppose.'

'I've spoken to Di but she has Mike back from New Zealand for Easter. Ginny is still over there, and Mike is only back for a week. So they don't want me there, panicking because I found a body. Anyway, I'm not alone. I've four guard dogs.'

'The terriers are hardly guard dogs, Mother, or the pointers. Perhaps you should get a rottweiler or something. But what about this letter? Can't you deal with it?'

'Evidently not. It's got to be you. Hopefully someone will report the man missing and find he just had a heart attack. The detective is coming round again tomorrow. Nice young man . . . '

* * * * *

When Ginny stepped out of the shower she had to hurry to answer the mobile.

'Hello, Ginny, is that you?'

'Hi, Mum. Of course it's me.'

'What time is it in New Zealand? I can never work out the time difference.'

'It's morning and a good time to phone. Is everything all right?'

Ginny glanced out of the window at the clear, brightening sky over the big paddock, remembering that it would be evening in the UK. With her shoulder holding her mobile in place, she wrapped her towel tight and tucked it in on itself. Then she bunched her hair at the back and let it spread over her shoulders onto the towel as she leant against the window sill. She missed her mother's chatting; she missed home. The voice she was listening to now was so familiar.

'We're all fine here. It's wonderful to have Mike back for a bit. But I thought you'd like to hear about your godmother. She's been on the telly. She found a body in the garden. A dead body.'

'Aunt Pamela? Oh no. At Ashly? Whereabouts?'

'She had Godley phone the police, so he was on the telly too.'

'Poor Aunt P. How awful! Was it murder?'

'They're treating it like it might be although she said the police thought not. They've had newspaper reporters phoning and television people wanting to take photos of the place. They had to lock the gates and, fortunately, the police blocked off the public path, otherwise they would've had people all over the garden. Pamela says there were no marks, not even any blood. The police won't know what he died of for a couple of days. Evidently checking for poison takes longer.'

'Who was he? And where was the body?'

'"Unidentified" as they say. Pamela says it was an older man. He was just off the public pathway. You can imagine the village – there'll be talk of nothing else.'

'So he may have just been out for a walk?'

'I doubt it. They didn't mention it on the telly but I've just spoken to Pamela again; she said he had a package on him, addressed to Charles. Of course, Charles isn't there – he's never home. He's in the South of France at the moment.'

'Ah, the plot thickens. Probably some disgruntled father. Or a drug dealer.'

'I'm sure it wouldn't be. Charles wouldn't be like that.'

'Oh, Mum, you know he's a prat of the first order. He'll probably fly back so he can stand beside his mother and have his photo in the paper. Sir Charles. God, I can't imagine what I saw in him. When's he coming back?'

'I don't know. I'll ring Pamela again tomorrow. Now, how's everything else? How are the horses?'

'The horses are fine. I have all four hunters to ride today but they're all pretty quiet.'

'Don't the people you work for help ride them?' Ginny could hear the worry in her mother's voice.

'Usually they do, just not today. It's all right, Mum, I'm not overdoing it; I've worked here all summer. Now the hunting's started, the horses don't need much work.' When Ginny had first come to look after the horses here, she had worked only part-time. She lived in this flat in the barn and could creep off each afternoon for a sleep. Now she had more energy and could work a whole day if necessary.

'I know. Mike says you're almost back to normal. I just worry.'

'You don't have to, Mum.'

* * * * *

The next morning, the phone rang continually. Pamela seemed to waste endless time explaining to insistent reporters that, no, they hadn't recognised the man and no, there was no news. The phone hadn't been this busy since CJ's death – when Charles had become the new Sir Charles.

The police had been very efficient and after initial questioning had restricted themselves to the trees, taping off the entrance to the path, and insisting they lock the front gates. Pamela was surprised the gates even worked. They hadn't been shut for years.

She placed the phone back in the wall bracket in the back corridor and walked into the kitchen.

'Godley, that was a different police officer.'

The Ashly kitchen was noticeably warmer than the corridor. Pebbles was sitting at the door; she knew dogs were not allowed in the kitchen. The other three were in their beds lined up under the telephone shelf, but Pebbles was hoping Godley would change the rules for her. She would have dearly loved to lie against the warm Aga.

There was a substantial scrubbed wooden table in the middle of the kitchen. The tray sitting on it had a small dish of butter and a breadboard with a fresh loaf of bread. Godley was heating something on the stove, and Pamela could see that the small dining table in the adjoining room was already set for lunch.

'The policeman's insistent that Charles looks at this package. He won't let me do it. Something to do with privacy. Totally unreasonable.'

Godley moved the pot off the hot element and turned to give Lady Scawton his full attention. 'I see the papers are full of it all. *Unidentified . . . may have some connection to the family . . .* that kind of thing.'

'The police say that the only link they have to his identity is this package addressed to Charles and the letter inside. The man had money on him but no wallet. Only Charles can deal with the package – I told them he's away for a fortnight.'

'Did they say how the man died?'

'They speak just like they do on telly. Their early enquiries do not reveal foul play, but they're waiting for forensic reports. At this stage their main concern is his identity and maybe Charles knows him.'

'Well, Ma'am, could Sir Charles come home just for the day? It's only Nice and he probably has a car at Luton.'

'Good idea, Godley. It's an unnecessary expense but perhaps he should.'

Godley went into the passage and, picking up the handpiece, checked the green file beside the telephone. He dialled the number and asked for Sir Charles. There was a pause.

'Please wait,' he said slowly and brought the handpiece to Pamela.

'They're speaking French.'

She took the phone and listened. 'Allo . . . Oh, pardon. Il doit être frustrant. Je suis tellement désolé.' Pamela replaced the phone. 'Was it the mobile number you tried?'

Godley dialled again. 'Good morning, Sir Charles. I have your mother.'

Pamela took the handpiece and pushed her hair back behind her ear with her other hand.

'Is that you, Mother? What's the latest? My phone has been flat out all morning.'

Charles sounded strange. Was it a bad line, or was he drunk? At midday?

'I'm sorry, Charles. The police are insisting you look at this package they found. They need some clues. I wondered if you could possibly come home, just for the day . . . No, the police won't allow me to . . . I know, I'm sorry. Oh, darling, that would be such a help. I hate to disturb your holiday.'

As she put the phone down, Pamela sent out a small puff of breath as she realised that was one problem solved.

'He says he'll try and get back here tomorrow just for a few hours,' she told Godley. 'There's an early flight and he'll phone to confirm. He isn't pleased, but I really can't help it.'

'You do have your solicitor for lunch tomorrow, Ma'am.' Godley was pouring tomato soup into a bowl on the tray as he spoke.

'Oh, dear. Charles won't want that. Patrick's coming to look at the leaking roof and discuss money – or the lack of it. I'd better put him off.'

'Weren't you wanting Sir Charles to become more involved with the house?'

Pamela looked at Godley for a moment and pursed her lips. She returned to the warmth of the Aga, leaning with her back to the rail.

She felt so undecided. For years she had organised the household, the garden, even the farm – everything in CJ's life before he died. Then, she always knew exactly what to do; now she seemed unable to organise anything.

Before he died, her life had centred around CJ. He hadn't been ill until the last month, but for years he had complained if she went anywhere and would harp on that her duty was to be there with him. It had really been easier to stay around home. He'd have those ghastly nightmares. Although they hadn't slept in the same room for years, she knew when they occurred. They would affect him for days afterwards and make him more cantankerous than ever. His cranky nature had long put off casual visitors. She would take him for drives and listen while he pointed out that the town was too busy or the countryside deteriorating. She sensed that she was deteriorating too.

She remembered how guilty she'd felt at the funeral – not about his death. The doctor had reassured her that it wasn't her fault. It was just relief.

Yet somehow, months later, she felt as stuck here as ever. Surely she should feel free but she didn't at all. Life just drifted on as she responded to whatever happened – dead bodies in the garden, the roof needing to be repaired or the Batchelor boys asking for a farm stall to sell the vegetables they grew in the walled garden.

Godley had fetched something from the larder.

'Yes, you're right Godley, as usual,' she said as he came back. 'The house and everything else does belong to Charles now. Patrick is a lawyer and if the letter is something...' She sighed. 'It's just that Charles is never here to do anything. Since CJ's death...'

Decisions were needed. She used to be exasperated when CJ gave her instructions she didn't need, yet here she was, wishing his son were concerned enough to make a few decisions so that she didn't have to.

Godley smiled sympathetically. 'I know, Ma'am. We did hope that with his father's passing Sir Charles would become ... more involved.' Godley hesitated. 'Indeed, he was fine last time he was here.'

Pamela looked at Godley. They both knew Charles was rarely at Ashly House, and when he was, he just took everything for granted. He refused to listen to Pamela complaining there was not enough money to maintain the place.

'Charles should get married,' she suggested. 'That would settle him down and make him concentrate on his affairs. Someone like Ginny would have been fine.'

'I doubt that would have worked, Ma'am,' Godley said.

'No. I know,' agreed Pamela, 'and it would help if his wife had money. Or perhaps if she were an accountant. Of course, CJ wanted him to marry Lizzie Shefford. "Bound to be a good breeder", he would insist.' She smiled to herself.

Lizzie was the daughter of Lord Shefford, second cousins and a family with large estates in the next county and a seat in the House of Lords. But Lady Elizabeth turned out to be a 14-stone heavyweight – a 'throwback', CJ insisted. She was married now, and it was she who ran the farm shop at Shefford Place. Pamela had arranged to go there and see what was involved in setting up something like it at Ashly. Oh no, when was she meant to go? Had she missed it, with all the drama of the body? No, she was due to go to lunch there on Friday, at the end of the week, and was looking forward to it.

Both Pamela and Godley knew that Lizzie would never have been to the taste of the present Sir Charles, who preferred the sleek, usually blonde, London society girls. The last one was called Antonia. Such a pretty name, except Charles had called her Ant all weekend.

* * * * *

Charles got into the driving seat of the hired Peugeot. It was still barely light. As he drove through the open wrought-iron gates of the villa, Joanna was already chatting about collecting him that night.

'Will you be back in time for dinner? We're due to meet the others at that fish restaurant on the front. That *loup de mer* was excellent the other day. What do they call it in English?'

'Bass.'

They were driving down the hill through Villefranche's narrow, stone-walled streets. The water in the bay was glassy and still. The streets were almost empty, with just the boulangerie open.

'How's your mother doing, apart from the body?' Joanna asked.

'Fussing. Hence why I'm going back for the day.'

'Hmmm. She did lose her husband barely six months ago, lives in a great big house by herself and now has the shock of finding a body in the garden. It's not surprising.'

Charles knew Joanna was right. He supposed he should've gone back yesterday.

'Maybe.' It was too early in the morning for a deep discussion.

'She'd be lonely after your father died,' Joanna continued.

'I thought she'd be relieved. He was totally unreasonable. I was able to move out years ago but of course she couldn't. Yet now I realise that she probably didn't want to. She can't think for herself. She likes to be told what to do.'

'The house and estate are yours, aren't they?'

'Yes, but it's all in trusts and there's probate and all that. Basically I pay for Mother to live there. I mean, she has to live somewhere. She does nothing.' He sighed. 'When Father was alive, he wilfully restricted the amount of money I spent. Now the trustees and Mother are just as bad. Without a patron I wouldn't even be able to play polo. Yet I bet the trustees get paid before I do. One of them will be there today, no doubt telling me there isn't enough money for the new roof.'

'Can't you sell the house? Put your mother in a flat in London or something? Or in a cottage in Sussex?'

'Evidently the house is entailed. We can't even sell the farm until Father's estate is sorted, and they say that could take a year or more.'

'Well, thank goodness you earn something playing polo.'

Charles didn't answer. At the moment he was earning nothing. His patron from last season, a Russian count, was off-air; the season was about to start and nothing was finalised. His horses were meant to be in work at Cowdray by now, not languishing in their winter quarters at Ashly.

They were already at the airport, and Charles pulled up in front of the terminal. Rather than get out, Joanna climbed over to the driving seat as Charles stood on the pavement, checking his pockets and wondering whether he had everything he needed. Charles leant down to kiss her.

'See you tonight.' Instead of a quick kiss on the cheek, he took her chin and kissed her on the lips. As he did so, his hand went down to her thigh and the shorts she was wearing, but Joanna had anticipated and pulled back.

'The sign up there says 'Kiss and Fly'. In English. So fly.' Her smile was very forgiving. 'Good luck with the trustee.'

* * * * *

After viewing the damaged roof from the garden, Pamela led the solicitor back into the house. She had loaned him CJ's old Barbour to keep warm over his neat London suit and she took off her own jacket as well and hung them both on the hooks. As they walked together along the corridor from the back door, Godley appeared from the kitchen with a tea towel in his hand.

'I've stoked up the fire in the study, Lady Scawton. It's warmer in there.'

'Thank you, Godley. Charles should be here soon.'

The two terriers began to bark.

'Oh, that might be him now. Or the policeman.' She glanced out of the window that overlooked the drive. 'No, it's Charles.'

Instead of turning into the study, Pamela opened the door which led to the huge flagstone hall. The solicitor followed her, both of them shivering as they felt the drop in temperature. The solicitor aimed for the large log fire blazing in the hearth while Pamela went and opened the big wooden front door, letting in another blast of cold air. She quickly closed the door behind Charles as he headed to the fire too.

'Hello, darling, did you have a good flight?'

'Bloody cramped seats, but at least it was on time. One advantage of Mr EasyJet living in Nice. He wants to get to lunch on time. Hello Patrick, good to see you. Christ, it's cold in here. When did Godley light the fire – ten minutes ago?' Charles shook the solicitor's hand as they all went through the door to the warmer study.

When the house was built, this smaller room would have been part of the servants' quarters, perhaps the staff dining room or the butler's pantry. The family would rarely have been in here. After the war, in the late 1940s, the then-baronet – Charles' grandfather, James – had made alterations to the house to allow for fewer servants and had made this a cosy sitting room. Now heating the reception rooms in the main part of the house had become impractical and expensive, and Pamela found it more convenient to shut off that part of the house for most of the time. She just used this study and the kitchen and small dining room – the nursery dining room they called it.

This study was small compared to the front rooms: the great panelled dining room, the spacious sitting room, the library only slightly smaller and further down the house, the ballroom. But this was Pamela's favourite room, with its white-painted bookshelves down one wall and her Victorian writing desk in the corner. A computer sat on the table in the corner and old magazines were piled high on the coffee table in front of the large, soft sofa. The spring sun flooded in, belying the temperature outside.

Charles went straight for the fire and immediately stood with his back to it. 'March and it's still freezing. Will we ever get a polo season?'

'I was about to ask when the season starts,' said Patrick, taking a seat in an upright chair beside the table. His briefcase was on the floor beside him.

Before Charles could reply, Godley appeared at the door, bringing a young police officer with him.

'Charles,' Pamela said, 'this is the officer who has the letter.' She turned to the policeman. 'Good afternoon.'

Godley went out and closed the door as Charles took over.

'Now, I gather you want me to open some package. Mother told me about it.'

'Thank you, Sir Charles. You've come back from France, I understand. I apologise for the inconvenience.' The plain-clothed policeman seemed unsure of himself. 'As of an hour ago, we do seem to have a lead on who the deceased is, Sir, but perhaps you will recognise him.' He handed Charles a photograph.

As Charles looked at it, Pamela saw him wrinkle up his face. 'Oh, God, no. He looks really dead doesn't he? No, I've never seen him before.' He handed the photograph back as though it were contaminated. 'Who is he?'

'He has yet to be officially identified.' The policeman deflected Charles' question by producing a small package. 'Forensics have checked this. That's why it's unsealed. We can still only presume he was coming to deliver the package and are hoping you may shed light.' He handed a lumpy envelope to Charles.

'Your tent is still up around where he was found,' Pamela reminded him.

Simultaneously, Patrick asked, 'So no foul play?'

The policeman answered the solicitor, obviously assessing him as a professional and warming to him. 'At this stage it looks like natural causes, probably a brain aneurysm. We hope to confirm tomorrow.' He paused, turning back to Charles. 'Once you've read it, perhaps you could keep the papers in this folder; just until we confirm the cause of death.' He produced a clear polythene folder.

Charles looked at the package, turning it over. The other three watched in silence.

The white envelope was a thick doubled-over A4 size envelope. Just the name *Sir Charles Scawton* – no address – was written in copperplate handwriting on the envelope. They watched in silence as Charles unfolded it to its full size. The envelope wasn't sealed and Charles shook it slightly until he found the open edge.

A small tissue-wrapped package fell into his hand as Charles pulled the papers out. He held the package out to Pamela who glanced at the policeman and waited for his nod before taking it. The letter looked creased, and had a note pinned to it. The smaller-sized note was in a strong, clear hand and easy to read. Charles held the papers flat and read the note out.

Professor Cook, Victoria University

'Where's Victoria University?' asked Charles, looking up and breaking the tension.

'Isn't Manchester Victoria University?' answered Patrick.

'Well, that must be a clue for you, Sergeant.' Pamela was standing beside Charles, watching as he continued reading.

Beth's letter – this is as far as she got before she died but she made me promise to send it to you. She said she was looking forward to you delivering the stone to the Scawtons and telling them the whole story or warning them, as the case may be. It all sounds most mysterious.

Have a good trip.

Good luck,
Diane

'Oh no, warn us about what?' Pamela said, looking up as she unwrapped the tissue paper. 'This is odd. It's a sort of green pebble. It's pretty rough, except the end is smooth.' She turned it in her hand. 'And you can see right through it. It looks like a half-cut gem of some kind.'

'Just wait, Mother, I'll read the letter.' They could all see the writing on the crinkled paper was a spidery hand-written script. Charles walked over to the table where Patrick was sitting in the upright chair. Charles spread the letter onto the table.

'This is hard going.' Charles was leaning over the table, squinting at the writing. He picked the letter up as he began to read.

Dear Sir Charles

We have never met and now that is unlikely, although your family and mine are so entwined.

This stone was given to my mother by the Scawton family. She only told me the secret when she was older and made me promise to seek the satisfaction she had failed to get. It was her dying wish that someone should confront your family. At first we did not know whether the story were even true, until we found proof.

The adoption laws in this country have been changed so I suppose . . .

He paused, allowing Pamela to ask, 'Oh dear, what on earth is that about? And where did this stone come from? Go on.'

There was silence. They could hear the logs crackling in the fire. Then Charles stood up straight and looked over at his mother.

'Nothing more,' answered Charles. 'Look for yourself. That's all there is.'

2

England 1919

Halfway down the wide staircase, the Dowager Lady Scawton stopped and looked at the portrait of her husband. It had been painted before the war. The artist, Fuchs, was the foremost portrait painter in London and had even painted Queen Victoria. She remembered the endless sittings had tested Freddie's patience but the Austrian had portrayed Freddie in exactly the right pose, with Jess, the spaniel, sitting at his feet looking up at him.

Jess had gone years before but Freddie's death was only a few months ago. How she wished he were here now! For a moment, Lady Scawton clasped her hands together and then touched the pearl brooch at her neck, before smoothing down her ankle-length skirt and lifting it an inch to continue on down the stairs without tripping. She turned towards the morning room. She had arranged to meet William although earlier she had seen him disappear across the lawn towards the stables. Thank heavens William had returned from India before Freddie's death and was of the same energetic nature as his father; and thank heavens he had not been affected by the war in the same way as his younger brother Edward.

Since inheriting not only the title and the house but the 5000-acre estate as well, William had been extremely busy trying to acquaint himself with the running of it. Before and even during the war, she and Freddie had assumed Edward would help administer the farms. Before he enlisted, Edward had spent time with John Brown, the estate manager, and had known all the tenant farmers and their foibles. Now, of course, that kind of work for Edward was out of the question. The shadow of the boy who had returned from the war had been no help to his father and was now such a burden to his brother.

Much to her surprise, William was already in the morning room, sitting in Freddie's high-wing chair and reading *The Times*. A near-full whisky glass was on the table beside that odd half-cut stone William had taken to carrying around with him.

'Good morning, Mama.' He folded the newspaper and stood up. 'They seem to think the flu epidemic is coming to an end at last. May I pour you a sherry?'

The flu epidemic had affected everyone. Only recently, an elderly cousin had died and the kitchen maid, Aggie, had lost her mother.

'Thank you, William, a sherry would be pleasant. The dry one. I thought you took all those Indian stones to be made up into necklaces?' She indicated to the rough gem, still sitting beside William's chair. He glanced at it as he walked towards the table and the sherry decanter.

'I did. I think I told you, the jeweller is going to make a necklace and a tiara with the other stones. I kept this one though. I quite like it as it is. I don't know why.' He handed his mother a small sherry glass and then picked up the uneven stone, rolling it in his hand.

'It's probably flawed,' his mother said. 'That would be why they never finished cutting it.'

'I like the way it changes colour. I suppose it reminds me of the trouble those Russians had, grabbing their half-cut jewels and fleeing right across Afghanistan – and how everything has changed so in the last few years.'

'I'm not surprised the man wanted to give you something. From what you used to tell us, if the British Army had not been keeping the peace on the North-West Frontier, those people would never have reached the border.'

'No, well . . . ' William knew he should never have kept the gems. He had missed handing them in at Peshawar. By the time he found them, there seemed no other course than to keep them. He slipped the stone into his pocket.

'William, you wanted to discuss Edward, I think.'

'Yes, Mother. I do,' he said, turning back to her with a puckered brow.

In 1914, there had never been any doubt that William would enlist. It was war and they were British. Despite his father wanting him to join a Guards regiment, William had been determined to join some of his Winchester friends in the Somersetshire Light Infantry. After a long training period, they were sent overseas. There was talk that they would be sent to the Dardanelles or perhaps Mesopotamia where the British already had successes at Amara and Shaiba. Instead they were shipped to India. Even though Afghan tribes were threatening the North-Western Frontier, it seemed a long way from the main theatre of war.

Many months later, they finally embarked back to Suez and Egypt to fight the 'bleedin' Turk' as the men called them. There, the reality of war became apparent. The heat was unbearable, the equipment poor, disease rife and Gaza seemed an impregnable fortress. When the Anzac mounted troops appeared, William realised his mistake of choosing to fight in the PBI – the Poor Bloody Infantry. A cavalry officer at least had a horse. In one of the battles, a Winchester friend was killed right beside him. Such incredibly bad luck. William escaped with a leg wound. After an uncomfortable time in field hospitals, he was shipped out. He expected to be sent to Egypt but his division has been broken up and he found himself back in Bombay. So, as it turned out, he was back making do with border skirmishes on the frontier, while the main centre of the fighting was everywhere else and, by now, mainly in France.

The family expected Edward to miss the war altogether, but of course it had dragged on. Edward had enlisted as soon as he was 18. To the relief of his father he joined a proper regiment – the Life Guards, or the Guards Machine Gun Regiment, as it became. Edward's battlefield was France. William knew now that the letters from home had not conveyed the difficulties there. He knew it was mud instead of heat and he could imagine the same exhaustion, the dirt, the same endless waiting that he had known in the Middle East, followed by the adrenalin rush of the attack as orders were taken, orders given. What the letters had not conveyed but which the stories and pictures he had seen since did, was the incredible devastation. And not just on the French and Belgium countryside.

The fighting in France had such a huge effect on everyone. Britain won the war but when William came back, after nearly four years away, he found a different country. London looked dirty and grey; Ashly looked smaller than he remembered and rather parochial. People talked about the war as though it was only ever fought in France. There was little mention of Turkey, or Gaza and the Middle East, let alone India. William hadn't even seen a German soldier. Had he been fighting a different war? No villager seemed grateful that he had been defending the far end of the realm.

People no longer had the same respect for Britain or its leaders either. Even his generation, the ones who would inherit this new world, appeared to have an insolent air. Britain seemed less united, not more. The labour unions had become much more active; even the police had been on strike and there were divisions over whether women should have the vote.

But the biggest difference was in Edward. William was aghast when he found his brother so changed, so broken. He had seen people coping with their injuries with great fortitude, a lost limb or obvious pain, but he had also known fellows who weren't able to cope. In Basra one young chap, who had earlier been at Gallipoli, came into the officers' mess, ranting and shaking uncontrollably, and then disappeared outside where he shot himself dead. Surely Edward wasn't one of those?

When he arrived back, his father had discussed how he tried to find jobs for those who had worked for them before the war and had now returned debilitated. It was costing the estate and it was often unpopular with the women who had worked diligently on the farms during the war, but his father insisted it was essential and William agreed. Allowances had to be made for those who had been injured.

Making allowances didn't seem to help Edward. According to his parents he had no physical injury. But he was so altered. William remembered that he had been so jealous when Edward, as a tall gangly 14-year-old boy, had won the point to point on Cristobel – the youngest winning rider ever. He had been a brave, modest, smiling fellow before the war. Now he was a limping, irascible, unpredictable, damaged man. In spite of William promising his father he wouldn't discuss the war with Edward, William tried to engage him in conversation, thinking it might help but Edward's mind seemed to drift elsewhere. When William suggested he ride a horse, 'Can't do it, old boy', was the reply of a defeated old man not a 20-year-old. Dr White called it neurasthenia. Everyone else called it shell shock. At William's insistence, Edward had been sent for hypnosis treatment in London, but had returned after a few days and it was doubtful that the treatment would have worked anyway.

It was when William became engaged to Henrietta that things came to a head. Henrietta was only sixteen and was terrified of Edward, both of his looks and his volatility. Her father had made it quite clear that his young daughter could not be expected to preside over a household where the war could never be mentioned or the house revolved around what he called a madman. As Henrietta's father was Lord Shefford, his opinion was paramount. William knew the engagement would be a social boost for the family's future, especially now his father had died. He had agreed with the principle of Edward living somewhere else, but Edward was still his brother and Ashly his home. He had suggested Edward move to London but this idea had fallen on deaf ears. Edward had never been a city person.

Surprisingly, Edward had agreed to emigrate to the colonies.

William still thought this rather extreme but perhaps an extended trip or even a few years abroad would be the solution. To his astonishment, his mother also thought it a perfect solution but William was still uncertain how Edward would cope. He had made the arrangements and now explained them to his mother.

'I have booked a passage for him on the *Remuera*, but I wanted to ascertain that you are quite happy that he goes to New Zealand. It is about as far as he can go.' His mother glanced for a moment towards the large windows that looked out towards the drive. William followed her gaze. It was a grey day.

'We have to do something, William, now that you are engaged to Henrietta. I agree totally with Lord Shefford. It would not be fair on her. The rest of us are able to suffer his afflictions, his limp when he has no leg injury and the ghastly tic which disfigures his face so, if it were not that his behaviour is so erratic. He never looks happy, he argues with everyone, just as he did with his father . . . ' She paused.

William knew she was remembering Edward's last argument with their father. 'I know you blame him for Father's death but a heated discourse over whether the glorious victory the vicar mentioned in his sermon was indeed glorious is hardly evidence of murder. Father did die of a heart attack.'

'William, the war ended nearly a year ago. Edward came home like this; nothing has changed. Before you came back, he destroyed his bedroom furniture. Twice. That's why we moved him to the nursery wing. Dr White suggested peace and quiet would help but his behaviour has not improved one iota. We creep around, not mentioning the war in case he descends into a fit. He imbibes to excess every night. No, Lord Shefford is right. We cannot live like this, not any longer. We have all been affected by the war but everyone else has pulled themselves together and moved on.'

'We could try some more treatment, send him up to Scotland to the man Dr White suggested.'

'And have him return here a week later, as he did when you sent him to the clinic in London, refusing to stay there because they were all mad? No, William. He is happy to go abroad, you know he is, and it is the desirable outcome. I am disappointed that he didn't choose Rhodesia where we have friends, but he does seem quite positive about New Zealand.'

William was annoyed that Edward had chosen New Zealand. When William had returned from India he found his father had employed a New Zealand groom to break in some young horses. William disliked the man. He had that impudent air of many Antipodean colonials and looked untrustworthy. William had no proof that the man was homosexual but he was far too familiar with Edward and William suspected he was trying to entrap him. Even though William had insisted on the man's dismissal, he suspected it was the groom who had attracted Edward to a New Zealand lifestyle.

'We just need to find a man to go with him and look after him,' his mother continued.

'That is the problem, Mother. We have advertised and cannot find anyone. The New Zealand government arranges a free passage for men who want to go there. The passengers don't need to be responsible for anyone else. Edward himself . . .' William frowned, unsure of how to go on. They were both standing either side of the fireplace. William leant down, picked up a log and added it to the half-burnt ones on the fire.

'Yes?' his mother prompted.

'The only one he would consider going with would be Mary.'

'Mary? The maid? The one who looks after his room?' Lady Scawton suddenly became incensed. 'I knew I should not have allowed that. We failed to find a valet for him after the war and he takes so much more looking after. When we moved him to the nursery wing, Mrs Howard assured us that Mary had experience looking after unruly patients in the hospitals. Now I suppose she has taken advantage. She must go at once.'

'Wait, Mama. He's going to need some kind of nurse. I pointed out to Edward that single women were housed away from other passengers on the boat and taking Mary would not work. So he proposed to her.'

'Proposed? Proposed marriage? Is she pregnant?'

'That's not possible.' William said too quickly. He hesitated. Edward himself had confessed his lack of erection but this was not a subject William wished to discuss with his mother. Yet now he was going to have to explain. 'I don't suppose you know. Edward is unable to ... He told me months ago. Part of his problem is that he cannot ... fulfil any husbandly duties.'

'Oh no.' She sat down in one of the wing chairs beside the fireplace and began to fan her face. William remained where he was; his mother would not want him to fuss over her.

'You mean he could be one of those ... woolly woofter people?' she asked.

William was quick to correct her. 'No, no, no. Edward isn't queer in that way, don't worry." He tried to sound convincing, although the incident that had incited the dismissal of the groom had involved the man embracing Edward, and William had never been too sure whether Edward hadn't responded inappropriately. At the back of his mind, he did fear the wretched shell shock might have turned his brother, but he couldn't bear his mother to think on that.

He explained further. 'He just can't, er, you know, jig-a-jig. I have discussed it with Doctor White and he confirmed that it is not unusual among soldiers with Edward's problems. Much as, theoretically, they can father children, if they cannot have an erection, their wife will not bear their child. That is why I doubt anything improper has been going on with Mary.'

His mother looked at him sharply. She was trying to steady her breathing, holding a hand to her chest. William knew he looked embarrassed by the conversation and no wonder.

She was listening carefully as he spoke. 'He must have someone, and would he find a wife anywhere else?'

She was recovering now and pursed her lips, cogitating. 'William, you are about to marry an Earl's daughter. It would be totally unsuitable for your brother to marry a maid, even without children. Edward is your brother and she is common. What would everyone think?'

'They needn't know. Mother, I want him to be looked after. I gather New Zealand is extremely unsophisticated and probably no one would even notice that she was inferior. They could marry on the boat or on the way to the dock. I know she is uneducated and doesn't speak properly but if Edward likes her ... no one would know.' He paused. 'There is only one problem.'

'And what is that?'

'Mary declined to marry him.'

His mother sat in a stunned silence for several minutes while William carried on. 'I know, it's a turn-up for the books. She felt he was too far above her.'

Lady Scawton remained silent. Since the war, everything was so topsy-turvy. Getting domestic staff – and men in particular – was proving so impossible. They had to use some of the maids to serve at table. Now William was proposing Edward marry one of them. And she had declined him! Only a few days ago, she had passed a tractor being driven by a girl who was wearing unbecoming men's overalls. Had the girl forgotten the war was over? Dressed in men's clothes and no doubt promiscuous with it.

William eventually spoke. 'Are you sure he should still go? Is there not any alternative? He is your son and my brother. And he isn't as bad as Crazy Joe in the village.'

'Indeed he isn't, William. That boy should be in an asylum. And yes, Edward does have to go somewhere where the chief topic of conversation is not the war. As well you know, if Lord Shefford is going to allow you to marry his daughter. Besides, you say he is happy to go.' His mother put her hands together in front of her chest and, after a few moments, carried on. 'No, I think it might be the answer after all.

Of course Mary will marry him. I know from the housekeeper that she is completely estranged from her father after he remarried before her mother was cold in the ground. She has nothing here and she is very supportive of Edward.'

She was remembering the ghastly scene that had prompted all this. William had arranged a shoot, the first engagement they had hosted since Freddie's death. Long mourning periods had become impossible since the war, when death had become so commonplace. A small shoot seemed a good way to inch back into society and for Lord Shefford to announce his approval of William's engagement to Henrietta. At the start of the day they all assembled in the hall, Lord Shefford among them. As they were getting ready to leave, someone outside accidentally let off a gun. The next thing Edward, who had refused to partake in the shoot at all, had appeared at the top of the stairs ranting out of his mind and totally naked. She still almost fainted just thinking of it. At the time, she had tried to hurry the ladies back into the morning room. Henrietta was only sixteen after all and, of course, Lady Shefford was there too but she did remember it was Mary who had appeared from nowhere and guided Edward back to his room.

'Perhaps it could work. She's a good maid. Why don't I speak to her? If you are sure about the children.'

∗ ∗ ∗ ∗ ∗

Lady Scawton was pleasantly surprised by Mary when she came to the morning room for a little talk. The girl was not unattractive. She seemed quite confident and very loyal to Edward. Mary implied that she had no real desire to travel but agreed that Edward could not go alone. Her reasons for refusing to marry him really did seem to be, as William had intimated, purely one of social standing. Lady Scawton was well aware that socially it would do Edward no good at all to have a wife who could not pronounce her 'h's, but he needed someone to accompany him.

She was surprised the girl had not found a husband. Mary told her that there was a man she had nursed during the war, of whom she had been fond. On his recovery, he had disappeared, presumed killed. Not an unusual story alas. Mary was now twenty-three.

'At your age, Mary, let us be frank. You are unlikely to find another man. There are plenty of girls younger than you and even the government agrees there are just not the numbers of men available now. Of course, you have a secure job here at Ashly, and I suppose in time you will see yourself looking after your father. Or more likely your stepmother when your father passes on. Surely it would be more worthwhile to be married to Edward in the colonies? The security of marriage and to see the world as well...'

It seemed to work. Mary agreed to marry Edward and, as importantly, to keep the arrangement secret. Thanks to William's organisation everything went smoothly and the time went quickly. Edward himself seemed to get some purpose in life and not just mope around. Both his mother and William still tiptoed around him, being careful, as always, in what they discussed. William said he dare not even mention Edward's favourite horse, the black thoroughbred, which had been sent off for retraining after the Kiwi groom had left. It now looked as though the horse had been stolen but William did not want to provoke an argument by mentioning it.

This limited the conversation to New Zealand – about which even William did not know much – and general news. They could discuss the endless industrial strikes, the increasing violence in Ireland and of course Mrs Pankhurst. Responsible women were already allowed to vote but it seemed she wanted all women to be able to vote, even the unmarried and uneducated. Edward agreed with the sentiment and his mother refrained from provoking an argument on the topic.

When the time came, the staff were informed that Mary was to be transferred to work in the family's London house and they all departed together. William had arranged for Edward to marry Mary at a small parish church in Edgware, on the way to Tilbury. This was followed by a quick lunch in the George Hotel where, to Lady Scawton's relief, both her sons and Henrietta began to include Mary in the conversation. It could have been embarrassing otherwise.

As they gathered on board the *Remuera* to farewell the couple, William presented Mary with the necklace he had made up from some of the Russian jewels, as he called them. The tiara was enchanting and would be worn by Henrietta at her wedding, but the necklace had turned out rather ostentatious – typical of an inexperienced young man commissioning a jeweller who, it turned out, was a Russian émigré himself. The necklace had a few diamonds and emeralds but it had too much filigree silver. It also had some of those rather strange stones that changed colour under different lights, like the odd half-cut stone William kept as a talisman. However, garish or not, it was exceedingly generous of William to give the necklace as a wedding gift.

Standing with William and Henrietta on the dockside, they watched the *Remuera* set off. Beside them were parents farewelling family, waving and cheering with tears in their eyes, as the ship's horn sounded. Of course Lady Scawton was sad to see her son go, but she knew even Edward was looking forward to the start of a new life. She was pleased to see him waving from the deck, his arm linked through Mary's.

Yet less than two weeks later, he was dead.

✳ ✳ ✳ ✳ ✳

The news had been so sudden and so unexpected that Lady Scawton had felt as though she were living in a fog ever since the telegram had arrived.

REGRET TO INFORM YOU THAT CAPTAIN EDWARD
SCAWTON MISSING BELIEVED LOST OVERBOARD
DURING STORM STOP LAST SEEN BY DECKHAND WHO

*WARNED OF CONDITIONS STOP SEARCH HAS REVEALED
NO SIGN STOP MRS SCAWTON UNDERSTANDABLY
DISTRESSED AT UNFORTUNATE SITUATION BUT UNDER
WATCH OF DOCTOR SIGNED CAPTAIN CAMERON STOP*

William had visited the offices of the New Zealand Shipping Company in London. Their reports explained little more than the telegram. Now, a month later, they had arranged a memorial service for Edward at the Ashly church and, of course, the reception at the house afterwards. Lady Scawton had been surprised at the number of visitors who had turned up. Almost as many as to her husband's funeral earlier in the year.

She waited until most of the well-wishers had gone before walking out through the open French windows to the terrace. She touched her black hat, checking that the heavy veil she had worn in church sat tidily. It was an unseasonably warm winter's day, so different from Freddie's funeral. Then it had been quite the reverse, a summer day but with a chilly nip in the air. How life seemed to be turning upside down. At least at Freddie's funeral there had been a body to mourn.

The wording of the telegram still reverberated in her head. Lady Scawton tried not to dwell on the thought that Edward might have died intentionally, perhaps regretting the marriage to Mary, or distraught at leaving the family. She mustn't think of that.

She heard a footfall and turned to see Lord Shefford approaching her. She stretched her hand towards him as he approached, realising he wanted to speak to her.

'My dear cousin, how you must be feeling . . . ' He took her hand in both of his. 'I feel guilty because we all thought it such a good idea that he go overseas.'

Lady Scawton stretched taller, stifling her morbid thoughts as she replied. 'The idea was an excellent one and, although it had a tragic end, we had the comfort of seeing Edward happier, I think, than at any time since he had been home.'

'I am relieved by that and I hope you are too.'

'In some way, I just wish . . . ' Lady Scawton began but then felt her thoughts would sound churlish.

Lord Shefford encouraged her to continue and so she did. 'Last year was such a difficult one, even though we won the war. Edward was never the same as the boy who went away. As you heard in William's eulogy, his record in the army was excellent. We know now that the conditions in those trenches were so appalling – even for the officers – but when he came on leave he never intimated that he did not wish to return. He said he enjoyed the camaraderie. We had no idea it would affect him so dreadfully.' Perhaps she was just gabbling on but it was such a relief to explain and Lord Shefford was such a good listener.

'At the end of it, he was so changed. Not just his appearance. He became almost socialist in his thinking. Do you remember that Sassoon man, who had put out that anti-war article and would have been court-martialled if they hadn't agreed he was not right in the head? Edward would tell his father how he agreed with Sassoon. He would never have thought like that before . . . ' Her voice faltered. 'And then to die like that. Someone who went through what Edward had, surely doesn't just fall overboard.' She took a deep breath and glanced at Lord Shefford. 'I just hate the thought . . . '

Lord Shefford cut her off. 'I know what you are thinking, my dear. But you say yourself he was not in his right mind. Nor had he been since the war. What you have to remember is that in all essence, Edward did die in the war. What was left afterwards was but a shell.'

Lady Scawton nodded, unable to answer in her concentration to hold back any further emotion. Together they turned and went back towards the drawing room doors. She looked up to see William and Henrietta together by the door, thanking Doctor White and his wife who were just leaving.

She sighed to herself. If the Edward who was her son died in the war, how fortunate that she still had William.

3

From the warmth of the study, with a cold mist hovering at the windows, Pamela had listened as the trustee clarified the quote from the roofing contractors. Charles had already departed for France.

Dealing with Patrick had always been CJ's domain although, thank goodness, when CJ died she did already know about the trusts and where the money came from, or was supposed to come from. It hadn't always been like that.

'With the roof repairs, I've itemised what the insurance will pay for,' said Patrick. 'It's less than half, I'm afraid. There is no way the trust can pay the balance. We can't really do anything until probate is declared.'

'Let's hope for no big spring storms. The tarpaulin up in the attic isn't going to hold forever. When do you think there will be money to pay for it?'

Patrick's expression changed. She resented seeing such sympathy in his face. She went to sit down on the sofa. Her husband had died – she didn't need pity, she just needed to understand.

'Charles' demands don't help,' he continued. She tried to listen carefully. 'CJ never spent anything like what Charles seems to spend. The school fees at Winchester were your husband's biggest concern, and you have to remember that for most of CJ's life, there was plenty of income. He had the Lloyds income for years and when that stopped, interest rates were high. Even the farms used to bring in a reasonable income – until, of course, he sold them . . .'

'To pay off Lloyds.' She knew she sounded bitter. 'There's only the home farm left now. When we married there was a huge acreage and I gather before the war it was even bigger. CJ used to say that his father inherited 5000 acres.' She already knew that the home farm of barely 90 acres hadn't been profitable for years.

'Yes, it was a large estate.' Patrick agreed. 'There was a lot of industrial property too. Old Sir William set the house up in trusts in the '30s after the Depression to avoid death duties. It also meant his reprobate son couldn't sell everything to pay off gambling debts. Not that CJ's father, Sir James, was in any way reprobate,' he added quickly. 'He was a charming man, wasn't he?'

Pamela smiled. Yes, indeed.

'It wasn't just Lloyds, Pamela,' he continued. 'Since the financial crisis of 2008, interest rates have been nothing, income has dropped and Charles is wanting more. I'm relieved that you have your own small trust. At least Charles can't get that, small though it is.' Again, that voice of condescension. Pamela didn't divulge that it was the income from her trust that had provided the salmon he had eaten for lunch earlier. She remembered back to when CJ used to inform her how much money would be available to spend on the household. In those days he never explained where the money came from and even when she asked, he intimated that she would never understand. Thank goodness she had now learnt about these wretched trusts.

'So what do we do, Patrick? Or what do I encourage Charles to do? Does he have to sell the home farm? At least that's in his own name.'

'Charles won't be able to sell anything until CJ's probate's complete, and that could well take a year or more yet and, of course, he can't sell the house even then, because that's entailed.'

'Charles doesn't seem to want to live here. How do we maintain it? Can we give it to the National Trust?'

'CJ tried that, years ago. Unfortunately the house has little or no historical value and the National Trust didn't want it.'

'CJ never told me that.'

'I realise he told you very little.'

Pamela hated the commiseration in Patrick's voice. He made her feel so ignorant. She was mentally exhausted by the time he left.

Once alone, she banked up the fire in the study again. Godley and Mrs Short had gone home, and the dogs were lying flat out in front of the fire. She didn't feel like dinner. Maybe she would boil an egg later. She drew the curtains and then sat down on the sofa, slipping off her shoes and picking up the television remote.

'Bentley,' she addressed the pointer. 'CJ used to infer I was too thick to understand all of this and Patrick expects me to know all about it. I wonder if Charles understands it. I doubt it, except he was born into this life. Perhaps he learnt by osmosis.' She waved the TV remote around the room. 'It's no wonder he expects the money to keep flowing. Money was never a problem when he was a child. It was never even mentioned. Not like my family. My father used to talk about money all the time but, in this house, it was never ever discussed.'

The pointer raised his head, flapped an ear and, not caring about her father, returned to his prostrate position.

Pamela's father had owned a huge department store called Kingsley's and each school holiday reminded her how much it cost to educate her at Benenden and her brother at Marlborough. He wanted Pamela to become a lady, he said. There was never any mention that she might join the firm – that was for her brother. After school she had been sent to France as an au pair to learn French while her father told his business friends she was in a finishing school. She had to return to England early when her father died.

By the time she had become engaged to CJ, her brother had already taken over the shop and it was on the downhill slope. Her father's reputation, so carefully built, became tarnished and, within a surprisingly short time, the shop went broke, leaving her family dysfunctional and she a penniless nobody, newly-married to a Scawton and constantly being reminded of how lucky she was. Even after all this time, comments about suspect breeding and trade rankled with her and she knew how dependent a reputation was on money.

At that time, there was no shortage of it in the Scawton family. When Charles was born, years later, he was expected to have the best of everything. He was the heir and the only one. Right from the start it was Norland nannies, clothes from Harrods and the wonderful little pony, Robin, for his second birthday. The cost never came into it.

Her body sagged against the softness of the sofa, and she stroked the faded Liberty print on the sofa cover. She had chosen it years ago and would have just booked it up on the account, without even asking how much.

* * * * *

Early the next day, a policewoman phoned to say they had identified the deceased. He was a 79-year-old retired maths professor from New Zealand, Professor Geoffrey Samuel Cook. He had travelled alone from New Zealand and was meant to be in Oxford for a genealogy conference. When he didn't register at the conference, the police were able to establish his identity. He was married and his wife had been informed. There were no suspicious circumstances surrounding his death.

Professor Geoffrey Cook. Did that the name sound familiar? Geoffrey? Geoffrey Cook? Nothing came to mind. Poor fellow. What was he doing visiting Ashly and with that strange stone? She felt sorry that he had died without anyone knowing and had lain there for so long before being discovered, just a raincoat-covered body, lying at the other side of the garden all night. It would have been dark soon after 4.00pm and few people used the public path anyway. His poor wife, to have him dying while he was on the other side of the world. She was sure his wife would not have felt the relief she had felt when CJ had died.

Pamela relayed the news to Charles in France. 'The policewoman said he had booked into The Rose and Crown in town, but the publican just assumed he was a no-show. It now transpired that, having left his bag at the station, he walked all the way to the village, where a local schoolboy had told him that the public footpath was the quickest way to the house. He died from a sudden brain aneurism at approximately 3.45pm.'

Charles seemed indifferent. 'What was some old professor doing tramping around England by himself at his age anyway?' The man was 79. Yes, she supposed that was old – Charles would certainly think it was.

Patrick had asked to be kept up to date and Pamela phoned him as well. He was more concerned. 'So why was this professor delivering the letter to Charles? Could you send me a copy of the letter and the note? I think it mentioned the adoption laws. They did change the Adoption Laws around 2005. Charles would have been quite young then.'

'But Charles isn't adopted. Believe me, I know,' she quipped.

'But sometimes he does seem . . . indiscreet.'

'Are you thinking that he might have got someone pregnant?'

'It does seem the most likely. I read in the Sunday paper only last week that Charles was at some party with the Honourable Clarissa Something who's married. They were surmising . . . '

'Oh, I know. Clarissa's an old friend of his and Charles was best man at her wedding. It's just the scandal papers making up stories.'

'It seems he has an eye for the women.'

'They have an eye for him. Last season he had problems with Count Rodetski's wife and had to put her off. Or so he said.'

'How involved is he with Count Rodetski?'

'The count's his patron. He pays for Charles' polo.'

'Oh dear, does he? There are rumours in the city of Rodetski being involved in a fraud case. Hard to know whether he's Russian mafia or not.' Pamela could hear the concern in his voice.

'Charles is doubtful he's Russian at all – or a count for that matter – but he seems to have plenty of money.'

'I don't think he is one of the modern oligarchs. Tell Charles to be very careful. I'm surprised the man still has the affront to spend a lot of money on polo.'

'Could he be the cause of the letter? Blackmail or something?'

'I don't think Russians are into blackmail by letter, Pamela.'

'Via a professor from New Zealand. No, I agree.'

As Pamela put the phone down she wondered why New Zealand. The letter did sound threatening but where did New Zealand come into it? Charles had been to Australia to play polo, but she couldn't remember him going to New Zealand. He wasn't even complimentary about Australia. 'Miles from anywhere' was how he described it.

The only people she knew in New Zealand were Ally's children – Ginny was her godchild and Mike was at university. Ally Williams had been a stalwart friend over the years and she had already spoken to her several times since the drama of the body had begun.

'Did your family ever have any involvement with New Zealand?' Ally had asked when Pamela phoned. 'What on earth was this Professor Cook coming to tell you?'

'That's what we don't know,' Pamela had answered.

'The stone thing you mentioned must be the key. What is it? Perhaps you should find out.'

After finishing the call, Pamela stood up from the arm of the sofa, where she had perched while she listened to Ally. She walked over to the table where the gem was sitting on the tissue paper, noticing at the same time how the oak logs were really hot now and the fire was throwing out the heat.

The stone rolled comfortably in her hand. It still looked like an uneven jagged marble except the one shiny end, which had this strange, dark reflection. If it was an uncut jewel, it seemed very large and if it was a precious stone, this unknown professor was very casual about carrying it, just wrapped in tissue paper. She stared at the cut end and held it up to the reading light. She was sure it had been a green colour before, but now, under the light, it reflected a definite pink aura.

She remembered some of the Scawton jewellery. The ridiculous tiara her father-in-law had lent her to wear at her wedding had jewels that changed colour, pale pink to pale green. They had been much more translucent and paler but this stone could be one of those. The tiara had long been sold so she couldn't compare them now.

She rolled it again; it almost felt warm. She turned her head towards the dogs. 'Who was Professor Cook, dogs? Why did he have this stone?' Florrie raised her head from the floor, enquiringly. 'Was the fact he came from New Zealand important?'

✶ ✶ ✶ ✶ ✶

Polly climbed the concrete steps to the unit and unlocked the front door, thankful to be home. The pharmacy had been busy today, and the Auckland traffic was getting worse. From the doorway, she turned to see her 13-year-old son Simon still getting out of the car. He had spilt his heavy pile of books over the back seat and was cramming them back into his school bag. He stood up, his arms full as he shut the Mazda's back door with his foot. There were still shopping bags in the car but they could wait. She walked the short distance to her bedroom. There the wide window overlooked the front path and the bare wooden fence the landlord had put up last year.

The phone rang, surprisingly loud. Most of her friends used her mobile but this was the landline. It had to be Uncle Pete. 'Local calls are free in New Zealand. Make the best of them,' he'd say. She picked up the handpiece from beside her bed.

'Polly, good evening,' came the strong cheery voice.

'Hi Pete. Are you okay?'

'I'm still here, that's the main thing. Unlike poor Geoffrey Cook. I just heard on the radio that he died.' Polly tilted her head and looked around her bedroom. Geoffrey had been her mother's friend. She glanced at the photo on the chest of drawers – Simon standing between Mum and her, taken at the school sports day a couple of years ago. Polly sighed as she sat down on the edge of the bed, straightening out the folds on the duvet with her free hand. Now they had both died, Geoffrey and her mother.

'I thought Geoffrey usually went to America,' Pete continued, 'but the radio said he was in England. At some conference. Rather sad really. Beth would have missed him.'

'Well, she wasn't married to him, and he wasn't at her funeral.'

She heard a faint chuckle from her uncle. 'Oh, I know you didn't like him, Polly, but Beth was pretty fond of him. He was away when she died – you know that – but he had visited her a few days before.' Polly sighed and knew she was being unfair on Geoffrey – and her mother.

'I know – she did like his company,' she admitted. 'I wonder what will happen to his wife?'

'I don't even know if she's still around. He's got that mad brother too, the one who used to be on telly.'

'Oh yes, that's right. Those science programmes. I used to enjoy them as a kid.'

'Anyway, I thought you'd like to know, and maybe there'll be something on the news tonight.'

Polly half watched the six o'clock news on the TV while she cooked dinner. No mention of Geoffrey. When Simon had been dragged away from her laptop and went off to bed, she sat down in front of it and googled 'Professor Geoffrey Cook, Maths'. Who would want to be a professor of maths, for heaven's sake? It was just numbers – the least interesting side of her pharmacy training. Simon was okay at maths but got his best marks for history and English. The screen flashed up a list of references. She clicked the first one, Victoria University of Wellington, School of Mathematics and Statistics.

> *'We regret to announce the sudden death of Professor Geoffrey Cook, renowned mathematician, teacher and . . . He had travelled to England to attend an international conference on genealogy at Oxford . . . missing . . . Found on a little-known public footpath which skirts the garden of Ashly House, the home of Sir Charles Scawton and his widowed mother. It was she who discovered him . . . Professor Cook was well known for his research into the probabilities of hereditary traits . . . '*

Polly's eyes widened and she went back up the screen. *Ashly House, the home of Sir Charles Scawton.* What was he doing there? Had Mum told him the story?

He was a prying old goat, always asking about family histories. Mum would have told him that Aggie – Polly's gran and Beth's mother – came from Ashly and maybe he was interested enough to go and have a look. Ashly probably wasn't that far from London and Oxford; they were all in the same part of England. She looked out of the window. It was dark now, but the lights in the room lit up the planks of the fence outside. She rose and unfurled the window blind. It dropped down, its dark grey panel giving an orderly look to the room. She glanced at the clock. Too late to phone Uncle Pete now. She would call in the morning.

She didn't sleep well. She kept thinking of her mother Beth and of her grandmother Aggie – or Nan, as the family called her – and of the missing stone. The stone had disappeared after her mother died. She and Uncle Pete had thought it stolen, but maybe it hadn't been stolen. No, Beth wouldn't have given it to Geoffrey. Her mother and she were the only ones who knew Nan's secret, and Beth would not have told that to anyone else. Surely!

* * * * *

In the morning, she opened the back door of the unit and looked at the early morning grey sky, wondering whether it was going to clear into another hot day or whether the solid, grey cloud would continue as a gloomy reminder that winter wasn't that far away. It acted as a backdrop to the skyline of houses and trees and the tall apartment block not far away in Remuera.

Turning back into the unit, she called out, 'Simon, it's after seven. You should be up.' She went back into her room and sat down on the edge of the bed. Picking up the phone she dialled the number she knew by heart. Pete was bound to be awake by now.

He answered on the third ring.

'Good morning, Polly.'

'Hi Pete. I didn't see anything about Geoffrey on the news, but I googled him last night. Did you see where he died?' There was a slight pause. She realised she had rushed in when she should have asked Pete how he was feeling, given him time to think. He didn't seem to mind too much though.

'Didn't he die in England? Wasn't Geoffrey in Oxford or somewhere, at a conference?'

'No, he was at Ashly. Ashly House.'

'Ashly? In England, in the village where Aggie was born – Nan, my mother?'

'Not just the village, Pete. The house. Ashly House. The house where Nan had worked. Where . . . ' Polly stopped. She had forgotten Pete didn't know the whole story.

'Why was he there? Beth must have told him that Aggie came from that village.'

Polly knew her annoyance at Geoffrey would come through in her voice. 'He was always quizzing about where everyone came from. Mum told him I was adopted and he was always asking me about my birth parents. He was a prying old man. She was bound to tell him about your family, how Aggie was the one who came out to New Zealand and that she came from Ashly.'

'He was interested in genealogy. When Beth was ill we talked about it with him. He was interested that my mother Aggie came from England in about 1920-something and that my grandfather on the other side was Irish and my grandmother Māori."

'Geoffrey'd have made a meal out of you having a Māori grandmother. I'm surprised he didn't suggest we vote for the Māori party.'

'You're too hard on him, Polly. Your mother probably would have married him if he didn't already have a wife.'

'I just found him so dry. A maths professor, for goodness' sake. But you're right, Mum did fancy him, and it wasn't a good situation with his wife either. But hey, Pete, do you think Mum might have given the stone to Geoffrey? Maybe it wasn't stolen like we thought.' She could almost hear Pete thinking at the other end.

'I'm sure I saw the stone beside your mother's bed in the hospice right up to when she died. In its box. Why would she have given it to him? Aggie only ever gave it to family members and after she died and Beth looked after it, she only lent it to family – she lent it to your cousin Steve when he went for that interview to Sydney, do you remember?' There was silence as they both pondered.

'But if she knew Geoffrey was going to Ashly?' Polly stopped. She didn't want Pete asking why he might have been taking it there.

'For good luck you mean?' Polly could almost hear him thinking. 'When Beth lent it to any of us, she gave it, box and all. You've still got the box haven't you?'

'Yes, I have.' There weren't many reminders left of her mother. She had got rid of all the clothes and most of her furniture when they sold the house. She just had a few photo albums and scrapbooks in the cupboard with the box. And Mum's ashes. Her stomach lurched. She still missed her mother so.

'I doubt she would have given him the stone,' Pete said. 'I think, because she had told Geoffrey about Aggie being born in Ashly and maybe working at the house, he was just wondering what the place was like. He had a day to kill. Well, I can't imagine anything else.'

'You could be right,' Polly agreed. She didn't need Pete asking any more questions. 'Pete, I'd better go. Simon's got to get to school and me to work. I'll call in, maybe not tonight but tomorrow.'

'Wonderful, Polly. Go on then and thanks for phoning.'

As Polly replaced the phone, she glanced at the clock beside the bed. She pushed the thoughts of Geoffrey out of her mind and stood up, calling out, 'Simon, are you up?' in a loud voice. She heard a muffled grumble from the bathroom next door as she grabbed her black skirt from the shelf in the wardrobe and opened a drawer to take out the folded dark grey T-shirt under the one on top.

Then she stopped. Years ago, Aggie had asked Beth to go back to Ashly and meet the Scawtons. Polly now remembered a conversation in the hospice, only a few days before her mother died. Beth, knowing she could never get to England now, suggested yet again that Polly go to England instead. Polly had dismissed the idea and told Beth so. It hadn't seemed that important at the time, and Beth hadn't complained.

If Geoffrey had come to see Beth after that, and was planning to go to England anyway, maybe Beth suggested Geoffrey go instead of her. No, surely not?

Polly thought about the stone. The family rock. Aggie's stone that changed colour. It hadn't been in the box when the hospice gave everything back. Pete had enquired. Diane, Mum's main nurse, wasn't there and the hospice people didn't know what had happened to it and so Pete and she assumed it was stolen, maybe by that dodgy looking maintenance man. Now Polly wondered whether Beth had given it to Geoffrey. Perhaps that was where it went. She couldn't worry about it now – she needed to get to work.

* * * * *

Hi Mum, the email on the laptop screen started. Ginny had finished writing it and was about to read it through. She leant back in her chair, stretching her arms above her head. For once there was no hurry; it was night in England and her mother would be asleep. She got up from the chair and padded barefoot across the rug towards the kitchen, noticing as she went how untidy the room was. The television was showing some cooking show, a neatly aproned woman with glass bowls of ingredients on the bench. She could hear a car backing out of the drive between her barn and the house and stretched her head forward to see her boss drive out in the Range Rover.

She pressed the button on the jug and reached for a mug and a teaspoon to make a cup of coffee. Damn, nearly out of coffee. She'd have to go shopping later. She would send off the email first and maybe head off to the supermarket. It was good to have the day to catch up on things.

With a coffee in hand she returned to her chair. She could hear the woman on the telly taking a cake out of the oven. 'Perfect,' she heard the woman say, 'springs back to the touch'. Of course it was going to be perfect, thought Ginny; they'd do another take if it wasn't. She reached for the remote and turned the sound down.

She looked back at the laptop screen.

Hi Mum

Day off today so time to write. The breakfast show on telly this morning showed Ashly House. Evidently Aunt P's body was a Kiwi. Quite a famous one too – some maths professor called Geoffrey Cook. They only showed the house from the gate at the end of the drive. Prof Cook had gone to some conference in Oxford. Why was he at Ashly though? It's miles from Oxford.

Apart from saying he died from natural causes, they didn't say much. Didn't even mention Charles for once. The professor looked pretty old in the photo they showed.

Mike is due back on Thursday so I'll catch up then . . .

She checked the rest of the email. It all looked okay. She pressed *Send*.

* * * * *

Once the papers had printed that there were no suspicious circumstances, the interest went out of the story and apart from sympathetic comments in the village over Lady Scawton discovering a dead body in the woods, life returned to normal. Pamela was able to keep the appointment with her Shefford cousins.

Although she was more than happy to catch up with the cousins socially, Pamela did have an ulterior motive in the visit. She wanted to look at their farm shop. Ashly House had a large, sheltered garden area behind the wall next to the stables, originally used as the vegetable garden. CJ's father, James, had put in a grass tennis court there but in recent years the area was just used as a spare field for the horses, until last year when old Batchelor, retiring as full-time gardener after years of service, suggested his two sons use the area in exchange for maintaining the gardens around the house.

The two boys – well, they weren't boys, of course, and weren't much younger than Pamela – had brought in digging machines and trucks of soil and had developed a neat and tidy area. The whole place looked extremely professional. Now they were suggesting a vegetable stall next to The Red Lion in the village. It was Pamela's idea to set up a farm shop rather than just a stall and since the Shefford cousins had one of the best farm shops in England, it seemed a good opportunity to see what might be involved in setting one up.

As always, she was impressed by the grandeur of Shefford House. It was much larger than Ashly and far older, with a wonderfully exciting history that involved generals and explorers. Josephine, married to Lord Shefford, was a tall, slim woman with a demeanour Pamela always envied. A similar age to Pamela, she had been stunning as a younger woman with a mass of black hair. Bouffants had been all the rage then. Heads would turn when she came into the room. As a mature lady of the manor, she still turned heads. Pamela would have loved to have developed that attention-turning look but knew she would always look second-class next to Josephine's chiselled features.

'Pamela, it's lovely to see you. We don't see nearly enough of you,' Josephine commented as she ushered her into the large dining room with the high ceiling. 'Sit where you like. Ever since you phoned about the farm shop, Lizzie has been dying for you to get here, haven't you darling?'

As Lizzie came through the door, Pamela noticed that Josephine's daughter was every bit as tall but had missed out on the striking looks. Lizzie was a similar age to Charles – slightly older perhaps – but had the misfortune to have the figure of a discus thrower and indeed, Pamela seemed to recall, she held the school record in her time. Her oversized physique had not endeared her to the debutante world, which must have been hard on her when her sister had become a model and who was now married to an international racing car driver. Or maybe not, since Lizzie had disappeared off to some distant university, taken a commerce degree and then made a good career for herself establishing the family's farm shop.

'Hello Aunt P. For weeks I've been badgering Mummy to get you over here and then you had that bloody thing about finding the body. That didn't help.'

Pamela felt the warmth in their welcome. 'It's lovely to come. I don't think I've been here since your wedding. When was that, three years ago?'

'All of that and we were on holiday when Uncle Charles died.

Missed the funeral. Daddy said it was a good send-off though.'

'It was. People have been so kind since.'

'Now help yourself to anything you want.' Josephine pointed to a spread of cold meats, home-made patés, cheeses, fruit and fresh bread. 'We've kept it simple. I know you're really here to pick Lizzie's brain over the shop so you don't want to spend half the day eating.'

'This looks lovely. Did this all come from the farm shop?'

'Of course, Aunt P,' said Lizzie. 'We eat the profits. That's one of the problems. But do try that funny-looking paté. We have a new chef and he comes up with some strange combinations. That one has beetroot in it.'

'Now, Pamela, tell us about this letter and stone business,' enquired Josephine. 'You didn't know the man, you said, and so what was the letter about?'

Pamela explained as much as she knew.

'And Charles had no idea either? It sounds most strange,' Josephine commented.

'I should have brought you a copy of the letter,' answered Pamela, for a moment relieved that some other members of the family were intrigued when Charles had not seemed at all concerned. 'There's Victoria University on the envelope but no address or anything and because he died from natural causes the police don't really want to know.'

'It must be worrying for Charles – and you. The professor obviously came with the intention of delivering it.'

'And telling us something,' Pamela finished.

By the time the coffee was served, the three of them had discussed the body, the letter and the stone, the family – including Lizzie's pregnancy, which Pamela hadn't even known about – and the hunting season. Even the state of the nation came into the conversation and, of course, the food.

Then Lizzie took over.

'Now, Aunt P, I need to show you the shop. Are you really thinking of putting one in at Ashly?'

'Do you remember that huge walled area where the tennis court used to be? It was a market garden in the war and now two local gardeners have resurrected it. They suggested a vege stall on the corner of our land where it comes out onto the village green. The idea sort of grew from there.'

'Do you need planning permission?' asked Lizzie. 'I can't remember that end of the farm.'

'Well, it's not "us" at the moment. There's an old hay barn down there, so they just suggested using that. It was my idea for the shop. Additional income for the estate. By their own admission they're gardeners, not business people. So when I suggested we turn it into a farm shop, their eyes glazed over. That's why I thought I had better find out a bit more about it all.'

'Well, let's go and have a look at ours, then. Come on.'

Pamela smiled at Josephine who waved her away towards the receding figure of Lizzie.

The farm shop, established at one end of Shefford House, was a far cry from the converted barn Pamela had imagined for Ashly. There was a large gravelled carpark, cut off from the front of the house with a hedge. Two buses and about twenty cars were parked there. The shop entry itself was adjacent to a busy café which seemed full, the recent coachload of customers still queuing. In the shop there were different counters for meat, cheese, fruit and even a bakery. The whole area was tastefully arranged.

Pamela was fascinated as Lizzie explained how the shop had grown from a tiny butcher's shop from which they had tried to sell the pork grown in the Shefford piggery. That didn't work at all and they had converted the old stable block into the present busy supermarket, as her father called it.

After asking numerous questions on the products, organisation, staff, stock-taking and ideas for marketing, they ended the tour in Lizzie's office, a small upstairs room overlooking the carpark.

'How on earth did you learn how to do all this? I'm most impressed,' Pamela complimented Lizzie.

'With difficulty, Aunt P. It was pretty rag-tag ten years ago, and I was lucky that Daddy was happy to plunge money into it.'

'It must have cost a fortune to set up.'

'We started small. Daddy was very reluctant. I had to give him quite a bit of "Look how much my sister spent doing the season" stuff before Daddy would even look at the business plan. And it wasn't really until a couple of years ago that we started to make a profit.'

'I don't think we could ever set up anything like this at Ashly.'

Lizzie stopped and looked hard at Pamela. 'At dinner last night, Daddy was saying that your father used to own a department store before he died. A farm shop sounds simple compared to that.'

Trust the Sheffords to remember that, thought Pamela. The shopkeeper's daughter. 'My father was more concerned with bringing me up as a lady than letting me near the business. It wasn't the done thing for daughters to work in the family shop. My brother did but it would have been better if Dad had let my brother start at the bottom like he did, instead of putting him in at the top. It all went broke.'

'So Daddy said. He said your brother had some weird ideas, which your father would never have agreed to. Mummy said she remembered the shop as a child and said it was a bit like Harvey Nichols or Fortnums. I'd no idea.'

Pamela smiled. It seemed the circle had turned. Pamela's barrow-boy heritage had suddenly become respectable.

'Hmm, the shop never handled food though and the problem at Ashly would be getting the money to set one up. At the moment, there isn't enough money for Charles to live on, let alone taking on a new venture.'

'Have you got enough money, Aunt P? You had a bad time with

Uncle Charles and Lloyds, when he sold the farms. Mummy was always worrying about you.'

'Goodness, Lizzie, no, I'm fine. It just takes time to settle all CJ's affairs.'

'This business with the body and the letter doesn't help either, does it? And Charles being away all the time.'

Pamela wanted to change the subject from her problems. 'So what are your biggest problems with your shop here?'

Lizzie thought for only a moment. 'Staff, undoubtedly. Getting reliable staff. Chefs can be temperamental and come and go. We have a good lot now. Suzie does the books, but I do most of the buying. In fact, I'm already panicking. I really want to take three months off when this baby comes and I'm just dreading having to find someone who's good but who isn't going to change everything and cost us a fortune.'

Although it was on a considerably larger scale than Pamela had realised, she loved the idea of the shop – dealing with local suppliers, keeping a high standard of both food and presentation, and having enthusiastic salespeople. The closest farm shop to Ashly was on the other side of town and sold mainly meat. It had no variety and little flair. A grumpy ex-butcher ran it, but it was still full whenever Pamela visited. Surely one at Ashly could do better than that – if only there were some money to set it up.

4

England & New Zealand 2013

A visit from Charles was an excuse for Mrs Short to cook a good meal. The old cook was officially retired but Pamela knew she liked to earn a bit of extra money and so she still employed her when the budget would allow.

Pamela found Charles had already arrived when she returned from the supermarket.

'Sir Charles arrived just before you returned,' said Godley, walking over to the Aga and shaking the wide-bottomed kettle to see whether there was water in it. 'Would you like a cup of tea, Lady Scawton?'

Almost immediately, she could hear footsteps coming down the flag-stoned passage.

'Hello, Mother.' He walked over and kissed Pamela on the cheek. The terriers, who had followed him, wandered off to their baskets in the corridor.

'Hello, darling, how are you?'

'Fine, Mother, fine.'

'I'm just making a cup of tea, Sir Charles. Would you care for a cup?' Godley asked.

'Not for me, Gods.'

Pamela frowned at Charles' tone; she hated it when he used that nickname. She waited while Godley poured the tea into three mugs and handed her the first one. 'Thank you,' she said.

'There's yours, Mrs S,' he said as Pamela moved away from the front of the Aga, to give Mrs Short room to put a rhubarb crumble in the oven.

'Perhaps I will have a cup,' said Charles.

A 'please' would help, Pamela thought, as, out of the corner of her eye, she watched Godley reach up to the shelf for another cup.

'The polo ponies are looking well,' she told Charles. 'Sewell thought Dainty was lame, but it turned out she had a stone in her foot.'

'I thought Sewell didn't work anymore?'

'He's retired, but he still likes to keep an eye on things. Will you be sending them down to Cowdray straight away?'

'Trying to, Mother. The bloody Count has gone AWOL and I have to sort a few things.'

He sounded unsure. Perhaps something had happened and Patrick's rumours were correct. She had mentioned his warning to Charles before but, at the time, thought that it fell on deaf ears. 'What would Patrick know?' had been the retort.

It was evening before Charles said anything more. Godley had disappeared back to his cottage in the village and Mrs S had left the evening meal ready in the bottom of the Aga.

Charles poured a glass of wine for his mother, while Pamela stood at the sideboard dishing the baked chicken onto two plates and telling him about visiting the Shefford shop.

'You wouldn't believe the variety of food or the number of people in the shop. Lizzie has done an incredible job.'

'And you think the Batchelor boys could run something similar? I doubt those boys could run anything.'

'The shop was my idea. And we don't have the money to set one up, so the problem doesn't arise. Come and help yourself to vegetables. At least the brussels sprouts came from their garden.' She handed Charles an empty plate, not sure he was even listening. 'We're going ahead with the pigs, though. They arrive in a couple of weeks, when your horses have gone. You know I can't make mashed potato like Mrs S. She gets hers just so smooth.' She carried her plate to the place laid at one side of the table.

Charles, with plate in hand, stared into the vegetable dishes, and said, 'We have a bit of a problem, Mother.'

With the sprouts? thought Pamela. No, this sounded more serious.

Charles carried his plate to the other side of the table and sat down, shaking out his serviette and placing it on his knees. 'Money.'

She felt relieved. At last Charles was realising there was a shortage of income and was ready to discuss it.

'I lost rather a lot in the casino,' he continued before she could comment.

'So?' Pamela was annoyed and silently asked herself why he was spending money in the casino.

'For God's sake, Mother. Can't you see I can't live on the income I get?'

Pamela felt deflated as Charles continued. 'Patrick says there isn't any more, which is ridiculous. Father always had plenty, even after Lloyds. You'll have to speak to Patrick. He treats me like a boy.'

Charles had been in Deauville playing polo when CJ had died. He had even been reluctant to come home which had upset Pamela. He had returned, accompanied by some blonde girlfriend. He had spoken brilliantly at the funeral, stayed a couple of days and disappeared back to Cowdray in time for the last tournament of the season. Since then, except for Christmas, Pamela had seen as little of him as ever. If she thought his father's death would bring him back to manage his affairs, she was mistaken. She heard more news about him from the *Horse and Hound* or *Daily Mail* than from him. Now there was Facebook. Someone there was always telling her his latest antics.

'I have spoken to Patrick, Charles. There's a recession on. The income isn't there. We can't repair the house. We can't sell anything because of probate and we can't sell the house anyway. Patrick suggested we lease it out.'

'Christ, who on earth would want this house? You've let it get quite shabby. All the money you spend on Godley and Mrs Short, cleaners and gardeners and it still looks a shambles.'

He had finished his chicken, and Pamela got up from the table and took his plate. He sounded so like his father. It was always her fault. It probably wasn't worth telling him that Godley and she did the cleaning, that Mrs S was retired except when he came.

'Would you like some more?'

'I saw there's rhubarb crumble for pudding. No, I won't have any more. What happened to the letter from that old man? And the rock?' asked Charles.

Pamela was relieved to change the subject. 'Ah, it's in the study. I told you the man was a professor from New Zealand, didn't I?'

'Yes, of course you did. And you don't know what the stone is.'

When they returned to the study, Charles took the letter out of the envelope and put the stone on the table without looking at it. Pamela picked it up. With her thumb, she stroked the smooth side.

'The jeweller on the High Street has no idea what kind of stone it is,' she said. 'He suggested sending it to a gemologist in London to be identified; I said I'd take it back if we needed to. You know I think it's an uncut version of one of those odd jewels in the tiara the family used to have. The police had no idea. It's too clear for an opal and too pink for a topaz.'

Charles was reading the letter. He raised his head and glanced at the stone.

'It's more of a rock than a jewel. Mike would know. He studies that kind of thing. Pity he's not around.'

'Ally's Mike? Of course.' Pamela stopped rolling the stone and looked at it. 'He is here. Ginny didn't come but Mike came back for Easter. He's about to leave again, back to New Zealand, hopefully to finish his PhD. He's bound to know what it is.'

'*Dear Sir Charles*,' he began to read out loud. Then he stopped. 'Hang on – this is dated July. The writing is in the crease of the letter. July last year. When Father was still alive. This was meant for him.'

'Really? Let me look.' Pamela took the letter. CJ had died in August. Yes, this was dated July. That was six, no, eight months ago.

So, it could be to do with CJ. It was to do with adoption. Adoption and CJ. Pamela's mind raced but she said nothing.

* * * * *

Charles hesitated as he looked up the number on the handwritten phone list in the kitchen corridor. Ally Williams was one of his mother's best friends, and Charles had grown up with the family. He had been there when their daughter, Ginny, had fallen off the balcony. Ally probably still blamed him, even though it had happened several years previously.

He knew Ginny was in New Zealand now but if Mike was back, he could probably identify the stone at once. At least that would solve one part of the story. He pressed the buttons on the phone.

'It's Charles for you, Mike.' Charles could hear Ally Williams calling. She hadn't sounded that friendly but had been polite. He heard clattering down the stairs and Mike pick up the phone.

'Charles?' Mike sounded surprised. 'Hello Charles, where are you? I thought Mum said you were in France.'

'I was. Just got back. I hear you're about to go back to New Zealand.'

'Yes, just packing now, leave in ... oh ... less than an hour.'

'Well, I just have a problem. You may have heard about the body Mother discovered.'

'Oh, yes. The "butler had to call the police" stuff. Poor Godley. Mum said the dogs found it. Sounded very mysterious, but I gather they've discovered who he was and it wasn't a grisly murder but a Kiwi professor. Rather disappointing really. We would have come to Aunt Pamela's trial. Mum could have sat there like Madame Defarge.'

'Who?'

'Oh, never mind. So why are you phoning, Charles?'

'There was a letter on the body with some kind of rock . . . jewel . . . marble. Anyway, we don't know what it is, and I wondered whether you could look at it. I can come round right now.'

'Well, you'll have to be quick. There isn't much time. I have to leave no later than ten.'

They finished the call and Charles quickly picked up the stone and disappeared out of the back door. He hadn't been to the Williams' farm for years but knew the way from childhood. There was a wide grass verge and their house was set farther back from the road – a low rambling place with a large tree-filled garden in front and the stables and a yard behind.

Charles checked his watch. He got out of the car to find Mike waiting just inside the front door.

'Haven't been here for yonks,' Charles commented.

'No, indeed,' said Mike, 'and Mum is going to panic if I offer you even a cup of coffee. We have to leave in a second. What can I do?'

'Well, as the rock expert, I thought you were the one who would know about this? What in hell is it?'

Charles pulled the stone from his pocket and handed it to Mike.

'I'm not an expert. Well, not yet, anyway.'

'A PhD in geology is a start.'

'I haven't even got that yet.'

'Why do you have to do it in New Zealand for God's sake? It's the other end of the world.'

Mike was looking at the stone, turning it carefully in his hand. He took it to the open door for a better look.

'This is really interesting. I've never seen anything like it before. I'm pretty sure it's not a New Zealand stone. Why did the Kiwi professor have it? It could be African – a topaz or something? Feels harder than that though.'

He looked at Charles.

'I really haven't a clue what it is,' Mike confessed. 'You'd best get a mineralogist to look at it. Take it to Oxford. No, even better, the Natural History Museum. They would identify it. Is it important?'

'It was with the letter on the body. The man was trying to deliver it – or so the police thought.'

'What exactly did the letter say? Did it say where the stone came from?'

'It said the stone was given to the writer's mother and it had to do with a secret. Actually, the letter was written last year so it was aimed at Father. He was still alive then. Mother has no idea what it's about. We hoped identifying the stone might help.'

'Well, I'd be interested to know what it is as well. Let me know when you find out.' Mike was still turning the stone in his hand as they both heard Ally call. 'Mike, we have to leave. I'll get the car.' They heard the back door bang as Mike looked over at Charles.

'How's Ginny?' asked Charles, thinking he should at least ask after her.

'She's well. Just didn't feel up to a long journey back for Easter. I see quite a lot of her. She's working not far from Auckland.'

'I'm glad she's back working.'

'Yeah, well, working part time, I guess. Still goes to sleep every afternoon but she looks great.'

'She always did.'

'Yeah, well,' commented Mike. Charles picked up his tone. Don't let's talk about the accident, he thought.

'So, can you get this identified in New Zealand?' he asked.

'Mike,' came the call from the back of the house.

'Yes, but it might be valuable. Take it to the Natural History Museum. Or a jewellery manufacturer might know.'

'The fewer people who know about it the better. You take it and just post it back when you find out. I can't believe it's that valuable. We can't do anything with it. Unless it's an emerald or something.'

'No, it doesn't look like one or anything I've ever seen. I would quite like to identify it. It's so unusual. Do you mind? I'll get it back to you. Not sure how but there are always people who can bring it back.'

'Mike, for God's sake!' came the voice.

'I'd better go. The voice is rising.'

'I can hear.' Charles turned towards the open front door. 'Go on, take it. I'll go. Give Ginny my regards. And let us know.' He left the door open and, as he got into his car, he saw Mike put the stone in his pocket, pick up an overstuffed bag and disappear towards the back of the house and the garage. Perhaps he shouldn't have left it with him. He supposed he felt guilty about Ginny or something, but he was amused that Mike was enthusiastic about finding out what it was. Obviously Mike had never seen a stone quite like that either.

* * * * *

Pamela was sitting on the sofa in the study. Earlier, Charles had disappeared, along with his team of polo ponies. She was quite relieved. Of course, she loved seeing him but she could never quite relax when he was around. It must be because he was so energetic.

There was a documentary on the TV but Pamela was oblivious to it, instead staring downwards at the faded pink Liberty print covering the sofa and wondering about the letter. The pointers were stretched out on the carpet in front of the fire, idly watching her in case she decided to move; the terriers were tucked in either side of her on the sofa. She glanced up at the letter, still sitting in its plastic cover on the coffee table in front of her. She knew it by heart now.

Dear Sir Charles

We have never met and now that is unlikely, although your family and mine are so entwined. This stone was given to my mother by the Scawton family. She only told me the secret when she was older and made me promise to seek the satisfaction she had failed to get. It was her dying wish that someone should confront your family. At first we did not know whether the story was even true, until we found proof.

The adoption laws in this country have been changed so I suppose . . .

Adoption and changes in the law. Now she knew that the letter had been intended for CJ, not for Charles, she realised what it was about – CJ's secret adopted child in Ireland.

She stroked her chin with one hand as she remembered back. CJ had been in the army, and was chosen for some secret outfit, not the SAS – he'd failed to get into that – but some intelligence operation. It was something to do with Northern Ireland. He wasn't allowed to tell her. It had all been very hush-hush.

They had only been married for a couple of years. CJ was very gung-ho in those days, more like Charles was now. He was always good company and exciting to be with. It was not surprising that she had fallen head-over-heels in love with him.

CJ had been thrilled to be chosen for a special mission, even though he wasn't allowed to say anything about it. He was only away a couple of weeks. When he came back, he still wasn't allowed to say much, and so she never did find out why he had to go.

It wasn't long after that episode that CJ began to become quite withdrawn, which was so unlike him. Pamela had been hoping to get pregnant. She hadn't and had begun to worry. She suspected that this was what was worrying CJ too – no heir. He was still working at what he called 'The Office' in London and denied there was anything worrying him. She didn't like to press the point.

A few months later, out of the blue, he told her that during the Irish operation he had stayed with a family in Southern Ireland but close to the border of Northern Ireland. The family had a son and two unmarried daughters. He had now heard that one of the girls was pregnant, and he was going to contact her and give her some money. He thought Pamela should know.

The news was so unlike CJ that at first Pamela was perplexed. Then, of course, she realised – CJ was the father of the child and that was why he was telling her. That was why he was worried about it. She tried to bring the subject up again and began to realise that CJ's sullen mood was probably because he was in love with the girl. She had dared not discuss the subject for fear he'd admit it and say he wanted a divorce. She had hoped in the months that followed that she might too have become pregnant but that didn't happen. Nor did CJ's demeanour improve. When she knew the girl must have had her baby, she tried to discuss it again. All he said, when Pamela chivvied him, was that the girl had had a boy and it had been adopted out.

'It's all over. Now don't bring up the subject again,' he'd declared. She tried to be thankful that her marriage was still intact.

Pamela's doctor sent her on what then became an endless round of gynaecologists to find out why she wasn't getting pregnant. Yet at the back of her mind was CJ, getting some Irish girl pregnant without any trouble and not being able to acknowledge it.

It had been the most miserable time in her life. Charles' mother had become ill, and then died. She and CJ had moved into Ashly House with CJ's father, James. Pamela was now expected to run the house. There were staff everywhere and she hadn't a clue how to organise them or even what they did. She left it all to the fierce housekeeper, who just looked down her nose at her and told her as little as possible. She felt a total outsider, one who couldn't even bear an heir. She knew everyone – even her father-in-law – was looking at her for a sign of pregnancy. It took years before he stopped mentioning, 'when you have children' or 'when there are little Scawtons running around'.

CJ was no help, telling her she was overreacting and being stupid. He was drinking heavily and even the butler remarked on the amount of whisky the house consumed. She wasn't sure what she should do. She knew CJ's morose behaviour was her fault, and she couldn't do anything about it.

At one point, she suggested to CJ that, if he wanted to get divorced and marry someone else, she would cope.

CJ just laughed at her. 'You couldn't go. All you have is us. If you leave, you wouldn't have a thing.' He never said he didn't want her to leave.

Pamela knew he was right about her having nothing. Her father's legacy had turned to dust with the shop. Her brother was much older, and her childhood had been quite lonely – the happiest hours were spent helping at the local riding school. She had enjoyed being an au pair in France but meeting carefree CJ at 17 had been by far the best thing that had happened to her. Fun, sports cars, horses – he introduced her to a whole world of excitement. Her mother, so embarrassingly proud at the wedding, had died suddenly and her brother, broken after the demise of the shop, had moved overseas. Her childhood world had disappeared. By then, all her friends were CJ's friends and she didn't like to confide in them, but CJ was correct – she had no qualifications and nowhere to go.

So she just carried on. At parties, other wives' conversations seemed totally involved with their children. CJ had become rude and abrupt in his demeanour and offended many of his friends. At home he began to get terrible nightmares, and when she woke him up he would become violent, often hitting or punching her or pushing her out of bed. He left the army on the pretext of taking over the running of the farms. If Pamela hoped that, without the travelling and the pressures of the army, life might pick up, then she was wrong. If anything, CJ became more unpredictable.

The pregnancy problem would have been easier now, she surmised, with IVF treatments available. There was talk of it then but the gynaecologist she visited considered it a new-fangled idea with very low rates of success. He suggested she give up smoking, which was hard when CJ was a chain smoker, but she did manage it. In a magazine, she read that if you did a headstand on the bed after 'you know what' it would ensure the sperm went the right way. She never did try that, but she did have endless tests and day visits to the hospital. Once she was so sore she couldn't drive home and CJ had to send someone to come and pick her and the car up. On her arrival back home, he just told her to toughen up.

CJ still wanted sex with her and every time she would hope he would return to his old loving, carefree days. He never did. Every time she was reminded of a son adopted out in Ireland, a son he was never allowed to acknowledge.

When she finally did become pregnant, what should have been a happy time became another trial. She hoped her pregnancy would lift the pall of CJ's moods, but it didn't. The morning sickness never left, and she spent most of the nine months in bed, sure she was about to lose the baby. When Charles was born safely, she just felt exhausted. A nursemaid and a nanny took turns in looking after the baby, insisting that Pamela rest up. Flowers filled the house, visitors came, her father-in-law congratulated her for doing her duty and as soon as they left, Pamela wept. CJ disappeared to London.

She moved to a bedroom closer to the nursery so that she wouldn't wake CJ when Nanny brought Charles for the night feeds. Somehow she just stayed there. It was the same room she still used now, opposite the old nursery.

It was only a year later when James, her father-in-law, was killed in a car crash and CJ became Sir Charles. Although she knew many now considered CJ quite eccentric, out of courtesy he would be invited onto local committees in place of his father. Usually he would refuse or propose Pamela go in his stead.

'All they want is the title. You'll do,' he would tell her.

Yet in doing that, CJ gave her a lifeline. She enjoyed helping out in the village, being on the church committees and organising the local horse shows. She was flattered to be considered the representative of the younger generation even though CJ never allowed her to become too involved. He always reminded her that she was only there as a figurehead.

The pony club was the only organisation where he allowed her to do more than be a committee member. Charles was about five when he joined the local branch. Nanny professed to be scared of horses and Pamela was allowed to drive the Land Rover with the pony in the trailer. The committee were delighted to welcome Lady Scawton, especially her old schoolfriend Ally Williams, who later asked her to be godmother to her youngest daughter, Ginny. Charles, as an enthusiastic rider, took to the pony club polo with gusto.

CJ never did bond with Charles. He always looked at him as though he were some strange visitor in the house. She would tell CJ how well he was riding and insist on buying good ponies but CJ would never come and watch or take any interest. Pamela encouraged a teenaged Charles to spend more of his holidays with his Winchester friends – he was an only child, after all, and needed other children around. She would suggest CJ join them at polo but he scoffed that it was only kids playing. Pamela enjoyed her involvement with the children and rose up the ranks to be the local district commissioner, with several friends suggesting she'd enjoy the organisation on a national level.

That was when the shit hit the fan, as they say. She opened a copy of *Country Life* to find an advertisement for their own farms. It prompted a huge row between them, CJ accusing her of caring more about the 'bloody pony club' and she accusing him of shutting her out. Finally, CJ admitted that as an underwriter of the failing Lloyds insurance, he owed more than two million pounds.

Immediately, memories of her own family's financial failing surfaced; the consequent fallout in relationships was not going to happen again, not to this family. She resigned from almost all her activities, spending more time at home and insisting that she learn more about the family finances. She was introduced to the 'old' Trustee – a professional of her father-in-law's age who glossed over any details and had no intention of discussing them with a woman. She was relieved when Patrick, the 'young' Trustee – a mere 50-year-old – was slightly more forthcoming. He confided that other Lloyds debtors were not selling but going to court, and he considered it unnecessary to sell up so drastically but CJ was adamant. The farms, except for the 90-acre home farm, were all sold, and Lloyds was paid off.

The Scawton reputation was saved although it didn't take long before she realised the lifestyle they had enjoyed for so long could no longer be maintained. She was never sure CJ really understood that, and Charles certainly never took it on board. Fortunately, as Patrick said, CJ's financial demands were few. His carping whims did not cost money, just her attention. Even if she rode a horse for more than an hour, he'd complain that she was ignoring him. It was a battle to insist CJ take more interest in watching Charles play polo.

Yet now this letter reminded her that CJ's secret must have been eating him up for years. She looked at the letter. It must be to do with the Irish child, though goodness knows why a maths professor should come into it. It had to be intended as blackmail. She needed to try and find out about CJ's past, about his affair, about the child. CJ had kept silent for so long. Who was the Irish mother? Had CJ been in touch with her? How could she find out?

She felt a large nose pushing against her hand.

'Okay, Florrie, you want to go out,' she smiled at the pointer's friendly face. The terriers began to bark. She got up and walked to the French windows, then waited for them all to return from the garden before heading to bed, still thinking of how she could find out about CJ and the affair.

Early the next morning she remembered. Among the letters she had received on CJ's death was one from an army officer who mentioned he had known CJ when he went to Ireland. As far as Pamela knew, the affair with the girl was the only time CJ went to Ireland. Perhaps this man would know. When Godley arrived, she was already in the study, going through the pile of letters. She found the card, from a Colonel O'Malley, and he had even included an email address.

She turned on the computer.

* * * * *

The world was really quite small, Ginny surmised. Ally had written this 13,000 miles away in England and it had whizzed through the ether to land on her phone in New Zealand. She loved getting emails from her mother. They were always full of news and this one was no exception.

So glad that Mike arrived back in NZ OK. Thanks for letting me know, you know how hopeless he is at telling me himself.

Saw Aunt P and told her you were happy to try and find out more about the professor.

She thought that was a good idea. The envelope was from a Victoria University. Aunt P thinks that is Manchester University. She said she might contact you as you did all that work for CJ helping him write his memoir and, although he tore it all up before he died, she thought you might remember some of it or it might be on your computer somewhere.

It is good to see Aunt P more resolute although today when I phoned she was quite secretive. She says she thinks she knows what the mystery is about after all and is going up to London to speak to one of CJ's army friends. She has never met him but he wrote to her when CJ died and she needs to check something.

She did show me a copy of the letter and the note. It was rather vague, talking about secrets, revenge, and adoption. It certainly sounded a bit threatening and the letter was written in a spidery uneven handwriting. The note with it was written by someone called 'Diane'. No address. If you can find out anything about Professor Cook over there, I'll let Aunt P know and she can contact you herself.

Better go now. I hear Dad's car.

Love you.
Mum.

Ginny stood up and stretched, bringing her thoughts back to her world in New Zealand. She had finished working the horses and she should start cleaning the gear but already felt weary. Maybe she'd have a sleep first. She moved over to the sofa and stretched out.

She would google Professor Cook and see what came up. She did have Sir Charles' memoirs on her computer but in the three months she had worked for him, she couldn't remember anything remotely secret. It had been the first job after her accident and was only for a couple of hours in the morning. He had been such a grisly old shit and unbelievably bossy, although all she had to do was take notes from his dictation. His memoirs consisted mainly of things he had done as a young man: a teacher he hated at his first boarding school (he didn't say why), a rugby accident at Winchester where he ended up in hospital and was lucky not to be paralysed, shooting on people's estates, riding in point-to-points, house parties. Then his army life, which seemed to be just moving from one army base to another, and his hunting and playing polo. He never mentioned anything remotely juicy. He talked about his father a lot but never ever referred to Aunt P. Or maybe they hadn't got that far.

He was so grumpy Ginny wondered how on earth Aunt P put up with him. Her mother agreed. She had no time for the old bugger and told Ginny to walk out if he became too much, especially if he threatened her or became too familiar. She needed the money at the time and he didn't threaten her and certainly didn't try anything. They only got as far as him being recruited for what he called 'Intelligence' when he got the flu badly and was really ill. After that he decided he didn't want to write his memoirs anyway and in a fit of pique tore up all the papers Ginny had given him, leaving her without a job. He died not long afterwards, by which time Ginny had taken a job looking after horses and had booked to go out to New Zealand to do the same thing there.

It was much better thinking of horses and Ginny was remembering the most useless eventer in the yard where she'd worked before she left England. He was called Plum and she loved exercising him. She fell asleep thinking about it.

5

England 1921

Lady Scawton had sat at her writing desk in the morning room for some time, quite still. There was only one item in front of her, a letter neatly written, a letter much handled and read. Her hands were folded on the ink pad in front of her as though the letter might contaminate them. It was addressed to William and had arrived some 18 months ago, some six months after Edward's death. It had been written by a doctor, a Doctor Wolstencroft.

Dear Sir William Scawton

My name will not be known to you. I emigrated, with my wife and five children, from England to New Zealand on the 'Remuera' with your brother and sister-in-law. I met your brother only briefly a few times but was impressed by his quiet demeanour and the kindness he showed to Mrs Scawton. I am sure, in less tragic circumstances, I would have appreciated other qualities.

Yes, Edward was always polite and did have a kind nature.

The tragic incident happened during the end of a three-day storm. When we set out the weather was fair although the captain did warn us that we had a storm ahead, which indeed was how it turned out. Seasickness took over most of the passengers, including your sister- in-law, who was confined to her cabin. As

74

the storm abated, it was Mrs Scawton (Mary as she has become known to us) who realised that her husband was missing. A search was raised and the captain and crew were very thorough in looking.

Her eyes wanted to fly down to the bottom of the page, to miss this part of the letter. She had read it so often.

It seems that one of the crew, changing shifts at 4.00am, had seen Mr Scawton near the rail on the deck. He warned him that the seas were still very rough and the conditions not suitable for promenading. He advocated following him to the shelter of the passageway. When the door to the passageway clanged shut, he realised Mr Scawton had not taken his advice and later regretted not going back to ensure he was safe. The sailor was exhausted after a long watch and did not think longer on it until questioned later in the day.

Both he and the captain agreed that sometimes passengers would want to go on deck even in such a storm. They would go there to get some fresh air and to relieve feelings of nausea. The air in the cabins would become fetid after a long period of inclement weather. Usually they realised the danger.

Every time she read the letter, she felt such desolation at this part. It was so obvious that Edward had intended to commit suicide and had waited until the crewman had departed. So tragic! She took a deep breath. At present she needed to stop any more thought of Edward – that was not the reason she was reading the letter again.

On his disappearance Mary was distraught, as you can imagine. As the permanence of his disappearance became apparent, she grew resigned to the inevitable and at all times behaved with great decorum. Her main worry was for your family and Dowager

Lady Scawton in particular. She had hoped to be able to return to England as she felt the reason for the immigration with her husband had disappeared. She was distressed when she received your telegram but of course adhered to your wishes.

Lady Scawton remembered, when the news of Edward's death had arrived, the New Zealand Shipping Company had offered Mary a passage back to England by transferring her onto another ship at Balboa. In the telegraphed reply, William had advised her against this and for her to continue the journey. She frowned again at *behaved with great decorum*. Lady Scawton knew what the letter was about to reveal.

We arrived in Auckland on 2 March, some ten weeks after leaving England. My wife had become very fond of Mary and so had the children. It was with pleasure that we were able to provide her with accommodation. Mary is an able nursemaid and my wife, who is expecting our sixth child in a few weeks, appreciates her help with the other children. As Mary herself is now some 16 weeks pregnant, she will remain with us until her own baby is born.

Mary herself has embraced her new circumstances with her natural enthusiasm and although she cannot feel she can write her own letter and does not wish to trouble you, sends her commiserations on your loss. She has confirmed that, following your instructions, she has made herself known at the Bank of New Zealand and with the money deposited there has paid outstanding accounts including those arranged for her husband's horse. There are still a few months before her confinement and she is wondering whether you have any opinion on her future.

Yours faithfully
Douglas Wolstencroft, Medical officer
4 April 1920

So there it was. When the missive had arrived, she and William had agreed that if Mary was with child then it could not have been Edward's. It seemed that she had had a liaison – probably with the doctor himself – and, from the timing, soon after their departure too. It was obvious to both of them that this was what had pushed poor Edward to take his own life.

If the doctor was not the father, he may well have believed the child was actually Edward's. There was no reason why the doctor should have known that Edward could not consummate the marriage. Perhaps Mary had told the doctor the child was Edward's, or perhaps the doctor and she had concocted the story. Whatever the circumstances, there was only one reason for the lie – and that was extortion. An immediate reply was sent at the time. It had been Lady Scawton herself who had penned and signed it. The letter was short and made the point that they were quite aware that the baby could not be Edward's. The letter had not invited any more correspondence and, indeed, none had come.

She had searched out the doctor's letter again, after so many months, for a reason. What if Mary's child had been a boy? With William without a son and heir, there was still a danger of blackmail from this woman. She had little doubt that, by now, with the baby born and the initial attempt of extortion stymied, the doctor would have abandoned her. Even in the colonies, Mary would find it difficult to raise a fatherless son, which meant her thoughts could return to extracting further help from the family by inferring Edward was the father. She smiled to herself. Freddie always insisted that victory comes from anticipating what might happen and being ready for it.

It was a pity that Mary could not have warned the other Ashly maids of the dangers of dalliances. These girls were so stupid. Flattered by a young man's attention, particularly a man of a higher social status, they would misread the flirtation as undying love and have to suffer the consequences. Earlier that morning Mrs Howard had informed her of the kitchen maid, Aggie's fall from grace. Mrs Howard's initial reaction, of course, had been to dismiss the unmarried girl for becoming pregnant, but Aggie had been working with them since she was a child, they knew the family and Lady Scawton needed just a little time to make some enquiries.

* * * * *

Luncheon had been a light affair. There had been no guests – only the three of them. Henrietta excused herself early as she was due to visit friends near Tring, informing them that she would be back in time for dinner.

As William followed his mother out of the dining room, he commented, 'You are out of sorts today, Mother. Is anything wrong?'

His mother was still a fine figure, tall and imposing. Her hair piled up on her head was quite grey now. Although the new short fashion of hair suited Henrietta's elfin face, his mother preferred the older, more elegant style with her long hair held in place with tortoiseshell combs. She would tell Henrietta that she doubted her patience – or her maid's – could have coped with the excessive use of the curling irons.

'I am melancholy, William, I must admit,' his mother agreed.

'Why not walk over to the stables with me? I was going to see the groom ride that new young hunter we got from up north. It's a lovely day.'

His mother put her head on one side and then agreed that a little sun would help. There was a wide-brimmed straw hat lying on the hall sideboard, which she had used earlier that day and now she arranged it carefully over her head, tying the long sashes under her chin. She did so slowly. She wished to discuss an idea with William. She was just not sure how best to broach the delicate subject.

'So, what's brought on the ill humour, Mama?' he enquired as he opened the front door for her.

Lady Scawton waited until she had descended the steps and was quite out of earshot of any staff before she spoke. 'Oh, I was thinking about an heir,' she answered as she tucked her hand through his arm. Nothing like cutting to the chase, as Freddie would say.

'Oh.' William paused.

His reaction made his mother hesitate. Of course, William was embarrassed to discuss the subject. When they had married, Henrietta had seemed perfectly healthy and according to her own mother was very much in love with William. Yet there were still no children. After a year of trying, Henrietta's mother had encouraged her to Harley Street to be examined for any problems. One of the specialists had also seen William.

'I still can't believe it,' complained William. 'Nor can Henrietta. After her seeing those specialists and suffering the embarrassing examinations, the man seemed certain it was the mumps I contracted. I was thinking it was something I picked up in India. Meanwhile, Mama, I can assure you we have not given up. Both of us are well aware the title requires an heir and miracles can happen, the man assured us.'

His mentioning the mumps had confirmed her suspicions. William's bout, in his first year at Winchester, had been a bad one. She did not have to consult a Harley Street doctor to know that mumps could lead to infertility. If William did not have a son, and that maid in New Zealand heard about it, she might think her son, conceived on an illegitimate shipboard romance, would inherit. That would not do at all.

She put on a brave smile. It was not a subject one discussed normally, and she took a breath to draw herself up. 'The family isn't dependent on just a title, William. We are respected for what we do, how we govern, on what we own – not just what title we hold. It is important that we behave accordingly. To keep standards up. I am sure you realise that. Your heir must be brought up among us.'

'Of course he would be, Mother. What are you trying to say? You're going round in circles.'

They had walked across the drive together and had reached the archway to the stables. Now she turned and wandered away from the archway and towards the iron railings looking out on the park, instinctively walking away from where others might hear. Her son followed her. There was a patch of sunlight there. While his mother put a hand on the top rail she saw William pull thoughtfully at his moustache. She needed to discuss this subject carefully. She had seen William speak to Aggie only the other day. She knew he had a certain air about him, a certain confidence with the ladies. First, she needed to ensure he was not involved.

At last she spoke. 'The little kitchen maid, Aggie, is carrying. I know during the war you would have had the odd liaison, which may not have been suitable. I do not wish to know about them. I just need to know there could be no repercussions if Aggie should be dismissed. Please confirm that you have not been tampering there.'

William might have reacted strongly, denying any odd fling, but she knew how Freddie used to behave, and William was a good deal younger and more virile and although married to the lovely Henrietta, men did have this tendency to prove themselves with others. She knew now that Aggie's baby could not have been William's even if he had succumbed, but any allegation by the maid would be embarrassing.

She was relieved when William did not seem too offended.

'Aggie? I know the one. She's been with us for years. No, Mother, you are quite safe. She's not to my taste. She probably has a fellow. Is she going to marry him?'

'She says he has gone off to America. Suddenly. Of course this might indeed be true.'

William frowned. 'Oh, one of those. There were plenty of those after the war, weren't there? Too late now for her to say he was killed in the war.'

'She was just a wild child when she first came to us. By the end of the war, Cook used to rave on about how good she was in the kitchen.

Now, understandably, she's changed her mind and can't wait to get rid of her. Says she won't have fallen girls around her.'

'Poor Aggie. What will she do? Her father's the blacksmith, isn't he? He won't be pleased.'

His mother overlooked the sympathy he showed for Aggie. 'Aggie daren't tell him. She only told Mrs Howard last night. She will have to leave the village, or everyone is likely to know. If she is lucky, the baby will be adopted out. It's all her own fault.' She looked at William who seemed to be squinting and looking out over the parkland. His moustache moved as he pursed his lips. He had put his hand in his pocket and produced that odd rock he carried around with the cut glass side. He fiddled with it.

'It seems so unfair that Aggie gets an unwanted child when Henrietta and I need a miracle to get one at all. Aggie seems healthy. She has four brothers – one was killed in the war, wasn't he? So, she is even likely to have a boy. She has been with the family for years. If she daren't tell her father, do we help her at all?'

Although Mrs Howard had wanted to get rid of Aggie at once, Lady Scawton had agreed that it was not that easy to find replacements and in this permissive age, allowances had to be made. As yet there were no visible symptoms of Aggie's problem so that she could work on for a few months.

'Yes, I think we could help her, William. I have heard of a religious establishment in Croydon where they take in such girls. I will enquire but I see no reason why she should not go there. Now come, William, we need to continue to the stables or we will miss seeing this new young hunter of yours.'

6

New Zealand & England 2013

There were weeds and the odd pansy growing through the cracks in the paved pathway as Polly and her son walked up to her uncle's cottage. Even in the New Zealand March evening, it was still warm and light. Daylight saving didn't change until April.

Polly wondered why her uncle had asked them to come this particular evening. He sounded quite positive. They climbed up the low wooden steps to the front door. The whole house needed a good scrub and paint, but she knew it wasn't going to get it. Pete loved it as it was, old, with the garden overgrown.

'Did you shut the front gate, Simon?' she asked. 'We don't want to let the dog escape.'

'Course, Mum.'

The front door was unlocked. Polly sighed. Uncle Pete should keep it locked all the time.

The dog rushed out from the kitchen, not bothering to bark but wagging its tail wildly. Simon rushed towards it.

'Mutty, here, boy.' Before Polly could get to the kitchen, her uncle appeared, stick in hand, greeting her from the kitchen door.

'Tēnā kōrua.'

'Hi Uncle Pete, can I take Mutty out?' Simon asked immediately.

'Just in the garden, not into the street. He's had a good walk today.' He stopped in front of Polly, and she had to lean down to kiss him on the cheek; he seemed to be getting smaller, she thought. Simon disappeared out of the open door, leaving it ajar.

Uncle Pete had put a bottle of wine and three glasses out on the green Formica table in the kitchen. She was about to ask who the third was for, but Pete explained at once.

'Diane phoned. The nurse who looked after your mother in the hospice – you remember her, don't you? She's calling in on her way home.'

Polly gave a small whoop of surprise. 'Of course I remember. Mum thought she was great. I thought she'd left the hospice? I haven't seen her since the funeral.' She had liked Diane, who'd been really caring with her mother.

As though on cue, they heard the front gate click and Mutty give a couple of barks. A woman was talking to Simon. Polly turned back to the hall as she came through the door with Simon and Mutty.

'Diane, Pete has only just told me that you were coming. Simon, do you remember Gran's nurse at the hospice?'

Diane answered for him. 'You probably don't remember, Simon. You must have grown half a metre in the last year, too.'

Polly wondered why Diane had wanted to come. It was a nearly a year since her mother had died – she must have met so many other families since then. Simon and the dog disappeared into Uncle Pete's bedroom to watch the television. In the sitting room, the French windows were ajar, and Polly went and closed them. The evening would cool down shortly.

As Pete followed Diane into the sitting room, he was asking about the hospice and whether she was still working there. He set the tray of glasses on the coffee table and sat down in the chair in the corner, carefully pouring the Chardonnay into the three glasses as he listened to Diane.

'I loved working at the hospice but after a bit you become too emotionally involved and I had to move on. I became close to so many families but after the funeral I never saw them again. Thank you for this.' She raised her glass. 'It's wonderful to see you.'

'It wasn't an easy time for us then, especially for Polly. She's looking great now, though, isn't she?' Uncle Pete sounded so proud.

'Don't be silly, Pete.' Polly smiled.

Diane continued. 'I read about Geoffrey Cook dying. He used to come and see Beth. I met him a couple of times.'

So that was what prompted the visit, thought Polly.

'Yes, we heard about it, too. Very sudden,' agreed Pete. 'Good guy. Beth and he were friends for quite a while. Rather sad that they both should have gone.'

Polly remained silent, just taking a sip of wine.

'He was interested in genealogy,' Pete continued, 'and Polly said he died in the place where Aggie came from in England. Aggie was Beth's and my mother and Polly's grandmother. Beth must have told him about England and he was having a look.'

'That's what I thought,' said Diane.

Polly noticed she looked embarrassed and frowned as she wondered how Diane would have known.

'That's really why I came to see you. Just before Beth died, Geoffrey and she had a long talk. I was in and out and left them as much as possible because it obviously wasn't anything to do with me. As he left, he was promising her something, and she told him she would send him a letter about it.'

Polly felt herself frown. Obviously Beth had told Geoffrey about Ashly and the Scawton family house – it was too much of a coincidence – although Polly couldn't believe her mother had told him about Aggie's secret.

Aggie had sworn Beth and her to secrecy. She had made Beth promise to take the stone back to England, and Polly knew her mother had stewed on this when she realised she could never go. She tried to make Polly promise she would go but Polly refused, failing to see why it had been so important to her mother when Aggie had been dead for several years and Beth herself was dying. Now she wondered whether she had explained it all to Geoffrey and asked him to go. No, surely not.

Polly sat pursing her lips and trying to suppress her anger. She glanced at Pete, who was looking animated and interested.

'After he went,' Diane continued, 'she began this letter, only she was so tired that she couldn't get far.' She paused. Polly wondered what was coming next. Surely Beth hadn't told Diane too!

'She didn't tell me what it was about. She said it was a secret.' Polly could almost hear herself give a sigh of relief as Diane continued. 'She asked me to send the letter to Geoffrey and, when she got as far as she could, she took out that little stone she kept in a box beside her. "Send this with it. He has to have proof," she said.'

Pete half got out of his armchair and reached for the bottle of wine. Polly knew the action was to hide his surprise or annoyance. She put her hand over her glass, realising that she was frowning. Diane was looking at Pete anyway and not noticing Polly. Diane was happy for another glass of wine and Pete poured himself a half glass. He shouldn't be having that much, thought Polly, her frown deepening.

'She also swore me to secrecy about sending it,' Diane continued. 'Obviously I had no idea what they were talking about, but when she asked me to post the stone to Geoffrey with the letter . . . ' She took a sip of wine. 'Apart from briefly at the funeral, I didn't see any of you afterwards, but I always felt guilty because I didn't know if the stone was valuable or not or whether you'd missed it. One end looked just like coloured glass, but it might've had sentimental value for you. It obviously did for Beth or she wouldn't have had it there.'

Polly gave a small involuntary groan. She couldn't help it. Diane looked at her briefly but then looked back at Pete who, Polly knew, would be disappointed too.

'We did wonder what happened to it when we found the box empty,' Pete told Diane. 'We asked the hospice. Perhaps they never asked you.' He sounded annoyed, almost disbelieving. No wonder.

Diane seemed not to notice. 'I did wonder whether I should tell you at the funeral even though Beth made me promise not to. I never heard back from Professor Cook but, when I heard he'd died and it was outside the Scawton home, I recognised the name from Beth's letter. Then, of course, I felt guilty that I'd never mentioned it to you.'

For a moment, even Pete didn't say anything. Polly certainly didn't trust herself to speak. She was angry with Diane, angry with Geoffrey Cook and angry with her mother – especially her mother, who had sent Geoffrey there to confront the family and tell them Nan's – Aggie's – story. And she had sent the stone – the stone that changed colour.

That stone was part of their family. She and her cousins had all played with it as children, taking it inside and out so that it would change colour when they held it against the electric light. Green in natural light, pinkish under artificial light. Even her mother would point out that it changed like people change.

It was gone now. Polly felt as though part of her was gone too – as though she was now stuck in only one colour.

*****

They had decided to meet at the Auckland Museum. There was usually plenty of parking for Ginny, and Mike could run up the hill from the university. Mike was late, as usual, and Ginny was already sitting in the autumn sun on the wide steps of the huge stone edifice which overlooked the whole of Auckland harbour. The museum stood majestically above her, surrounded by mown lawns, with a park of ancient oaks beyond. The gentle sea breeze drifting in from the harbour stopped the day from being too hot.

When her brother finally arrived, Ginny realised that his long skinny body hadn't been running at all. 'I got a lift,' he admitted. 'At least I'm not all sweaty. It's too bloody steep to run up the hill. I don't mind walking down or you can give me a lift back,' he suggested.

'Anyway, how are you?'

'I'm fine, Mike. Being up here isn't even like being in the city and there's plenty to look at.' She pointed to the expansive view out to the Hauraki Gulf. Across the water was the bush-clad volcanic cone, Rangitoto. She had been musing that it was exactly like the classic shape of volcanoes she used to learn about at school. 'But now I'm getting hungry,' she told Mike. If she dwelled on the volcano, Mike would start a geology lecture. She got up and they went up the steps together, turning back to look at the harbour again before they went in.

'It's raining in England. Showers, the internet said, and cold,' Ginny reflected. 'Much better weather here in Auckland.'

They chatted as they went through to the café at the back of the building. Ginny had only been here once before, but Mike knew where to go. It was a bright and airy café.

Ginny chose a chicken wrap while Mike had a pasta salad and a muffin. They took their food to a table while the coffee was being made. Ginny knew it would be Mike's main meal for the day.

Once they were seated and had started eating, Mike said, 'We think identified Charles' stone. It's a type of chrysoberyl. I told you it was pretty unusual.'

'The stone? Chryso-whatsit? Why's it so unusual?'

Ginny had never followed Mike's passion for geology. She had gone to Southampton to study business, but then all that had come to a halt with the bloody accident. She had been stuck at home trying to get her head together while Mike had finished his Masters degree and had come to New Zealand for his PhD.

Ginny could see him as a geology professor already, although he insisted he was keen to get out of university and not teach. He had such a teacher kind of air, she thought: enthusiastic and kind of vague.

'No one here knew exactly what it was but a mineral expert from Vic was visiting and he identified it. It's a chrysoberyl, beryllium aluminium oxide. He got pretty excited about it actually. The pseudochromatic coloration means it is an alexandrite which is extremely rare. He was pretty sure it came from Malyshevo, even without doing an X-ray powder defraction . . . '

'Whoa there, Mike. You lost me miles ago. It's a what? And where did it come from?'

'An alexandrite, named after the Czar. Originally mined in Russia. All alexandrites are rare although there are some in Tanzania, Brazil and other places. But he's pretty sure this is a Russian one, mined from the Urals, where they were first discovered. The ones from there are really rare. Plus it's of incredible quality: very clear. And it's huge. And I just carried it in my pocket all the way from the UK.'

'So it's a jewel, like a diamond. How much is it worth? Do you have it with you?'

'Christ, no, it's at the university. It's worth much more than a diamond. The Russian alexandrites are the rarest. He says this one would be worth thousands.'

'What on earth was Professor Cook doing with it on the Scawton estate?'

'That's the mystery, sis. Did you find anything else about Professor Cook?'

Ginny knew Mike had always loved mysteries. She was the kid sister and, as a teenager, he would take her on 'mystery' tours through the woods and fields of home, often across the old Scawton estate. Most of his mysteries would involve some history or geology of the place. Once, he took her on a long bike ride to show her an old charcoal oven, deep in the woods, and they both returned covered in filthy black dust. Mum wasn't best pleased, and was pacified only by Mike telling her, 'Well at least my sister wasn't racing around with boys and getting pregnant. She might even turn out to be a famous archaeologist.'

'I can email Professor Cook's obituary from the newspaper to Aunt P,' said Ginny. 'Professor Cook sounded pretty erudite. Wrote a whole lot of articles on maths and genealogy evidently – that was his speciality. He's survived by a wife and his brother who was some kind of TV scientist. There's a memorial service next week in Wellington.' She stopped to take a mouthful of the chicken wrap. 'The university's press release said he was found in the garden at Ashly House. Then it just went on about his articles. There were a whole lot of other famous Geoffrey Cooks when I googled it. I also found there are some Scawtons in New Zealand too. Scawton Millers actually. But it doesn't matter now because Mum said Aunt P thought she knew what the story was.'

'You said Aunt P had asked if there was anything in old CJ's memoirs you wrote for him.'

'I've checked the file. It's all deadly dull. I remembered it was boring at the time.'

'Hmm. I'd still like to know why Prof Cook had this chrysoberyl on him, what it was about. What about googling the conference he went to or the name of his wife or phoning Wellington?' suggested Mike.

'The administration people?' Ginny asked.

'You'll need the Maths Department. He was in England for a conference.'

'Oh, God, you and your mysteries. Okay, I'll try and find out more.'

'The man was carrying an unbelievably rare stone which presumably belonged to someone else.' Mike said. 'We need to find out who owned it.'

* * * * *

The mysterious stone was certainly not on Charles' mind. In the gentle sunshine of Sussex, he was riding his favourite horse, a polo stick in his hand for the first time that spring. He sent the small white polo ball floating around the mown grass. He would have preferred a proper game with seven other players on one of Cowdray's good grounds but so early in the season, with the ponies barely fit to ride, a gentle stick-and-ball was all he could expect. He was looking forward to the first game. He hadn't seen the Count and had barely seen the polo manager but assumed everything was as it was last year with the Count as the patron paying for everything and only appearing to play the matches.

Alas, the pleasure of the afternoon did not last. The manager was waiting by the stable door when he rode back. Charles was about to make a quip about the grass being too long but noticed the man's solemn expression, reflected by the girl groom who led his horse into the stable without a word. It had to be bad news.

'As of today, Charles, there's no Rosetski polo,' the manager explained.

There had been rumours, but this was a bit dramatic.

'What the hell? Is Rosky ill or something?' Charles began, thinking that he would have heard if Count Rosetski had died.

'The Count is overseas and will not be back for this season or the next. I've been contacted by his accounting firm. The stables are to be vacated, the count's horses sold or at least leased. The house has already been closed down – Rosky hasn't been there for months anyway – and now I have a few weeks to close everything else, which means we want your stables empty. The new security guys on the gate will ensure nothing is stolen.'

'What about my horses? I can't just move them.'

'The accountants are coming down in a day or two. They'll be taking inventories of the horses and all the equipment. We don't want an argument and you having to prove your horses are yours. If I were you, I would get your horses out of here. Like now.'

'Sorry to talk about money but what about payment?'

The manager waved his hands as though they were full of papers.

'All our contracts are unsigned and useless. No money. I'm on a reduced rate for a month and so are the grooms while they're here. Everyone else – zilch. Sorry about that.'

'And where is Rosky?'

'Now that is a good question, Charles. He's Russian. So he could be in one of Putin's dachas on the Black Sea or he could be freezing in Siberia. Who knows?'

'Bugger,' was all Charles said.

* * * * *

As the train gained speed out of the station, Pamela's spirits lifted. Off to London. Now the commuter rush was over, the train was almost empty. She settled into the seat, smiling at the young girl opposite. She was quite a pretty girl, even if she had a slightly pinched face, but she had too much makeup on and those earrings were over the top.

The train wasn't the express and at the next station a large lady opened the door and, pushing past her with a bulging case, knocked Pamela's handbag off the seat. As the whistle blew, Pamela, the woman and the young girl were scrambling to pick up the purse, wallet and the detritus from Pamela's handbag.

'I'm so sorry. I should never have left it open,' said Pamela as she retrieved a lipstick from the floor.

'Silly cow,' mumbled the girl. Pamela thought she was talking about her, but then saw the girl was looking at the retreating figure of the woman, towing her case up the aisle.

'Shh, she'll hear,' chided Pamela. 'I shouldn't have left the bag there.'

'Here, there's still an envelope down there.' The girl leant down again and picked up an envelope, glancing at it as she handed it back to Pamela.

'It says *Lady Scowton*. Are you a lady then? Like Lady Di was?'

Pamela smiled. 'It's Scawton, but yes. Not quite like Lady Di, but my husband was a Sir.'

'I've never met a Lady.' Pamela was unsure what to say and watched as the girl pulled at her high boots. As they slowed into the next station, the girl suddenly came to life again.

'I suppose you live in one of them fancy big houses, do you?' she asked.

'Well, I suppose so, although the house isn't too fancy at the moment.'

'Why not?'

'The roof is falling in, and there's no money to repair it.'

'Down to your last million, I suppose.'

Pamela pursed her lips giving a faint smile. Maybe a change of subject was advisable and she asked, 'Where do you live?'

'Aylesbury. With my parents.' They both looked out of the window as the train began to move again.

'Do you work in London?'

'Nah, I couldn't afford the rent up there.'

Then the girl turned back to Pamela and continued. 'Got a day off work. Going to see my sister. She's just had another baby. A girl.'

'That's exciting then.'

'Yeah, it is. Don't often get a day off during the week. Dad had an accident and can't work now, and I have to work in the pub at the weekends as well, just to help the olds pay the rent. My boyfriend wants me to move in with him, but I can't see how we could ever afford it.'

'It's hard, isn't it?'

The girl suddenly went silent and looked at Pamela as though to say *how would you know?*

'It's good that you help your parents though.'

'Don't have any choice, really. Not like . . . ' The girl looked at Pamela and stopped. Not like me, thought Pamela. That was what she was going to say.

As they drew into London, Pamela stared out of the window again. The tenement houses were hidden behind dirty graffiti hoardings. The trees in the street looked to be struggling, still bare and brown.

When the train had stopped at Euston, the two got up, and Pamela thanked the girl for helping her earlier and wished her good luck. The girl gave a quick nod, her eyebrows denoting you-live-on-another-planet, as Pamela went to open the door.

Pamela got out of the taxi at Simpson's in the Strand. She so rarely came to London that this was a treat. The restaurant had been a favourite of her father-in-law and she used to bring Charles here when he came up from school to go to the dentist. She noticed the new wheelchair ramp on the pavement step outside. The hallway was brighter than she remembered, now pale green with bamboo coloured pillars rather than the old dark panelling.

She acknowledged the maître d' and said 'I'm Lady Scawton. I'm due to meet Colonel O'Malley . . . '

Before she could go further, the maître d' raised a finger and asked her to follow him towards a man sitting alone in one of the booths down the right-hand side of the magnificent Grand Divan dining room. If this was Colonel O'Malley, he looked a large man, his hair very close cropped or maybe bald. He had a kind, creased face and pleasant demeanour. He stood up when he saw her and shook hands formally, almost with a little bow, a sort of non-military salute, thought Pamela.

She had wondered why he had suggested a restaurant to meet in, rather than wherever he worked. Perhaps he was retired. As she sat down opposite him, she quickly realised this place was ideal; it was not too crowded, and it would be a good place to talk.

After the initial, rather difficult, small talk with the waiter hovering for their orders, she realised that Colonel O'Malley was waiting for her to mention CJ.

His voice had a soft Irish accent as he spoke. 'I don't know how I can help. I didn't know your husband very well. I was only involved in the one mission with him, and that of course was years ago, but I was intrigued by you saying I could maybe help with some mystery.'

'Colonel O'Malley . . . ' she started.

He interrupted her. 'Why don't you call me Mal, Lady Scawton?

Everyone else does, including a whole lot of those who shouldn't.'

Pamela noticed the twinkle in his eye, which went so well with the lilting voice. He was older than Pamela but still looked fit. She began to relax.

'And you call me Pamela. Titles are so formal. Now,' she paused, 'I know it was years and years ago but you worked with CJ and I know he spent a short time in Ireland on some special mission. We now have had a letter, which may refer to that, and I wanted to know exactly what happened there.'

Colonel O'Malley – Mal – raised his eyebrows for a moment; he obviously remembered. She waited.

'I know exactly what you're talking about. Unfortunately, I'm not so sure how much I can tell you, even after all this time.'

Mal was frowning now and looking down at his plate. He touched the knife on the place setting. Pamela was trying to fathom whether he was saying it was still-secret-not-to-be-revealed stuff or whether he was embarrassed because he didn't want to tell her about CJ's affair with the girl.

They had both ordered roast beef, and the trolley was being arranged beside their table. The waiter carved thin cuts of rare beef onto her plate. It looked delicious.

As the waiter wheeled away the trolley, she saw Mal glance at her, with an almost guilty expression. She hoped he would answer the questions that had remained unanswered for over thirty years.

Speaking slowly, he explained that the mission had been to gather information on a newly formed branch of the Protestant UDF – Ulster Defence Force. It was right at the beginning of the Troubles in Northern Ireland. If they had known then what they knew now, the mission would never have been contemplated.

Charlie, as Mal called him, was chosen because he was easy-going and fitted in anywhere. Pamela knew what Mal meant. She tried to remember CJ like that but images of what he was like during the next thirty years kept creeping in.

'CJ was never the same afterwards. Did anything happen?' she asked.

'The idea was to meet up with people from the north and find out exactly what the UDF were plotting against the IRA. The border was still pretty fluid, and the idea was that Charlie stay with a family on the southern side of the Northern Irish border. One of their daughters was engaged to a guy on the northern side. It was just a casual visit, no weapons or anything. Just information gathering. Charlie was there a week and I know got on well with the northern guy who arranged a meeting with UDF members. In a barn.' Mal hesitated, which confused Pamela; he didn't look to be a man who hesitated. 'Only it went horribly wrong. Charlie was late to the meeting – I can't remember why. When he finally reached the barn, the northern contact had been ... hurt.' Mal hesitated again. 'It wasn't pretty. It had been an IRA ambush and they were a cruel lot.'

'You mean he had been kneecapped or something. Didn't they do that?'

'The guy died.' Again he hesitated. By the way he said 'died' Pamela imagined that maybe he had not been dead when CJ had arrived, but she didn't like to ask. 'Charlie had to stay there for quite a while, until dark, before he could leave. There were no mobile phones or communication in those days; he did well to get himself out. I can't really tell you any more.' He hesitated. 'Except that he was one of the first people I ever sent into the field and I always felt guilty about what happened.'

They finished their beef in silence. She was sorry the mission had gone wrong, but it sounded as though it wasn't CJ's fault. Pamela wanted to broach the subject of the girl. That was what she really needed to know about. There was silence as the waiters took their plates and brought the menu for dessert.

'Charlie lived with this family for a week,' she blurted out, 'and you say there was more than one daughter. Did Charlie have an affair?'

The Colonel looked taken aback, clearly embarrassed and confused.

'Look, he isn't here now. I just need to know,' she continued.

The waiter returned to take the order for dessert. Pamela declined anything. The meat had been perfect. Perhaps some coffee. The colonel patted his stomach and agreed. He now smiled at her and his eyes had a twinkle.

'He certainly stayed in their house, and I know he was – what – sociable? But I don't really know whether he had an affair.'

Then he suddenly seemed to catch on to what she was talking about. 'Are you talking about the girl being pregnant?'

Now it was Pamela's turn to be taken aback. So he did know.

'A few months after it all, the girl whose boyfriend was killed contacted us.' He hesitated again only for a moment. 'You have to understand the difficulties some of the families had in those border towns. She was Catholic, unmarried, and had become pregnant to a Protestant northerner, with the Reverend Paisley ranting against the Catholics at every turn. Her family sent her to Dublin to have the baby, and she wrote to us – to the army – asking for money. We refused of course. It was nothing to do with us. We would not have acknowledged anything about the operation by then, but I did tell Charlie and I know he felt sorry for her and blamed himself for the girl having a fatherless child.'

Pamela tried not to show any emotion. She looked at Mal and his fleeting expression of guilt told her that he had revealed more than he meant to.

He continued, almost to himself. 'He shouldn't have told you anything about her. Did he tell you anything else?'

Pamela shook her head. She was almost speechless. 'CJ was never the same after that mission,' she said quietly. 'His whole personality changed.'

Mal looked at her in surprise and his expression changed. 'At the time I did realise Charlie might've had a problem. I put him on to the medicos. I found out later he was diagnosed with PTSD – post traumatic stress disorder. They were going to treat him. I lost contact with him after that. I was stationed . . . elsewhere.'

'I thought it must have been the girl who had caused him to change,' Pamela explained.

Mal looked down at the two coffees the waiter had poured and then around the room. Pamela followed his gaze. The room looked very comfortable. Most tables seemed to have two or three people talking quietly.

Mal continued, 'It wasn't her – well, not directly. It would have been the mission – the informer getting killed – which would have affected him. He blamed himself. That's how PTSD works. Didn't the treatment work? By the time I came back to London, he had left the army.'

Pamela just shook her head again. She was trying to concentrate. Her mind was still on the Irish girl and the adopted child – who it seemed was not fathered by CJ. Not CJ's . . . Charles was CJ's only son.

'So you had to cope at home with a changed character and you didn't know why?' Mal seemed to understand.

She tried to concentrate on answering Mal's question. 'He kept everything about his job secret. That was the only thing he ever told me, that this girl was pregnant and had asked for money. Whenever his father or I mentioned that he seemed . . . different since he went there, he denied it. Yet his temperament was entirely altered. He began to drink heavily, he was unsociable, unhappy. He had dreadful nightmares. He was just not the CJ I'd married. His whole personality had changed. I thought it was the girl, or otherwise something I'd done.' She paused. How stupid that sounded now! 'If we hadn't had money and frankly, if he hadn't had the title, he wouldn't have been able to get away with his behaviour at times. Locally, he was just considered rather unpredictable and eccentric.'

Her mind was still on the adopted child. It wasn't CJ's child. He had not fallen in love with an Irish girl he couldn't have. Whatever had changed his personality was not that child. It hadn't been because she had been unable to get pregnant when she was expected to. It wasn't that at all. It wasn't her fault.

When Mal said goodbye, he held both her hands as he explained, 'From what you said, I suspect CJ never completed the treatment. It's too late now, of course, and I don't know if it would have worked anyway, to be fair. The treatment in those days was so different. I'm sure our guys never realised it was so bad or that he made life so difficult for you. It's all treated quite differently now but back then – well, there was really only a bit of counselling and then "You'll be okay now" – but it must have been very hard for you.'

Pamela began to choke up at his words and had to swallow hard.

'Thank you.' She didn't trust herself to elaborate. A short time later, she left him standing on the steps of Simpson's in the Strand. It was beginning to spit with rain which gave her an excuse to hurry into a taxi. She had intended to go shopping but, as the taxi driver commented on the darkening weather, she realised she couldn't face it. She asked to go to Euston Station instead. She wanted to go home.

7

England & New Zealand 2013

All the way home Pamela felt she was about to start crying but there were too many people around. When she got out of the train, she saw someone she knew by sight but just acknowledged them and didn't slow down. She hoped they would think she was late for something and couldn't stop.

By the time she got home, Godley had left for the day. Pamela had taken one of Mrs Short's casseroles out of the freezer that morning but now she didn't feel hungry and put it in the fridge. The dogs were keen for a walk and it seemed a good excuse to take them out onto the lawn and walk up to the footpath where all this had begun. The rain had cleared at last, the days were getting longer, and the cold snap had given way to rather balmy spring weather. From the edge of the woods, with the four dogs diving into the bracken with their noses to the ground, she turned and looked back at the house – it was far from being a huge stately home, but it was still big, by any stretch of the imagination.

For nearly forty years she had lived here. A year or so after they were married, when CJ was still in the Army and often away, she and CJ had moved from a cottage on the farm to the end bedrooms overlooking the garden. Here she didn't have to be alone in the house at night. It didn't seem that long ago, she mused, as she looked along the house to the old nursery wing where she now slept.

Tears began coursing down her cheeks as she stood, rooted to the spot.

'This is so stupid,' she said suddenly. She pressed her hands over her eyes for a moment, but the tears still came as she remembered looking out of those end bedrooms and wondering if CJ had even cared about her at all when his heart was in Ireland. All that was so totally wrong and now it was all too late.

She gave a large sniff and dug into the pockets of her jacket to see if she could find a handkerchief but there was none. For a moment, she just stood there, letting the teardrops make rivulets on her cheeks. No matter, there was no one around, no one who really cared if she wanted to stand in the middle of the garden and be miserable. She remembered the privileged life she had been handed on a platter by her husband and rued the incredible waste she had made of it all.

She wiped her damp face with a hand and turned away from the house to check on the dogs. Through eyes still blurry, she could see Florrie chasing a blackbird at the far end of the lawn and the terriers, deeper into the woods, trying to find a rabbit. Bentley was close to her, looking up at her and wondering which way she was going to go.

'You know, Bentley, that's what I'm wondering too,' she told him.

With a sigh, she remembered back to when she had taken over the running of the house. She had known so little; CJ, and even James, had been no help. Suddenly in charge of employing new staff, one of her first tasks had been to interview Godley as the under-butler, and she had started off by telling him how much he would be paid. Within minutes, he was explaining to her what she should be asking and what information she should be expecting.

'You shouldn't mention the money at all. Ladies don't talk about money.' Naturally he got the job.

Now, as she wiped her tear-stained face, she became annoyed, not with the house or the family but with herself because she'd been so naïve, because she should have realised it wasn't an affair with the Irish girl that had changed CJ and because she had done nothing. She'd been totally self-centred and had a fixation when she hadn't become pregnant. On the odd occasion when she had discussed it with CJ, he hadn't blamed her at all – she just hadn't believed him.

As CJ became progressively unreasonable, no one but she seemed to notice. The servants, his cousins, the friends he hadn't already offended, they just accepted it. No one ever suggested that CJ had a problem that could have been treated, not even the doctor, or maybe CJ was on his best behaviour when he saw the doctor. Her father-in-law, James, just thought CJ's anger was normal but at that time James had a dying wife and her death had really broken his heart. Not long after her death, his old Land Rover had rolled down a bank on the way back from a shoot. He wasn't wearing a seatbelt and was half thrown out of the car and killed instantly. That was when CJ and Pamela had become the new Sir Charles and Lady Scawton.

She longed for the carefree CJ she had married, to apologise to him for not realising that he had witnessed something so dreadful that it had triggered all those nightmares. She wanted to tell him how sorry she was that she hadn't tried to help him more. Instead she'd been hung up about not getting pregnant and had been fixated on what a failure she was.

And Charles! So like CJ in many ways. He and CJ should have been able to enjoy each other's company. Instead, she knew, Charles had been terrified of his father – as had half the village. Now only she – and Colonel Mal – could remember the CJ she had married, the good-looking, social, exciting husband whom she'd loved so much.

'If only I'd . . . ' she began out loud. The dogs were still too busy to listen. Even Bentley had wandered off to sniff around the roses.

She had achieved so little in her life when all the opportunities had been there. Even running the pony club had led nowhere.

She wondered what she would do now. Probably, as Lady Scawton, in a large country manor, she would just continue to play her part, representing the older generation on village committees perhaps. Except nowadays no one seemed to want her on committees, charities seemed to be professionally run, and she had no training and no experience for anything sensible like social work. She would like to do something worthwhile but every idea, even setting up a small farm shop, needed money they didn't have.

No, her future was to stay here and, after Godley retired, which he would have to do eventually, she would turn into a Miss Havisham, disintegrating with the house. She stared up to the broken roof.

With another large sigh, she called the two terriers from the beech trees and the path, and mused how sad it was that it had taken the dead body of a stranger, who had been carrying a threatening letter and a mysterious stone, to prompt this whole trail of memories and revelations.

* * * * *

By the time he got back to London, Charles was thinking more sensibly. He would need to find another polo job, but the season had already started and it was bloody late to try and find another patron, particularly one who could keep his ponies. He had phoned the Cowdray manager from the car, but all the players seemed to have their plans sorted and the wretched Argentines had taken all the good jobs. He parked the car and walked round to his flat.

He unlocked his door, while juggling a shopping bag with two bottles of wine. Joanna had moved into his flat after they came back from France and at least she kept the place tidy. She had texted him to remind him to buy decent wine for tonight's hostess to make it up to her, insisting that he had offended her at an earlier party.

'What did I say?'

'You said the necklace she was wearing was a trifle common.'

'Did I? It probably was.'

'It was an heirloom from her American father. All diamonds and pearls.'

'Oh, I remember, the diamonds were enormous. They couldn't have been real.'

'I can assure you they were. Daddy deals with the father – they have a huge outfit in Wisconsin.'

'Well, Wisconsin isn't Santa Barbara or Palm Beach, is it?'

'They still use dollars there. Now make sure the wine is good.'

Charles was still smiling as he thought to himself how there was more to Joanna than just tits and legs but, by Christ, the tits and legs were good.

He picked up the pile of envelopes on the table – nothing but bills and bank statements except there was an envelope with the Cowdray Club crest. He opened that one first, realising it was an invitation to the Cowdray Polo cocktail party. He picked up and opened the bank statement and realised there wasn't enough money there to cover the cocktail party ticket and the bank statement didn't even include the automatic payment for the rent. Bugger. His phone buzzed its tune and he dug it out from his pocket to look at the screen. It was his mother. He remembered that she had left a message earlier but he had been too preoccupied to bother to get back to her. Now he pressed the green button.

'Mother, how are you?'

'Charles, I'm fine. I've been in London to see someone. Have you a moment to talk? Are you at Cowdray?'

'No, just got back to London. It's bloody bad news. Rosky's pulled the pin, and I've got to get the horses out of his yard. I have no job.'

'Are the horses all right?'

'Yes, they're okay. I just have to move them. Might even have to bring them home.'

'Well, let me know. Adrian manages all the farm pretty carefully now. He has cattle in the big paddock and needs to know if your horses are going to need it again.'

'The horses really need to be stabled.'

'Oh no. We've altered most of the stables for the pigs; they're due any day. You won't be able to stable them.'

'What pigs?'

'I'm sure I told you. Adrian has organised a new pig venture for the stables.'

'For God's sake, Mother, my ponies are far more important.'

'They don't produce income. Anyway, let me know what's happening. I rang you to say I thought I had the answer to the letter, and it was to do with your father in the army. Well, I was quite up the wrong tree. I met this man your father worked for and found out about . . . '

Mother seemed to be prattling on when Charles was more concerned about his horses and trying to calculate how to pay the hire-truck to take them back to Ashly.

His mother was still talking. 'Do you know I had no idea? How awful is that?' She had been saying something about Father.

Charles tried to catch up with her rambling as she said, 'Of course, we still don't know what the letter is about.'

'The guy was some crank wanting to be paid off. And he's dead now.'

'I would still like to know. Someone wrote that letter, and the professor brought it all this way. There is a tone of passion in it.'

Charles' thoughts were still on the polo. He needed to find someone who would pay him to play and to keep his ponies. He might try Windsor or Cirencester.

'Charles, are you listening?'

'I'm more concerned with polo. That's really more important.'

*****

Ginny knew Aunt Pamela was never one for too much small talk, even on the phone from the other side of the world, but she had never noticed what a piercing English accent she had.

When Ginny and Mike were small, and Aunt Pamela ran the pony club, her voice could be heard at the far end of the field where the rallies were held. She used to wear a battered old hat or even worse, a scarf, like the Queen used to wear, tied under her chin. 'Come on, children, lunch now. Unmounted. In the barn. Go and deal with the ponies but please don't canter over there. A walk will do . . . ' It was a voice that did not brook disobedience.

'Ginny, dear, how lovely to hear you. I assume your mother or Mike told you about the stone and Professor Cook?'

'Yes, Aunt Pamela,' Ginny answered. 'Mum told me you wanted me to dig around a bit and I saw Mike yesterday. He was raving on about the rock.' She couldn't remember enough details to tell Aunt P about it and realised that she should have listened more carefully to all that technical stuff that Mike was going on about. 'I'd better get him to email all the techy stuff about it. And Victoria University, which Mum mentioned was on the envelope, is probably Wellington. The professor worked there.'

'Oh, well done, Ginny! Was there anything in CJ's memoirs? I never read any of the papers you did for him. He tore them up when he got ill, as you know, but Godley said you used your own computer and might still have the notes. That might shed some light.'

The work she did for the old bugger was a year ago.

'Yes, I've still got all the files on my computer, Aunt Pamela,' Ginny interrupted. 'I didn't see anything about jewels, cut or uncut, or even remember him talking about them. I can put the files on Dropbox, and then you can read them for yourself.'

'What's Dropbox? Do you have to post them?'

'No, it's a kind of software. I'll email instructions. Can you manage?'

'Godley's quite good on the computer. He'll probably know.'

'The files are pretty rough, so don't criticise the spelling mistakes and things. I was just trying to make sense of what Sir Charles said.'

'You can't remember him speaking about a jewel or a rock like this?'

'My memory still isn't that good, but I'm sure I would have remembered if there was a family secret involving a rare jewel. Your family didn't really have many secrets.'

'Hmm,' came the disbelieving voice. 'I suspect CJ's memory was selective. Families always have secrets. He probably just went on about how he won the point-to-points and was in the army. He probably skipped over the secrets.'

Ginny couldn't disagree.

'Well, send me what you have,' Aunt P continued. 'Godley and I are going through the old family papers. There are boxes of them, of course. New Zealand must be the key just because of Professor Cook, but there is no mention of New Zealand here. Ally said your job was finishing soon and you might have a bit more time. Maybe you could speak to Professor Cook's wife and see who wrote the letter?'

There was a pause. Working for the Scawtons again was not an exciting proposition. Aunt P was okay. She had known her forever and grumpy old CJ was dead now, but if she was going to be a Scawton detective she didn't want the new Sir Charles interfering. No way.

'How are you, dear? How are you coping?'

'I'm fine, Aunt Pamela. I'm still not too good at concentrating or even reading for a long time but getting much better. Working with horses is fine. I don't really have to think too much.' Ginny paused, realising she was twirling a strand of her hair unconsciously. It might be okay working for Aunt P and it might be something a bit different. 'I'm not sure how good I'll be, though. I'll have to write everything down.'

'Why don't you send me Drop It or whatever it's called, and I'll try and find out where the professor's wife is from the police here.'

The voice had softened, thought Ginny.

'And Ginny, dear, I haven't told Charles I'm phoning you. He's more concerned about his polo. We'll find out about the stone before we tell him anything.'

Ginny smiled to herself. Maybe Aunt P was on her side. She had no real reason to blame Charles for the accident but just felt no desire to speak to him again, either.

'I heard from some of the polo guys that Count Rosetski has disappeared. Doesn't Charles play for him? Where are his ponies?'

'I gather they're still in the Count's yard. It sounds a problem.'

'Oh my lord, does the Count own them?'

'Certainly not. Charles just has to find another team to play in. That's why he hasn't got time to worry about this letter and Mike's rock.'

They finished the conversation. She was a good old bird, Aunt P, and it was bad luck that Charles should have turned out such an arrogant bugger. She had long deleted him as a friend on Facebook and certainly wouldn't put anything about the stone on there. Not if it was as valuable as Mike thought.

✶ ✶ ✶ ✶ ✶

It was early the next morning when Pamela woke to hear the phone's insistent tone. She put her hand out to answer it and the duvet fell to the floor as Bentley and Florrie both appeared at her feet to demand attention. She grabbed the phone and sat up on the edge of the bed, glancing out of the window – it was still dark – and then at the clock. 6.30am. She took the receiver from the cradle and put it to her ear, trying to pick the duvet up off the floor at the same time, but Florrie was standing on it.

'Hello?' She was more concerned about getting the duvet up and shook it to move the pointer. She was cold.

'Aunt Pamela? It's Mike.'

Mike? Oh yes, Mike Williams. 'Oh, Mike, how good to hear you. How are you? You sound as though you are next door, not the other side of the world.' She was getting things organised now. The terriers were both on the bed and the duvet was back over her. Bentley was sitting impatiently looking at her, waiting to go outside.

'I'm fine. Ginny suggested I phone and tell you about the stone. I haven't got Charles' number.'

'I'm afraid Charles isn't here anyway. He's in London. What have you found out?'

'Well, that's the point. I didn't want to email. Charles' stone is very rare, and probably very valuable. I feel guilty because I just carried it in my pocket all the way from London. But it's an alexandrite and my professor doesn't even know how valuable it is.'

'A what-did-you-say?' Pamela was concentrating now. She hadn't heard of a jewel of that name. 'Valuable' sounded interesting, although she couldn't imagine it was going to be the winning EuroMillions ticket. She was holding the phone close to her ear; her other hand had stopped stroking Bentley and was holding her nightdress to her throat. 'It didn't look like a diamond or anything,' she commented.

'No, it's much rarer than that. Can you use a computer?'

'Of course.'

'Google *alexandrites*. And you'll see what it is. I can email you some information. Most of the modern alexandrites come from Africa, but this one came from the Urals. It's Russian. They don't mine them there anymore. It's uncut so it doesn't look like much, but when you really look at it you can see what it would be like. They change colour. It's called the alexandrite effect.'

'And how much are you talking when you say valuable?' Pamela couldn't help interrupting. Maybe it was the winning lottery ticket after all. Maybe it could help fund the new farm shop. No, the roof would need repairing first.

'I don't know. The professor says it's looks huge although it would need cutting before it was a jewel so it wouldn't be quite as big then. Thousands, he thought.'

'Pounds? And two thousand or a hundred thousand pounds?'

'Maybe not quite a hundred thousand.'

There was silence. Definitely enough for the roof. Suddenly she realised that if the stone was worth a lot, maybe the writer was intending to blackmail them for much more. After all, the old man, even if he had been a professor, had been carrying a valuable stone to *help identify me* or whatever the letter said.

'Is it okay if I email the details to you?' Mike asked. 'Ginny said it was better than contacting Charles.'

'Please do. Charles is busy with polo and the letter was actually addressed to CJ before he died. Did Charles show you the letter, Mike?'

'No, but Ginny's finding out about Professor Cook. She's going to email you the obituary and is trying to find out where his wife is. She also found there are Scawtons in New Zealand. Are they related?'

'It is such an unusual name. I thought we knew them all. I suppose anyone with that name would have to be related. The letter said the stone was being returned to the family but didn't say why.' She paused. 'Where's the stone now?'

'The head of department has it locked in the safe. I suggested he keep it there.'

'Good. Let me know what happens. Now, give me your email address just in case. I've got Ginny's. I'll email what the letter says to you both.'

After Mike had given her his mobile phone number and his email, she put the phone down, which was a cue for Bentley to put his head on the duvet. Time for a cup of tea, put the dogs outside and get that letter again. She got out of bed, picked up her woollen dressing gown from the chair and slipped into some sheepskin slippers. She went downstairs, the dogs running on ahead.

* * * * *

The large truck had left and now there were horses everywhere in the Ashly stable yard, tied to every available place. The girl groom was running around from one to the other, as the afternoon began to turn dark and drizzly. Pamela was standing in the stable yard with the phone to her ear.

'Charles, at last you're answering. Where've you been? What on earth are we to do with these horses?'

Ten horses had been unloaded. Most were standing quietly but they couldn't stay tied up for too long.

'I left a message for Adrian on his phone and told him to tell Sewell. Did they arrive all right?'

'It seems so, Charles, but Kathy here, who came with them, is expecting some of them to be stabled.'

'We managed to get them out of Rosky's stable, not without some difficulty. I've nowhere else to put them. They should only be there for a couple of weeks until I find somewhere. They need to be stabled.'

'Adrian is on holiday in Spain. He's the farm manager and has nothing to do with your horses and as I said on the phone last time we spoke, most of the stables have been converted for the pigs.'

'I know. I heard. That's why I left him a message to convert them back.'

'There are certainly not enough stables for ten horses.'

'Oh Christ, how many stables are there?'

'Probably four. I was only going to leave a couple of stables, enough for a hunter or two.' Charles seemed to be ignoring what she was saying.

'They're all meant to be in work. I was assuming Sewell would help Kathy ride them.'

Pamela was watching Kathy unbandaging the horses one by one. Sewell, CJ's old groom, was well past retirement and wouldn't be safe riding half-fit polo ponies. She supposed some of the horses could be stabled and the others turned out in the orchard. No, too many for there – the front paddock would be better. She wished Charles were here himself, instead of giving orders on the phone.

'For God's sake, Mother, keep the horses safe. Some of them need shoeing – you'll have to organise a blacksmith and feed and straw too. Kathy can stay there but you'll have to lend her the pickup to go back to Cowdray and get her stuff.'

'Who is paying for all this?'

'Well the farm can. Or the estate.'

'Adrian covers the farm costs. This pig conversion is just using material we have on the farm already. The estate has no money.'

'Oh, Mother, you're being quite unreasonable. This is an emergency. Surely you could help muck out the stables. I'm busy trying to find a team to play in. I think I may have a job with that ugly little man who owns the buses. It's only fifteen-goal – he's a useless player but at least it's a job.'

'That's good. Has he got a large yard?'

'No, I still have to find somewhere for the horses. Can't you convert the stables back in the meantime? The ponies need to be in work.'

'Charles, I suggest you get up here and look for yourself.'

'Mother, no wonder Father despaired of you. This isn't much to ask and it's not as though you do anything else. Kathy can ride the horses and I don't need you harping on about money. The least you can do is be supportive.' The phone clicked off.

Pamela had wandered back out of the yard towards the driveway. She put the phone back in her pocket and stopped. Of course Charles was quite right. He was under pressure; it was unreasonable of her to be angry at him.

She huffed out a deep breath and called out to Kathy. 'We can turn some into the big field through that wall or a small group can go in the orchard through that gate over there. That big field has plenty of grass.'

As Kathy waved acknowledgement, Pamela began to plan. Converting the stables back was impractical, and most of the horses could live out in the field perfectly well for now. The pickup wasn't licensed and so Kathy would have to take Pamela's car. She didn't really need it at the moment.

She had wandered back into the yard and up to one of the horses. It was Dainty, her favourite.

She spoke quietly to her. 'So you're back again, are you Dainty?

We'd better get those bandages off then.' She knelt down on one knee to undo the travelling bandages. While she unbandaged, she wondered what there was in the freezer. Kathy would need a meal. The old housekeeper's bedroom would be the best place for Kathy to sleep because it would be warmer than the front of the house. She needed to make up the bed and air the room.

She knew she should be more supportive of Charles but sometimes he didn't make it easy for her. He sounded just like CJ used to, except CJ hadn't always been like that.

In the early days, CJ would cajole her with a laugh. 'Come on, you, you can do anything,' he would encourage her. Poor Charles had never seen that side of him and had grown up only hearing his grumbling. This hadn't made it easy for Charles, and it was no wonder he'd picked up a bit of his father's carping tone. She needed to help him where possible and, of course, she could help muck out the stables. She moved to Dainty's back leg to take off the next bandage.

* * * * *

Right, thought Ginny, Detective Williams into action – Wellington first and Victoria University. She put in the website address and trawled about the website trying to find the Maths Department. The website kept going to courses to study – engineering, statistics rather than give details about dead professors. She gave up and decided to google *Scawton* again. Last time it came up with Charles' affair with the Argentine singer from 'What If', the sister of a top polo player. Their latest album was still being played around the world. This time she added *NZ* to the *Scawton* and the screen changed.

There was the website *Scawtons.co.nz* but when she went there, it said: *This website is under construction*. Dead end there. She found a report from a farming paper on some kind of new shop, which was called *Scawtons*. There was a photo of a Sally Scawton Miller holding a lamb, and Ginny wondered whether that was her name or whether the Scawton was there because she owned the shop called that. The girl looked rather attractive. There were other articles on farming, sheep and horses but all with a *Miller* added to the *Scawton*. So the family must be Scawton Miller.

She went to another link. In this article a horse called Grand Exit, owned by Bob Miller from Havelock North, won a steeplechase. That didn't seem a good name for a steeplechaser. This Bob Miller was quoted as saying the horse could win the Grand National but was that the New Zealand or English Grand National? She read on. *My grandfather won the race with a steeplechaser called Ashly.* So these Scawton Millers must be related. Too much of a coincidence. God, it said Ashly had won in the 1920s. They didn't sound the kind of family to send an uncut Russian jewel off to England with a maths professor, but perhaps they were.

Mike had said to phone these Scawton Miller people rather than email. Through the *White Pages* she found no Scawton Millers but she did find three *Robert Miller*s in Hawke's Bay and only one in Havelock North. He probably had nothing to do with Aunt Pamela and she felt embarrassed to think she might phone on false pretences. She practised what she would say – 'I was wondering . . .' No, that was too vague. 'I have a friend, Sir Charles Scawton', but she didn't consider Charles a friend any more. Perhaps she could use the fact that Aunt P was her godmother, her godmother in England. No, 'aunt' sounded better. 'I have an aunt.' No one would know she wasn't a proper aunt.

She needed to phone before her courage ran out.

She heard the phone ringing and a hurried voice answered, 'Hello, Anne Miller speaking.'

Ginny began 'Excuse me . . .' and explained that a friend in England was asking whether their family might be related.

'What was the name of your friend?'

'Scawton. She lives at Ashly and I noticed your family used to have a horse called Ashly or I assume it's your family ... I wondered if you were related.' It sounded so lame.

'Sir Charles Scawton?' The voice barely paused. 'Yes, of course we're related. Can you just hold the line while I get my husband?'

Here was a lead. It wasn't a wild goose chase after all.

'Bob Miller here.' He had an older voice. Ginny explained that Sir Charles Scawton lived at Ashly and she wondered whether they were related.

'I suppose you're the secretary?'

Ginny reeled. She tried to stay calm. 'Well, no. I'm phoning from New Zealand. For Lady Scawton who . . . '

'That's Sir Charles' wife, is it? Couldn't she phone herself?'

Ginny was nonplussed, not sure how to handle this. 'She's in England. She lives in Ashly and her husband died last year. Lady Scawton is the present Sir Charles' mother. She was just wondering if . . . '

'I know where they bloody live. Well, you get her – or this Sir Charles bloke – to contact us herself. She's welcome to make our acquaintance but I don't want to speak to her damned staff. Bloody hell, she can even come and stay at our bloody stately home if she wants.'

The phone went dead. Ginny took a big breath, wondering who on earth this man was. She was sure she hadn't been rude to him. She blew her breath out; she had no doubt, now, that the man was related to the Scawtons because he was just like miserable old Uncle CJ. Well, Aunt P could stuff it; she could phone her own relations, from England.

She picked up the phone again and dialled Mike's number. As usual, he didn't answer, so she left a message. 'Can't find the Professor's contact and got an earful from Scawton relations. So bugger them all. They can do their own detective work.'

It was evening and she was watching *Masterchef* on TV by the time Mike phoned back. She turned the sound down while one of the contestants prepared a dish with crab. Her mother cooked seafood without nearly so much stress, although that dish on telly did look pretty tasty.

'You had problems, chicken?'

'Don't chicken me. I phoned this Scawton Miller guy. He's obviously related to crabby old CJ and was really rude. I'm not speaking to people like that.' Mike listened in silence until Ginny had finished venting. before he said, quietly, 'I guess you haven't seen the *Sunday News* today?'

'No, why?'

'The *Sunday News* has an article – hang on, I'll just read it out.' Ginny could hear the rustle of paper. 'Headline is "NZ Maths Guru Murdered?"'

Ginny gasped. Professor Cook? At Ashly? She held her breath as Mike continued to read.

A memorial service was held for mathematician Professor Geoffrey Cook in Wellington. A Fellow of the Royal Society of New Zealand and a former committee member of the NZ Mathematical Society, he was on a visit to England when he died suddenly, reportedly from a brain aneurism.

Yes, well they knew all that.

However, after the service his brother, Theodore Cook, intimated that there was more to his death. 'They killed him' he told our reporter. When questioned further, the doctor, who hosted a popular children's television series some years ago, said that his brother was visiting a powerful family about a secret they didn't want revealed. 'They dealt with him and made it look natural,' he said. The Sunday News contacted the New Zealand Police, who said it was a matter for the UK authorities. As far as they understood, there were no suspicious circumstances and the matter was not being investigated.

8

England 1921

Ashly House was what her family called her 'other 'ome'. Aggie had grown up with four older brothers. Before she lived at the big house, she had been a wild 12-year-old, spending more time out of school than in. She and her brother Tom used to scarper off from school to watch the soldiers training on the Commons. They would then re-enact them, pretending to be their older brothers who were already trained to kill Germans and awaiting to go to France. So her parents were relieved when she was taken in at the big house, as the scullery maid, to live in while her brother Tom went to work on a local farm. That was over six years ago now, just after the war broke out.

She remembered how impressed she had been with the space at Ashly House. She had shared the attic room with two other maids but no one had to share beds. At first she found the work hard. She was expected to scrub everything, from the big dishes they used for cooking, to the stone flagged kitchen floor. She was only little at the time but the other maids were friendly, although Mrs Parker, or Cook as she was known, was fussy and strict. 'Go and wash this again' became a byword.

By the end of the war, Aggie had worked her way up to being a kitchen maid, although she knew this was only because so many of the other maids had left to work in factories. She still had the washing up because there was no scullery maid at all now but Cook used to tell everyone she was the best kitchen maid. That was until disaster happened.

Oh, how she missed her mother – if only she hadn't died of the flu and if only Mary was still working here. Aggie and Mary had shared the attic room after the war, when Mary came back from working in the hospitals. Mary's own mother had only recently died too so she understood how Aggie had felt and afterwards she had been like a big sister, warning her about men only wanting one thing and how she needed to be careful. Mary would have been furious with her now, although she would have been sympathetic too, and would have told her what to do.

Mary had left Ashly the same time as Mr Edward went to New Zealand saying she was going to work in the Scawton's London house, except when Mr Edward drowned she never came back for the memorial service. All the other London staff did but they said Mary wasn't working there. Thinking about it afterwards, Aggie had realised that Mary had been acting a bit strange before she left, even buying that lovely new dress and hat. If she had planned to leave the Scawton's employ, there was no reason for her to travel in the car with them. She said she would keep in touch and Aggie knew that Mary could write perfectly well – much better than Aggie could – but she never heard anything.

That left Aggie to cope with this problem by herself. She'd seen her father that afternoon but had lost the courage to tell him. Instead, she came back to Ashly and confessed to Mrs Howard, the housekeeper. Mrs Howard asked sensible questions. When did she last have 'those'? Had she ever missed before? Was she sure? Mrs Howard assumed, correctly, that it was the boyfriend who was the father. Did he know? Was it just in the morning she felt so sick? Worst of all, did her dad know?

By this time, Aggie was crying but Mrs Howard didn't seem to mind. In fact, she understood how difficult it would be to tell her father. He wasn't particularly religious – grace before dinner and the morning service on Sunday was about the extent of it – but Aggie knew he wouldn't cope with his only daughter getting knocked up. Now Mrs Howard was saying that Lady Scawton would allow her to stay at Ashly House for a few weeks, provided no one knew except Cook. She would have to leave before anything began to show. While Mrs Howard said she was lucky to be able to stay that long, Aggie was panicking as to where she would go then.

Cook gave Aggie a right telling off, saying how disappointed she was, how she had never imagined her as that kind of girl. Aggie never got the opportunity to tell her that she had been going out with her beau for over a year and she was sure he was about to propose. She had no idea that he would go and get some fancy job up north and that the boss would offer to take him to America to learn about car engines – in some place called Detroit. The other maids, most of whom came in daily from the village now, were surprised at Cook being so mean to Aggie all of a sudden but Aggie was relieved that Cook never let on. At least Cook was good in that way.

About two weeks later, Mrs Howard called her in to the housekeeper's room. She sat her down and told her again how fortunate she was. Because she had worked there for such a long time, Lady Scawton had arranged for her to go to some home near London, run by nuns where she would stay until the baby was born. The baby would then be adopted out. Usually the home didn't take girls until they were about to give birth but they had agreed to take on Aggie to work in the kitchen. Mrs Howard said that she had already spoken to Aggie's father and explained that Aggie would be furthering her experience by working in the family's London house. It was up to Aggie whether she wanted to tell him any more. She advised her not to.

The next day Aggie was allowed a few hours off to go and say goodbye to her dad. She wasn't feeling quite so sick now and was allowed to take some vegetables from the Ashly garden so she could cook dinner for him and the two brothers who still lived at home. Dad was working late at the forge and Tom, the brother she was closest to, chatted to her while Aggie cooked. He was full of how he planned to go to New Zealand. He could get a good job on a sheep farm. The New Zealand Government, or the sheep farmers themselves, would pay his fare. Aggie reminded him that Mr Edward had gone to New Zealand and drowned on the way, but this didn't seem to put Tom off. He saw it as an adventure and suggested that she come too.

'It would be better than working for the Scawtons in a steamy old kitchen for the rest of your life,' he said.

Aggie knew he wouldn't want to hear about her predicament, but she had to tell someone. He was shocked at first and they agreed that if Aggie told Dad, God knows what would happen.

'And what about after, sis?' asked Tom. 'Is Mrs Parker going to think you're no longer an 'ussy? She – and Lady Scawton – are never going to treat you the same.' Aggie knew he was right. No one was going to want to know her. She was a fallen girl.

'But I can't stay at this nuns' place in London after I've 'ad the baby. Mrs 'oward said.'

'So, you'll have to come with me to New Zealand.' They sat in silence for a while, until Aggie saw the potatoes boiling away and moved the pot to the cooler part of the stove.

'That's what you'll 'ave to do,' Tom said. 'You'll need a new start. You've been slaving away for those Scawtons forever and if you come back here, someone in the village will know.'

Aggie suddenly saw that Tom was right. After the meal, she suggested to her father that she might go to New Zealand with Tom. Her father looked shocked. He thought London was quite far enough but after a bit of persuasion, he said he wouldn't stand in Aggie's way if she really wanted to go.

The men couldn't understand why Aggie burst into tears before she left and wasn't more excited about working in London.

Her father gave her a hug. "Ow are you going to cope with getting to New Zealand, lass, if you're this nervous about going to London?'

*****

It was the first time Aggie had ever been to London. She had been as far as Watford on the train, but this time she was going all the way to Euston.

The train chugged slowly out of the station, covering the windows with black steam. The train seemed as reluctant to leave as Aggie.

Euston was the biggest station she had ever seen. The trains went right inside a high vaulted ceiling like a giant church, and the noise was deafening. There were so many people, all jostling and pushing. She still had to find her way across London to Waterloo and get the train to Croydon. Hours later, she was exhausted and relieved when she rang the doorbell of Duckham Lodge which, according to the sign, was the 'Mission of Hope'. The nun who opened the door asked her name and introduced herself as Sister Anne. She almost smiled at Aggie and seemed very calm and peaceful. She led the way to the matron.

Matron was a tall and skinny nun with a large hooked nose and beady eyes. She looked down her face like a nasty big bird eyeing up Aggie as though she was a worm. She sighed a lot too, which made Aggie feel even smaller, especially when Aggie was so tired and trying not to cry. Matron explained that Aggie would be working in the kitchen. Aggie would be expected to use the little chapel regularly and, of course, attend church on Sundays. She asked if Aggie were healthy or had any problems but never gave her time to reply. It wasn't a two-way conversation.

None of the nuns spoke very much. They kept to themselves and lived at the top of the house. Newborn babies were in the middle of the house and the girls in the basement. Aggie had never lived with so many girls at once but none of them were there for long enough to make any real friends. Some of them insisted that their intended had died; others, like Aggie, were just angry because their boy had pushed off. One said she had been seduced by a titled gentleman but then the girls began to doubt her because it was obvious that the titled gentleman hadn't been the only man she'd had.

All the girls were expected to work right up until the birth. The girls complained the work was arduous but it was no harder than at Ashly. A bell would go at 5.30am and Aggie would get up and start chivvying the others. Depending on what their duties were, they would start cleaning, setting up the kitchen, or helping with the washing. There was a small room set aside as a chapel, and they were expected to pray in there, for forgiveness, at least ten minutes twice a day. Those rests, on her knees, were the best time of the day. The girls were marched along to church twice on Sundays. The sight of up to twenty heavily pregnant 'naughty girls', as the locals called them, marching in a waddling crocodile, must have caused great embarrassment to the neighbours but for most of the girls it was the only time they ever left the property.

Aggie's work was in the kitchen. The meals were very plain, often with no pudding, or maybe just a small tumbler of jelly. They were much smaller portions than at Ashly and there were many more people to cook for, but Aggie soon realised that the years in Cook's kitchen had trained her well.

She had always known her baby would be adopted out. It was the one piece of advice Mrs Howard had instilled in her.

'Don't be tempted to keep your baby, Aggie. My niece tried that and ended up in the workhouse. She still had to give her away and she herself ended up in the asylum for a while. Don't even think about it.'

Even so, at one moment of homesickness, the baby felt like the only friend she had in the world, and she asked Sister Anne why she couldn't keep him or her. Sister Anne would have none of it either.

'Would you scar your baby for life by telling everyone she was born out of wedlock? She, or he, would end up in the foundling home. Or were you planning on taking her to New Zealand?' Matron censored and read all the letters the girls received and so they all knew Aggie's plans. Aggie began to cry, and Sister Anne softened.

'I assure you, our babies do go to people who want to bring them up as their own. It isn't like the old days.'

Aggie knew she was right. Only a very few of the girls kept their babies. They were the ones upstairs who spent the day trying to find a job or somewhere to live before they had to leave the home. They kept their babies but instead of feeling relieved, most of them would just weep miserably. No, adoption would give the baby a good opportunity in life, like the Wilson twins in the village who everyone knew were adopted after Mr Wilson came back from the war with only one leg. They were happy four-year-olds now. Perhaps her baby would have parents like that.

It was definitely best if Aggie went to New Zealand where she wouldn't be reminded but she was full of dread about that too, even though Tom, in his letters, was so excited. Aggie tried not to think of how far it was, or how Mr Edward had died on the way.

When the time came for one of the girls to have their baby, the nuns would take her to some other part of the house. All the girls were scared about what happened then. Sister Anne was the most approachable of the nuns but even she just said, 'The Lord will protect you.' Aggie asked her whether it hurt a lot.

'Of course, there is hurt. Just as you hurt the Lord by getting into this position. You have to pay. Just trust him to watch over you and look after the little one you will bring into the world.'

The other girls were more helpful and one of them explained exactly what would happen. To Aggie, it sounded horrible and so it proved to be. When the contractions were more than she thought she could ever bear, one of the girls fetched a nun and they helped her upstairs to a room where there was just a narrow bed and a cross and a picture of Saint Francis on the wall. There was the most dreadful pain but then a flannel with a nasty smell was put over her face. When she awoke, she was in another room with two beds, the other bed empty. Aggie turned her head to see Sister Anne, with her 'almost' smile, looking at her. She had a cup of water and helped her drink it. Aggie tasted more than water in the cup and afterward went straight back to sleep.

Springtime sunlight was shining through the window when Aggie awoke again. Her first thought was the baby. She wanted to see what had been growing in her for all those months. She hoped that Sister Anne would appear but when she did, Matron was right behind her.

'Ah, you are awake,' Matron began. 'Good. I have been speaking to Sister Anne. Cook has had to go back to Dublin suddenly and so hopefully tomorrow you will be back in the kitchen. The other girls are asking for you and we all enjoy your Yorkshire pudding.' Aggie nodded weakly. She wanted to ask about the baby, but Matron never wanted any questions. She swept out muttering 'fine' and Sister Anne stopped Aggie as soon as she mentioned the baby.

'It's best you move on straight away. And your baby too. Enough to know he is healthy and will have a good family. Rest while you can if you are to start back in the kitchen tomorrow. It's Sunday too.'

So it was a 'he' – a son.

Sunday usually meant brisket, slow roasted with what vegetables there were, and Yorkshire pudding made in the hot oven. The thought of food made her nauseous and she wondered where she would get the energy from. At least Aggie would be excused from attending morning service if she was cooking. She had nothing to thank God for.

Sister Anne was still there and, looking through the window, remarked on the sunshine. 'Spring is here,' she said.

Aggie felt guilty at her heathen thoughts. 'What date is it?' Aggie asked.

Sister Anne thought for a moment. 'The second of April today.' So her son had been born on the first of April. April Fool's Day. It wasn't much of a joke.

* * * * *

It was only a few weeks later that the *Rotorua* was due to sail. Aggie wasn't allowed visitors at the home but Tom had kept sending letters to keep her up to date. The miners were about to strike. He was afraid the railways would be on strike too but fortunately that didn't happen. Tom had arranged to meet Aggie at a pub beside the docks at Tilbury.

Ever since the birth, Aggie had been working harder than ever. She was still allowed her ten-minute breaks in the chapel but now whenever her thoughts turned from her work, she would start weeping. She knew she should be relieved that her baby had been adopted out. Sister Anne had told her he went straight away, and so he was no longer in the house. Her greatest sorrow was that she never even saw him, to know what he looked like. She hated the nuns for that and hated the Scawton family for making her come to such an uncaring place.

Yet when she walked out of the home, suitcase in hand, she felt she was leaving half of her behind. She wept quietly as she walked along the street to Croydon Station, shivering in the fresh air. She found The Anchor at Tilbury where Tom told her to meet but hesitated before going in. She wasn't used to entering pubs. Two men appeared at the door. She looked up to see Tom, but it took her a second to see the other man was Dad.

His grisly beard and his face burnt dark from the flying embers in the forge all looked so familiar. Aggie threw her arms around him and burst into tears.

'Ee, lass,' Dad murmured.

They spent a few hours catching up with all the news. Her father had seen Mrs Howard and she was full of the news that Lady Henrietta had just had a son and heir. No one had seen Lady Henrietta for months, he said, as she had been with her parents until after the birth but now she had arrived back and was installed in the newly decorated nursery wing.

Aggie winced involuntarily. No Mission of Hope for Lady Henrietta. Her baby had been born with doctors and nursemaids at the ready.

She could imagine the fuss there would have been when she arrived back with the baby although Aggie was surprised there had been no mention about her being with child when Aggie left. In fact, Aggie remembered being embarrassed because her maid was complaining about Lady Henrietta's monthlies. No maid should talk like that.

Dad brought her back to reality. He pulled an envelope and small package out of his pocket. Mrs Howard had given it to him, saying it was a reference from Mrs Howard and something from Sir William and his mother, because she had worked there so long. Aggie unwrapped it. It was some kind of small rock with one smooth side of pale pink glass. She held it in her hand, wondering why Lady Scawton would give her such a thing. She couldn't remember her giving any presents to maids except at Christmas.

It wasn't long before Tom and Aggie climbed up the gangplank onto the boat. Aggie knew she would be put on a separate part of the boat to Tom, in among the other single women. It seemed no time before the horn went and the ship began to move.

As the ship moved out into the middle of the river, Aggie clasped the rail of the deck, one hand still holding the stone. Just a few bits of pleasure up in the woods with her beau had led to all this. It had ruined her life. There was no one else to blame though and she just had to make the best of it. When she looked at the stone, she was sure it had been pale pink in the artificial light of the pub, but now in the afternoon sunlight, it had more of a greenish tinge. As Aggie wondered how the stone had changed colour, she pondered the changes in her life too. She would never forget the son she was leaving behind, never, she swore to herself, however much she changed.

She clasped the uneven sides of the stone even harder as she felt the tears running down her cheeks.

9

England & New Zealand 2013

Just as Charles opened the back door, he heard the telephone ringing. Godley appeared, hurrying to pick it up. He had a black and white apron tied around his waist.

'Ashly House,' Godley said. Only butlers could answer the phone with that cool all-the-time-in-the-world voice. There was a pause as Charles shrugged out of his quilted jacket and bundled it on top of the cupboards to his right. Only half his ponies had been exercised and it was hopeless trying to work them when they couldn't use most of the stables. Perhaps he should make them take out the wooden partitions put in the stables for the pigs – the pigs weren't here, his horses were.

'And may I say who is calling?' Godley continued. 'Please wait.'

'James Corey, Sir Charles, for you.' Godley said, his hand over the handpiece as he held it out towards Charles.

Charles frowned, wondering who would phone him here at Ashly. Everyone knew he didn't live here. 'Who's James Corey?'

Godley raised his eyebrows and gave a small shrug, still holding the phone out.

It occurred to Charles that it may be a polo patron wanting him for his team, so he hurried forward to take the handpiece from Godley, but as the speaker began to introduce himself, Charles' hopes died. It was a bloody journalist.

'Who did you say you write for?' he asked, about to cut him short. Then he stopped. He had spoken to reporters before. Some even had his mobile number and phoned at all hours. They would twist comments around if they could, particularly ones like this who worked for *The Sun*. It didn't do to just fob them off too quickly. He didn't need any bad publicity.

This man was going on about the body and Charles was quick to answer.

'Surely that would hardly be news now. Although the poor man was found here, he was old and died of natural causes. There was nothing suspicious. It all happened weeks ago.'

'Professor Cook was the man who died outside your house, wasn't he? Your mother found him.'

'So I understand,' answered Charles, careful now with his words. 'I was away overseas. It gave my mother a huge shock.'

'There was a memorial service for Professor Cook in New Zealand, and his brother reported that in fact he had been murdered – probably by your family. What relationship did you have to Professor Cook?'

'Absolutely none. Neither my mother nor I knew the man. We'd never seen him before. He died on a public footpath which happens to run through the edge of the estate and has done so for years. Why the man was there we have no idea.'

'So the man wasn't visiting the family?'

Charles paused. There was that silly envelope, and he could hardly lie when the man was found so close to the house.

'As I say, we have no idea who the man was and had certainly never met him. Have you spoken to the police?'

'His brother intimated it was murder and your family were involved in a cover-up.'

'My mother may live here but I doubt she would be able to conceal a murder. Why would she want to? She didn't know him and it was she who reported it to the police.'

'Your grandfather was high sheriff of the county.'

'My God, that was years ago.' The man was just digging. 'There was no murder. The poor man died suddenly. I think it was a brain aneurism, wasn't it? He came from New Zealand and I have no idea why his brother should think he was murdered.' Charles felt he was gaining traction.

'Thank you for your comments, Sir Charles. Do please contact me if you think there is anything more.'

Charles replaced the receiver and turned to find his mother at the end of the hall, listening.

'Some reporter about the body,' he explained, placing the handpiece back into its holder and pushing the phone further towards the window, wondering whether anything he had said could be misconstrued.

'No one's rung for weeks,' Pamela commented. 'Why on earth was he ringing now?'

'The man's brother announced at the professor's memorial service that it was murder and we covered it up.'

Pamela walked down the passage, her shoes squeaking on the flagstone floor. Charles failed to notice the shock on her face.

'It sounds like a game of Cluedo,' he said. 'Professor Cook in the dining room with the lead piping.'

✶ ✶ ✶ ✶ ✶

Although Ginny had told Mike that this was absolutely the last phone call, she was going to make on behalf of Aunt P, she was quite interested to find out why the brother thought the professor had been murdered. She knew Aunt P and Godley were the only ones in the house when he had died. She tried to imagine how they might have poisoned him with some concoction Godley knew about, and Godley and she would have dragged him out and manhandled him across the garden in the wheelbarrow before Aunt P would have pretended to find him the next day. No, she just couldn't envisage it.

She waited until late in the afternoon when, from her window, the shadows of the trees were extending right across the paddock. When she pressed the numbers, the phone took a while to get answered. There seemed to be no message service; the phone just rang and rang. Maybe she had put in the wrong number and so she pressed 'End' and started again, making sure the numbers were correct.

It gave the same ring but hello came as an annoyed voice. Oh, Lord, she hoped it wasn't going to be another rude person.

'Excuse me, are you the brother of Professor Cook who died in England?'

'Where are you from?'

'Er . . . '

'Why do you want to know?' the voice persisted.

'I'm phoning for the lady who found your brother.'

'He was found by some highfalutin' lady . . . '

'Exactly, I'm phoning for Lady Scawton.'

'Scawton, that was it. That was the family he was visiting.' The voice seemed agitated.

'According to Lady Scawton, she never met your brother.'

'You see? They deny he was ever there. Exactly what I thought. Goodbye.' The phone went dead.

Ginny couldn't believe he'd just cut her off. Her initial frustration became anger and she looked at the number she had written down, intending to dial again. Then she stopped.

Bugger them, she thought, that's enough. She was not going to have this malarkey when no one would speak. It was just too hard. As tears welled in her eyes, she decided she'd send this phone number and the wretched Bob Scawton Miller's number to Aunt Pamela and she could phone them herself. She was fed up with the lot of them.

* * * * *

The pharmacy where Polly worked was in Valley Road. She liked working there and could fit her hours around Simon although she had to work the occasional Saturday morning. The owner played golf on Tuesday and Thursday and as today was Tuesday, there was only Polly and an assistant in the shop. The rush of Monday prescriptions was over and, as usual, Tuesday was quiet.

She was sorting the new packets of Atorvastatin. The name was always changing depending on what drug company Pharmac purchased from. These were called Zarator. She piled them in the corner of the shelf when she felt a tap on her shoulder.

'There's someone to see you.'

Polly walked round the end of the shelf to see Diane there. She frowned, but then remembered Pete's reprimand and tried to put on a bland face. She hadn't seen or heard from Diane since they had met at Pete's and afterwards she had listened to Pete reminding them that Aggie had given the stone to Beth and if Beth wanted to give it to Geoffrey she could – it wasn't Diane's fault. Beth had sworn Diane to silence anyway. Polly was still angry but couldn't do anything about it. Pete didn't know why her mother had given the stone to Geoffrey or why Geoffrey had gone to Ashly to give it to the Scawtons. Polly wasn't about to tell him.

Diane looked a little apprehensive. 'Hello, Polly, I know you're at work. I just wondered if you had a moment.'

Polly supposed she had been a bit unfair on Diane and, anyway, she could do with a break from the pill counting. 'I wouldn't mind having a coffee next door at the cafe. Would you like one?'

It was a tiny café – more of a bakery with a coffee machine. They chose to sit at the one table outside.

'I know you weren't pleased with my sending that letter and stone for Beth, Polly,' Diane began. Polly said nothing. 'Now there's this. I don't know what to do. Did you see it?' She produced a newspaper, the *Sunday News*, folded over into quarters. Polly hadn't seen a newspaper for days; she got her news off the radio on the way to work.

Polly read the headline 'NZ Maths Guru Murdered?' and frowned as she realised that no, she hadn't seen it and it hadn't been on the radio.

'I keep thinking, if this were true, it would've been on all the news. It sounds a bit hearsay,' said Diane. She hesitated, giving Polly time to read right through the short article.

'I was worried though,' continued Diane, 'in case the letter and stone had something to do with it. So I contacted the *Sunday News* and got the name of the journalist who wrote the article, and I phoned her and asked her about it.'

'Oh? What did she say?' Polly had never heard of anyone doing that.

'She was an older woman, I think, or she sounded like one. She became quite cagey when I said I'd met Professor Cook. She wouldn't give me his brother's contact details, but in the end she did say that he was drunk and weird and she doubted the whole thing were true. She said the police had been quite offhand when she enquired and came back saying they had absolutely no evidence of murder or that it was covered up or anything.'

Polly read the article again. *There were no suspicious circumstances and the matter is not being investigated.* She looked up at Diane, still frowning.

'I was quite relieved after I spoke to her,' Diane continued. 'I just didn't want you or Pete wondering whether it was true. I don't think it is.'

Polly stared back down at the newspaper, realising that Diane was embarrassed. Perhaps Geoffrey would still be alive if Diane hadn't given him the letter and stone. Or at least he might not have died on some strange English country pathway. Except he was old, and he was going to die somewhere. Pete's voice came into her head. 'Don't take it out on Diane.'

She spooned up the froth from her cappuccino as Diane spoke again. 'I don't know why they put it in if there's no truth in it.'

Polly answered. 'It sounds like a Sunday paper story. If the other news services haven't picked it up . . . I wonder what the family are thinking?'

'Doesn't Geoffrey's wife have dementia? I expect that's why the brother would be the spokesman.'

'No, I mean the Scawton family,' said Polly. 'I wonder what they'll do with the letter and the stone.'

'You mean the Sir Charles who Beth was writing to? The letter didn't say much. Beth said that Geoffrey would tell them about it. Do you know what it was all about?'

'I think you said she didn't finish the letter,' said Polly, not committing herself.

'She didn't. The letter was barely a page. It said the Scawton family were *entwined with hers.* That was the word she used. *We've never met but your family and mine are so entwined. The stone was given to my mother.* Something like that. *She made me promise to seek the satisfaction she had failed to get.* She had an old-fashioned way with words.'

Polly wasn't sure whether that was a compliment or not and didn't comment.

Diane continued. 'Then she began to say something about adoption and the rules changing but never got any further. Do you know what she was wanting to say?'

They had both finished their coffee and Diane was still a bit flustered, Polly noted. Yes, Polly knew the story, but she wasn't going to tell Diane. She stood up and Diane got the message.

'Of course,' Diane said as they went to part, 'we don't know if Geoffrey actually got to the Scawtons. He might still have been on the way there.'

'You mean he might not have given them the stone and the letter? Where would they be then?'

'I suppose Geoffrey's effects would have been sent back to his wife

– or maybe to his brother and his brother found something among them, which made him accuse them of murder.'

Polly knew she had been little help in placating Diane but that was too bad. As she walked back next door to the pharmacy, she stopped. She was still holding Diane's *Sunday News*. Perhaps the stone had been sent back to the brother and maybe she could contact him.

* * * * *

The Williams' house had a welcoming air, even when it was raining. It sat comfortably among trees, a big elm overshadowing the lawn opposite the door. Small light-green leaves were beginning to show and causing the rain to drip unevenly on to the patchy grass below. The house was much more welcoming than Ashly House which sat outside the village and had a long bare drive. The trees there were mostly on the far side of the house.

Pamela parked outside the front door, as close as she could so that she didn't have to get too wet. She got out and ran to the porch, wiping her shoes on the large coir mat and pushing open the heavy wooden door. The unlocked door swung open at her touch.

She heard Ally call out, 'Hi, Mappy. Come on through to the kitchen.'

Pamela smiled at the kindergarten name. Ally was the only one who still used it.

Pamela ran her hand through her hair, but it had barely got wet. She turned into the passage by the stairs, drawn by the aroma. 'Hello, Ally. Lovely smell of coffee.'

'You come so rarely. I thought the least I could do was to put a proper cup of coffee on the stove. We'll stay in here, though – it's still so cold everywhere else.'

Pamela looked around the comfortable farm kitchen, bowls and saucepans piling up on the draining board and pots of jam and sugar sitting in the middle of the table. Newspapers were neatly stacked on the chair at the far end.

'Mike's still excited about that rock of yours, or Charles' rock or whatever.'

'Yes, I had an email from him getting very technical about it. I had one from Ginny too.'

'Ginny?' Ally interrupted. 'She should be doing something better than grooming hunters although she is talking about getting a proper job at last, or training for something.'

'It has been a long time, hasn't it?'

'The accident was a bitch of a thing, you know. When you think that, at the start, they said they thought she was fine. Just a hit on the head and maybe a bit of concussion, they said. I remember being so relieved.'

'I know. So were we.' Pamela felt uncomfortable. Charles was with Ginny when she had the accident and it'd been he who had taken her to hospital. Although Ally had never blamed Charles, saying it was 'just one of those things, he didn't know the balcony rail was going to give way', Pamela had always felt guilty; Charles said he was dropping Ginny back after a party, but she wondered what they were doing on the balcony in the middle of the night.

Ally continued. 'It's been more than three years of falling asleep, not being able to remember, too tired to get out of bed, drugs, counselling, God knows what. It's a strange thing, the brain.' Ally paused to pour the coffee into two mugs. Pamela was already sitting at the table. Ally had a check gingham tablecloth on it. You didn't often see tablecloths nowadays.

'What exactly did she have again? I know you told me.'

'In the end they called it a TBI – traumatic brain injury. The brain was okay but just couldn't cope with the hit on the head. I'm very thankful it's all over and she's nearly back to normal. Now, to change the subject, when I spoke to you a couple of days ago you were off to

London to see someone about the letter. What happened?'

Pamela smiled to herself and took a sip of coffee. Maybe Ally knew she was still embarrassed about Ginny's accident and was happy to change the subject.

'Oh, I'll tell you that in a minute. But I really came because I was worried about the email I received from Ginny. On my behalf, she's been digging around about Professor Cook but she kept getting fobbed off and sounded rather miffed. I didn't want her getting worried about it.'

'She hasn't told me anything, and I think she would have if she were too concerned. Now, what happened about the letter? You said you were going to London to find out.'

'That was most interesting. Did you know I found out that CJ had that post-traumatic stress disorder – PTSD – and I never even knew.'

There was silence as Pamela remembered Ally had never liked CJ. When Pamela had resigned from the pony club, Ally had berated Pamela and pleaded with CJ; Ally and he had ended up in a big argument.

'You never knew CJ when we were first married,' Pamela continued, trying to justify CJ's behaviour.

Ally smiled briefly. 'He gave a very amusing speech at your wedding I remember. After that, we lost touch and never really saw each other until pony club.'

Ally was sitting at the table holding her coffee mug between her hands. She suddenly put it down.

'Mappy, I know I shouldn't speak ill of the dead, but we did always wonder why you married CJ. He never seemed very kind to you and was always so crabby. Such an imperious Sir Charles. The kids were terrified of him. Ginny was quite relieved when she could stop working for him.' She paused. 'Did he ever mistreat you? Was he violent?' Ally was looking straight at Pamela.

'CJ? Absolutely not. He never touched me like that. The family gave me everything I have.'

'If he had post-traumatic stress disorder, why didn't he get treatment? Wasn't he in the army? Is that where he got it?'

Suddenly Pamela was crying. Tears coursed down her cheeks and she couldn't speak. Ally rushed round the table and gave her a quick hug, and then found a paper towel to give her.

'Oh, God, I didn't mean to offend you. Really, I didn't. It was just that we thought you were such a brick to stick with him when he was so mean to you.'

Pamela nodded and smiled at Ally, unable to speak for a minute. She shouldn't be crying like this and embarrassing Ally.

'Pamela, I know CJ was difficult to live with.' Ally spoke much more softly now. 'We watched you run the pony club brilliantly and knew that it was compensation for a lousy home life but I didn't mean to offend you.'

'You didn't. You didn't at all. It's just . . . ' She shook her head at Ally with tear-stained cheeks and smiled. She really didn't know why she had burst into tears.

'At school you were such a lively soul,' Ally carried on, 'and some of that appeared at pony club. The kids loved you but then CJ got in the shit with Lloyds and sold the farms. Even so, you shouldn't have had to resign and, when I spoke to CJ about it, he was so rude about you. I still get cross thinking about it. Afterwards you just . . . deflated. That wasn't you. I hated CJ for doing that to you.'

Pamela dried her eyes again and sat up straighter. 'Now I must look awful.'

Ally smiled. 'You look fine.'

'When I married CJ, he was fun,' Pamela explained. 'Outgoing, sociable, more like Charles is now. He hunted, played polo, tennis, all those things. We had a great life. CJ's behaviour changed just before he left the army. I thought it was because I wasn't getting pregnant and he'd had an affair with the girl who had a child – a son – and he had to give her up because he was married to me. That's what I thought for years.'

'Why didn't you leave him, if he was so mean? No – worse than mean – cruel.'

Pamela shook her head. 'He wasn't really cruel. He'd had to give up the affair for me, except now I know there wasn't an affair at all. It never really occurred to me to leave. Ashly was my home. What would I do? My own family had disintegrated, and I had no money; I wouldn't have been able to take Charles. I did think CJ had depression but that's very common and I couldn't see CJ being happy taking Prozac.' Pamela wiped her eyes again and told Ally about the army colonel. 'All along his problem was this post-traumatic stress disorder. The army doctors had known.'

Ally was sympathetic. 'Why didn't he have treatment, then?'

Pamela gave a small shrug. 'I think he did have a bit in the army but CJ never admitted anything was wrong. His father, James, was alive then and it never occurred to us that it was something which could be treated.'

'And now you feel guilty because CJ was difficult to live with and you thought that was just how he was?' Ally held the coffee pot up towards Pamela. Pamela nodded, smiling as Ally continued. 'And you should have forced the doctors to treat him, although CJ would have refused? You lived with him like that for twenty years or more.'

'Over thirty. What a waste.' It made her sound so foolish. Now it was Ally's turn to smile.

'Well, you didn't really waste it. The pony club never ran so smoothly. The chairman said you were wonderful on the hospice committee and weren't you on the committee that helped with raising the funds for the church repairs? You didn't exactly do nothing.' Ally helped herself to a biscuit from the plate and continued. 'CJ obviously had the opportunity to get treatment and didn't. You can hardly blame yourself.' She took a small nibble from the biscuit as she carried on.

'You know, CJ died months ago and you're stuck in that house by yourself. What are you going to do?'

'Charles still has his horses at home, and Adrian has pigs arriving any day to go into the stables. We have to do something with the house and the roof's falling in.'

'That house is a mausoleum and you live in one corner. You need a house in the village or something.'

'I have thought to move into the Lodge. The tenants are leaving, but I would still have to look after the house. Charles doesn't want to live there.'

'What will he do with it? Sell it?'

'We can't do anything without probate. I'd like to start a farm shop but there isn't any money for that. Then there's still all this business with the body and Mike's stone. Godley suggested I go on a holiday but that was before all this letter stuff. I can't see me on a cruise when someone's about to blackmail us or I'm accused of murder.'

'Murder?'

'The dead man's brother insists it's murder and we covered it up. Charles had a man phoning from *The Sun*. I've called the police since and they're sure there was nothing suspicious. They suggested the man's just upset about his brother and wanted someone to blame, but it was accusation enough to make the papers. Ginny emailed the cutting from the New Zealand papers. It was quite a big article.'

'The letter spoke about adoption. There was no one adopted in CJ's family, was there?' Ally asked.

'That was why I went to London. I thought there was, but I was wrong.'

'Mike thinks the New Zealand Scawtons may have something to do with it because Professor Cook came from New Zealand and because they were so rude to Ginny on the phone.'

'I didn't even know there were any Scawtons out there until Ginny found them.'

'So? Why don't you go out there and meet them? While Ginny is still there. She said they invited you.'

'Perhaps I can visit poor Professor Cook's wife and find out about the letter and why the brother thought we'd murdered the poor man.'

'Exactly.'

Pamela was quiet for a few minutes. 'I do have a friend who lives in Singapore. I could stay with her on the way.'

'Well then. Go to New Zealand and sort the whole thing out.'

Pamela bit her bottom lip. 'Do you think I should?'

Driving back to Ashly, Pamela thought about New Zealand. She would like to find out about the stone. Ginny seemed to be having problems and not getting much information. Ally had suggested skyping her but she'd have to ask Godley about Skype. Perhaps he'd know how to do that.

'Just go for a couple of weeks,' Ally had encouraged her. They couldn't do anything about the roof repairs for now; Adrian would be in charge of the pigs; Godley could handle the house and she really wasn't needed at the moment. In fact, she wondered if she ever was needed. She could have three days in Singapore and ten in New Zealand; there was just about enough money in her trust account to pay for it.

She turned down the drive, the house looming ahead of her across the park field. The rain had stopped and behind the silhouette of the house, the battleship-coloured clouds were clearing and moving away. Yes, perhaps she could go.

10

England & New Zealand 2013

The black London taxi slowed as it turned into the crescent of white Nash-designed houses, the traditional black iron railings and white facade hiding spacious offices as well as affluent apartments. Charles indicated the number and the taxi double-parked. Both Clarissa and her husband were good friends and, as he reached the top of the steps and Clarissa opened the front door, he lent forward to peck her on the cheek. He was surprised when she stepped back to open the door wide.

'I meant to phone you, Charles. David's plane was delayed. He's not back yet. Come on in.'

Charles could sense something wrong.

'He's landed and is on the motorway,' Clarissa continued. 'Emirates brings him back in a corporate car. Would you like a drink or something while you wait?' Charles looked around the hallway. He was always impressed by the daring red of the thick plush carpet, while the pale walls and plain gold-edged mirror made the place look chic. Clarissa, turning towards the kitchen area, was wearing a pale green jersey dress which clung to her body.

'Does it give us time for anything else?' As she turned back towards him, Charles flashed his eyes towards the staircase with a smile on his face. He had known Clarissa for years, long before she met and married David. At parties, they had shared different concoctions of drinks and drugs and when alone she would rarely let an opportunity pass.

'For Christ's sake, Charles. Isn't it time you grew up?'

That wasn't going to work, thought Charles as he wondered what was irking her. At one stage there were few secrets between them, but the confidential tête-à-têtes had become less frequent, along with the sexual encounters.

She continued talking while he followed her. 'We've known each other too long. And you've bloody well stuffed things up.'

Ah, so she was blaming him for something. Bloody women, always expecting you to guess what their problem was; Joanna was just the same.

Clarissa led him to the back of the house. It was one long room, with a kitchen, dining table and sitting area.

'Do you want a beer, Charles? Or will we wait until David is back?'

'No, I'm happy to wait. Tell me what the problem is.' Clarissa was rather attractive when she was upset. Her colour was heightened, and her movements became flamboyant.

'You owe David money,' came the short answer. 'He's hoping you're coming today to give the money back. I doubt you are.'

Charles tried not to grimace. Clarissa knew him too well and had guessed that he was hoping to borrow another few thousand, not pay any back. Now it was sounding as though it wasn't worth trying.

'Before he went away, David said the last lot was it. "Well beyond the call of friendship, damn him," were his words. I'm not allowed to ask you to dinner until you have paid some back.'

'Oh bugger. I can't repay until the bus man's started to pay. It all looks good and he has a son who will be in the team. Not brilliant polo, but it'll be okay. Until then, I'm bloody skint.'

'Charles, for heaven's sake, you're always short of money. Sell something. You own all those polo ponies and a socking great house you never live in. I suppose that's in a trust, is it? Grease up to the trustees then.'

'The trustees are not being helpful. I need the ponies, and I'm not allowed to sell the house. I tell you, there just isn't any money to live on. Once Father's probate is through I suppose I might get a bit more. Meanwhile, I'm at my wits' end.' He tried to sound deserving of sympathy.

'You never have enough money. Why don't you do something about it?'

'What can I do? Don't say I should get a job. I'm trying to be a polo player. What else could I do?'

'Well, marry Joanna. She's moved in with you, hasn't she?'

Charles looked at Clarissa in surprise. 'What on earth! I can't do that. It's not that I don't enjoy Joanna. She's actually quite alluring, but I don't know that I want to spend the rest of my life with her.'

Clarissa, sitting at one of the chairs at the table, fiddled with the green china apple she had picked up from the bowl on the table. Charles was standing with his back against the fireplace and realised she was deliberately avoiding catching his eye.

'Well, you're going to need an heir and it's time you were married.'

'Before I turn into one of those boring old rakes, leering at every girl? I'm far too young for that. *Hello Magazine* called me one of England's most eligible bachelors, although they did mention that I wasn't as rich as some, bugger them.'

'That's why you need Joanna.'

'Well, if I had to marry anyone, Joanna would be all right, I suppose. Except for her parents. Have you met them? Her father can only talk of trucks and her mother is what you call common.'

'I know. I met them at her 21st. Father is a trifle ordinary, I agree, but he's stinking rich and Joanna's his only daughter. She isn't stupid either.'

Charles frowned. Joanna never seemed short of money, but she didn't drive a flashy car or have a lot of jewellery. He hadn't really considered her rich. It was more her body he enjoyed. He wondered whether he could remain faithful to her, to the exclusion of even

Clarissa. He had quite fancied that redhead at the party the other night and supposed that wasn't a good sign.

'It's the forever bit that I don't like the sound of. You know me.'

'Nothing is forever, Charles. Yes, I imagine being a dutiful husband would be a problem for you and you'd have to be faithful for a few years. Until you had a son or two. Wouldn't it be worth it for the money?'

'He's probably the kind of father who wouldn't let her have any money.'

'Bullshit. Where do all those designer clothes come from? And you have the one thing he can't give her.'

'A title.'

'Exactly: Lady Scawton. Smites of respectability and breeding. Exactly what he wants. Propose and the floodgates will open, I can guarantee.'

∗ ∗ ∗ ∗ ∗

Ginny sat by her laptop ready to go.

'Aunt Pamela, hello. Good, you've found Skype okay. I can hear you. Can you see me?'

'Yes, dear, I think it works. Godley tested it. I can't see you . . . Oh yes, I can. There you are. I haven't got a camera on this computer so you can't see me. Just as well but, yes, that's you and you're looking very well. And Godley says this doesn't cost a thing.'

They discussed the wonders of Skype but even without seeing her, Ginny could tell Pamela wanted to get down to business.

'I've lots of questions. I'm really sorry you've had to speak to such rude people. I haven't phoned the relations yet. I thought I would speak to you first. You spoke to Professor Cook's brother but what about his wife? Is she at this Victoria University too?'

Ginny loved Pamela's directness; she was just straight into it.

'Vic University is in Wellington, Aunt Pamela. Mike and I couldn't find out where the wife is.'

'The nice policeman here checked and said that they were asked to send all his effects to his brother, not his wife.'

'His brother's the one who accused you of murder. He sounded odd. Mike says he's some kind of scientist.'

'The police here say they have absolutely no evidence of murder and Professor Cook died of a brain aneurism. Charles wants to sue the man for libel. Now tell me about these Scawtons.'

'Scawton Millers actually.'

'They were rude to you as well but still invited us to stay. Is that right?'

How was Ginny going to explain it? She tried not to show any expression in case Aunt P noticed on the video. She sat still in front of the camera.

'I've never heard of them,' Aunt Pamela continued. 'I don't remember CJ or anyone knowing any Scawtons who went to New Zealand. Scawtons are pretty rare, with only one boy per generation. He must be a very distant cousin. Did he elaborate?'

'No, not really.' Except with 'bloody hells' Ginny thought.

'The letter was addressed to *Sir Charles Scawton* quite clearly. Not Scawton Miller. What did this Scawton Miller relation say?'

'He said perhaps Lady Scawton or Sir Charles would like to contact him themselves. Or you could come and see them.' Ginny didn't elaborate on the 'bloody acquaintance' bit, or the 'our stately home.'

'Well, dear, I thought I might come out and take them up on the invitation. The police here say they're sure it wasn't murder, but I want to find out about this stone and clear it up.'

'Come out here?' Ginny was amazed. She had never heard of Aunt P going anywhere. She used to stick to old CJ like a limpet and her mother used to say the week at pony club camp was Aunt P's annual holiday.

'The Scawton Millers live in Hawke's Bay,' she continued. 'You could hire a car and drive I guess.'

'Would you be able to come too, dear? I wouldn't like to drive in a strange country by myself. I'd pay you of course.'

'Hmm. I probably could, Aunt P. You'll need to phone them yourself, though. I did send you their number, didn't I?'

'I would need to meet the scientist brother too and find out why he thought the Professor was murdered – there must be some reason – and also find Professor Cook's wife. I'm sure she must be wondering what kind of place her husband died in and perhaps she knows what all this is about. Can we do all that in ten days?'

'I don't see why not. Where would you stay when you arrive?'

'Is there a hotel or pub close to you? Somewhere cheap.'

'No, not really, and you can't stay in a pub, they're not like English pubs. I've got a spare room in the flat. You could stay here.'

'Perfect. That would be ideal. Now, how are you, Ginny? Are you well?'

As soon as the conversation was over and Skype turned off, Ginny phoned Mike. 'God, Mike, what have I done now? Aunt Pamela is coming to stay.'

'She's coming to New Zealand? Good, she can do her own digging.'

'No, it isn't good. She's coming to meet the obnoxious Scawton Millers and Professor Cook's brother. I stupidly offered her the spare room and now she's coming to stay here. What do I do?'

'Well, she's not an ogre.'

'She's Mum's friend. She's old and she's used to having a butler. She wants me to drive her to Hawke's Bay. Although she did say she'd pay me.'

'Well then, stop whinging.'

* * * * *

Charles was driving the BMW fast and erratically. He was annoyed at the truck that was going so slowly in the middle lane, and he was also irritated by his mother because she would harp on about money all the time. He swung out to the fast lane, causing a car behind him to flash its lights.

'There's too many cars on the motorway for this time of day,' he complained.

'Charles, for pity's sake, all the way you've ranted and raved while I'm trying to enjoy this trip to your ancestral home,' Joanna said.

Charles moved his head in a circle in an attempt to relax.

'I'm sorry, darling. It's Mother I'm annoyed about. She used to be quite sane and capable but now I don't know what's got into her. She rattles on about money and now she's talking about going abroad. She doesn't know what she's doing.'

'She probably feels insecure. Your father didn't die that long ago, and my grandmother was like that before she moved to the retirement home. They become frightened.'

'I suppose so. Damned truck.' On the wet road, the spray, as he overtook the large truck in the middle lane, made visibility almost impossible. 'It's not one of yours, is it?'

Joanna peered across, through the window. 'No, it's Liverpool Transport. Daddy wants to take them over and has been getting Marcus to work on it.'

'Well, tell him when he does to put decent mudguards on the trucks.'

'Yes, sir,' laughed Joanna, pretending to salute.

Charles frowned. He was clear of the truck now and back thinking of his mother.

'Mother didn't sound frightened. She keeps rattling on about the letter and the stone. She already has Mike and Ginny trawling through New Zealand finding out about the old codger who died. Now she wants to go there.'

'Mike's the friend who's a PhD student, isn't he? The one you gave the stone to?'

'Yes – we've known the family forever. I took Ginny to a party, years ago.'

There was a groan from Joanna. Charles remembered she'd said that she was tired of hearing about girls Charles had taken out. Usually they told her themselves about how they had slept with him, or would reminisce on Facebook, complete with photos of parties. She should be glad that they considered him exciting.

'You're quite safe, I never slept with her, but I was there when she had the accident.'

'Oh, is she the one who fell off the balcony?'

'Yes.'

'What happened?'

'She was at uni and there was a party close by. I thought she might like to go. She was too young and hopeless. Didn't want to drink or smoke, you know the kind. We went back to her flat, had an argument. She went out to the balcony and the rail gave way. She didn't fall far and landed on the grass below. By the time I got down there she was coming to. I took her off to hospital and she was released the next day, supposedly okay. But in fact she had something wrong and went all weird. I think she may have had the problem before. She was always falling off horses.'

'What were you arguing about?'

'Oh, nothing really.' He glanced out of the window. Damn Ginny. He should never have been there and should never have got so angry with her. She was just a tease. He gripped the steering wheel tighter.

'You mean she wouldn't sleep with you?'

'It's the next turnoff we take for Ashly.'

'Silly girl. She didn't know what she was missing.' She put her hand on Charles' lap and felt the zip of his trousers. Charles smiled weakly, trying not to respond. It was good to have someone on his side.

The car swung through the large stone gates. The oak trees were hanging over the gates and rhododendron bushes hid the entrance to the Lodge. The drive opened up into a grassed park with black wrought-iron rails lining both sides of the drive. Cattle grazed in the field on the right. One, with a large white face, looked up over the rails as Charles swept past. He slowed down, realising there was a pothole just where the drive bent left towards the large house towering ahead of them.

'Well, the house isn't exactly tiny,' commented Joanna beside him, 'and it's got lovely lines.'

'Mother only lives in one end of it. The rest is pretty shoddy.' Charles' eye was caught by two horses standing by a gate in the stone wall leading to the stables area. A girl released them, and they trotted away to join the others already in the field.

'What the hell?' exclaimed Charles. 'She's meant to be catching the horses, not letting them go.' He glanced at his watch and the car promptly hit another pothole, making the engine surge angrily.

Swinging the car past the gravelled drive at the front of the house, he drove straight round to the stable yard at the back. A large truck was backed up into the yard and Charles assumed it was the truck to collect his horses. He parked beside it and leapt out. Out of the corner of his eye, he could see four dogs rushing towards the car, barking, and Godley coming out of the back door.

'Kathy, Mother,' he yelled towards the yard. He could see at least one horse tied up in a stable.

'Oh, there you are Charles,' he heard his mother call. 'Just in time to help with the pigs, darling.' She poked her head round the top of the truck ramp, waving a walking stick in the air. 'I twisted my ankle and can't move too well.'

'Why is Kathy turning horses out when they should all be going into the truck? What's happening?' he shouted out to her over the gate, not wanting to go into the mud when he was clean.

The stable yard was surrounded by a 4ft-high stone wall, which was probably just as well, as suddenly a lot of little pigs were running down the ramp of the truck, squealing loudly and bringing a flurry of dirty straw with them. One darted off towards an open stable door, several ran in circles and others disappeared under the ramp of the truck.

'Charles, help. The dogs . . . ' The two pointers were standing at Joanna's door. One dog was trying to put his head inside the slightly open door, and Bentley was standing back barking.

Charles called to Godley. 'Gods, for Christ's sake, lock the pointers up. Joanna can't even get out of the car.' He turned back to the mayhem in the yard.

'Shut the feed room door, Kathy,' Pamela was calling out as she hobbled down the ramp. Several horses were neighing, and one was banging on the wall. 'Someone needs to see to Dainty. There isn't a top door to that stable.'

Charles walked through the gate and found a snuffling melee of little pigs at his feet. He'd cleaned his shoes before he left London and now booted out at the pigs, making them squeal and run away. Through the top of the stable door, he could see Dainty kicking out at the wooden wall.

'Why isn't there a horse next door to Dainty?' he called out.

'More pigs are going in there in a moment,' called a voice.

Pamela and a wrinkled old man dressed in corduroys and a check shirt were both holding light wooden hurdles and herding the piglets towards a stable at the end of the line. Charles stood frowning as the pigs disappeared into the stable.

Pamela, regaining her walking stick to help, hurried to climb the ramp of the truck again. Kathy and Sewell scurried to the still-kicking Dainty.

'Morning, Sir Charles,' the old man said, nodding his head in greeting as he moved towards Dainty's stable. 'You're just in time.'

'Sewell, what . . . ?' But the man was scuttling quicker than Charles had seen him move in years and disappeared into Dainty's stable.

'Mother, what on earth is going on?' he called out.

From the top of the ramp she shouted back, 'Well dear, your horses were all in the yard. The horse truck was meant to come earlier but never came. Now the pigs have arrived, as you can see, and your horses are not enjoying it. Horses don't like pigs. The pig man has been very patient in waiting until Kathy turned most of the horses out again, but we do have to unload the pigs. You could help by picking up that hurdle at your feet.'

Charles was furious. He had deliberately delayed the horse truck because he had wanted to show Joanna the horses and wasn't going to flog down the motorway too early in the morning. He hadn't bothered to phone about it because it shouldn't have mattered. Now he watched as Sewell appeared with a fractious Dainty on the end of a rope. The mare's eyes were flashing as she gave a small buck, but Sewell took no notice and within a minute the mare had quietened.

'Hi Charles, what's going on?' Joanna called from over the wall where she and Godley were standing, close to the iron gate. Charles was about to introduce Joanna, but his mother had disappeared back into the pig truck and when she reappeared she was giving orders again.

'We are about ready. Godley, if you and Charles' lady – hello there – could just shut that gate. The pigs are little and could get through it.'

With that, about a dozen little pigs rushed down the ramp. As if they had heard, they tore straight towards the iron gate and several dived through where Charles had left it open. Joanna stepped back in a hurry and tripped, falling backwards on to the gravelled drive. Two terriers appeared, having escaped from inside the house and, barking, began to chase the piglets as Godley helped Joanna up. She was unhurt but one high heel had broken.

'Get the pigs, Godley, they're getting away,' called Pamela. Fortunately the pigs had decided to avoid the terriers and surged back into the yard, the two dogs in hot pursuit.

'My God, are you all right, darling?' Charles rushed over to the gate where Joanna was up and smiling bravely. While Charles commiserated over the broken shoe, Godley shut the gate.

'Just stop them getting out there again,' called Pamela, still at the top of the ramp. 'Terriers, stop that chasing.'

Sewell and Kathy were herding the piglets down towards the next empty stable amid squeals as they resisted and looked for escape routes. Charles took no notice and was helping Joanna towards a low wall by the back door where she could sit.

Just at that moment, a large horse truck drove into the yard. Charles beckoned the driver to drive forward, even though it was obvious there was little room to turn around. His car already blocked the way.

The squealing lessened as the pigs were safely ensconced in the stables, with the terriers now sniffing outside their doors.

Charles took over, wanting his horses loaded immediately and bewailing 'Why weren't they bandaged and ready for travelling?'

Although the pig truck driver was grumbling, wanting to get away, it was obvious the horse truck was now blocking the exit. Charles insisted it would be quicker to load the horses and get rid of the horse truck first.

Sewell and Pamela led the horses forward, stopping while Kathy quickly bandaged their legs before loading them so they wouldn't get injured on the trip. Charles, standing beside Joanna, was still fuming. His shoes were ruined, and Joanna could have been hurt. He just stood with his arms crossed, watching the others load the horses. Joanna remained quietly sitting on the wall holding her broken shoe and looking somewhat dishevelled.

At last the horses were loaded. Kathy said a quick goodbye and climbed up into the front seat of the horse truck. Charles spoke to the driver who began to reverse the truck into the main drive. Immediately he turned to help Joanna to the car; they would need to buy her new shoes and he was in no mood to deal with his mother. Pamela was already directing the pig truck to turn around safely. Charles revved the BMW, sent up another spray of gravel and joined the exodus.

*****

Pamela stood beside the Aga, holding a piece of paper. There were several flights available to Singapore and then New Zealand. She just had to choose which.

Ally Williams had offered to look after the two terriers, and Godley was happy to take on the two pointers. He and Mrs Godley lived in the village, and he said that Mrs G insisted that the two dogs move into their cottage while Pamela was away. She never seemed to mind when Pamela walked them along to visit, and Pamela knew Godley enjoyed the dogs' company as much as she, although this was for nearly two weeks.

She had told Patrick, who sounded more encouraging than usual, and said the break would be good for her. He also felt that Charles was appearing to take more interest in the estate.

'He has a few ideas on what to do with the house. He says he's sure he'll do better than having pigs in the stables.'

'Oh dear,' commented Pamela in a tone that made the solicitor laugh.

'I am sure the house will still be there when you get home.'

She was still standing there when the phone rang. She walked out into the corridor to answer it while the dogs watched her from their beds against the wall.

'Mother, I have been expecting an apology.'

'Good morning, Charles? An apology from whom?'

'Your behaviour was despicable. You never even acknowledged Joanna, let alone helped her when she fell. I was extremely embarrassed. The whole thing was a disaster. What on earth got into you?'

Oh, yes, the pig debacle. She began to laugh. Once it was all over,

Sewell, Godley and she had enjoyed the lunch Mrs Short had made for Charles and his girlfriend and kept roaring with laughter at the pigs' antics.

'Them pigs don't round up like sheep or ducks,' commented Sewell.

'And horses hate them. Dainty was going berserk,' said Pamela.

'Oh, she were just reminding us she were a lady,' added Sewell.

'Well, Sir Charles' lady friend could have easily hurt herself. Those high heels were enormous. I'm not surprised they broke on the gravel,' said Godley.

It now seemed, from the tone of his voice, that Charles hadn't seen the funny side.

'It was messy, wasn't it? But the horse truck was late. The horses were meant to have left before the pigs arrived. And I was sorry you rushed off – we were all prepared with lunch and everything.'

'It shouldn't have mattered the horse truck was late. I wanted to show Joanna all the horses and the house, but it was a complete nightmare.'

Surely a nightmare was an overstatement!

'We did load them in a hurry. Did they arrive safely?'

'They were fine. They're next door to the bus man's yard, but I was horrified at your behaviour, Mother, I must admit. Horrified. What has got into you?'

'What on earth do you mean?'

'You hardly noticed Joanna. You were very rude, and we can't have the yard full of pigs. The smell in the house will be horrendous.'

'I'm sorry you thought it was a nightmare and I was sorry not to meet your girlfriend. Godley said she was lucky not to hurt herself.'

'She's fine, Mother, but there are still potholes in the drive. You need to get repairs done.'

For a moment, Pamela remembered CJ speaking with exactly the same tone. Why have you not done so and so? It's your fault. You've not done it correctly. She had heard that tone for years and years.

'Charles, there's no extra money at the moment to fix the drive. They're left on purpose so that the taxman can fall in the potholes and realise there are no hidden millions.'

'You're on about money again. Obviously your priorities are wrong.'

'Yes, they probably are.' Perhaps changing the subject was more tactful. 'Did the horses settle in?'

'Yes, we have our first game next week,' he said, his voice sounding a little more conciliatory. 'Of course the horses are barely fit. Now, didn't you say that you were thinking of going to New Zealand?'

'Yes. I am. Singapore and New Zealand. I want to find out about this letter.'

'New Zealand is all hills, sheep and bungy jumping, and you can't possibly go by yourself. You've never been anywhere.'

'I went to America with your father. We even went to France. Your father said the drains smelt. Paris was lovely though.'

'New Zealand's far further and this stone business isn't that important. Besides, you don't know anyone. Where will you stay?'

'Ginny seems happy to have me stay with her in her barn. We're driving down to see these relations.'

'Mother, you can't possibly stay in a barn and as the polo season is starting, the bus man is expecting Lady Scawton on the sidelines. No, Mother, you can't go.'

Suddenly Pamela began to have doubts; perhaps it was a fantasy, getting on planes and flying all round the world by herself; she felt exhausted thinking of it. Besides, if they were letting out the house, she should stay and help.

Her heart sank. She had watched Charles play polo hundreds of times. Even at the start of last season she would drive CJ to the games and CJ would sit in the car and grumble, although she would enjoy walking up the sideline to see the ponies. Now it seemed she was expected to spend this summer traipsing around England watching Charles playing club polo and drinking Pimm's with his new patron.

She didn't care how many buses the man owned.

'I would like to get to the bottom of this letter and murder business,' she suggested, with a flicker of hope.

'You know it wasn't murder, even the police agree. The letter was all just some attempt at blackmail which failed because the guy died. I'm still checking whether we could sue the brother who accused us of murder, but there's no point in you going out there. You can put the stone on display for visitors to look at instead.'

'What visitors?'

'I've been speaking to some consultants about turning the house into a guest hotel, operating it ourselves.'

Pamela was taken aback; Charles had never mentioned speaking to any consultants. She had discussed with Patrick letting out the house but running the house as a B&B certainly wasn't on the agenda.

She heard the back door click behind her. The dogs got up but didn't bother to bark as Godley appeared, smiling at her as he went into the kitchen with a bag of bread and milk. He signalled to the kettle and Pamela nodded. The dogs lay down again.

'You know, dinner with Lady Scawton stuff. High class,' Charles was continuing. 'You could look after them.'

'Oh, I'm not sure I'd be able to run a hotel.'

'Oh, no, I quite agree. It'd need to be done properly. Professionally.'

'Surely the best option is that we let the house out and I move to the Lodge.'

'Who'd want the house? Some foreigner who'd want to put a temple in the front garden or who knows what? It's not in Gloucestershire or Oxford or anywhere fashionable.'

Pamela despaired that he should have opinions like that.

Charles continued unabashed. 'So you can see why this is not time to traipse off to New Zealand. I'll bring these consultants down and you'll see what we mean about a hotel.'

As the conversation finished, she resigned herself to cancelling the idea of New Zealand. It would save money.

She explained to Godley that Charles didn't want her to go and sat down at the table.

'You need a break, Lady Scawton,' he argued, 'and it's not for long.'

'Yes, but perhaps I'm just obsessed with this letter business. After all, it's CJ's family, not even mine. We haven't found anything untoward, have we? We've been through all those papers.'

'Wouldn't you wonder for years what it was all about? The man died trying to get a message to you. It would haunt you.'

'Charles wants to run the house as a hotel and put the stone on display. You know, "blackmail gone wrong" stuff.'

'That sounds a good idea,' said Godley. 'Getting someone to use the house as a hotel – I don't mean putting the stone on display.'

Pamela had already discussed with Godley the idea of letting out the house. She could move to the Lodge and Godley could retire, as he had been asking to for years. He could still come and help her when Mrs Godley wanted him out of the house. There was plenty of space for the dogs, as the fields in front of the house would still belong to Charles. Charles could decide whether to stable his polo ponies or have pigs and it wouldn't be her concern.

'The only trouble was that he talked about "we" running it rather than a hotel company. He suggested I stay here as a sort of hostess.'

Pamela suddenly had visions of the Ashly hall painted lime green like Simpsons-in-the-Strand, full of modern, hard sofas covered in white velvet, with upright padded leather chairs or perhaps those see-through dining chairs and glass-topped tables. A B&B with dinner. It didn't appeal. Just as being Lady Scawton on the sidelines at polo didn't appeal either.

'You know, Godley, I think two weeks away would be excellent. I think I will go to New Zealand after all.'

11

New Zealand 1931

Aggie woke to hear Michael beside the bed, pulling on his clothes. He whispered. 'See you later, Aggs. I've told Mickey to milk the cow when he gets up.' Mickey was barely eight years old. The cow wouldn't get much of a milking. Maybe there would just be enough for the children's porridge.

She pulled the blankets over her. This was the only time she had to herself, before Mickey started getting dressed and woke the two younger boys as he did so. She could hear the birds just beginning their dawn song. It would increase into a raucous chorus once the tui started. She was sure the birds here were much louder than she remembered the birds in England being.

Her life now was such a long way from England, from the life she had known growing up. The homesickness she had felt on the boat and when she had first arrived in Auckland had long gone. She was too busy being a mother now and wouldn't have swapped her life with Michael for anything, even though she worked harder than she ever did at Ashly cleaning the dishes, or in that awful home working in the kitchen.

It was only when she thought about her dad or got letters from home that it would hurt. The latest letter was from her brother Jack, forwarded to her from her brother Tom in the Manawatu. It told them that Dad had died. It hadn't been unexpected. She knew he was ill and would have loved to have been there to nurse him but knew that would have been impossible. At least he had a peaceful end and his arthritis wouldn't be hurting him now.

Jack told them that the church was full for the funeral. They'd used the church hall for tea and cakes afterwards and the committee refused to let his family pay anything for it – they reckoned Dad was such a stalwart in the village. The vicar's wife arranged it all and made her special sponge cake which she said Dad always liked. Even Sir William Scawton had come to Dad's funeral and he had brought his son, James. Jack said he seemed a dark, strong boy.

She knew that Lady Henrietta had been pregnant about the same time as her own firstborn son was born, ten years ago now.

Whenever she thought about England, she wondered about that first son, the one she never knew. She imagined him adopted out in London, his father working on the railways or something, with lots of other children around. She hoped he'd have siblings, like the O'Briens out here, over by the railway line, who had five girls and then adopted a boy.

She would always mourn not being able to see him – just once. Those mean nuns had prevented her. It wasn't as though it had been a stillbirth or he had died and wasn't there anymore. Somewhere he was alive and living – and was her son.

She wished there were someone she could tell her secret to, just as much now as then. Only Tom knew about her first child now. She had never told Michael because she knew, being Catholic, he would never have forgiven her. Michael's mother might have understood – she was Māori and was always great at helping Aggie out with the boys, but she might not keep the secret to herself. Aggie certainly wasn't game to let Michael's father find out – he had a fierce Irish temper.

She thought of eight-year-old Mickey and how he had been as a baby. He hadn't been that easy, although he'd been quiet compared to Sean who had colic all the time. Was her lost baby like dark, brooding Micky or did he scream like Sean? She knew it had been the right thing to adopt him out. It would have been too unfair for him to grow up in the village as a bastard but if Lady Scawton and Cook had been a little more sympathetic and the nuns a bit more understanding . . . If she could have had some idea of where he went and could have been able to have a look at him at least once. If . . . if . . .

She'd always blamed Lady Scawton. Looking back that was probably unfair because it was the nuns who wouldn't let her see him. All Lady Scawton had done was arrange for her to go there and it wasn't Lady Scawton's fault she'd got into trouble in the first place. It was just that people like the Scawtons held such a moral sway over the village. Jack had mentioned Sir William coming to the funeral as though it was a special honour when Dad had slaved away shoeing the family's horses for years. When she'd become pregnant, Mrs Howard was more concerned about what Lady Scawton would think; and the way Cook had treated her, as a fallen girl, was horrible. They insisted she should be grateful because Lady Scawton had arranged for her to go to the nuns' home and work like a Trojan cooking, when she'd only been sent there so that no one at Ashly House had to be embarrassed. Lady Scawton probably advised the beak-nosed matron how to treat her.

There must have been a kinder way to adopt a child out. Having your first child wasn't something you ever forgot about but those nuns not even telling her where the baby was going or letting her have one quick look – that was cruel.

All she had now was an odd stone, which changed colour and had forced her to change too. It was compensation for not going back to the village and asking for her job back, but it would never be compensation for not knowing about her son.

12

New Zealand 2013

Ginny went upstairs to change out of her wet clothes. She'd stripped off her parka and left that downstairs. New Zealand rain was harder than England and riding in the rain wasn't fun. It always made her knees cold. She was just pulling on a clean pair of jeans when she heard her mobile phone ring. She hobbled from her room to the sitting room and, seeing the phone on the table by the window, went and swiped the screen.

'Hello?'

'Ginny, it's Charles. How are you?' For some reason, her stomach gave a lurch. She hadn't spoken to Charles for years. How did he even know her number?

'Hello, Charles.' She really didn't know what to say.

'I was trying to get hold of Mother. I gather she's with you. She's not answering her phone.' Ginny remembered Aunt P said she was giving this number for emergencies. Lordy, she hoped something hadn't happened.

'She's arriving tomorrow morning. Is everything all right?'

'Oh, bugger, I thought she was with you already. She must have given me the wrong time.'

'Shall I ask her to phone when she arrives? It isn't bad news, is it?'

'No, not at all. I just wanted to tell her something. Make sure she phones when she gets there.' Charles didn't sound as though it was bad news. If anything, he sounded excited and slightly drunk.

'Okay, then . . . er . . . How's the polo?'

'Going well. I'm playing down at Ciren this year. Might get a couple of 15-goal tournaments. Not high-goal unfortunately.'

'Yes, I heard the Count had disappeared. That was bad luck.'

'Well, I think it might turn out for the better in the end. So, is Mother really going to be staying with you?'

Ginny felt guilty that she hadn't arranged anything better. 'She'll come here to start with. I'm so sorry she's not here.'

As Ginny swiped the phone shut, she wondered why she felt so uneasy and why she was apologising. It wasn't her fault that Charles had phoned too early to get Aunt P. He was so up himself. Nothing was ever his fault.

She finished zipping up her jeans, wondering how on earth she'd ever fancied Charles; he was so sleazy. As kids, she and Mike had always envied him – the big house, the champion pony, which made him a champion rider, a brand new Land Rover and smart trailer – anything he wanted, everything Ginny would have liked.

As a teenager she was flattered when he took an interest in her. He was older and she thought so worldly. She was at uni when he phoned to ask her to go to a party close to Southampton. He'd picked her up in his fancy Audi and taken her to a large house near Winchester. She hadn't known anyone else and found the women were all immaculately dressed, looking ready to be photographed for the front cover of *Vogue* while she was wearing the only dress she possessed, which her mother had bought for her to go to the Hunt Ball the year before. Even though she'd washed her hair, it felt messy. The men leered at her and she realised that, to them, she was just another of Charles' girlfriends. Not a friend, just a bird.

As one of the obnoxious men so aptly put it: 'You're not really Charles' normal style. You must have hidden talents.' He guffawed as she squirmed with embarrassment.

Charles had wanted her to stay and party all night. There was too much dope and drink around and she felt lonely and uncomfortable.

She insisted she leave soon after midnight, pretending she had to do an assignment the next day. Fortunately it wasn't far and he could drive back to the party after taking her home. She didn't really care.

Her flat was the top floor of an old house and had a view over the city. She remembered it had been a balmy night. Charles followed her up the stairs – which probably meant he expected to sleep with her. She remembered climbing up the stairs, opening the front door and wondering how she was going to get rid of him without being rude. Her two flatmates had gone home for the weekend. She honestly couldn't remember anything after that. Sometimes she thought she remembered what happened. Did she lean back against the rails with Charles leering towards her? Did he try to grab her as the rail broke? Or was that her imagination? Did she remember lying on the grass and Charles peering down at her, helping her up? Or was that just her imagination again?

She did remember being in the hospital with a nurse who kept waking her up. She remembered that. Mum had come in later in the morning and cried when the doctors said it was only concussion. Charles had disappeared by then, although Mum had said it was he who had taken her to hospital. By the evening, she was discharged and Mum took her back to her flat. The landlord had arranged for the rail to be fixed; her mother went on home and that was the end of that.

Or so she thought – but in fact, it was just the start. Three days later her flatmates made her phone home and her mother came and collected her. All she could do was sleep.

∗ ∗ ∗ ∗ ∗

Polly had found out the address of Geoffrey's scientist brother. He lived in the west of Auckland, near Piha – not just west but way out west. She had been there once with her mother, years ago. She remembered Piha as a windswept expanse, big sand dunes with marram grass and

Lion Rock sticking up on the edge of the beach. She also remembered getting there through twisty bush-clad roads which had made her feel carsick. That was why now, having turned off the coast road down the narrower Lone Kauri Road, she was driving carefully. She didn't want Simon beside her complaining of nausea.

Overhanging trees meant the road was dark and still wet from the rain. They came to a dilapidated A-frame house, which looked like a church. It had no number but there were few other buildings around. She stopped the car and got out.

The immediate quiet of the bush took her by surprise after the loud music Simon had been playing in the car. In the damp silence, the soft buzz of crickets felt threatening.

She knocked on the door under the protruding roof. Almost immediately it was opened. The man was tall, skinny, wrinkled and not unlike Geoffrey. He even wobbled like Geoffrey.

'Are you Theodore Cook?' she asked.

'Come in, come in.'

She noticed his brown cardigan was mis-buttoned and when he turned, it was threadbare at the elbows. His cord trousers looked no better – misshapen and old. The man looked shambolic. Polly turned and signalled to Simon that this was the right house. She needed her son for moral support.

She trod carefully onto a timber floor, noticing how the boards creaked. The house was not as large as it looked and was seriously overcrowded. The slanting roughsawn-timber ceiling was all dusty rafters and cobwebs. She turned to introduce Simon, but the man had gone ahead to the far side of the room where he almost disappeared among the old furniture, the unlit potbelly stove and piles of books. Polly wondered whether the place was safe.

Simon had a different reaction though. 'Cool,' he said, walking confidently in, and past the wooden kitchen bench piled high with yet more books, empty tins and plates, which to Polly, didn't look quite clean.

'Don't touch anything,' Polly whispered. 'For goodness' sake.' She tried to remember whether she had hand sanitiser in the car.

Theodore invited Simon to rifle through the books on the table beside the empty dust-laden stove. Polly was wondered what was in them.

'Good of you to come to my humble abode,' the man was saying as he straightened up from moving piles of books around and sounding as though he had invited her, instead of her asking to come. When she had phoned him, he had acknowledged that he had Geoffrey's suitcase from England but hadn't elaborated on any proof of murder or whether the stone was in the case. The man had seemed so vague so that she had asked if she could come and look herself.

'Allow me to get you a cup of tea and perhaps a lemon drink for you, young man.' Polly saw Simon was warming to this unkempt stranger and tried to attract her son's attention but failed as the lure of all those books became too much. Simon had picked up a large book with trains on the front and then he changed it for another one. Theodore had moved to the kitchen bench where he filled a chipped enamelled electric jug in the sink full of dirty dishes. He pushed the electric cord into the back of it. Polly remembered her mother having one of those old jugs years ago – they were positively dangerous.

As the man reached into the sink for a dirty cup and rinsed it under the tap, Polly answered. 'I don't need anything, thank you.' There was no way you could trust whatever was in that cup. Undeterred, the man went to an old fridge Polly hadn't noticed and pulled out an old glass whisky bottle, its label torn. He poured a pale juice into the cup and before Polly could stop him, walked over to Simon and handed him the mug. She knew it would be rude to snatch the mug and insist Simon didn't touch it. Perhaps the liquid would be sufficiently chilled to be okay and it was too late anyway, as Simon was already sipping it and thanking the man. Theodore wobbled around the pile of large books on the floor, haphazardly arranged or maybe just fallen there. He pulled out a large book with a torn cover of stars and handed it to Simon.

Then he lurched back to the bench and turned to Polly.

'You sure you won't have tea? It's very good. Peppermint. Helps the digestion, and relaxes you, don't you know? Made by a lady down the road. Very refreshing.'

'No, I'm fine.' Automatically she remembered that peppermint can also interact with diabetic medication. She assumed Theodore was not diabetic and watched as he made himself a cup.

'I was so sorry to hear about Geoffrey ... er, dying, so far from home.' She tried to sound caring. 'You think your brother was murdered?' She suddenly felt guilty about bringing up the subject so quickly.

'Who? Geoffrey? Oh yes.' He had obviously been about to join Simon by the fireplace but then changed his mind, putting his mug on the bench and pushing aside more detritus. Polly sat on a tall stool on one side of the bench, while the man now leant against the other side. He looked at her, as though noticing her for the first time.

'We weren't close, you know. He was always racing around going places – Australia, England. He loved digging in the past. Ridiculous.' He sipped from his mug.

'You said he was murdered.'

His face suddenly wrinkled up. 'Did you read that silly article? I was a bit pissed when I said that. He probably wasn't murdered. Is that why you are here? I ...' he paused, an anxious inflection in his voice as he tried to divert her to having some tea. 'You sure you won't?'

Polly shook her head. 'I gather you knew why he went to England?' she asked, wanting to get him to concentrate on what she had come to ask.

'He had a lady friend – what was her name?' he asked.

'Beth?'

'That's right. He died going to her old home, Ashton? With that strange rock. He was going to see them.'

Polly sat up straighter and for a moment, trying to ignore how odd the man looked. 'Ashly. Did he tell you about the stone?'

'Oh, that stone. He showed it to me, the day before he left. Never seen anything like it. Dug out of the earth but with a strange dichroism. It changes colour.'

'I know. The stone belongs to my family. That's why I'm here.'

'Why you're here?' The man's brow furrowed again and his whole face seemed to wrinkle with it. Polly hadn't noticed his hands were also wrinkled and they shook as they held the mug.

'Yes, I just wondered whether Geoffrey still had the stone when he died and maybe it had been returned to you."

'He died in England.'

'Yes, but when I phoned you said his belongings were sent back to you.'

The man's face cleared; his smile was crooked with a couple of missing teeth. His sudden openness unnerved Polly even further and he spoke. 'Oh, you mean the suitcase. The suitcase is in the cupboard outside. I took out all the papers and books – a couple of his books are around here.' He rifled through a pile of books on the bench, coming up with a battered address book.

The man flicked through the pages and handed it to Polly. She recognised Geoffrey's closely written, almost squashed, handwriting. The script was so unlike his tall loose frame. He would throw his arms around to tell some unfunny story to which he – and her besotted mother – would laugh raucously. She sighed, remembering that there hadn't been much laughter at the end when Mum was ill. She flicked through from the end of the address book and came to 'W'. She recognised one name.

'This is my uncle, Pete Walsh.' Polly held out the book and pointed at the name. _Beth's brother_ was written beside the name. Perhaps it would give her some credibility in Theodore's eyes.

'Beth's brother, eh?' He peered where she was pointing.

'I'm Beth's daughter,' she said. She wasn't sure he was even listening until he gave a sudden small leap and started shambling towards the front door, leaving it open behind him.

Polly stood to follow and called to Simon to come too but he was engrossed in some large book. She could see Saturn with its rings. He was reading, with one hand stroking a large tabby cat, who was lying in a cardboard box lined with a dirty towel. The cat didn't look particularly healthy; it was probably riddled with fleas.

'This is a neat book, Mum.'

'Just watch that cat.' You never knew with cats.

She went to the door and peered out. The green bush seemed so close, looming overhead and still dripping damp. She could see Theodore at the corner of the deck, opening a small wooden door. She stepped towards him and nearly tripped as he backed out of the door with a suitcase draped in cobwebs. The suitcase couldn't have been there more than a week or two but looked as though it had been there for years.

'This is what they sent back. They were going to send it to Marion, but not much point is there? She's far too doolally.' Polly knew Geoffrey's wife had Alzheimer's and lived in a home in Hamilton. It was the one reason why Polly had not complained too much about Geoffrey and Beth's friendship.

Theodore put the suitcase on an old backless wooden bench, almost tipping it up. He pulled out a pair of brown shoes, large but clean, a bag of toiletries, a pair of striped pyjamas, a soft green sweater Polly could imagine Geoffrey wearing and several neatly folded pale check shirts. There didn't seem much.

'You know this isn't bad. I might take it.' Theodore picked up the green sweater and shook it out. It wouldn't stay clean for long, Polly thought.

There was no stone, no letter from Beth.

'There were no other papers?'

'His papers were just his itinerary, details of the conference, that sort of thing,' said Theodore.

Together they stuffed everything back into the suitcase, except for the green jersey.

'There was no letter from my mother? Among the papers?' Polly asked.

'No, I thought your mother died.'

'She did. She died last year.'

'That was why he went to that place, Ashton. He wanted to see the family there. What was their name? He had this story he had to tell them.'

'Scawton. Sir Charles Scawton. Do you know the story?' She sighed at the thought that Geoffrey might have told him the story.

The wrinkled face looked up at Polly.

'That's the name. Scawton. It was them that found him. No, I had no idea what it was about. He just showed me the stone. Do you want this stuff?'

Polly shook her head. 'No, thank you.' She watched as Theodore took the suitcase and wobbled back to the open shed door.

'You said you thought the Scawton family had your brother murdered.'

'The silly journalist wrote the article.' He shut the shed door and weaved his way back along the wooden boards to the front door.

'But you must have said you thought they did?'

'Well, they were the last people to see him, and it was a strange place to die. They could have killed him, given him a pill or something.'

Polly sighed. A pill to cause a brain aneurism was pretty unlikely. 'The article said the family might have covered up the murder. Was there anything about it in what was sent back to make you think that?'

'Think what?'

'Perhaps something in the papers about the stone or anything from my mother or the Scawtons?'

The face furrowed again. 'No, the papers were all about his conference and genealogy papers. You know that was what he was interested in?

The probability of recurring genetic traits in families – myopia, colour blindness – that kind of thing. Digging in the past, all overtaken now by DNA sampling and genetic research. Waste of time, really.'

Theodore looked wistful for a moment. 'Would you like a drink of something? I might be able to find some of the neighbour's plum wine.'

They were still standing outside on the deck. Polly would have liked to ask again about any papers but doubted Theodore could have found them in the chaos inside. 'So you only saw the stone that one time, before Geoffrey left for England?'

Theodore nodded. 'I would have known if it had been here,' he said.

Polly supposed he would. She was distracted by Simon, appearing at the front door and looking along at them.

'I wondered where you went,' he said.

Polly glanced around at the dark green bush, the large menacing fronds of ponga almost touching her. There was no stone. No hope. It was time to leave.

* * * * *

Aunt Pamela strode out of the airport arrivals hall at Auckland, immediately commenting that New Zealand was much further away than she had imagined and how pleased she was to get here. As her godmother kissed her on the cheek, Ginny was taken aback at the familiarity. Aunt P wasn't really the kissing type, but Ginny still found herself warming to her enthusiasm. She'd remembered her as taller, more distant.

'It's lovely to smell some fresh air,' Aunt P said as they walked across the car park. It was barely daylight. Ginny sniffed the air but could only notice aviation fuel.

'Sorry about the messy car.' Ginny was suddenly embarrassed by the battered blue Corolla. It was quite reliable but wasn't too smart and she realised that she should have borrowed the new farm ute. Aunt P didn't say anything but maybe she was just being polite.

'I am so glad you live on a farm. That apartment life in Singapore would drive me dotty.' Ginny backed the car out of the parking space and once on the road back to Karaka, asked about Ashly.

'Oh, the house is just the same, falling down, but they're building more houses on that old airfield on the other side of the village. It'll mean even more people in the village. The village post office closed down. Did your mother tell you?' Ginny had only been away from home for a year but there seemed to be lots of changes.

Back at the farm, Pamela climbed the wooden stairs to the top of the barn ahead of Ginny. Ginny was still nervous about having Aunt P to stay, especially after Charles' derogatory tone on the phone. She had cleaned the place from top to bottom but now wondered again how Aunt P would fit into the tiny spare room after the huge space of Ashly House. After all, Aunt P was her mother's friend, not hers.

Pamela was polite about the flat, saying it was perfect. Ginny was embarrassed, knowing it was not perfect; it was tiny. She left Pamela to unpack, have a shower and settle in while she went and caught the four horses that needed exercising. The couple who employed her would both be riding today. The day before Ginny had told them her aunt was a 'lady' and Caroline, the boss's wife, had suggested that in that case perhaps Pamela should stay in the big house, but it was too late to alter the arrangements now.

She was saddling the first horse when Aunt Pamela came down from upstairs. Ginny introduced her employers and they chatted politely while Ginny put the fourth horse, which had lost a shoe and was lame, in the stable. Ginny was surprised at how deferential Caroline was, apologising that she had to stay in the flat – just because Aunt P had a title for Pete's sake. It was enough for Ginny to change her mind. She wasn't the Queen and the arrangements had been made; even Aunt P thought the flat good enough.

As they walked the horses out of the yard, Ginny glanced back at Aunt Pamela, who was looking quite envious, standing there alone. Perhaps she would have liked to ride too.

Ginny was relieved that Mike was coming to dinner that evening. When she'd arrived back upstairs after riding, Aunt P had greeted her with a tea towel tucked into her waist and a cloth in her hand. 'I gave the bathroom a good clean after I used it.' It was all Ginny could do not to point out that she had spent all day yesterday cleaning the wretched place. It was spotless. She smiled weakly as she wondered how she was going to cope with all this for ten whole days.

She'd been able to disappear off to clean the dirty saddlery and then had fallen asleep for part of the afternoon – Aunt P was going to have to get used to that. Fortunately Pamela had taken herself off and walked for miles round the farm, and Ginny was calmer by the time Mike arrived for dinner.

'Now, dears,' Pamela began when she had finished helping Mike lay the table.

Ginny was within earshot, just heating the lasagne she had made the day before and wondering what was coming now. Mike could deal with Pamela's demands.

'First of all, I think I had better be Pamela. You're too old to have aunts and it's going to confuse everyone.'

'Good idea,' said Mike. 'As long as we don't have to call you Lady Scawton or Ma'am.'

Ginny smiled. Mike was so laid back.

'Mike, don't be silly,' Pamela said. 'Although, the title can be useful, particularly in Singapore. Wonderful when you're booking a restaurant. They'll always find a table.'

Ginny brought out the lasagne. She was trying to remember the last meal she had eaten at Ashly House. It was probably served on the dark, polished dining table with Godley leaning over her shoulder and saying 'More water, Miss Williams?' Now she pushed the salad over to Pamela, and said, 'Please help yourself. Unless you popped Godley into your suitcase.'

'Oh, I wish, dear. He's retiring, you know.' They began to discuss some of the local village news. The meal was cleared away before anyone even mentioned the letter and the stone.

'Do you have the alexandrite, Mike? That was what you said it was, wasn't it?'

Mike stood up to put his hand deep into his trouser pocket and pulled out the crumpled tissue paper. He spread it out on the table, revealing the rough stone and turning the smooth face uppermost so that it caught the light from the centre of the room and glinted pink. Ginny watched Pamela pick it up; a softer look came into Pamela's eye, as though she were happy to greet an old friend, and she turned it to catch the light again.

'I'd never seen anything like this.' Mike explained, 'It's a chrysoberyl but a very unusual one. It changes colour and becomes green in daylight. That's called the alexandrite effect.'

'Yes, I remember now. The gems in the tiara we had did that, although they seemed much paler in colour. You say it's worth – how much?' asked Pamela.

'The mineralogist expert who identified it was pretty cagey about that. Thousands anyway. It's going to be a collector or gemologist who's going to buy it, because it isn't fully cut.'

'And it's probably flawed,' said Pamela.

'No, it isn't. That's why it's so unique. He says the clarity is excellent. Many of the modern ones aren't as clear. There is no one in New Zealand who would even know how much it's worth. He suggested taking it to Amsterdam or Paris. Or London, I guess.'

'Hmmm.' Pamela was still looking at the stone. Ginny noticed that she was beginning to look quite tired, and her face was lined after the flight, even if her manner was still lively. They had cleared the dishes away and Pamela had placed the stone back on the centre of the table.

Suddenly Pamela got up and went into the spare room, coming back a moment later with a clear folder. It was the letter and the note.

There were marks on the photocopy where the paper had creased but it was still legible. Ginny could see that Mike was intrigued, reading the letter carefully.

'No wonder you thought it was threatening. *Returned to the family.* Yet you never knew about it?'

'Sir Charles certainly didn't mention anything in his memoirs,' added Ginny.

Mike had one hand on the table. He had a thin brown sweater over his open shirt, but his arms were slightly longer than the sleeves and it made his tanned hands look larger than ever. Pamela was staring out of the window at the dark, sitting as though she were the chairman of the local village committee, her hands clasped together on the edge of the table. Her face looked pale and the lipstick she always wore had worn off.

'The first thing to settle is the professor's brother,' Pamela said. 'The one who thinks I murdered the poor man. Our lawyer in England says that what the newspaper had printed is hearsay and not libellous, but Charles thinks we might have a case against the man if he doesn't immediately retract his statement.'

'Really? I don't think there's been anything in the papers since,' Mike said, raising his eyebrows.

'Wasn't he one of the rude people Ginny spoke to? Presumably that was because he thinks his brother was murdered. We meet him first don't we, Ginny?' asked Pamela.

Mike put the paper down and gave Pamela his full attention, pushing at his tousled hair. 'Ginny asked me to phone him to arrange it. He started off prickly but then eased up when I explained I was just a PhD student and not a journalist. He said he did a PhD, but he couldn't actually remember what on. Said he didn't want any more enquiries about his brother, and he was never that close to him anyway and he didn't seem to know who you were until I pointed out you were the one he accused of murder. "Lady Thing", he called you. He says he goes into Titirangi once a week to visit the library and you're to meet him in a café there.'

'If he's so intelligent, surely he'll realise we can sue. The lawyers in England say a court case would be difficult but, as Charles says, we don't want this thrown up every time the family is mentioned in a newspaper – you know how they are. Charles insists I should be very forceful with them.'

'Them? I thought you were just meeting this man,' said Mike.

'He may have his solicitor there too.'

Ginny frowned. Mike had said he had arranged a casual meeting, not a lawyers' confrontation.

There was a slight silence before Pamela admitted, 'I just want to find out why he thought we'd committed murder.'

'Well, this'll be your chance,' concluded Mike.

'Then we go to see Professor Cook's wife, don't we?' Pamela continued, changing the subject from the professor's brother. 'If his brother doesn't know what all this is about, hopefully his wife will.'

'It's funny. She's in Hamilton, in a retirement village, when he lived in Wellington. I said you'd phone before we went,' said Ginny.

'Then you're off to see your relations in Hawke's Bay,' added Mike.

'Yes, ones I didn't even know existed. But I've brought the family tree and some old family photographs. I thought they might be interested. They're Bob and Anne Scawton Miller.'

'Didn't you say the relations were difficult, Ginny?' asked Mike.

Please Mike, thought Ginny, don't mention how rude the man was.

Fortunately Mike was back to fingering the stone and said, 'You do wonder how a Russian gem mined in Malyshevo – that's close to Ekaterinburg where the Russian royal family were murdered – came to New Zealand. Why hasn't it been cut and made into a fancy necklace somewhere? Where's it been all this time?'

* * * * *

Polly knew her uncle would be inquisitive.

'So what was Geoffrey's brother like?' he asked.

'Weird, Uncle Pete, far worse than Geoffrey. He lives miles up in the Waitakeres, damp bush all around, in a disgusting house, untidy and filthy. I'm surprised we weren't poisoned. And he was more interested in talking to Simon than to me. I can imagine what Geoffrey's house was like now.'

Polly was glad to be sitting in Pete's tidy kitchen, even if the kitchen stool she was perched on was a bit wobbly. At least Pete had a lady come in twice a week and clean the place, and had the dishes washed and put away.

Pete laughed. 'Geoffrey wasn't weird. He lived in an apartment in Wellington I think. Maybe he was a bit eccentric, but he was always interesting.'

Polly gave an involuntary grunt. It seems for the older generation there was a fine line between 'interesting' and 'peculiar'. Theodore was over the top, just like his name. Theodore for pity's sake.

'So the brother still thought poor Geoffrey was murdered?' Pete had put his stool by the oven; presumably he had been cooking something on the stove and needed the stool for support. The light on the oven was on. He wasn't that steady on his feet and Polly wanted to warn him to make sure he didn't fall.

She kept to the subject though. 'Not really. He thought that perhaps the Scawtons could have given him a pill that caused the brain aneurism. I suppose it isn't too far-fetched, but I haven't heard of anything that will do that. Not one pill I mean – you'd need a whole lot.'

'And why did they want to kill him?'

Polly pursed her lips and frowned. She knew why they might want to kill him, but she wasn't going to say. 'Because of the stone, I suppose.'

'But you said earlier that the stone wasn't among Geoffrey's things, which meant that he must have given it to the Scawtons before he died. If it was originally theirs and Aggie had stolen it or something, then they had it back. They didn't have to kill him to get it.'

'Aggie didn't steal it. You know she was given it by the family.'

'So why did she want to give it back?' There was a pause before Pete sighed. 'I know you know the whole story, just as Beth did . . . Beth wouldn't say either.'

'Nan told us but made us promise not to tell.'

'It all sounds very mysterious. Presumably it involved returning the stone and Beth sent Geoffrey off to do that.'

'She wanted me to go to England, but I couldn't afford to do that. Anyway, the stone is ours. Or was.'

'I'm blowed if I can see why they would bother to murder him for it, if he'd already given it back to them.'

'Oh, I think that was just this silly man's idea. For Geoffrey, the effort of getting there was too much. He had just done a long trip all around the world and given them the stone back.'

Pete leant down from his stool and opened the oven. A puff of steam came out and he shut the door and turned the temperature down. The comforting smell of meat wafted across to Polly.

'Hmm, it smells all right, Uncle Pete. I'd better go.'

'You can have some if you like. It's only a supermarket pie. Not sure what kind. Chicken, I think.'

'No, I have to collect Simon.'

'Well, I'm glad poor Geoffrey wasn't murdered. Bad enough dying over there by himself.'

'It was rather sad that there was just a suitcase of stuff sent back. I don't know what happened to his body or anything. I never asked – but at least we know that Geoffrey must have given them the stone.'

13

New Zealand 2013

First thing in the morning, Ginny would bring the horses into the yard for feeding and then return upstairs for a cup of coffee and a catch-up on Facebook or emails before starting on the riding. That morning, when Ginny thought Aunt P would be severely jetlagged, she came back upstairs to find her up and dressed and the table laid for breakfast. Pamela was digging around in the cupboards for cereal.

'I think there might be some cornflakes somewhere,' Ginny said. 'I don't want anything.'

Pamela looked at Ginny and raised her eyebrows. 'Why not?'

Ginny couldn't eat this early. Breakfast was an older generation thing. 'I'm not hungry,' seemed a pretty straight answer. 'Coffee will do.'

'You need something to start the day. Couldn't find cornflakes but here are Coco Pops. I'll get something healthier for tomorrow. Or would you rather toast? You have to eat something – we've got this big meeting today, plus Mike's adventure.'

Ginny sighed. She might as well agree. She could see Aunt P was not going to allow her to get out without anything. 'Toast, then.' This Theodore Cook had not sounded a 'big meeting' kind of person. Mike said he was vague. A small café in Titirangi didn't sound like a battle site, and Mike's suggestion of a walk on Karekare was hardly an adventure.

'Who are you phoning at this hour?' was the next question, which came as Ginny was looking at her mobile.

'I'm not phoning anyone,' she answered. 'I'm just catching up on

Facebook and there are a couple of texts. I hardly use the laptop at all now. It's better for Skype but that's about all.' Honestly, her mother was far more up with the play than Pamela. Pamela now explained that indeed, she was a member of Facebook, mainly to track Charles, she said. When Ginny admitted she didn't follow Charles, Pamela gave her an odd look.

'Well, I don't think we'll be able to text or Facebook this retirement village. Didn't they ask us to phone when we were coming to see Mrs Cook?' Pamela asked.

'Yes,' said Ginny and returned to look at the screen. 'I'll get the number in a minute.'

'You phone, because you spoke to them before. Is it all right if we go tomorrow? On the way to this Hawke's Bay.'

After finishing half a piece of toast and a cup of coffee, Ginny dialled the number and explained that they would like to visit Mrs Cook the following day. The nurse asked her to hold the line and someone else came on the phone and asked to speak to 'Lady Scawson' herself. Perhaps Mrs Cook was ill or something.

Pamela took the phone. After a brief introduction with Pamela explaining that Professor Cook had died in Pamela's garden and she wanted to ask Mrs Cook some questions, there were a few 'yes' and 'no' answers from Pamela and then a long silence while Pamela listened with a questioning expression on her face.

Finally the call ended with, 'Thank you so much for telling me. No, if you say so, it wouldn't be suitable.' Ginny was intrigued, realising there must be some problem.

Pamela looked at the phone carefully before clicking the call off. She handed it back to Ginny with her face puckered up.

'Oh dear, that's a dead end.'

'What do you mean? Is Mrs Cook ill? Can't she see us? Oh Lordy, she hasn't died?'

'The poor woman has Alzheimer's.'

'You mean she can't remember anything?'

'No, nothing at all. She thinks her husband still visits her and calls him Jimmy. As the nurse said, she wouldn't appreciate our visit and wouldn't be able to tell us anything. Oh dear.'

'When I phoned before, I did find out her name is Marion, so she isn't the Beth in the letter. Or the Diane for that matter.'

'The nurse said I could contact Mrs Cook's lawyer,' said Pamela, 'but I can't see him allowing us to trawl through Professor Cook's private papers to find a clue to some friend of his who isn't his wife.'

'Maybe that's why the brother seems to be the one accusing you of murder.'

Pamela shot Ginny a withering look, before breaking into a smile. 'It isn't every day I'm accused of murder, is it? Especially when even the police think I'm innocent. All the same, I'm not looking forward to meeting him. I know he's going to be aggressive.' A few minutes later she added, 'I'd rather be going straight to the Scawton Millers. Perhaps they knew Professor Cook.'

If they've got over all the 'bloody hells,' thought Ginny.

* * * * *

Charles cursed his mother for choosing this time to go traipsing around the world. He should have been far firmer in telling her not to go. Now he had to do everything by phone.

'Mother, it's Charles.'

'Hello, darling, how are you? Well, I'm here. About as far away as I can be after an excellent flight. What's the weather like?'

'I'm fine. We won our first four-goal match yesterday, so the bus man is very happy.'

'Darling, that's wonderful. We are just about off to see the brother of Professor Cook.'

Charles sighed. He still felt he should be able to sue the man who had wrongly accused the family of murder, but both Patrick and another lawyer he spoke to thought a written apology would be the best he could get. He doubted his mother would be able to extract anything more. She'd just let the man get away with a false accusation.

'Mother, you need to attack from the start, especially if he has his lawyer with him. Put him on the defensive at once.'

'Charles, you told me all that before I left. You want a written apology. Is that what you rang about?'

'Yes and no. Mother, I'm getting engaged.'

'Engaged, Charles, engaged to be married?' This was a new turn.

'Of course, Mother, don't be stupid. I'm getting engaged to Joanna. That was why I wanted you to meet her, only you were so rude, you know, with all those damned pigs.'

'Charles, how lovely. She must be nice for you to think of marrying her.'

'I just thought you'd better be the first to know. We'll wait till you're home before we announce it officially.'

'That's very exciting. Joanna? What's her surname?'

'Thomson. We've been down to the house, trying to make up from when you had the wretched pigs arrive. I hadn't really concentrated on the house before. It certainly does need something done and Joanna has some good contacts.'

It had all gone according to plan, just as Clarissa promised. He had proposed, they had gone for drinks at her parents. He supposed he was meant to ask her father's permission but heck, Joanna was already living at his place. The parents should be thankful.

They had enjoyed champagne while her mother fluffed, calling him her 'future knight in shining armour' and his father strutted around talking about trucks and companies and suggesting perhaps he'd like to be involved in the firm. It was the last thing Charles was wanting – to be involved in a national trucking company or 'logistics' as Joanna called it.

When he explained that his main worry was the estate and house, which was falling down, it was her father who suggested Joanna take it on as a project.

'We don't want to live there, Daddy,' Joanna pointed out.

At least they were all on the same page there. Ashly was in the middle of nowhere. The home counties were not quite suburbia, but it wasn't Gloucestershire and not as attractive as Berkshire or Sussex. Definitely the wrong place.

This visit to the house had gone much better than the first one with no distractions from pigs or his mother. Godley had arranged coffee – proper coffee for once – and had left the dogs in his cottage. He and Joanna were able to have a good look around.

'Oh, I'm so glad she went,' his mother was now saying. 'Did she like it? Will you live there? How are the dogs? Godley's emails say they're fine, but I'm not sure he isn't just being polite.'

'Oh, for God's sake, the dogs are fine. Joanna doesn't like them and no, we have no intention of living there.'

'She doesn't like the dogs?'

'They scare her, and they make a mess. It's Joanna's friends who suggested we could turn it into a hotel or something.'

'When were you thinking of getting married?'

'Obviously we can't get married in the polo season. Maybe next spring, before the polo starts. First of all, you need to meet her parents.' Joanna's mother was already talking about who should be invited. 'They want to hold a cocktail party as soon as you get home before Jerry has to go away.'

'By that time we'll know about this mystery.'

'And you will have the apology from the man. Or we'll be suing.'

* * * * *

Pamela dialled Godley's number, hoping he was still up. She knew it must be after nine there. She was relieved when he answered on the second ring.

'Godley, is it late with you? Oh, I'm so sorry but thank you for answering. How are the dogs?'

'Lady Scawton, how are you? No, this is a fine time. I was just watching the telly. The pointers are well, except Bentley sits on the sofa.'

'Oh, Godley, I told you not to start letting them up there. They can sit on the floor. They don't sit on the sofas when we use the big drawing room.'

'Don't worry, Mrs G is quite happy. Bentley shares it with her. I'm pleased you rang. Lady Elizabeth phoned a while ago. She said if you could, please would you phone her.'

'What, from here?'

'She seemed to think so. Shall I give you the number?'

'It's too late to phone now, but I'll phone in the morning. I hope it's nothing bad. Did she say?'

'It didn't sound as though it was bad news. It was about the farm shop.'

'Thank you so much, Godley, and I'm glad the dogs are feeling at home. Now, what I was ringing about was that I have just been speaking to Charles who says he is thinking of getting engaged. To Joanna. Godley, I think she's the one who broke her shoe, poor thing. Isn't she? And they went off in a huff.'

'They came down this morning and had a good look around the house,' Godley explained. 'They were talking about making some improvements and are bringing some consultants in a day or so.'

'She doesn't like the pointers.'

'Yes, I know. I locked them up while she was here, but I think it's just that she isn't used to them. A city girl.'

'Godley, do we know anything about her?'

'I've googled the name. She's the only daughter of Jerry Thomson. He has a son, but she's the only daughter.'

'Jerry Thomson. Thomson Transport? That really common man on the telly ad?'

'Exactly. The "From one to a hundred" millionaire. I imagine he'd be very excited about his daughter marrying into a good family. She does seem a little more down to earth than she did the first time, and, excuse me for saying so, but by the way she behaves I imagine it will be her money doing any alterations to the house. There doesn't seem to be any shortage according to Google.'

'Ah, that explains it. I'm glad you think she's nice.'

'She seems pleasant, Ma'am.'

'Well, perhaps she can keep Charles in the lifestyle he'd like to be accustomed to. The farm certainly won't do that. What's the weather like?' They talked about the weather in England and the weather in New Zealand. Godley said there was still a nip in the air in the evening.

Joanna's father sounded like her own. Pamela remembered how excited her own mother had been when she had become engaged to a titled family. It wasn't always happily-ever-after though. Perhaps Pamela would give Joanna a woolly dressing gown for an engagement present; she'd certainly need it if they changed their mind and lived at Ashly during the winter.

* * * * *

As Ginny drove across Auckland, Pamela complained. First of all there was the wet weather. Ginny wanted to point out that it rained in England – she didn't think that had changed since she left. Then Titirangi was further to go than Pamela had understood.

'It's still part of Auckland.'

'It all seems red roofs and white houses. Why red roofs?'

'There's a few grey roofs,' replied Ginny.

'I suppose so.' Pamela went quiet for a while. Then she remarked on Titirangi's strange name. Ginny remembered that England had Barton in the Beans and Upper Snodsbury for Pete's sake.

'I know this meeting is going to be difficult,' Pamela confided.

'He may have his solicitor there. Charles insists I must expect some recompense for the accusations of murder, or at least a written apology. I am just going to have to be very assertive.'

Pamela surely wouldn't find that hard. Maybe it was just the title thing; Pamela wasn't unpleasant like old CJ but just expected things to be done her way. Ginny was dreading having a whole week of Pamela being assertive.

They found Titirangi and the library and saw the café opposite, where they were to meet. They parked and hurried in the rain towards the café sign, outside an attractive cottage. Pamela marched in through a white-painted front door with little leadlight-glass panels and a bell that tinkled. Ginny paused by the outside table under an awning and looked around. The village was empty, except for an old man walking down the road in the rain. He held a sort of floppy flag on a stick, which Ginny realised was an umbrella, only it wasn't open, it just flapped feebly on the stick while he proceeded to get wet. Ginny turned to point him out to Pamela, but the door was already closed.

Once inside, Ginny saw Pamela was already standing at the counter peering at the menu. Ginny frowned as she heard her explain, with her loud English accent, that she was trying to work out the exchange rate. The bell on the door rang again and Ginny turned to see the old man come through, holding it open while he shook the umbrella and left it propped outside the door. He looked dishevelled. The girl behind the counter called out 'Good morning, Theodore – your usual then?' as he waved a hand and shambled over to the table by the window, taking the wet battered hat off his head and putting it on the chair beside him.

Pamela had already left the counter and marched towards the man as he sat down.

'Doctor Theodore Cook?' she almost shouted. The man nodded and his face wrinkled in an extraordinary fashion. Ginny wasn't sure whether it was a smile or a grimace. 'I'm Pamela Scawton.'

The man looked up in surprise and muttered, 'I thought I was meeting a Lady Scawton.'

'Indeed, that is who I am.'

Ginny walked towards the table as Pamela sat down opposite him. He looked half-beaten already and Pamela had a business-like air. This wasn't going to be much of a match. She wondered where the *Boston Legal* guys were that he was meant to have with him.

'Would you like me to order you a coffee, Pamela?' Ginny asked.

'That would be nice, dear. Just a cup of tea, thank you.' She turned towards the man. 'This is my goddaughter, Ginny.'

Dr Cook's face suddenly lit up, if you could call it that. Ginny was taken aback by the spooky smile. A tooth was missing.

She was about to ask Dr Cook whether he wanted anything, when he pointed to the girl behind the counter. Ginny turned, realising the girl must know what he liked. There was a short silence as the only other couple in the café were leaving.

Before the door had even closed, Pamela had started, her voice carrying. 'I found your brother – he was already dead, I'm afraid to say – at the far side of the garden, beside a public footpath. There was absolutely nothing suspicious about his demise. You cannot just go about accusing our family of murder, you know. We have a considerable reputation and I imagine there is quite a case for defamation.'

Ginny watched from the counter as Dr Cook seemed to crumple into his chair. His coat was an old tweed jacket, damp from the rain. It had probably been quite respectable once but now was almost as worn as he was. The shirt underneath, a checked open-necked one, didn't look clean. His hands, strangely, looked cleaner than the rest of him but old and wrinkled, with raised veins.

'Slander?' he muttered.

'Indeed.' Pamela was away now. 'What on earth made you even think your poor brother was murdered?'

His voice was quiet, almost tentative. 'You live at Ashton?'

'Ashly, yes. Our family owns Ashly House.'

'Geoffrey went to visit your family, on behalf of a friend. She'd died. He had this stone. Very unusual.' Ginny could hardly make out what he was saying. He was mumbling and looking sideways at Pamela.

There was no doubt what Pamela was saying though. 'We know that, we have the stone. Do you know about it?' Pamela's voice had softened a little, perhaps. 'And the letter?' she added as an afterthought.

'He showed me the stone before he left. It changes colour.'

'Yes, I know, but do you know why he was carrying it?'

'It's the optical absorption. Different light, different colour.'

'But why was your brother carrying the stone?' Pamela raised her voice again with that imperious tone. It seemed the man had gone into a reverie while Pamela repeated, 'Your brother. Carrying the stone. Why should you think we murdered him?'

Suddenly, the man returned to the present and looked at Pamela. 'Who took the stone?' he asked. Ginny noticed Pamela's perplexed expression.

'Your brother, of course. We want to know why he was carrying it?' Ginny squirmed at Pamela's tone.

The old man spoke slowly. 'I've no idea. It was all to do with the lady who died. Her daughter came to see me and asked me about it too. Odd woman, rather critical, I thought – could have worked for Social Welfare. Boy was fine though.'

'Excuse me. What are you talking about?' Pamela's impatience was obvious even to the waitress behind the counter. Ginny saw the waitress bend her head to peer out of the window; she followed her gaze and saw the rain had stopped.

'Now, let us get this right,' Pamela began again in her clipped accent. 'Do you believe your brother was murdered?'

Even if the old man did think his brother had been murdered, she doubted he was going to admit it with Aunt P interrogating him like that. The man just looked mystified again.

'Well, then,' Pamela continued. 'I've flown around the world to find out why you accused us as you did, and I need some recompense for the damage caused to our family. Or we could sue, take you to court.' Pamela's voice reverberated round the room, particularly the court bit. The voice was at odds with the comfortable furnishings and cluttered artwork on the white-painted wooden walls.

Ginny saw the old man's face wrinkle again, not in a smiling way but with a worried, almost frightened expression. She was sure the man was about to burst into tears. His hands were visibly shaking. Ginny felt she should do something to stop Pamela, to stop her harassing him like this.

At that moment, the woman who had been behind the counter appeared with a tray and hurried to the table. She rattled the empty tea cup in front of Pamela and almost slammed the small teapot down. Ginny looked up to see her whisper something to Dr Cook, who then looked up at her, nodded, stood up unsteadily and followed her.

The woman turned triumphantly to Pamela. 'Dr Cook prefers to drink outside, and I was just pointing out that it's stopped raining.' The woman helped him to his feet. Ginny blinked as the man shuffled away towards the door. She was thankful. Aunt P's tirade seemed so totally over the top and was so embarrassing. Now she saw a look of surprised confusion on Pamela's face.

'But . . . ' Pamela started.

As the doctor disappeared out of the door, Pamela's expression suddenly changed and she immediately got up and marched towards the door.

'Stay here, dear,' she commanded Ginny. Ginny cringed as she saw Pamela was going to attack him again.

Ginny watched through the leadlight panes on the window as Pamela approached the table outside. The waitress was under the awning, leaning over Dr Cook seated at the table and turned defensively towards Pamela, but Pamela slipped into the bench opposite and began to talk. Perhaps she was apologising, as the waitress seemed to soften in her stance. Both kept glancing at Dr Cook.

It was difficult to see Pamela's expression through the warped glass as she angled towards Dr Cook, but he didn't seem to mind. He sat up straighter as Pamela produced the stone from her pocket. The waitress turned and came back through the door.

'That's a strange lady, your mother,' she commented to Ginny.

'She's not my mother,' answered Ginny.

The waitress stood beside Ginny and the two of them stared through the window.

'He's pretty fragile, is Theodore,' said the waitress. 'He didn't need your . . . that woman . . . going at him like that.' Ginny nodded in agreement but wasn't sure what to say. Outside, there seemed peace.

'He used to be my science teacher, you know. He had his own television show. A long time ago.' There seemed little movement outside but then Pamela extended an arm out and Dr Cook nodded. There didn't seem to be any further argument and indeed Dr Cook seemed to relax and become a little more animated. Ginny wasn't sure whether to go outside too but decided to remain where she was. She went to get her coffee.

Eventually Ginny saw Pamela help Dr Cook to his feet and, her hand on his elbow, guide him inside. As he shuffled in, Pamela turned to the waitress.

'We'll go now. Thank you. It's a bit cold for Doctor Cook out there. Ginny and I are going on to Karekare Beach to have a look.' She nodded at Ginny. Ginny didn't say anything but just followed her out, the bell tinkling again.

The rain had stopped, and the wind had got up. Neither spoke as they returned to the car. Ginny didn't comment on Dr Cook and was still embarrassed by the way Pamela had attacked him. It was so rude and unnecessary and so bloody typical of the Scawtons. They thought they knew everything.

The road to Karekare was narrow and wound downhill. Ginny had to concentrate. Apart from Pamela commenting on the tropical forest around them and Ginny pointing out that it was subtropical and in New Zealand it's called 'bush', neither spoke until they reached a carpark with a signpost which read *Beach*. Ginny didn't think it very beach-like, but Pamela suggested they park the car and walk.

'It's not raining.'

The scene in the cafe faded as they walked along a damp sand track between the tall clumpy grasses. The desolation and grandeur of the place overtook Ginny. Sheer tall rocks towered on either side. Large seabirds called to each other as they wheeled over pools of water and drifted in the wind over the clumpy grasses. Once they had walked past the lifeguards' hut, Ginny could see the flat expanse of dark sand. With a wind beginning to whip around them, they looked out at the huge waves surging towards them with the noise of thunder. White-tipped surf crashed and rushed at them while the rocky cliffs loomed above. This was no standard seaside beach – this was raw nature. The beach was empty and windswept. Ginny couldn't remember seeing anything like it. She glanced at Pamela who seemed equally impressed.

They walked a little way, but then just stopped and looked. Pamela wiped a hand over her eyes. Perhaps she had the wind in her face. They turned to walk back up the track.

'Karekare means wild surf, so Theodore said.'

Ginny didn't answer.

Pamela's voice seemed quieter or perhaps it was the surroundings. 'You were angry with me in the café.'

It wasn't really a question. Ginny's anger had dissipated in the enormity of the landscape and it made her – and any stupid anger – feel rather unimportant. She shivered in the cold wind now as they began to walk back up the track.

'You sort of attacked the poor man. It seemed so over the top,' Ginny began, not sure how to continue as she tried to avoid stepping into a puddle of wet sand.

'He was just so . . . just so not what I was expecting,' Pamela responded. 'I was expecting an aggressive man who was determined we had murdered his brother.' Ginny didn't answer. 'Not a poor old man, who was grieving for his brother and had been too drunk to remember saying anything until it was printed in the paper.'

There was a pause.

'So, you didn't gain much?'

'He had a visit from a woman who was asking about the stone,' Pamela said. 'She seemed to know about our family although he called her the Welfare lady. He's going to try and find out how to contact her.' They walked on in silence, with the roar of the sea behind them and the cawing of the sea birds as they wheeled around.

'You know, he lives somewhere up there.' Pamela pointed to the steep hills around them and Ginny could see the several odd isolated houses almost totally hidden in the bush.

'Will he find her? The contact I mean: the Welfare lady.' By the way Pamela had spoken to him inside the café Ginny doubted that there would be any information forthcoming.

'He was a bit vague,' Pamela agreed, sighing. 'Charles is not going to be pleased . . . '

'Because you didn't get the written apology,' Ginny finished for her. She couldn't see the point of getting any kind of apology anyway.

They walked on past the lifeguards' hut, built on top of a blockwork shed, as they followed the path towards the carpark, still witnessed by the giant gulls circling over the low clumpy grasses.

'Is Charles a bully, Ginny?' asked Pamela suddenly, taking Ginny by surprise. 'You went out with him. Did he bully you at all?'

Ginny didn't know what to say. She knew it was Charles who had encouraged Pamela to be so assertive. As Ginny recognised the carpark ahead, she suddenly felt tired and realised that she wasn't looking forward to driving back on these wet and narrow bush-clad roads.

'Are you still there?' smiled Pamela a moment later.

'No, Charles wasn't a bully,' she answered slowly. 'I only went out with him that one time. It wasn't my type of party and when I wanted to come home early, he seemed happy to take me home. I can't remember why I fell off the balcony but no, he wasn't a bully. In fact at the pony club polo, he was always helping some of us on little ponies. He's quite good at teaching. I'd forgotten that. It's just that . . . '

'Just that?' prompted Pamela.

'He's a bit arrogant. Uncle CJ was the same. They just give you the feeling that . . . sort of . . . everything belongs to them and they're in charge.' In other words, Charles is totally up himself, she thought to herself.

Pamela didn't answer but just nodded.

There was a wooden carved Māori statue by a tree on the left. Ginny could understand that this place would be important to Māori; it had that feeling.

She dug in her pocket for the car keys, wondering how she would be able to concentrate on driving.

'Would you like me to drive, Ginny? You could have a nap.' Ginny looked at Aunt P with relief. Maybe the old bird wasn't so bad after all.

✶ ✶ ✶ ✶ ✶

It was still dark when Pamela woke to hear her phone ringing. It must have rung several times already before she had shaken off the early morning sleep and grabbed it. This was such a small flat that it was inevitable that Ginny would have been woken in the room next door.

Finding the right button to press, she whispered, 'Hello?'

'Pamela. I know you are in New Zealand, I spoke to Godley earlier. It's Lizzie Evans – Shefford, that was.'

'Oh, Lizzie, Godley did tell me to phone you. He was going to email the number. I hope it isn't bad news.'

There was a chortle at the other end. 'Well, it depends on how you look at it. No, everyone here is fine.'

'And the baby?'

'Coming alone fine and making me look fatter than ever.'

'Oh, don't be silly.'

'It's the baby phoning you really. She – or he – is due in July. Wonderful time to have a baby. The hottest time of year, everyone goes on holiday, the shop is at its busiest and the ice cream likely to melt. Great timing, really.'

'Babies don't know that!'

'No, well. I really want to take this baby stuff seriously and even though I'll be around and at the end of a phone, I need someone to do the shop. I've been interviewing people who might do it.'

'I quite agree you'll need someone. That's not a small task and certainly not one you can do when you're up all night feeding. It would be a wonderful job for someone though.'

'The agency singled out really well-qualified people. We ended up with three. The best one was a white South African, and I had practically offered him the job when he met my wonderful, black, Nigerian chef. They didn't take to each other and frankly, chefs are more important, and I have no intention of offending this one. So the South African failed. The next one was a woman who was 2 IC at some airport and I could see just wanted to change everything. The third one turned up two hours late saying it was my fault we lived so far out of London.'

'None of them were any good?'

'I had a long talk to Daddy, who finally pointed out that with each one, I have been going on about how they didn't ask the right questions and, even though you aren't as qualified, you asked all the right questions when you came here and really, all I need is an assistant for a few months – not someone to take over entirely. So he suggested that you would be ideal.'

'Me? I couldn't possibly do your job.'

'I'm not asking you to, but you wanted to know about farm shops in case you put one in at Ashly. What better way than to take over mine for a few months? I'll be around, so in effect you are my PA. Any stuff you don't understand, Carol's here and does all the accounts and the rosters. She's excellent. And touch wood, the chefs all seem lined up for the summer at least. Your job would be mainly monitoring products – quality control, I suppose – sorting out problems as they arise and making sure the icecream doesn't melt. Oh, and you have to keep Mummy from interfering – her ideas tend to cost too much. All stuff you would be excellent at.'

'Goodness me, I'd have no idea. Your shop seemed so much bigger than I expected.'

'Well, it would have the advantage of getting you out of Ashly. You could live in our guest cottage and even bring the dogs.'

'You mean live onsite? Well, I would have to really. I couldn't commute.'

'If the dogs misbehave we have wonderful kennels and there is always someone wanting to walk them. Godley told me he was thinking of retiring and if he did you couldn't possibly live at Ashly by yourself.'

'Oh, Lizzie, it's a wonderful idea. I would love it but honestly feel that I wouldn't be up to the job. I don't know enough.'

'Of course you do. Daddy spoke to the major, the one you worked with on the hospice committee. He gave you a very good reference – said you'd be ideal. He said you could turn your hand to anything, as we know anyway.'

'All your staff are professionals. Wouldn't they see me as an interfering relation thinking she knows everything because she has a title?'

'Yes, they will. I've lived with that all my life. One of my tutors at uni found out I had a title and always marked me down. I had to work twice as hard, but I still passed. I'm sure you would have coped with that kind of thing before. Now, don't worry. I don't need an answer now. I know you're tracking the stone and the writer of that awful letter and you need to sort that out first. I thought I would just suggest it and let you think about it. We'll get you over here when you get back and you can have another look at everything.'

'I wouldn't be up to it. I don't have to think this over.'

'Daddy said you'd say that, and that I was to take no notice. What's the weather like in New Zealand?'

They chatted on for a while before Pamela put the phone down, already deep in thought. She'd loved the atmosphere of the farm shop. It would be exciting to work there. She sighed. Realistically, there was no way she could do it, and there was no way she could leave Ashly House empty and falling down. Charles would never let her.

14

New Zealand. 1934

Aggie was leaning down off the bed, lacing up her good boots. She could hear Sean and Pete start an argument.

'It was Bo's fault,' called Sean. It was always better to blame the two-year-old. Bo wouldn't argue back, and they knew Bo's smile would win her over. It was the excitement, of course, the anticipation of a trip on the bus to the races. She shouted at them to calm down.

'How many eggs did you collect, Pete?' Aggie asked as she appeared in the kitchen. There were four eggs in a dish beside Sean's milk bucket. She peered into the bucket. Half full – Sean had done a good job. She put the bucket in the cool of the meat safe.

'Now, are we ready?'

Ellerslie was the only racecourse they could reach easily with the kids. Avondale was too far to take them, and they had to change buses. Michael trained a couple of horses down on the foreshore at Point England, along the edge of the Tāmaki estuary, close to where they lived. He and Mickey would spend the first hours of each day working them.

God knows, they didn't have enough money to have racehorses, but it was a dream Michael had harboured since he was a kid and the reason they lived where they did. He had bought two horses as weanlings; one was no good and Michael had swapped him for two others. Aggie always had a soft spot for the second original one. He was called Buttons. Aggie had suggested his name – he was out of Seamstress – and already he was a winner. As much as she complained about Michael and his horses, the two races Buttons had won did bring in a bit of money.

When the races were at Ellerslie, Michael would ride Buttons to the course and Mickey would ride one of the other horses to keep Buttons company. The rest of the family would go by bus.

It wasn't a big day at Ellerslie – like New Year's Day or Easter – but there was still a big crowd. Sean disappeared into the crowd immediately in amongst the big weatherboard buildings while Aggie held on to Pete and little Bo and managed to make her way up to the saddling stalls by the main drive, where she knew the other boys would be.

Saddling was the most exciting time. Michael and Mickey would fuss around Buttons, brushing every bit of dirt off him before Michael put the flat saddle on. Then Mickey would lead him around before heading to the paddock. Trainers and lads would call to each other, with jokey comments of good luck. Hopes were high. Every horse was going to be a winner.

Aggie was standing back from the line of wooden stalls, under one of those big oak trees, with little Pete holding her hand and Bo in her arms. She was trying to keep them out of the way of the lads leading the shiny horses or rushing around with buckets of gear. She noticed a man beside her, also watching Buttons. He looked well-to-do and educated. Like most of the gentlemen around, he wore a trilby hat and carried a walking stick. Michael must have called something to Aggie because the man turned and asked if she was to do with the horse. He said he liked the name, as his wife's maiden name was Buttons.

For something to say, Aggie asked, 'I don't suppose she were Mary Buttons then, from England?' She knew it wouldn't be her.

'Do you know her?' he asked.

No. Surely not? Aggie became excited. 'Mary Buttons, from England? From Ashly?'

'She's Mary Miller now, but yes, that's my Mary. She's my wife.'

Aggie couldn't believe it. Was this really true? She didn't even know Mary had come to New Zealand. Aggie wanted to introduce the man to Michael but of course Michael was busy as the steward was calling for the horses to go into the parade ring. The man gave her his address so that she could write to Mary. Mary had come out before they were married, with her first husband, he told her. They lived in Hawke's Bay.

Aggie wrote the next day to Mary. Mary Buttons that was. She waited impatiently for a reply, still not sure it was the same Mary she had known. At last the reply came, giving her all her news. Mary had married Mr Edward and had been on the boat when he drowned. Married him? Aggie couldn't believe it. She had never said anything when she left and when Mr Edward died, no one had ever mentioned Mary or even that he had a wife. If it were so, they must have eloped or perhaps Sir William didn't even know. Aggie had so many questions. Mary now lived in a big farm house and she invited Aggie to bring her family. Aggie dreamed of taking all the boys for a holiday and Mary and she being able to talk.

If Mary had run off with Mr Edward, then Aggie would be able to tell her the secret about her first son. Mary wouldn't tell anyone. She anticipated the relief of being able to talk about it to someone who knew the family and that witch Lady Scawton. Mary would understand.

In a second letter, Mary said that they were very busy on the farm and coming to stay might not be a good idea although she would still like to see Aggie. When Aggie read the letter to Michael, he immediately picked up the problem.

'And the smart man you met at the races was her husband? Likely he's a Miller from Hawke's Bay. They have the scouring business there – Millers. They would live in a big house and wouldn't want us to stay. You wouldn't be comfortable, love. They aren't our people.'

'Just because you're Catholic? That wouldn't worry Mary.'

'It might not have worried her when you knew her but she lives in Hawke's Bay now. Wouldn't want Holy Romans to stay. Beside which . . . '

'Beside which, what?' Aggie asked. She couldn't believe that Mary would worry about what church Michael went to.

'They probably read the article in the paper about me being half Māori.' Recently Michael had had a bit of publicity with Buttons winning. The newspaper article had mentioned his Māori heritage as well as his Irish one. Māori and Catholic – not good old Hawke's Bay Anglican Pākehā. Aggie had to agree with Michael. Her wild children wouldn't get on well with Mary's.

But Mary still wanted to meet – and Aggie did too. Michael planned to take Buttons to the Taupō races and so perhaps they could meet there. Mary wrote that her husband used to own racehorses too and Michael knew one of the horses they used to own was a famous steeplechaser called Ashly – Mary must have named it. So Aggie arranged to leave the children with Michael's parents and go to Taupō for the day.

The races themselves were a blur. Buttons didn't go in the end – he had gone lame a few days before – but Michael took another horse. It ran in the first race but did no good even though Michael had Aggie's lucky stone in his pocket.

'Didn't work this time, Aggie.' He handed it back to her after the race as Aggie went off to find Mary.

They recognised each other at once. Mary was dressed in fancy clothes and a matching blue hat. She took Aggie's hand warmly but certainly had that look of a proper lady, and Aggie felt dowdy in her print dress and old felt hat. They went and sat on a grassy knoll behind the grandstand to enjoy the sun. Children ran around beside them and a little further down – where the view of the racecourse wasn't blocked by the grandstand – families had gathered in groups. There were picnics laid out on colourful cloths. The women tried to keep tabs on the children while the men disappeared into the grandstand.

Mary was much more matronly than Aggie remembered but she was still wanting to talk and reminisce. She had three children and said she was pregnant with a fourth, although she wasn't showing. Aggie marvelled at how respectable she looked. Her voice had an English accent but with more of Lady Scawton's accent rather than a local Hertfordshire lilt.

There was so much Aggie wanted to talk about. Mary told how she had married Mr Edward just before leaving, with the permission of both Sir William and old Lady Scawton. She had been Mrs Edward Scawton when she arrived in New Zealand.

'And now you speak all la-de-da,' laughed Aggie.

Mary looked embarrassed but then laughed it off. 'I met this doctor and his wife, and I lived with them before meeting John. They taught me how to behave properly. I would never have been able to marry John otherwise.'

Aggie didn't care. This was still her Mary,

Aggie said she couldn't believe that Sir William and old Lady Scawton had allowed her to marry Mr Edward, but Mary said it was they who had suggested it, provided she told no one in the village. Aggie was reminded how Mary had felt sorry for Mr Edward and had enjoyed his company but she still could not imagine her actually married to him. Mary told how she had been really seasick and had been in the cabin when he had drowned. In a particularly fierce storm, Edward had gone out for some air and got blown over the rail. It was such a sad story. Aggie remembered how Mr Edward was a lovely man, just messed up by the war. She told Mary about the service for Mr Edward in the little village church but didn't tell her that no one ever mentioned he had a wife or that Lady Scawton had made them clear out his rooms – the old nursery – straight afterwards and forbade them to speak about him. 'It was too painful for Lady Scawton,' the staff were told. The old lady was dead now of course.

Mary asked Aggie about her life, and Aggie had been so looking forward to telling her. For the last few days she had planned to confess about her secret son but, now that Aggie realised Mary was so respectable, she wasn't sure. She didn't think Mary would understand. Instead Aggie asked Mary more about what happened to her when she came to New Zealand.

'When Edward died, I wanted to go back to England so much but Sir William said I was to carry on. I felt so guilty about Edward but hated Sir William for making me go on. The doctor's family I mentioned were in the cabin next door and became good friends. They looked after me and came with me when I had to attend the Board of Enquiry. The doctor wrote to the family explaining how it had all happened and telling them that I was pregnant. After Teddy was born, he showed me the reply from Lady Scawton. It said, more or less, that my son couldn't be Edward's and must be someone else's. For goodness' sake. Who did they think I was?'

Aggie began to laugh. Mary, married to Edward but going with someone else? Never – not the Mary Buttons she'd known. If Mr Edward had gone to the trouble of marrying Mary and taking her with him to New Zealand, there was no way Mary would have been unfaithful to him. She would have kept her side of the bargain, come what may.

'And so you 'ave a son? Mr Edward's?' Mary brought out a photo of him – he had same kind face as Mr Edward.

'He goes to boarding school in Whanganui,' said Mary. It seemed a long way to send him to school.

'Isn't there a school closer? Don't you want 'im at home? Why send 'im all that way?'

'All the family go to Collegiate. It's good for him. Makes him independent. The others go off to boarding school too, but the girls much closer, to Woodford House. Where do your children go?'

Aggie thought of her children. She would have hated Mickey and Sean to have to go away to some fancy school for months on end.

'So your son is Edward Scawton too?'

'No, he's called Miller. He knows his father was Edward Scawton though. We did wonder whether he shouldn't be Scawton Miller. That has a nice ring, doesn't it? Perhaps he should.'

'That Lady Scawton was a one, wasn't she? Did you ever hear from them again?'

Mary's expression changed. Aggie wasn't sure whether she was angry or upset.

'We did, actually. The letter Lady Scawton had sent after I got here was really horrid. I had no qualms about taking the money, which had been sent out for Mr Edward or keeping that necklace Sir William gave to me as a wedding present. I never wanted to hear from them again, but then there was an argument over the racehorse.'

'A racehorse? Was that the one called Ashly?'

Mary explained that Edward had sent his favourite horse out to New Zealand. 'Do you remember that big black horse Edward used to watch being ridden? Edward had arranged to ship the horse out before we left England. He won a lot of steeplechases, just as Edward thought he would.'

Aggie was amazed. Michael had said the horse had been famous but she'd never dreamt it was a horse that came from Ashly, a horse that her father would have shod!

'The problem was sorted out in the end and we've never heard from Sir William since.' A flash of concern crossed Mary's face but Aggie didn't want to spoil the conversation by asking more.

With the talk of the family and the household, she wondered whether this was the time to confess to having a baby, out of wedlock, before she left but she hesitated.

Mary was getting stiff sitting on the grass and moved to stand up. 'Let's go and get a cup of tea. There's a stand over there. And then you can tell me all about how you came to be here. I've been doing all the talking.' The moment had passed.

They walked over towards the tea stand and queued in silence. Aggie excused herself to go to the powder room. Suddenly, she knew she could never tell Mary her secret, not about her child in England. Mary had changed too much.

As they collected their tea and returned to their grassy knoll, Aggie told her how she had come out from England with Tom. She never mentioned why and fortunately Mary didn't ask.

'I am glad,' said Mary. 'I was always worried about you, Aggie. You were so headstrong, and I could see you getting into trouble when you were a young thing. Your dad must have missed you when you came here though.'

For no reason, tears began to roll down Aggie's face. Mary looked surprised but said she understood when Aggie said her dad had died and she'd never seen him again. Aggie never mentioned there was another reason, a secret she could never share.

As the excitement of the races continued around them, they talked about Aggie's boys, and Mary's children. Aggie showed her the stone the Scawton family had given her and how her family called it her lucky stone. Aggie tried to show her how it changed colour.

'The necklace Sir William gave me has two of those same stones. They change colour like that. Aren't they unusual? Sir William did mention their name when he presented the necklace, but I was so nervous I've forgotten. No one seems to know what they are over here. Some jeweller said they came from Russia but he might have been making that up.' They were outside in the sunlight and the stone just stayed pale green.

Aggie wondered at how different they were now. Mary, with her posh voice, her servants and someone to look after her children. She invited Aggie to come and stay – she even invited Michael and the boys – but Aggie knew she would never have embarrassed Mary by disturbing her ordered life.

A few months later Aggie found herself pregnant again. This one felt different, and indeed it was. She produced a girl and told Mary in the Christmas card she sent. She was Mary Elizabeth, or Beth for short.

15

New Zealand 2013

Pamela was driving as they headed into Havelock North. She seemed more relaxed than the previous day and didn't complain once. Even Pamela would have found it hard to compare the mountain vistas, the Taupō lake and the huge acres of barren farmland with England's home counties.

At Mike's suggestion they'd deviated to Rotorua and visited the hot pools and the Māori village. Ginny has been surprised at Pamela's interest in Māori culture – she kept asking the guides questions. Ginny herself preferred the boiling hot pools. There certainly weren't anything like those in England.

Pamela had asked to stop at a fruit shop coming into Hastings but seemed disappointed that the shop only sold fruit. She said she was hoping for more of a farm shop like in England, and Ginny promised to try and find a farmers' market during her visit.

As they drove towards Havelock North Pamela looked over at her. 'Goodness knows what these people are going to be like. You know, I'm quite nervous.' Ginny pulled herself up from where she had slouched, wide awake now.

'I can never imagine you nervous, Pamela. You're the least nervous person I've ever met.' Ginny remembered Pamela bullying Dr Cook, poor guy, although, from the rude way Bob Scawton Miller had spoken on the phone, she doubted he would be as easy to attack.

Pamela must have been thinking about the Millers too. 'Godley said Mr Miller was rude to him on the phone too,' Pamela said, 'but when I spoke to him myself, he sounded charming. Perhaps he's just a snob.'

They found Middle Road and a little while later heard the GPS say, 'You have reached your destination' in such a sombre tone the machine sounded disappointed.

The narrow farm drive meandered uphill, lined by large bare plane trees. With old wooden gates, once painted white, it had the feeling of a very established but slightly run-down farm. Through the wire fence behind the trees they could see large paddocks with sheep. As they reached the house, the drive went around a raised wall-edged circle of lawn. The garden was bushier here, and it looked as though in summer it would be lush. An old hose was snaking over the lawn; from its mouldy green colour, it looked as though it had been there for some time.

They stopped the car in front of wide wooden steps, which led up to a white weatherboard house with a long verandah. The paint was peeling in more than one place and, like the drive rails, the house looked in need of a touch-up.

As they got out of the car, Ginny realised the woman standing at the top of the steps must be Anne, and Bob came through the front door as they approached the steps.

'How lovely to meet you. You got here all right?' Anne greeted Pamela as she walked down the steps.

'Well, I never,' Bob called out, staying at the top of the steps. He was dressed in a crumpled short-sleeved open-necked Aertex shirt and an old pair of baggy khaki shorts. Ginny saw a look of surprise on Pamela's face. Maybe it was the shorts; his sturdy legs were tanned, and he wore fawn woolly socks and no shoes. 'Ah, the murderer! Come on in and you're – let me see – Ginny? You see, Anne, I was listening when you reminded me, eh!' He gave a guffaw.

Ginny followed Pamela and Anne into the hall, wondering whether Pamela would react to Bob's accusation. She watched as Pamela held out her hand, but Bob had turned and expected them just to follow him inside.

As they stood in a small panelled hall, with faded photographs in frames on the table and an old hunting print on the wall opposite a mirror, Ginny was reminded of England. They stood around rather awkwardly until Bob suggested tea and Anne insisted they come into the sitting room. This room was rather tidier than Ginny would have expected from the appearance of Bob, and she suspected Bob would have preferred tea in the kitchen. The sun filtered through the windows on to a pale, comfortable-looking sofa and there were two big armchairs with cushions. Pamela stood in front of the crackling fire, before Bob suggested she take a seat in one of the large chairs. Bob sat in the chair opposite. It all felt a bit stiff.

'We had the local reporter phone about the murder. He's not a bad joker. He phoned back a couple of days later to confirm that the police said they weren't going to investigate.'

'You mustn't mind Bob's sense of humour,' Anne explained.

There were a few tentative questions after that, Bob asking how the flight was and how did Pamela know Ginny. Pamela asked how big the farm was – 600 hectares. How many acres was that, she asked, and was it just sheep? Sheep and beef. How many workers did they have? Bob looked puzzled by that question. Pamela changed tack. Had Bob always been there? Yes, he had inherited it from his father. Then both Pamela and Bob started speaking over one another.

'I should apologise for the phone conversation . . .' started Pamela, Ginny smiled. Apologising wasn't a usual Scawton trait.

'Well, Anne said I was rude on the phone to your butler. I was a bit out of turn, I suppose,' Bob countered, 'but I was remembering the first conversation I had with him years ago.'

'With Godley?' asked Pamela. 'Had you spoken to him before?'

'Might not be the same butler,' explained Bob, 'How many butlers do you have, eh?'

'He's not really a butler,' Ginny couldn't help but say. Bob obviously had the wrong impression.

'Indeed he is,' came the sharp retort from Pamela. 'He was trained as a proper butler. When he first came, he wore a uniform.'

Ginny laughed to herself. Aunt P back to her stern self – perhaps it was the nerves she mentioned. The last time Ginny saw Godley he was helping to cut down a fallen tree on the drive. She didn't think chainsaw training would have been in the manual for a butler.

'Well,' continued Bob, 'it probably isn't the same butler. But years ago, when we were in England, I thought it would be good if we made contact. I phoned the house, and got the butler, who disappeared off to speak to Sir Charles and then came back and said "Sir Charles does not wish to meet you. There are no Scawtons in New Zealand or any of the other colonies. Nor does he have extra money to give to supposed poor relations. Goodbye." So you can imagine we weren't exactly excited when Ginny made contact or the butler phoned. Couldn't Sir Charles contact us himself? Bugger them all, excuse the expression, eh?' He gave an apologetic smile towards Ginny.

Ginny wondered if he was trying to be funny; he had been pretty rude as far as she was concerned. She looked at Pamela, who had gone rather pale. Ginny was sure the story about the butler was true, whether it was Godley or not. Uncle Charles was always so unpleasant and unsociable; he could easily have said all that.

Now she could see Pamela wasn't sure about Bob's tone either. 'Oh dear, that probably was my husband. CJ could be so suspicious and unwelcoming, couldn't he Ginny?'

'He could be pretty grumpy,' agreed Ginny. That was an understatement.

'I suppose it does sound odd to have the butler phone . . . ' Pamela began again.

'More tea, Lady Pamela?' asked Anne. Ginny was surprised to see Pamela straighten up.

'Well, first of all, please call me Pamela. I'm not Lady Pamela. I would have to be the daughter of an Earl to be Lady Pamela. I'm just Lady Scawton, or even Pamela Lady Scawton. Really, that's all another age. Just Pamela is fine.' Holy Nora, thought Ginny. Aunt P was back at her bossiest, telling the pony club children 'a walk will do'. Then she smiled to herself as she saw Bob raise his bushy eyebrows in surprise. No, good on her – Bob needed that!

There was a noise on the wooden floor outside the door, which suddenly flew wide open. A man rushed in, followed by a golden retriever with muddy feet. Anne immediately got up and shooed the dog outside. The man had a mass of black curly hair and he was dressed in jeans and a plaid shirt, but it was his angry demeanour that took everyone's attention.

'Dad, you'll have to come and help shed up.' The guy was clearly upset and looked as though he could really explode. Bob jumped up, then stood his ground, his hands at his sides, perhaps deliberately not reacting.

Ginny looked again at the guy. He was a good-looking Heathcliff type, not much older than herself. Pamela had shrunk back in her seat in surprise and Anne was now standing at the door.

Bob spoke. 'I'll be there in a tick. Tim. Meet Pamela. And this is Ginny.'

* * * * *

Tim's arrival broke the ice. Suddenly they all relaxed. Bob explained that they were due to start shearing the next day and he'd left Tim to put the sheep in the shed by himself. Ginny and Pamela both offered to come and help. Tim disappeared out of the door, and the golden retriever came back in, to be shooed out again. Bob took Ginny with him to help with the sheep while Pamela helped Anne pile the tea tray. She needed to change her shoes before chasing sheep.

Anne apologised for Tim's behaviour. 'Sometimes things get on top of him.'

'He looks very capable.'

'Oh, he is. But he had, or has, this problem, only he doesn't like everyone to talk about it. He's had treatment and is really so much better but just sometimes he does fly off like that.'

'You certainly don't have to apologise. My husband had post-traumatic stress disorder and I never even . . . '

'Oh, goodness, you'd understand then. It's not easy to live with, is it? We've had to make a lot of allowances.'

Pamela regretted admitting that CJ had the same problem as Tim. Now Anne would expect her to know all about it. She tried to divert her a little. 'The dog didn't seem to mind Tim. Ours used to cower whenever CJ lost his temper.'

'Sunshine adores Tim. She sleeps in his room and jumps on his bed to wake him when he has nightmares.'

Pamela didn't say anything. She was remembering CJ's nightmares. The dogs would have been in danger had they been in the room. Oh, why had she never realised CJ's problem?

The sheep were almost yarded up by the time Pamela reached the tin-covered woolshed. She marvelled at so many sheep and the size of the woolshed. There used to be sheep at Ashly before CJ had sold most of the farmland, but she could never remember them all being packed together like this, crushed together in the wooden pens upstairs with more in the yards outside. She wondered where the shepherds were – there seemed to be only Tim and Bob pushing them into the pens under the woodshed. The sheepdogs were expert at loading them, even running along the sheep's backs to make them move. She stood beside Ginny, not wanting to get in the way.

'We need to keep them dry,' explained Tim, now seeming quite relaxed. 'They can't shear them damp and at this time of year they take all day to dry, even if it's sunny.' His temper seemed quite forgotten and he invited Ginny to help him feed the horses and dogs down at the stables. He pointed to the farm buildings Pamela could see further away.

It barely seemed time for dinner when they all sat down in a dining room with a big mahogany table and, like the hall, rather an old-fashioned air. Tim seemed quite relaxed now and Bob was cheerful too. Both had showered, and Bob had changed into clean jeans from his long shorts. Pamela found a huge pile of rather overdone roast lamb placed in front of her. Anne piled on roast potatoes, carrots and beans and something called kūmara which her hosts insisted was like sweet potato. As she watched Bob smother his pile of food with gravy, Pamela wondered how on earth she was going to eat even half of her portion.

While Bob and Tim both admitted that they normally ate in the kitchen and what a pleasant change this was, Pamela's main concern was how not to leave too much food. Perhaps she could slip a bit to Sunshine, sitting quietly on the floor between her and Tim's chair.

As Bob offered her a glass of wine – 'a good local "Sav Blanc" unless she'd prefer red'. Pamela took encouragement from the bonhomie. 'Now I know CJ was extremely rude, but I did check, and we couldn't find any evidence of Scawtons in our family coming to New Zealand. We are an old family but Scawtons have been awfully shy breeders and there aren't many left. Each generation has only had one son for generations. My Charles is an only child. CJ did have one brother who was stillborn I think, but his father James was an only child. So where did your Scawtons come from?'

Bob answered her. 'My father was Teddy Scawton who was born here but his parents came from Ashly. We have my grandparent's marriage certificate – Edward Scawton and Mary Buttons. My sister-in-law has it with all the other papers. When did she say, Tim? I think it was 1920. My father was born nine months later. Just legal, I'd say. Edward Scawton died on the boat coming over so never knew his son.

My grandmother, Mary Buttons, married again to John Miller and Teddy became Edward Scawton Miller.'

'I wonder who that original Edward was then?' Pamela mused. 'Must have been a cousin. There is certainly no other male line listed in *Debretts*,'

'What's *Debretts*?' asked Tim.

'That's the sort of *Who's Who* of titles in England, right from the monarchy down. They are pretty accurate and give the lineage of everyone from a baronet up.'

'You mean every sir and lord that ever was? What is a baronet, anyway? I didn't think England still had barons,' asked Tim

'It's not a baron nor a knighthood. It's like a hereditary knighthood – knighthoods aren't usually hereditary. They don't make them anymore. The baronet's title is passed on to the eldest, natural-born son. Ours is pre-Victorian.'

'What did he get it for?'

'The baronetcy? I'm not sure. Do you know what he got it for, Ginny?' Pamela had already told them how Ginny had helped her husband write a family history and so knew even more than she did about the family.

'Uncle CJ said it was for giving money to the King to pay for the army. I think you're right. It was before Victoria.'

'So why does your son deserve to be a "Sir" now, generations later?' Bob asked. 'I mean, the Royal Family work quite hard and do a lot for Britain, but you read about all these playboys who are Lord Something or Sir Somebody. Most of them are on drugs, eh?' Out of the corner of her eye, Pamela could see Ginny look down at her plate, her hair falling forward and covering her face. She was pretty sure Charles wasn't into drugs; she knew he had smoked marijuana occasionally and drank but surely that was all.

'Oh, Bob,' came a rebuke from Anne.

But Pamela was not at all offended. 'Oh yes, I quite agree. I don't think my son is a drug addict, but he certainly doesn't take his duties seriously. He's more interested in playing polo.'

'Well, there you are then. What duties should he be doing?'

'We still have a small farm and a large house, which is falling down and costs a fortune. We used to own most of the village and half the local town as well. It's considerably less now, but I suppose we are still expected to help with local affairs – provide the house for the local gala, help organise the church and local school – and the old people's home. But no, there isn't anything specific. Charles will probably have to sell the house anyway.'

'So it's all a load of old codswallop? You just get to be Lady Scawton to maintain the class system. And pass it on from generation to generation.'

Pamela could see Anne looked embarrassed although Pamela found the argument quite refreshing.

'We do have knighthoods here, though the Labour Government stopped them for a bit,' explained Anne. 'You must admit, Bob, that the Governor-General sounds better as a "Sir".'

'Yes, but usually he's a good joker, deserves the title and it doesn't get passed on. Anyway, I think we should call them our own bloody title, not use some antiquated English how's-your-father "Sir".'

'Like the kaumātua,' said Tim.

Pamela wondered what the word meant but didn't like to ask.

'Something like that,' agreed Bob. 'Titles certainly shouldn't be automatically inherited by useless pricks who do nothing for it, eh?' The contempt sounded in his voice.

Pamela saw Ginny frowning at Bob's tactless outburst. She smiled at Anne to show she was not taking offence and answered. 'I think you're probably right, but there aren't any new baronetcies, so eventually they will all die out anyway. Under your system, if you inherit a title, what should you do?'

'You bloody well give it back. Get given your own title when you deserve it.'

'The title is only part of the inheritance. Do you give the whole estate back? Don't you have a similar thing here? Does everyone who inherits a farm deserve it?'

There was silence. Bob's eyebrows raised, and it was a moment before his face relaxed in one of his big guffaws.

'Well, you probably have a point, eh?' The atmosphere eased. Anne got up and began to collect the plates. Pamela rose too, although Anne signalled her to stay.

'Tim will help.'

'Now, knights or baronets or whatever, what about this mystery of yours? And this stone you talked about?' Bob asked. 'You found a body in the garden?'

Pamela explained about Professor Cook, relieved to change the subject slightly.

'Do you have the stone and letter here? Can we have a look?' asked Tim.

'Of course.'

Ginny offered to get the letter and after a few minutes reappeared with a pile of papers, a folder of photographs and the stone wrapped in tissue. She put the papers on the bare end of the large dining table as Anne followed her into the room with an apple pie and a carton of ice cream.

Pamela was concerned that dinner wasn't finished but Bob had risen from his end of the table and began to press flat the family tree. Even Anne had left the sideboard and came and picked up a photograph.

'This is interesting. Who's this?' she asked.

The brown-edged photo showed a couple, both with golf clubs in their hands. There was a thin golf bag lying on the ground in the background. Pamela took the photo and turned it over, reading what it said on the back.

'*Sir William and Lady Henrietta, 1920.* She was the daughter of Lord Shefford. That was why she was Lady Henrietta rather than Lady

Scawton.' The man was of about Tim's build, with a heavy moustache. He wore plus fours, a tweed coat with leather shoulder lapels and a tweed cheesecutter. The woman wore a calf-length skirt ,which looked to be made of a heavy material like serge and a large loose-sleeved shirt with a dark scarf hanging down the front. The outfit was topped with a felt hat with a large brim. She had one booted foot forward and leaned on a golf club as she watched the man putt at the ball.

'Hardly comfortable golfing clothes, are they?' Pamela said as she handed the photo back to Anne.

'But look how like Tim this guy's stance is,' said Anne. 'It looks like Tim in fancy dress. This man is left-handed like Tim too. Unless the photograph has been printed the wrong way.'

Ginny was leaning over the family tree with Bob and put her finger on 'William' who was born in 1898. Beside him, almost as an afterthought, there was a faint horizontal line leading to 'Edward b.' – the date was unreadable – 'd.1919'. It looked as though someone had tried to rub the line out.

'Here's Edward,' she said. 'William was 21 in 1919. Edward was younger. Which meant he was married young if it's him on the marriage certificate.'

'How interesting,' said Pamela, joining her beside the table. 'I don't remember anyone talking about Edward. I thought the other son had died as a young child. There's no plaque or gravestone in the Ashly Church. Yet he would have been James' uncle.'

'He died on the ship but that was definitely him,' said Bob. 'His wife inherited a bloody garish necklace and a good racehorse, which she and her husband raced. Called Ashly.'

'If he died on the way to New Zealand and there was a child, why don't we know more? Perhaps he eloped or was he the black sheep of the family? What disease did he die of I wonder?'

Anne picked up a photo of the house. 'Oh my, I see what you mean about a big house. It's huge. Three floors and all those windows.'

Tim had picked up another photo. 'Who's this one in the carriage?' he asked. 'She looks pretty fierce. Although the horses look very smart.' Tim turned the photo over. '*Lady Scawton, 1912.* Imagine going shopping in that?'

Ginny looked at the photo over his shoulder. The lady did look fierce, thought Pamela, sitting tall and straight and looking at the camera.

'So, where did the letter and stone come from?' asked Bob.

Pamela unwrapped the stone. 'The stone is most unusual and very valuable. An alexandrite. It changes colour. This one was mined in Russia and there are stones like this in the royal Russian jewellery.' She explained a little of what Mike had told them about the stone. 'I was hoping you might be able to shed some light on it all.'

Tim took the stone, and Bob read the letter out and the note, both now safely kept in a plastic folder so that it didn't keep getting folded more than necessary.

'Oh, this is a real mystery. You didn't tell me about this earlier, Ginny,' Tim chided Ginny. Pamela noticed how Ginny smiled at him.

Anne was talking now. 'Bob's father, Teddy – I never knew him – definitely called himself Scawton Miller. He died soon after the war, but the Miller family was large and fairly colourful. What was the story of your aunt, Bob? Didn't she run away with an Egyptian prince in Paris?'

'Oh, how wonderful,' said Pamela. 'Who was she?'

'No, no, she was a Miller, not a *Scawton* Miller,' said Bob. 'They all went off on a European trip in the 30s when she was about 15. When they were in Paris, she ran off with this Egyptian. They had a devil of a job to find her and when they did, the Egyptian prince or whoever he was did a quick runner, and she was returned to the family in time to catch the boat home. It was quite a scandal at the time. But Teddy was the only one who was a Scawton – Scawton Miller.'

'He married in the war,' Anne said, 'and had two sons and then two daughters. Bob was the younger son; Harry's dead now, but Harry's wife Margie's in Taupō. Could there be anything mysterious with your sisters, Bob?'

'Probably, but the girls married and took other names. Not Scawton,' Bob pointed out.

'The letter mentions adoption – *The adoption laws in this country have been changed*,' said Anne. 'Margie's two children are both adopted. That may be a clue. She's got old photos and everything, including the marriage certificate. She lives in Taupō and is hoping you'll spend the night with her on the way back.'

'Where is that jewel, Tim?' asked Bob. 'Let's have a look.' Tim and Ginny had been inspecting it and passed it over.

Bob picked it up, turning it over in his hands and holding it up to the light.

'It's valuable?' Tim asked.

Bob was looking at it, turning it to catch the light. 'If it changes colour, it will be the same as those in that ghastly necklace Margie has – the family heirloom from England, the one she's talking of selling. This stone is larger. But it must be the same kind.'

16

New Zealand & England 2013

Pamela awoke and listened to the birds beginning to chirp in the trees outside, even though there didn't seem to be any dawn light. She heard a door bang. Someone must be up. Her thoughts turned to the stone and how Bob, even though he had recognised it as a jewel similar to the ones in a family necklace, hadn't been impressed by it.

'Can't imagine it being valuable. It looks like coloured glass,' he'd said, as he jiggled the stone in his hand. 'Margie might know but our family never discussed the Scawton side really, except when I thought I might look you all up in England. Officially I'm a Scawton Miller, but computers don't like two names, so we keep to Miller. Except of course we've brought the Scawton name alive with the new shop, eh?'

'What new shop?' Pamela had asked. Anne explained. 'Our daughter Sally is involved in marketing and interested in the gift business. She and a friend have formed "Scawtons". She makes merino scarves from especially fine South Island wool and her friend has an incredible line of skincare. They've opened a shop in Taupō. I'm sure Margie will take you there. Since they've taken your name in vain, Pamela, I suppose you should check that our Scawtons aren't fraudsters and scoundrels.'

A shop called Scawtons reminded Pamela about Lizzie's offer. She would have liked to take that job – if only it wasn't such a responsible position. She could already hear Charles' reaction in her head. 'Totally out of your depth,' he'd say.

She picked up the stone, which was lying there in its tissue paper beside the bed. She stroked the smooth part with her thumb, wondering yet again where it really had come from and why it hadn't been turned into some jewel to adorn some celebrity's neck. It seemed to warm in her hand.

Her phone ringing disturbed her reverie and she quickly answered it before it woke anyone in the next-door room.

* * * * *

Charles had thrown a silk dressing gown on and was walking through to the sitting room, the phone to his ear. 'Mother, how are you?' Joanna was in the bathroom. It had been a quiet evening and they'd eaten at a local pub. Very ordinary food. He looked at the dial on the wall to turn the heating up.

'Charles, I never really congratulated you on your engagement. Should I send Joanna flowers?'

Charles was still squinting at the dial. The numbers were so small. Last time he turned it up too high. 'Oh, that can wait, Mother. You need to meet her properly first.'

'Yes, I suppose so. Why are you phoning? Has something happened? How is the polo?'

'No, everything is fine. We started another tournament yesterday. The bus man's pretty hopeless. We only won because the other side started arguing with the umpire in the last chukka. We've got our work cut out to win much.'

'Never mind, a win is a win and at least you've got someone to pay the bills.'

'I wanted to tell you the latest on the house.' Charles knew Godley would be reporting and he needed to get in first.

'Oh good. Have you someone to lease it?'

Charles pursed his lips. 'We're looking at turning the house into a small hotel and Joanna has friends who've done it before. We went to have a look at what could be done.'

'Oh yes.'

Charles failed to notice the scepticism in his mother's voice. 'They think it would be perfect for weddings. Just enough bedrooms. We would have to do the whole place up. Get it looking immaculate and redo the kitchen for caterers. Joanna's guys were delighted it was so big.'

It was Joanna's suggestion that they take her two designer friends to show Charles what the house could be like. Within minutes they'd imagined the house transformed into a wedding venue. The ballroom could lead directly on to the terrace and a marquee on the lawn if that was needed. Christ, they hadn't used the ballroom for years – not since his 21st birthday. No, they had used it for Father's funeral – for the tea – now he came to think of it. The whole village had been there.

Susie, one of the consultants, anticipated re-wiring and had said that the plumbing was always suspect in these old houses. 'You couldn't expect guests to listen to a lot of rumbling when they run a bath,' she'd said. He had almost forgotten his mother on the end of the phone.

'It would be good to see it all used, I must admit,' she was saying. Charles nodded to himself, pleased that his mother seemed enthusiastic and surprised that she hadn't mentioned the cost yet.

'We envisage you still living there,' he continued.

'Well, actually, I might not have to. Lizzie Shefford suggested I move over there and help her with the farm shop.'

'You? What help would you be? They have people running it, don't they?'

'But if you're turning our house into a hotel, you won't want me there.'

'No, quite the reverse. We need you to host it. To look as though you live there, shake the hands of the guests when they arrive, that kind of thing.'

He could imagine his mother at the front door greeting the guests. Godley – Charles knew he was hoping to retire but perhaps they could bring him back for weddings – would open the door for the bride and groom after their wedding in the village church and Mother would welcome them to Ashly House. The guests would all troop in, greeting Mother and saying how lovely it was, and then she would disappear to her apartment – Susie suggested they turn the stables into small apartments and she could have one of those – while the wedding party enjoyed the evening. Having Lady Scawton there would definitely add authenticity to the whole thing.

'Quentin thought weddings would be the best use. A similar house in Wendover is booked out years ahead. You'd be able to live in an apartment over the stables.'

'Mmmm. An apartment over the stables? Would the dogs like that?'

Charles suddenly had a vision of guests at the end of the wedding, coming out on to the steps at the front door and seeing his mother, in gumboots, tramping across the front paddock, the damned pointers and barking terriers going in all directions and Mother yelling at them. It would not be a good scene.

'You would have to be discreet.' He wasn't so sure now that using his mother as a hostess would work. It had been Susie's suggestion, but she'd never met his mother.

'What about the pigs?' Pamela was asking. Charles had avoided going near the stables yesterday. He'd already phoned Adrian about the pigs. It seemed pigs were some joint deal between his mother and Adrian and they agreed to leave the pigs where they were for the moment, until they were big enough to sell.

'The pigs will go. I've already phoned Adrian. Mother, it seems everything is happening while you're away. I did tell you. By the way, why were there three gardeners there when we visited? It seemed far too many. I thought we employed only Godley. Employing three gardeners is totally over the top.'

'They're the Batchelor boys.'

'You are the one always saying we have no money. Perhaps we need to cut down the staff . . . but, of course, that can all wait. Now, are you relaxing over there?'

There was a pause before his mother spoke. 'We're at the Scawton Miller's farm in the Hawke's Bay. It's early morning here, quite chilly actually. We're about to see the shearing today – a woolshed in action. And Charles, Bob Miller recognised the stone.'

'So you solved the mystery? What was it about?'

'No, but they have a necklace with similar stones.'

Joanna appeared and smiled at Charles as she made her way past him to pick up a magazine from the table. Charles felt a surge at her provocative sway. He was sure he could smell her perfume. He drew his dressing gown around him.

'Their grandfather came from Ashly,' his mother was saying. 'We tracked him on the family tree.'

'Well, I'll phone in a few days when we have some more plans, Mother. I have to go now.'

'Yes, I'll phone . . . ' He had pressed the 'End' button as she spoke, and watched Joanna. The magazine in her hand could wait.

* * * * *

The noise from the shearing shed was quite deafening, and there was a distinct smell of sheep manure and wool. The shed was small according to Tim, with just three stands – his brother's farm in the South Island had eight – but it still seemed busy and noisy. Pamela imagined a gang of men would be contracted but there were only the three shearers. She was surprised to see Tim and Bob were the workers, picking up the fleeces themselves and pushing the sheep into the pens. Ginny was already helping and sweeping the floor with a thin broom, while Anne had suggested Pamela help prepare the smoko – the morning tea, it seemed – which would be followed by lunch and tea.

At lunch, just as it had at smoko, the noise from all the machines stopped. There was a sudden silence except for a few sheep bleating and Tim busy shouting at the dogs while Bob was standing at a yard gate outside with his arm half out, obviously counting the shorn sheep. Lunch was set up on a makeshift table in the lean-to barn and the shearers took their place on a bench. One of the shearers, a wiry old man, had sweat still pouring off him while he sat at the table. He looked far too old to shear.

Hot sausages, cold roast lamb, a big potato salad and a smaller green salad all disappeared in no time at all as they sat around the table, accompanied by a faint smell of wool, tractor diesel and old hay. The shearers themselves seemed to spend the breaks talking about how many sheep they had shorn or what combs or cutters they were using. They were very polite to Anne and Pamela, the youngest shearer answering Pamela's questions. He'd been shearing since he was a kid, and explained with gusto that no, these bloody sheep were bloody easy cutting compared to the bloody merinos in the South Island, until the senior shearer told him to watch his language.

The three shearers got up from the table and wandered away, one rolling a cigarette, another changing the cutter on his handpiece. Pamela was still sitting at the table, with a mug of tea in her hands, and Ginny was sitting beside her, buttering a piece of bread, when there was a shout from the yards.

'You fucking dog, get out of there,' came Tim's voice. A large woolly sheep ran between the barn and the shed and more sheep followed, with a dog and then Tim in pursuit.

'You bloody mongrel, what the hell were you doing? Get in behind for Christ's sake.' Tim's face was thunderous as he ran past. Although Pamela was used to the language by now, Tim's tone was violent. Even the three shearers on the woolshed steps seemed paralysed with surprise.

'Tim,' yelled Bob as Tim strode past and went to follow the sheep up the track as they headed back to the hills. Tim had just reached the gate when he turned and came back, his fury showing.

'I'll have to get the bike. The fucking things will go right back up to the airstrip. I'll kill that dog.'

As Tim strode past the barn again, his father, showing more agility than Pamela would have given him credit for, ran to catch him up. They stood by the bike arguing, the voices loud but incoherent. Tim suddenly turned and with the same angry stride headed off back to the house.

Bob got on the bike himself, and calling the dogs, disappeared in a cloud of dust up the track, the dogs chasing behind except one old dog who followed at a leisurely pace, unable to keep up. 'Oh dear, I'd better go and speak to Tim,' said Anne.

'I'll go,' Ginny said. Both Anne and Pamela turned but Ginny had got up from the table and ran out of the barn before Anne could begin to say anything.

Stunned by the interruption, Pamela realised she must have looked worried about Ginny as Anne spoke.

'She would be as good as me. He doesn't become violent. It's just frustration, his brain.' She began to pile the plates up and put a plastic top on the salad container.

The machines in the shed started up again; Anne looked up at the noise.

'We'd better leave this and help in the shed until Bob gets back. Come on.'

The two women climbed up the steps to the woolshed and Anne pointed to Ginny's broom and showed her what she was meant to be sweeping. The old shearer at the end of the line had already settled into a rhythm. Pamela didn't realise that, out of deference to her, he kicked the first cut of wool – from the sheep's belly – out of the way before turning the sheep over.

'He won't do that again,' Anne whispered quickly into Pamela's ear.

'He usually just stands on them. He's just being nice to you.' Pamela was ready with the broom for his next sheep. His shears made smooth tracks in the wool across the sheep's stomach and by the time he turned the animal over, Pamela had swept that separate piece of wool away. Bellies went in a separate pile, she had been told. In no time at all, Pamela was throwing the shorn fleeces into the wool press while Anne climbed into the wool press itself and trampled them down to make room for more.

They could hear Bob come back on the bike.

Anne asked Pamela to stay and sweep while she went and cleared the lunch and prepared the afternoon smoko. 'Bob will be up in a minute,' she assured Pamela as she disappeared through the open wooden door at the top of the steps. Pamela was too busy to notice her going. The shearing machines droned on.

17

England. 1943

The bus slowed to a stop, and James stood back to allow two girls to get off before him. They were both in a green uniform he didn't recognise. As the bus drove off, he put his leather kitbag on the ground, leaning it against his leg. His greatcoat hung over his arm. He looked around. There was a large concrete bollard in the middle of the road – the bus driver had to drive around it, grumbling 'It's supposed to stop the bloody jerries.' Apart from that, the village of Ashly looked the same as ever, war or no war.

The houses he could see had crossed tape over their windows but so did every house in London. Someone – maybe his mother – had said a stray bomb had landed on one of the roads but James couldn't see where. It must have been further away. He could hear children playing in a garden close by.

'I want to be Hitler. You were 'im last time!' The voices stopped and then started again, this time making noises of aeroplanes and crashing bombs.

There were few people around and no dogs barking. James could remember a lot of dogs had been put down at the outbreak of war, even before he had enlisted. His father had kept their good Labrador bitch to breed from and had taken her up to Scotland with him. The two girls who had got off the bus with him had reached Andy's, the village shop. There was a jeep outside the shop but otherwise, apart from the kids, the village was quiet. It was going to be one of those wonderful summer evenings that would linger on until ten o'clock.

James sighed. He had written ahead and booked into the Red Lion. His parents had moved to Scotland while the Americans had taken over Ashly House; it was some secret intelligence base now. He picked up his bag and headed past the little church and across the village green towards the pub.

It had been a long day. He had come down from Edinburgh on the Birmingham train After the week of his leave in Aberdeenshire with his parents, his father had asked him to call in and check on the business on his way south, and so today had been spent in the iron works at Tring, going through the contracts with his father's partner. It was only nostalgia that had brought him back here for the night.

His father had always intended that James should work in the company once he left school, and James had been keen to do so. He had never been much of a book person. Probably his main claim to fame at Winchester was when he hit 99 for the first eleven to beat Eton at Agars Plough, just before he left school. So close. He was sure he could hit that last ball for six; instead he got bowled.

James had started work, as his father wanted, from the bottom up. Malcolm, the partner, put him in the blacksmith's shop first – the old-fashioned part of the business, as he said. His father had bought the original blacksmith shop from the Black family who lived in Ashly Village and had then moved the forge to Tring, amalgamating it with the engineering plant his father also owned. The company specialised in cast iron fencing but quickly got a reputation for strong tools and good machinery repairs as well as fancy wrought iron gates and hinges. All the door handles at Ashly were given new levers and the gates at the entrance were a work of art.

War finally broke out a year later. It was not unexpected. All during his last year at school, James had been quite active in the cadets and the masters had been speaking of war being declared even when Neville Chamberlain had returned from Munich in 1938 saying that it was unlikely. When Hitler invaded Poland, everyone knew that war was inevitable.

It seemed obvious to enlist straight away. James hadn't worked for long enough to be indispensable. His father was still there to supervise, and Malcolm was more than capable of running the business himself anyway. Contracts were coming in for war material, but James still decided enlisting was the right thing to do. He would have liked to join the Air Force after enjoying a couple of flights as a passenger in a Gypsy Moth, but his father was keen for him to join his old army regiment. The army won out.

All that had been nearly four years ago. Who would have dreamt the difference just four years could make? It felt like ten.

He reached the pub and the landlord came to the door to welcome him in. 'It's pretty rough and ready, Mr James, but you're welcome. Sorry, it's not Mr – it's Captain now, isn't it?'

He followed the landlord up the stairs to a tiny room with a wash basin stand and the leadlight window propped open to the late afternoon air. The window looked out over the village green.

He unpacked his washbag and put the notes he had made for his father in the case. He would have time to write him a proper report on the train tomorrow, but his father would be pleased that the demand for steel security fencing had shot up with a couple of good contracts from installations at Ashridge and Bovingdon. Raw materials were still a problem with both the steel and iron; no one in the factory seemed surprised that there was never enough steel. In some cases they'd used old iron fencing from atop stone walls – it had been put there to keep stock in but now it was refashioned into fencing to keep people out. Finding enough workers for the factory was the other problem. Good strong labourers were hard to find; King and Country had long since called them up.

Even so, James found the plant one of the busiest and most cheerful places he could have visited. Malcolm had trained up new staff although his father would be horrified to see they were women, including two who were the largest women James had ever seen; one of them said she came from Poland. Malcolm assured him they could do most of the jobs, even the tricky forge welding James had found so hard when he had worked there. The new younger men there had all been discharged from the army with injuries. One poor guy James met had lost a foot two years previously; he had been in the navy trying to get British troops out of St Valery. He seemed to be coping with the injury and tapped the false foot in his boot saying how he could drop a red-hot cinder on it and it wouldn't hurt.

James looked out the window of the pub again. He still had plenty of time to get up to the house – he wanted to see what had happened to it. He could hear the landlord in the kitchen but just went out of the front door and walked towards the woods and the public footpath he knew led from beside the pub. The path was now fenced on the garden side with high iron railings. It was one of the first changes the army had made on taking over the house and it had amused his father that the Scawton works got paid to fence their own property. He could still see the house across the garden, but the railings stopped him taking a short cut. He'd have to walk on to the main gate. Once out of the trees and beside the open parkland, the gardeners had planted a hedge beside the railings, which was already waist high. The main gates were closed with a sentry box and bar as well, and he could see the lodge a little further away. He called to the sentry.

No amount of persuasion could persuade the overly polite American corporal to let him through without a pass or at least a name to ask for. Disappointed, he turned back towards the village, looking longingly over the park fields towards the house. He had gone through the woods and had nearly reached the pub when he heard a bicycle come up from behind and he turned to see a young man.

'Mr James, have you come back to see what we're doing to your house?' It was John Batchelor. He was several years younger than James, who remembered him as just a snip of a boy, helping his father who'd been one of the gardeners.

'Hello, John, good to see a familiar face. I'd like to see what's happening in the house, but they wouldn't let me in. What do they do there? Is your father still working there?'

'No, Pa's in Suffolk. He's on Coastal Defence, sitting out on the dunes and watching the bird life mostly. I'm due to sign up in a month. I'll be 18.'

James shuddered. He could remember how enthusiastic he had been about enlisting.

'We can go through the farm if you like,' the lad continued, 'and see the garden end. It's all vegetables now. We're not allowed near the house, but you can have a look from there.'

They turned back along the path and then up the farm track. James could see that the farm was much the same. Young John explained how they had six land girls who worked hard, evidently doing all the milking and most of the tractor work. A couple of the girls were dab hands at the vegetables as well.

They walked up through the kitchen gardens to the gate, which led through the wall to the stable block.

'We aren't allowed further than this unless we 'ave one of them Yanks with us. This gate's locked. We have to ring through on this bell or phone up from the office when we want to get in.' He pointed to a new brass bell hanging by the gate. The gate, wrought iron, of course, had plenty of gaps, and James could see the back of the house was all much the same. The stables seemed to have been turned into some form of administration block. There were obviously no horses and several olive-green jeeps were parked in the yard.

'But how do you keep the garden tidy through there? Or do they do that?'

'They set days when they supervise us working there. We get the whole farm staff and mow and do whatever weeding needs doing all on the one day and they send a couple of overseers to watch us. They don't trust us.'

'Goodness me, that's extraordinary. It sounds like prison.'

'Nah, we're used to it. The overseers know us now and work with us. One is black as anything. Comes from Florida. Says his family were slaves once. The other one is a walnut farmer from California. Both of them complain about the cold weather,' John laughed.

They walked back together towards the village, and James thanked John for taking him. They parted outside the Red Lion and James stopped at the door, looking at the village pond over the road. They used to ride the horses through the pond on the way back from hunting to clean the mud off. It would save having to brush the horses down when they got home. He remembered his first little pony used to roll in the water, dumping him in the muddy water while the groom with him would nearly fall off his own horse laughing. After a couple of soakings, he would take a stick with him when the pony went into the water and would beat the little wretch if he began to paw and feel as though he favoured a dip.

＊＊＊＊＊

'Captain Scawton, if you've finished your dinner, Sir, there is someone here you might like to meet. He's been trying to get into your house as well.'

James had indeed finished his dinner. The landlord had suggested the rabbit stew because 'we can't always get it'. James realised the rabbit would have probably come from the Ashly farms and been shot by the landlord himself. He hoped, for the rabbit's sake, that the man was a better shot than he was a cook but there were plenty of vegetables, which the landlord informed him came mainly from the Ashly House gardens, and the stewed pears for dessert were delicious.

The landlord had left the bar to the attractive girl with hair curled round her ears and the pretty smile. Now James got up and followed him towards a man of about James' own age. He wasn't in uniform and looked as though he was in borrowed clothes: they were too big for him.

'This is Mick. He's a Kiwi flyer and was complaining that he couldn't get into the Ashly grounds this evening either. He says his mother used to work for your family. Before my time though. This is Captain James Scawton.'

'How do you do?' said James, 'A Kiwi, are you? I met a whole lot of your chaps in North Africa. Good fellows.' He proffered a packet of cigarettes and took one himself.

'Senior Service. I don't mind if I do, Sir. Makes a happy change from Woodbine. Thanks.' The New Zealander took a cigarette. James held out a match as they began to chat about the war. Mick had started as a navigator on Wellingtons, as part of 75 Squadron, the New Zealand squadron. Lately he had been in Short Sterlings, based up in Mepal.

'I got done in the knee by a bit of damaged fuselage during the last op and now they're shipping me home to be an instructor. I leave next week but my mum insisted that I should come down here and see where she came from, before I go back. I've been staying with an uncle over in Nettleden. They did say I wouldn't be able to get near the house and they were right. I could only look from the path, through those fancy wrought iron gates. Didn't they let you in, even though it's your home?'

James shook his head. 'Not a show, but I met a gardener and we saw a bit of the back part. Enough for me to see it all looks much the same.' James arranged to get the drinks: a pint of Double Brown and a whisky for himself.

'Good stuff this when you get used to it. Thanks,' said Mick as he took the tankard.

They chatted for a while. James explained that his parents were living in Scotland, and that they had an ironworks in the town which James had come to see on his way south.

'Was that the blacksmith shop, which my mum said my uncle sold to you lot?'

'Was your uncle Jack Black then, who died? I knew your grandfather too. Great old man. Used to shoe my pony. What was your mother's Christian name then?'

'My mum was Aggie, the only girl in the family of five boys. Mum left when she was my age and went to New Zealand with another uncle – Tom. Before that she worked as a maid in the big house here. A kitchen maid, I think.' Mick sounded excited to find someone who might have known his mother.

'Goodness me. I don't remember an Aggie. Maybe she left before I was born. Emily was in the kitchen when I grew up and a French chef. Emily was mean and would stop me trying to steal food from the cold store.'

They talked about growing up. Mick would agree with James that even as a kid, there was never enough to eat.

'Mind you,' Mick continued, 'it was the Depression and we never had enough money. We relied on Dad's racehorses winning before we got a decent meal.'

'I always thought there would have been plenty to eat in New Zealand. All those sheep. Some of your chaps seem so large, especially your Māoris.'

'Good fighters, eh?'

'The best. They don't hold back. Are you Māori then?'

'Not really. My Dad was half Māori, half Irish. I never admitted to the Māori side when I joined up, but now I'm quite proud of it. The Māori Battalion are doing us proud.' Inevitably the talk turned back to the war, the fighting, the advance to El Alamein, the heat and the sand.

'I tell you, at times it was bloody unnerving,' James admitted. 'Just to see those Panzers coming over the dunes would be enough to make you want to shit yourself. We all had our own way of dealing with it. I always seemed to be next to the soldier who would start praying out loud, which was a bit disconcerting.'

Mick smiled.

'I have the stone my mum lent me. I wouldn't fly without it. That came from your family too. In fact, she wanted me to show it to your father if he was around.'

'What stone?' James blew out cigarette smoke and looked around at the murky atmosphere. There were quite a few men in the pub now, mostly in uniform. A Home Guard group had come in, chatting happily. Mick dug deep into his pocket and pulled out something that looked like an uneven stone, shiny on one side.

'It looks like some kind of half-cut jewel. How did your mother come by it?' asked James.

'She said old Lady Scawton gave it to her when she left. I guess she meant your grandmother.'

James frowned, wondering why his grandmother would have given a maid a present like that. It seemed unusual. The jewel, even half cut, looked quite valuable. His grandmother had died years ago but James remembered her as a stern lady with grey hair piled high into a bun on the back of her head. The matron at James' school had been scary but never as scary as Grandmother.

'Sit up straight.' 'Nanny, haven't you taught this child any manners at all?' 'You don't talk in church, young man.' He could remember her voice to this day. She would usually sit in a high-backed pale green velvet chair – very upright even when she was old – and her blue-veined hands would be clasped in her lap, not interlocked but just overlapping, together and still. Her funeral was the first funeral James had been to, and they had to hold it at St Peter's Church in town because the village church was too small. It had rained and James had wondered whether it always rained for funerals; it seemed suitable somehow.

He took the stone. 'This end is perfectly smooth. What kind of jewel is it? It looks pink but not pink enough to be a ruby.'

'Yes, but in the daylight it changes. Come over here – there might still be enough light – I'll show you.' Mick took the stone and got up from his stool and went towards the window but it was too crowded there and so he walked to the open door instead. The twilight had lengthened and there was not enough light to show how the stone changed colour. 'It changes to green.'

'Oh, I know the thing. My mother has a tiara. She never wears it now, but it has stones that change colour. She says they're Russian jewels of some kind. It's most unusual. Is that what this is? Before it's cut?'

'I suppose so. I don't think my mum knows.'

'Well, if it is, it's pretty rare. This looks big though.' James wondered again why his grandmother had given a maid such an unusual stone. She must have been very fond of the girl.

'Well, it's our family taonga. My mum gave it to me and, now that I'm going home, I'll give it to my brother Sean to keep, until he gets home. I'm seeing him in a few days.'

A bell sounded. Closing time. There was a complaining mutter from the Home Guard group. The pretty maid with the curled hair was beginning to check the blackout curtains were still up.

'Are you peddling back in the dark?' asked James. The two were still standing by the door.

'There's a bit of a moon. And it isn't that far.' Mick went to leave, waved at the publican and then remembered to shake James by the hand.

The publican looked across at them. Two men from either side of the world. One a local lad, whose family had been here for generations, the other a foreigner and obviously not in the same class – but they looked remarkably alike.

18

New Zealand 2013

Polly was looking out from her bedroom toward the ordinary fence, as she called it. The morning was still only half light. She really disliked the plain wooden panels, not even painted. She had planted a bougainvillaea against the fence when they moved in, but it hadn't taken even though bougainvillaea was meant to be hardy. It was a sheltered spot, but the soil was dry and didn't get much sun. Simon had suggested putting pots of flowers in front of it but then they would need watering all the time. If the bougainvillaea had died for lack of water, the pots didn't have a chance.

She kept thinking about Diane. She still couldn't believe she hadn't said anything about the letter and the stone after Mum died, yet surely she must have known they would miss the stone. Diane was the only one now who knew what was in the letter, apart from the Scawtons, of course. If Diane had told them before Geoffrey had left, Polly could have gone to see him and . . . oh, what was the point? If, if, if. If her mother were alive none of this would have happened.

The phone shrilled. It was still early and so it had to be Uncle Pete. Anyone else would've used her mobile. She turned to the phone beside her bed and picked up the receiver.

'Good morning.'

She heard the cheerful voice. 'Uncle Pete, how can you be so happy so early in the morning? It's barely light.'

'I wanted to catch you before you left.' For a moment she wondered if there was something wrong, a chest pain or something. She sat down on the bed waiting to hear.

'I had a call from Geoffrey's brother. Theo or Theodore. The one you went to see.' Polly wondered why the mad doctor would have called Pete or how he got his phone number.

'He had a visit from Lady Scawton, as in the Scawtons of Ashly.'

Polly stomach gave a lurch. 'Sir Charles' wife?'

'His mother – the one who found Geoffrey. She's flown out because he'd said the family had murdered Geoffrey.'

'She flew from England? I only saw him a short time ago and he never mentioned anything about her coming. So did Lady Macbeth confess?'

'Polly, we know Geoffrey wasn't murdered – even he knows that. He was worried because she said she might take him to court – slander or libel or something. She hoped he could tell her about the stone. She has the stone and she showed it to Theo. So you see, Geoffrey did get it to the family and we know where it is.'

'We knew that already. When it wasn't with Geoffrey's things, he had to have given it to them.'

'The lady said she wanted to know about Beth's letter.'

'She must know already.'

'Evidently not. The man agreed he'd contact one of us and ask us to phone her.'

'There's no point in speaking to her. They aren't going to give the stone back or anything, are they? Particularly now they've been accused of murder.'

'He sounded agitated.'

'Theodore? He sounds like that all the time. The man's a nutcase.'

'He didn't sound that mad. He just wants us to contact her because she wants to know why Geoffrey had it.'

Polly looked out of the window. A ray of sunlight caught the glass, so she couldn't see the top of the fence. Polly smiled to herself, pleased that at least the stone was back in New Zealand. Then she remembered how it didn't belong to her family anymore; it had gone.

'You can phone her if you want. I don't want anything to do with it; we don't even know what the letter really said.'

'It's no good me phoning her. I don't know why Aggie wanted Beth to give the stone back, do I?'

'If Geoffrey gave them the stone, they know already.'

'I said we'd phone; he's given me her number.'

Goodness, Pete could be persistent. 'Well, I'm not going to.'

'Think about it. We might get the stone back.'

Polly gave a mean laugh. 'From a high and mighty English lot? I doubt it, I really doubt it.'

✶ ✶ ✶ ✶ ✶

Arrangements had been made for Pamela and Ginny to visit Bob's sister Margie in Taupō. She knew the family history much better than he did.

For some reason Pamela couldn't understand, Ginny said she had to make a quick dash back to Auckland and so would leave Pamela with Margie and drive on. Tim was hitching a ride with them to Taupō to pick up a vehicle. It seemed everyone was on the move.

Pamela had finished packing and had put her bag in the hall and walked towards the kitchen door. She could hear Bob and Tim talking.

'Time she bloody well went, Tim, eh?' came Bob's voice. Pamela hesitated at the door, thinking he must be speaking about her.

'She was handy in the shed,' came Tim's reply.

'Yeah, but that's about all. Shearing's finished and she's had her holiday,' answered Bob. 'Ginny got her under control, eh?'

Pamela was embarrassed. They'd only been here two nights. She realised now that Bob had resented her ever since she got here. With the title and all that stuff, she'd thought he'd been joking but obviously he hadn't been.

As she entered the room, Tim was heading out of the back door and Bob looked up at her. Surely they'd realised she'd overheard but his face didn't register any unease.

'Help yourself to a cup of tea, Pamela. Tim's just got to feed the horses before you go.' He just got up from the table and followed Tim towards the back door without another word. Pamela dare not catch his eye. Alone now in the empty kitchen, she turned and went back up to her bedroom.

She checked she hadn't left anything and through the window she could see Tim and Ginny walking up to where he kept the horses. They seemed deep in conversation and when Tim patted Ginny on the shoulder, Ginny turned and laughed. Pamela looked away and picked up her mobile. No messages. She sighed, realising the mystery still wasn't solved and all she'd done was offend Bob – she should never have come.

They left soon afterwards, with Pamela driving. Pamela would have preferred to let Tim drive, but Ginny had reminded her that, being a hire car, only she and Ginny were insured. Tim didn't seem to mind and folded himself into the back and then stretched out over the two seats.

They had passed over the top of the hills now and the road was heading downhill. There were huge tussocky paddocks either side of the long open road; hardly any traffic –just one large truck coming towards them in the distance. Ginny was fast asleep, leaving Pamela and Tim with their own thoughts. In the rear-vision mirror she saw Tim was gazing out of the window.

He seemed pleasant except for those outbreaks. Ginny didn't seem to mind them, which was just as well if she was becoming a bit keen on the boy. She wondered whether his temper tantrums would become less in time; they hadn't with CJ. They'd got worse. Perhaps the ongoing treatment now – drugs or counselling – would make a difference.

She was watching the road ahead as a truck came closer.

'Tim?' Pamela began. The truck swished by, the road ahead empty. Tim raised his head, catching her eye in the mirror.

'They said that you had post-traumatic stress . . . ' She wondered how best to continue.

'For Christ's sake, who is "they"?' Tim's voice thundered round the car. Pamela was taken aback and Ginny woke with a start. 'That was all years ago. It gets blamed for everything,' he went on.

'Goodness, I am sorry, Tim. I just wanted . . . ' began Pamela.

'I just don't want people to talk about it.'

'I'm so sorry,' Pamela repeated. Ginny, confused, turned in her seat to look back at Tim. Pamela watched him in the rear-view mirror. Tim was stony-faced as he stared out the window.

Ginny was fully awake now, and frowning. No one spoke. The pale green landscape flashed past, flat and expansive and appearing rather empty and wet. A road wound off to the right. Imagine living down that road, miles from anywhere, thought Pamela, trying to think of something to say but not daring to break the silence. There was a lonely pub there, one old ute parked in front of it. They drove on in silence until they came down into Taupō and the lake lay ahead of them.

'What a brilliant view,' Ginny commented. It sounded banal, but Pamela took it as chastisement – a 'Don't be silly, guys. What's all this about?' Pamela straightened in her seat.

'Yes, it's a great view,' she agreed. 'Look at those clouds.' There were black edges to the grey cloud overhead. Tim still sat in silence in the back.

* * * * *

Ginny hoped Pamela wouldn't mind them leaving her with Margie. She had forgotten her counselling appointments before and she didn't want to end on a bad note by cancelling this last one. She also didn't want to have Pamela telling her mother, who didn't know about the counselling and would probably have rubbished it. When the counsellor finished Ginny would tell her mother herself. Tim understood her predicament – he'd had counselling too.

Tim's Aunt Margie welcomed them in. She was a tall woman, a little overweight but with a easy manner and a large smile. A black and white spaniel ran out to add to the welcome. They chatted for a while, talking about Taupō and Tim's sister's shop using the Scawton name.

'We'll have to go and visit. Sal saw the film star – what's his name? Stit Rennie – in town the other day but he didn't come into the shop. He's living just along the road here in the Jones' big house on the point. The film company rented the house.'

Ginny was obviously impressed as she said, 'Oh, I saw him on telly when he arrived in New Zealand. Have *you* seen him?'

'Oh, goodness no. There are usually bodyguards around and he's only here for a couple of weeks. The most you ever see are big black cars going through the gate – you can tell them because they look like the Mafia. The Dawsons next door to the house say that cars come out of the gate at seven in the morning and don't go back in until dark. They're filming up in the Craters of the Moon. I must admit it would make wonderfully spooky scenery in a film.'

'Who is this man?' asked Pamela

'Oh, Aunt Pamela,' chided Ginny, forgetting to omit the 'aunt'. 'You must know Stit Rennie. He's really hot. An American superstar. He was in *Night Rides*.'

Pamela shook her head and confessed she wasn't into film stars. She had never heard of him.

⋆ ⋆ ⋆ ⋆ ⋆

Tim and Ginny had left together, leaving Pamela feeling a little insecure as she stood looking out at the lake shimmering in the afternoon sun. She felt a long way from home.

When Pamela produced the paper and the stone, she waited while Margie read the letter carefully and then showed her how the stone changed colour from the green colour in daylight to the pink under artificial light. Margie excused herself and disappeared for a good five minutes before coming back downstairs with an old-fashioned velvet-lined jewel box.

'Take a look at this. It belonged to Granny, Harry and Bob's grandmother, the Mary Scawton who came from England.' From the box, she took out an ornate and expensive-looking necklace and laid it on the table, emeralds and diamonds sparkling in the sun from the window.

'What an incredible necklace!' Immediately Pamela noticed the similarity to the Scawton tiara she remembered. This necklace had two alexandrites, one on each side set into the heavy silver setting. She pointed to them and laid her stone alongside them, the smooth face upwards. The single stone was much darker, perhaps because of the density from its uncut part, but it had the same translucence as the two jewels in the necklace. 'The stones are definitely the same, aren't they? The Scawton tiara I wore for our wedding had the same stones too. I wish I had brought a picture of it. It was sold years ago but I'd say it was made by the same jeweller. And she brought this from England?'

Margie nodded, adding, 'Harry always said she arrived in New Zealand with this necklace, my father-in-law Teddy and the racehorse.'

'And did the racehorse come from England too?'

'Indeed. Mary's first husband sent it out and Harry's grandfather bought it and then married Mary,' explained Margie. 'It was already called Ashly and turned out to be a really good steeplechaser.' She picked up the necklace and put it back in the velvet case. 'No one's worn this for years and it's been in the bank. I thought the family might sell it and put the money into Sal's new venture. When I took it to get valued, the jeweller commented on those two stones and said he wasn't sure what they're worth or even what they are; the rest of the necklace is all diamonds and emeralds.'

Pamela had picked up the uncut stone and was rolling it, feeling the rough exterior as she spoke. 'Mary's first husband was Edward Scawton, CJ's great-uncle. Why was this one stone left like this and not used? Why was it given away? The family called the tiara the Russian tiara, but I'm not sure that had anything to do with it, except we know this stone and, presumably, those two in the necklace were mined in Russia.' She placed the loose stone back on the tissue paper and there was a moment of silence before Pamela continued. 'Can you solve the letter too?'

Margie shook her head. 'No, I've really no idea what that's about. Maybe something to do with the jewels . . . The letter mentions adoption . . . '

Pamela was comfortable talking to Margie but didn't like to ask about her adopted children. She wasn't sure whether she was meant to know they were adopted.

Margie changed the subject. 'Do I sense a budding romance there, with Tim and Ginny?' Pamela agreed, but after the angry reaction from Tim about the post-traumatic stress disorder, she didn't want to talk about him either. They talked about the farm instead, and then about Margie's husband. He had died some years before.

Towards evening, they walked along the lakefront with Smoky the spaniel running madly around in excitement. Pamela explained about her own dogs and how she enjoyed walking them. Eventually Pamela asked about Margie's children and found that, like most mothers, Margie was happy to talk about them. Linda and Chris were now both adult and lived away from home. Linda lived in Rotorua and had a little boy, Margie's grandson.

A little later in the evening, with dinner over, they were seated either side of the picture window, which ran along the side of the sitting room, sipping on a cup of herbal tea. It was a clear moonlit night with the lights of the town twinkling as brightly as the stars overhead and a shimmer of reflection coming from the lake.

Margie spoke. 'You know, I've been thinking about this letter and the adoption thing. Why did this Beth talk about adoption? I can't see it concerns Harry's grandmother. They married in 1920 and Teddy was born in 1921 after Edward had died on the way out.'

Pamela agreed. The marriage certificate was still on the table and she read it again. Mary Buttons was 24, her father was a mill worker and Edward was 20. The witnesses were Sir William Scawton and an illegible name. Both bride and groom came from Ashly.

'Maybe it's nothing to do with this Edward Scawton at all,' Pamela suggested. 'I know it's a long shot, but Bob said your children are adopted. Could they have something to do with it?'

'I can't see how. We've never met any of the Scawton family and nor have the kids. The adoption laws were certainly changed here, oh, about 2004. Before then it was quite hard for an adopted person to find out about their birth parents, but this letter infers that whoever it is, has known for a long time. *Your family and mine are so entwined* the letter says.'

'I just don't like *the satisfaction she had failed to get*. It sounds like revenge,' Pamela commented with an involuntarily shiver. 'If it doesn't concern your children, perhaps it concerns another child, or the people who adopted the child, the adoptive parents like you? Perhaps the adopted child did something terrible and the adoptive parents blame the baby's original mother. Hereditary trait. Or maybe they were forced to adopt him.' This was an angle she hadn't considered. Of course, she thought – it sounded plausible. She should have thought of it before.

Margie just shook her head. 'That's too far-fetched. No one is forced to adopt a child.'

'You were saying earlier what trouble your daughter caused when she was a teenager: ran away, slept rough and was such a worry. I know this isn't to do with your daughter, but if this adopted child we don't know about became a murderer, wouldn't the adoptive parents have blamed the birth parents?'

She saw a flash of anger cross Margie's face. Pamela's stomach gave a lurch. She didn't know Margie that well and she was always offending people – Bob, Tim, old Doctor Cook and now Margie. She was relieved when Margie's face changed again, the anger lost. Thank goodness.

'You've no idea,' said Margie. 'Can you imagine the agony of not being able to have a child when you want one?'

Pamela was immediately contrite. Indeed she knew. 'We were married years before Charles was born,' she said. 'There was never any talk of adoption because the title was involved – the wretched title – but I do know about wanting children. Was that the same with you?' Margie nodded. Pamela continued 'I had all the tests imaginable. Gynaecologists galore. Now there's in vitro fertilization and all that, it probably wouldn't be such a problem.'

'Mine was before IVF came to New Zealand,' Margie agreed. 'We would've had to go to Perth and the chances weren't good. Oh, I went through all those tests you probably had to – injections on the 14th day, taking the temperature. When we decided to adopt, the Social Welfare kept saying we wouldn't get a child. So when, finally, we were allowed to adopt Linda, it was the best day of our lives. And Chris a few years later.'

While Margie was fondly reminiscing, Pamela returned to the letter.

'So if Linda or Chris had turned out to be a murderer and it was proved that it could have been a genetic trait, wouldn't you have blamed the original parents?'

Margie thought for a moment but was adamant. 'Blame the birth parents? I don't think it would have occurred to us.'

'When Linda was so difficult as a teenager, didn't you wonder whether it was an inherited trait?' Pamela persisted.

'Pamela, with due respect, every time Charles was ill as a child, did you think perhaps his natural father had tonsillitis at that age – that it runs in the family? Even if we had wondered, we didn't know who the birth parents were at that stage, and there was no way of finding out. We had a one-page description of the birth mother, but it certainly wouldn't have mentioned anything about her having criminal genes!' Margie was smiling now.

'Would all adoptive parents feel the same?'

'Forget the adoptive bit, Pamela. They are our children and we are eternally grateful for that. Even those who've adopted a child, and then had one or more of their own, feel the same. Oh, they may have found their children were difficult, me included. But there are probably as many natural parents who find their own child wayward.'

Pamela nodded in agreement as Margie continued. 'We only encouraged Linda to find her birth parents in the hope it would give her some sort of history. Genetics get talked about so much more now.'

'Did she find out?'

'Oh, yes and that was quite dramatic. We didn't know until after Linda had met her mother. Lovely lady, lives in Wellington. A bit of a free spirit. Very like Linda, so I suppose that trait was genetic.'

'Wasn't that awkward? Didn't it make you feel . . .' Pamela hesitated.

'Guilty, if anything,' Margie finished for her. Pamela was surprised – that wasn't the word she would have suggested.

Margie continued. 'Guilty that we had a daughter who, more by luck and Linda's own efforts, we had managed to bring up and who had turned into a great person. Guilty that we now have a wonderful grandson.' Pamela had never imagined adoptive parents feeling that way.

There was a silence before Margie picked up the letter again. 'I don't think whoever wrote this letter felt guilty. She felt aggrieved. Aggrieved because her family was *so entwined* with yours.'

19

England & New Zealand 2013

Charles parked the BMW outside the front steps. The windows were down. He had told Godley he didn't need him but now, with no Godley to greet him and his mother away, it all seemed rather silent. No dogs rushed out. He sat in the car for a minute, Joanna beside him, looking up at the house through the window. The house seemed ghostly.

'The other two said they would be here at 11.00am. Do you want me to phone?' she asked, moving a long lock of blonde hair back from her face. 'I don't want to hustle them though.'

'I suppose it's a good chance to have a look around. I'll just check Godley unlocked everything.' Charles got out and stretched. The sun was beginning to warm things up. It had been drizzling all through his polo match yesterday and he had ended up with everything slightly sodden. Typically, today – a day off from polo – was going to be fine. Joanna got out on the other side of the car.

'You can't smell the pigs from here, or hear them,' Joanna said. 'I would have thought you would have. They're round that wall, aren't they? It's all very quiet.' She sounded almost distasteful of the silence.

'You could never hear the horses when the stables were full.'

Joanna perched herself against the bonnet of the BMW.

'It'll be good to go through their ideas without feeling Godley's around every corner listening,' she mused.

'And reporting to Mother you think?'

'Don't be silly. I'm sure he wouldn't be.' Charles knew that, indeed,

Godley would report.

As he climbed the steps towards the front door, Charles felt the quietness around him. He couldn't understand why he felt guilty, skulking around his own house. This was all his now – not his mother's, not even his ancestors'. It wasn't his fault that there wasn't enough money to keep the bloody thing going and it needed updating. At Joanna's suggestions, her father had offered to pay for the upgrade, provided, as her father said, 'Either you live there, or you make an income from it'.

Joanna and he had never entertained living in it; she wanted to live in Gloucestershire and this was Hertfordshire so that meant they needed to use Jerry's 'income' option. Patrick and his mother had suggested leasing, it was easy commuting distance they said. Charles grimaced at the thought of commuting; when he had left Winchester, Father had suggested that he work in the city and he couldn't have imagined what for. Sitting behind a desk all day didn't appeal and, as any trip to London took well over an hour, it would mean two hours in a train each day. What a ghastly thought.

'Oh, here's the car now,' Joanna called out as a blue car drove through the oak trees at the gate and up the long park drive. He watched the car hit the pothole at the bend and slow right down.

The car drew up and parked beside Charles' car. Joanna walked towards it.

Charles still felt perplexed. It was all wrong; it was all too quiet. He turned and opened the front door. Thank goodness Godley had left it unlocked. He walked into the large hall and Joanna and the consultants came in behind him.

'The entrance is one of the most impressive parts. It gives a wonderful arrival,' commented Quentin, as he followed Charles through the open front door. 'I can see the bride and groom wanting photos on these steps. It's the one part we both agreed shouldn't be changed.'

'Good,' agreed Charles, smiling weakly as Quentin's partner Susie was looking around the hall as though she owned it.

'Except, of course, this hall would need to be modernised and those dreadful stag heads taken away. Joanna says the butler isn't here today.' Charles wondered whether they saw Godley as one of the accoutrements.

'We were arguing about the table. I thought sofas beside the fire but now I'm not sure the table isn't better. This hall is very daunting and cold – maybe a carpet would help.'

Charles had never found the hall daunting. With the fire going, it was always rather welcoming.

Joanna and the couple went on ahead into the big drawing room, with Charles following behind. He had grown up here; every corner had memories – children's parties, hide-and-seek around the furniture. His father's study, the library, was next door; as a young child, Nanny used to get him ready for bed and then walk down with him to the library where he would knock on the door. When his father answered, Charles would go in alone to say goodnight. His father would politely ask what he had been doing that day, and Charles would shake him by the hand and then run back out of the door to Nanny. It was the only contact he'd had with his father and it sounded ridiculous now, but it had seemed quite normal then.

It seemed the library would become a proper withdrawing room so that older wedding guests could mingle away from the music and noise. From the ballroom, the French windows looked out onto the lawn where, for larger weddings, they could extend with a marquee. Smaller weddings, or company conferences, would take place in the ballroom alone. A band, if needed, could play in the little music room off it. Charles remembered all the rooms being opened up when they had Hunt Balls or parties here but that hadn't happened for years. Even for Father's funeral, there was enough room in the ballroom alone.

They had moved into the dining room now, the consultants checking their clipboards.

'We anticipate this table going of course. I know it is magnificent, but we need this room to be adaptable. Of course, antiques are worth nothing now.' Charles had already found that out; he had got half what he had expected from the odd bit of furniture he'd sold.

'This will be ideal for conference cocktails or dinner parties. We thought it was a long way from the kitchen but actually, when we did the measurements, it's almost perfect. Caterers do need such a large area for serving and by taking away the study and knocking that wall out we can have an "in" for the food and an "out" for the dishes very happily. There's even room for an admin office in the corner.'

They walked through to his mother's study. It was so tidy. There were no pointers lying on the sofa, no *Country Life* or *Horse and Hound* lying on the coffee table. The empty fireplace looked unwelcoming.

'Of course, this room will need to go altogether. Goodness, it's still quite cold in here, isn't it?'

Charles changed the subject. 'Godley insisted on leaving something for coffee, so why don't we go through to the kitchen? The Aga's on. It's warmer in there.'

'Have you decided where your mother's going? Joanna thought she might be ready for a retirement village, but we have wonderful ideas for the stables apartments and could easily accommodate her there. I gather she isn't really the type to fit in with the wedding guests as a hostess. Rather too much dogs and wellies.' That was a little unfair, thought Charles.

'Oh, she can be quite presentable if she wishes. Joanna didn't see her at her best. I suppose she could move to the Lodge.'

'Well, I really think we need the Lodge. It would be perfect for us to stay in while the alterations are being done and then once going, the manager is going to need a house. It isn't really suitable for your mother, from what I hear. It's very close to the road. Guests don't want dogs rushing the cars as they drive through the gates.' It seemed their view of Mother was tainted by Joanna's.

'Or pigs in the garden, you mean?' he quipped. It was so annoying that Joanna had only met Mother at her worst. She wasn't like that, and there wouldn't be any pigs.

They walked into the kitchen and the consultants aimed for the warm Aga while Joanna inspected the tray Godley had left.

'A supermarket fruit cake. Well, better than nothing.' She switched on the electric kettle beside the sink.

'This kettle on the Aga will be just as quick,' said Charles, lifting the Aga lid and pushing the kettle onto the hob.

'If your Mother was in the Lodge,' said Joanna, 'she'd probably feel that she had to run things.'

'She's in New Zealand, isn't she?' asked Quentin. 'With friends?'

'She's travelling around the North Island,' explained Joanna, 'staying in a barn and investigating the letter that was left on the body she found on the estate. The body was a New Zealander.' Charles cringed as she made it sound so eccentric.

'Oh yes, of course,' said Quentin. 'That's when I first heard of the house. How awful for her to find someone dead in the garden. She's obviously still independent though, Charles.' Charles was reminded of her waving the walking stick around while she chased the pigs. Perhaps it was just as well she wasn't any more mobile.

'Obviously her moving to the Lodge isn't going to work,' said Joanna. 'Perhaps the workmen can work around her here until the stables are ready.'

'We'll find a way,' Quention suggested. 'We can start on the house but it'll take a while to get planning permission for the stables.'

Susie turned towards Charles and must have noticed the expression on his face as she said, 'I'm sure you'll be much more comfortable when you see what allowances we can make for her.'

Charles was suddenly tired of all this planning and changing. 'Why don't you carry on. I know Joanna wants to show you upstairs. I'll go and see what's going on outside.' With Joanna muttering, 'Good idea, bring your coffee with you,' she led the other two towards the front of the house, while Charles walked towards the back door.

* * * * *

Margie and Pamela were standing at the picture window looking out at the lake, both holding an early morning cup of tea.

'Of course, I don't mind being by myself,' Pamela said. 'A day alone to catch up with everything really appeals. I won't have to be polite to anyone, and I don't need to go anywhere. It's a lovely house to be in and there's a whole lake to walk beside. I'll cook dinner for when you get back.'

Pamela was wearing her light navy coat pulled on over the top of her cotton nightdress; the flimsy dressing gown she had brought with her took up no room in the suitcase but was too cold and Pamela was sure Margie wouldn't mind her wearing an overcoat. They were watching Smoky the spaniel outside the window, sniffing his way around a spiky aloe vera plant growing at the top of the wooden steps which led down to the foreshore – the reserve, as Margie called it. Margie had just explained that her grandson had his leg in plaster and her daughter had asked that she look after him for a few hours while she went to the dentist. They lived in Rotorua.

'You're welcome to come but you're probably better here rather than trying to keep a grumpy kid busy. Smoky will be happier too. If you really want to do dinner, there's some mince in the fridge but otherwise I'll try and bring something back. I'll be back tonight.'

After Margie had left, Pamela took her time getting dressed. It was amazing how long everything took when you weren't at home. It was already late morning before Pamela began to think of mince recipes. Her repertoire was extensive on eggs – boiled, baked, scrambled, even a pretty good omelette. She could fry a chop, or steak but not cook mince. CJ had called mince the butcher's rubbish and would only eat it if Mrs Short had dressed it up into her meatloaf or pie. Pamela found a shelf of recipe books and chose the book with a blonde smiling figure on the front who didn't look at all like a cook. _Herbs should be fresh_, the book said. Well, there didn't seem to be too many fresh herbs in this kitchen. She eventually settled on cottage pie from another book called _Simple Cooking_. No glamorous chef on the front cover, just photos of a delicious looking roast beef dinner and a lemon meringue pie, neither of which looked at all _simple_. Pamela searched for potatoes but failed to find any. Back to _Simple Cooking_. Ah, meat sauce, suitable for pasta, and _If no fresh herbs available, use dried_. Perfect.

✶ ✶ ✶ ✶ ✶

Polly was peeling the potatoes into the sink while Pete, leaning back against the kitchen bench, watched. She was pleased he didn't comment that most of the potato was coming off with the skin as she lacerated them in her anger. It was this whole stone situation and Pete and Geoffrey's mad brother trying to get her to phone this Lady Scawton woman. She should never have gone to see Theodore.

'Do you want me to do that while you do something else?' Pete asked as the knife sliced off another hunk of potato.

'This whole thing's just so pathetic, Pete. If this woman has the stone, then obviously she knows why Beth sent it back and knows the whole story. She just wants to come and gloat or something.'

'What _is_ the whole story?' Pete asked.

The knife hit Polly's thumb. She wanted to tell him but just couldn't; for the past year, he had been her safety net and she couldn't risk upsetting him.

'Oh, it was to do with Nan,' she said. If she told him, he'd be shocked, or angry – and anyway, the stone was gone now.

'Yes, perhaps you had better finish these potatoes,' she admitted. 'I'll just check on Simon next door. He needs to finish his homework before he turns the telly on.' She quickly disappeared towards the living room.

Simon was on to his homework, working on Pete's dining table. She stopped in the doorway, thinking for a moment. She had coped without her husband and she could cope without her mother just as long as people left her alone and didn't rake up the past. Pete was her ally, her support when she needed it. She didn't need to upset him. Besides, the secret wasn't really hers – it was her grandmother's and then her mother's. If she were to blurt it all out, Pete may not react well. Aggie had been his mother, the matriarch, and Pete's brothers were all a bit religious and Catholic. The story was best left buried. She could understand her grandmother wanting to confront the Scawtons, but now it was two generations later and it no longer mattered. If Beth had arranged for the stone to go back to the family as Aggie had wanted, then her grandmother's reputation should stay untarnished.

Pete had put the potatoes on to boil. 'I still think you should phone this woman.'

'Why? She knows the story.'

'She's out here from England and wants to meet the family who had the stone.'

'You ring her.'

'No, it's best that you do. You know the story. Your mad doctor says she isn't here for long – a week, maybe.'

Losing the stone to the family was bad enough; now it seemed Pete, or silly Theodore, expected her to applaud the whole affair. No way.

'I'm not going to meet her.'

'Then tell her that. I did say you'd phone. You're coming here tomorrow so if you haven't phoned by then, I'll remind you.'

'I suppose.'

* * * * *

Charles walked out the back door and towards the stables. Memories kept flooding back; perhaps it was because there was no one around. He went from the back drive through the old stone passageway to the tack shed, where everything looked the same as always. There was the familiar smell of old leather and the wooden rack, which hung high from the ceiling, swayed slightly. The bridles were clean and hung tidily, although cobwebs hung from the ceiling. His mother's hunting saddle sat on the closest saddle rack. He looked up to the far corner where dust hung in threads from the old side-saddle, even though it was covered with a blanket. He could never remember his mother riding side-saddle – not her style really.

On the wall beside it hung faded rosettes: rosettes he had won as a kid, a lot of red ones and quite a few champion rosettes too. He fingered a big one, blowing off the dust as he remembered winning that championship at the local county show; that had been a big affair. When he had come home afterwards, triumphant, his father had just nodded at him; his father couldn't even be bothered to tell him 'well done'. It took the gloss off the success although it was always the same – he never changed.

Before she went away, his mother had muttered about Father having post-traumatic stress disorder but it felt like she was just finding an excuse. He couldn't remember his father being any other way than a stiff upper-lip formal grump, an unpredictable ogre who put a threatening pall over everything. As soon as Charles went to Winchester and realised other people's fathers were rather pleasant and friendly, he decided it best to avoid him altogether.

He turned to go out the door. His eyes took in the stable yard and the orchard beyond; his friends told him he was lucky to have all this but they hadn't had to suffer a stifled childhood and watch his father lose most of the family money, leaving Charles a broken-down house, a mother who relied on him and not enough money to live the lifestyle expected of a baronet.

As he stood in the stable yard he tried to see the whole shambles of a yard as the consultants would. His father was gone now, and the pall of his presence could be lifted; Joanna was his way ahead, bringing the estate into the 21st century.

He heard a snuffling and remembered the pigs. He sniffed and wrinkled his nose; bloody pigs, although really the smell wasn't that bad. He looked over a stable door and immediately there were little grunts as the pigs rushed towards the door. He couldn't help smiling at their enthusiasm. He supposed it was not a good look even though they all looked clean and tidy and had straw to lie and bury themselves in. No, it was far too rustic a look. A tidy set of apartments would be better, and the two experts thought you would get three or even four small apartments along here if they used the barn at the end – perfect for staff quarters and somewhere for Mother.

He could see millions being spent – hopefully Jerry really did have unlimited resources – and perhaps it seemed churlish to think the house was going to lose its character. Joanna was quick to point out that he knew nothing about interior design, and she wasn't interested in hearing about how it had been in the past. It had made him feel he was just an accessory, especially when they said all those portraits on the stairs would have to go. He felt they were taking away his heritage. No one else would want them, and after he and his mother had gone, no one would even care who they were.

He shook his head, chiding himself. He had to make allowances if he wanted his and Joanna's children to be proud of him. His assets – the title and this bloody great house – would combine well with Joanna's wealth. His mother could look backwards if she wanted. All her generation harped on about the good old days, but he wasn't going to – he needed to make the best of what he had.

Joanna was right; Mother was a problem, stuck in the past. He had felt sorry for her having to live with his father for so long, but he realised now it was what she had wanted. She had a title, prestige and considerable comfort – at his expense now, bugger it – without having to work or worry. He'd just have to put up with her relying on him for everything, grumbling about the house and money and disappearing at the most inconvenient time to track boorish distant cousins in New Zealand.

When she came back, she would need to realise that things were changing. Joanna's parents had been over the moon at the idea of Joanna becoming Lady Scawton, but he had difficulty warming to them personally. Jerry was small, fat, and opinionated and Jill was far too air-brained but, as Clarissa had reminded him, it's the bank account that's important, not the accent. Jerry, Joanna's father, was already contributing to Charles' income by paying him to teach Joanna's nerdish younger brother, Marcus, to play polo. The kid had only just left school and was working for his old man. He didn't have much character but already he wasn't a bad rider and seemed to enjoy getting out in the open air.

With Jerry's and the bus man's money, life was getting back to where it should be. He'd even be able to pay some money back to David.

He leant on the metal gate of the yard, his heart still sinking at the changes there would be.

He decided it was the two consultants who annoyed him; they seemed to have no qualms about spending other people's millions. Charles was sure there would be difficulty getting building permits and permission, even though Ashly House didn't have any historical significance, but Susie insisted that with the house itself there were no outside structural changes planned and no reason why the alterations inside the house, re-wiring and plumbing, shouldn't proceed straight away. They even had a builder in mind and had contacted him. They'd suggested the three-way partnership with Charles' house, the consultants' expertise and Jerry's money. Perhaps it did sound positive and was a better solution than letting the house out to the tenants Patrick had in mind.

He walked through the yard gate towards the front garden. To his left another small wrought iron gate led to the vegetable garden. The gate there had the same pattern as the front gate, which had prompted the first argument with the consultants. Charles knew the gates had been made by his grandfather James, when the family had the ironworks. Surely the front gate, with its intricate pattern, could be electrified, not replaced with solid wooden gates as the consultants were suggesting.

He looked through the small gate now at the tidy rows of vegetables. Charles had never been into growing vegetables. He walked to the corner of the house and gazed over the lawns in the front of the house; the lawns and garden beds looked immaculate. This was where he had seen the three gardeners on the last visit. Three, for God's sake! They were no doubt skiving off today because his mother was away.

Roses were coming into bloom. It looked so peaceful with the beech trees edging the garden on the far side. It seemed rather a pity to turn all this into a busy conference centre or whatever.

20

New Zealand 1985

Polly walked through the school gates, opened the back door of her mother's car and threw her schoolbag on the back seat before slamming it shut and climbing into the front seat.

'Good day, Polly?'

'Suppose.' Her mother always asked the same pathetic question, every day.

'We just have to pick up Nan on the way back.'

'Oh, not from the races, Mum. I want to go home.'

''Fraid so, but it won't take long.' Polly humphed into her seat.

Her grandmother's favourite outing was going to the races and Beth insisted it was good she got out of the retirement home. Nan – her name was Aggie, but she was Nan to the family – was well into her 80s. For weekday meetings Beth would drop her off on her way to work and collect her and take her back to her retirement home at the end of the day. If it was a weekend meeting, Beth, or one of Nan's grandchildren, would go with her. Polly used to go quite often when she was younger.

It was boring now, though, and Nan was equally happy going by herself. Beth and Polly would watch the tiny figure, clutching her plastic holdall, marching into the racecourse as though she owned it. Beth used to say she had shrunk, but Polly thought she couldn't have been very big before. Nan preferred those windy stands at Avondale to the smarter stands at Ellerslie but then Nan always was indifferent to anything too 'posh' as she would call it and didn't like the big crowds. Plus, Polly knew that her grandfather, Michael, had trained at Avondale and it held a lot of memories for Nan. It was one of Nan's stories how, thanks to Buttons, they were able to move from Panmure where Beth was born, to Avondale, where Michael could become a full-time trainer.

The racecourse must have been pretty grand in its heyday but by now the buildings were looking run down. Nan would sit alone up on the top of the stand with a thermos of tea and a few biscuits. She could look all over the course and to half of Auckland. Nan said that when they first lived there, the view had all been green fields.

If it was cold, Nan would be wrapped up in her old overcoat, which looked like a blanket. Even on the hottest day she wore an old felt hat; she said she couldn't go to the races without wearing a hat. That and the stone were her good luck charms.

Whichever grandchild was with her for the day would be the runner. Nan always had a well-worn *Best Bets* tucked away and the old binoculars that had belonged to Michael. She wasn't bad at picking the horses and would usually finish with a few more dollars than she started with, enough for an ice-cream on the way home.

On this occasion, when they went to collect her, there were still two races to run. Polly and Beth climbed the grandstand and sat alongside Nan. Even Polly knew better than to suggest Nan leave before the last race. Polly would just have to do the runner bit.

As she climbed the steps to the TAB in the stand, she could hear Beth complaining to Nan. 'You know she's meant to be 18 to put bets on.' As she ran off, Polly imagined Nan smiling. Her grandchildren had been putting her bets on for years. There was no queue and Polly went to the nearest tote window and handed in the ticket Nan had given her. Nan had won $5.20. When, as instructed, Polly pushed $4 back to put on Number 13, saying 'Two dollars each way please,' the lady didn't say anything. She must have thought Polly looked 18.

By the time Polly climbed back up the stand, Beth and Nan

were reminiscing about the Depression. Beth said she could hardly remember living down at the Point in Panmure. Although Nan was always telling them how hard life had been then, she still seemed to remember it fondly.

Most of Nan's stories would be about the stone though. Either about how Grandad's racehorses would only win if the stone were in his pocket, or when, in World War Two, Uncle Mickey was due to come home, and he'd given the stone to his brother Sean who was still there. Two days later the boat was torpedoed and Uncle Mickey killed.

'Mum, it was an odd gift. You were only a maid in that Ashly House. So did they give all the maids gifts when they left?' Beth asked while she fingered the stone.

Nan gave Beth a strange look and Polly wondered what was coming next. Then the horses moved into the birdcage and Nan pointed out the black horse she had backed. It had a big white blaze. Polly wasn't really interested although she noticed it looked shiny and jumped around when the jockey vaulted on.

As the horses started to stream through the gate to the course, Nan suddenly turned to Polly and said, 'Have you done anything about finding your birth parents?' Polly was used to Nan coming out with extraordinary comments. One minute she would be talking about the racehorse and the next minute she would come out with something like this.

'You'll be able to find them now. They're about to change the law,' Nan went on.

Polly had known she was adopted ever since she was a baby. She also knew there was a private member's bill before Parliament allowing adopted children to find their birth parents, but that didn't mean she wanted to find hers, or even talk about them.

'So?' Polly hoped her grandmother would change the subject.

'You need to know where you come from, what's in your genes.'

'Nan, I don't.' Beth was the only mother she had ever known, her father in Australia was her only father. Occasionally she did wonder who'd conceived her but whoever it was had given her away. Willingly. It never really worried her, and she certainly didn't have a hang-up about it.

'Well, you should,' Nan continued. The horses were already walking around down at the start and being loaded into the starting gates.

'Nan, I have my family,' she answered. 'I've Mum and you and the uncles and cuzzies and even Dad in Aussie. I couldn't handle another family.'

There was a silence. It's my life, thought Polly. Why does everyone always tell me what to do?

She tried to turn Nan's attention back to the horses. She pointed out that the black horse Nan had chosen was the rank outsider. The line of panels in the middle of the course showed $70 for a win. Nan shook her copy of *Best Bets*.

'It ran a good gallop earlier in the week.'

Indeed, the commentator mentioned the shiny black horse as soon as the race started. 'And Cuzzio goes straight to the front. Coming up to the first turn, he's a length in front.' It was only a short race, but Nan certainly was getting her money's worth. He was still leading going into the last turn but coming up the straight the others caught him up and overtook him. In spite of Nan's urging from the stand, Cuzzio ended up about fifth.

'Too much distance for him,' said Nan.

Over the years, in spite of her lack of interest, Polly had learnt a bit about racing. 'Well, he's going to be hard pushed to find a shorter race. That one was only 1200 metres.'

As the horses came back into the birdcage, they watched Cuzzio being unsaddled. Nan pointed out that in any race there is really only one happy trainer, two or three others who are nearly happy and the rest all have to make excuses of why they didn't do better. Cuzzio's trainer was doing the making-excuses bit to the smartly-dressed owner who was standing beside him.

That race over, the small crowd started to rattle down the iron stairs at the end of the stand. Polly went off to find the toilets. She came back to find her mother and grandmother back on the subject of her adoption.

'Nan was asking if I minded you looking for your birth parents. You know I don't. It's a good idea.'

'I can't do it for two years, till I'm 18. And I've told you, I don't need to know. I'm happy as I am.'

'But it's important,' said Nan.

'Why? Not to me, it isn't. I am who I am.'

'You could have a famous mother.'

'More likely she was a teenage druggie. She's probably married now and would be just thrilled to have me turn up on the doorstep. Yeah, right!'

'Your birth father was Māori or part Māori.'

'So what?' Long ago, Beth had told Polly and Nan everything she knew. When she was pregnant, Polly's mother had lived in a Salvation Army hostel called Bethany. The matron there had arranged the adoption.

'So you need to know your whakapapa,' Nan continued. 'Are you from the same iwi as your grandfather? Are you Tainui?'

'I haven't a clue. Did they tell you, Mum?'

Beth shook her head. 'I think we were chosen as parents because Dad was half Māori and they wanted your adoptive parents to have a Māori connection. Social Welfare were relieved we fitted the bill. I don't think they were concerned which iwi. They certainly never asked. Māori were just Māori.'

Polly already knew Grandad had been Tainui from the Waikato but Nan didn't have any Māori though, so there was no reason for her to go on about Grandad's family.

'Well, you need to find out, child.' Polly bristled at Nan calling her a child.

'Nan, I don't. My mother gave me up at birth. She didn't care what happened to me. I have a perfectly good mum and dad, and I'm not going to go running off to some marae now to find out about someone who doesn't even want to know.'

'That's just what you think. Your mother won't have forgotten you and I'll tell you why. It's all tied up with this stone. I've never told anyone, but I will tell the two girls in my family because you need to know. But first you go and put on my money for this race; it's the last one.' She handed Polly four dollars to put on Number 1 – Seagrove. All for a win this time.

Something in Nan's tone piqued Polly's interest. As Nan patted her pocket where the stone was, she had a mysterious look on her face. Polly ran to the tote window, invested the money and then returned to sit on one side of Nan. Beth was on the other side.

Polly never really noticed the horses coming into the birdcage. She was more interested in listening as Nan told her of her first son. In England. No one knew about him – he'd been adopted out. Beth often watched the English TV programmes – *Upstairs Downstairs* was a favourite. Listening to Nan now, Polly could imagine Ashly House, the mean old Lady Scawton drinking tea from the best china while Nan scrubbed away in the kitchen. The part about the nuns' home sounded gross and Polly looked over at her mother. For a moment she wondered whether her own birth mother had been through something like that at Bethany. Beth had always spoken so well of Matron there.

'When you were adopted, Polly, Beth said that they did meet your birth mother and father and they were told lots about our family. Everything except the surname. In my case, I never saw my son and was never told anything.'

The horses were cantering slowly down to the start at the far side of the course. Even Nan didn't seem too keen in following the horse she had chosen as Beth asked her questions.

'You never told anyone? No one at all? And your father never even knew? And where did the stone come into it?'

'Tom knew about the baby. He persuaded me to emigrate with him to New Zealand. In the end, he told Dad I'd had a baby.' Polly's great-uncle Tom had died a few years before.

'I couldn't have gone back to Ashly,' Nan continued. 'It wasn't like it is now. Solo mothers and unmarried mothers are two-a-penny now. Then, even though the baby was adopted out, if anyone had known I'd had a baby . . . well, not even the vicar would've been kind to me. Cook had already accused me of being a fallen girl. No, there was no way I could go back. Tom's idea seemed a good one.' She paused and watched the horses being loaded into the starting gates.

Aggie's two 'girls' sat, silenced by her story.

'Oh, would you look at that?' Beth said as she pointed to where the horses had started. It had been a false start. One horse must have pushed through the starting gate before they were officially opened. Some horses had already taken off and were being pulled up before the first turn. One insisted on galloping on and was close to the second turn before the jockey managed to stop him and turned to trot back to the start. They watched as the stewards began to load them all again.

'Why did Lady Scawton give you the stone if she was pleased to get rid of you?' Beth persisted.

Polly thought Aggie was about to say something, but the horses were all loaded again, and Nan's attention went back to them. This time the horses started properly. The commentator said that Nan's horse was in the main group, but Polly didn't even see it until they all passed the post. One, two, three, four all together. Nan's Number 1 came in second.

'No good, Nan. You only backed Seagrove for a win. Shall I throw away the ticket?'

'Just wait, young Polly. You never know until they've all weighed in.' As though on cue, a siren went, like an air raid warning. 'There. You see. The stewards are objecting. I thought there was some interference.

I could still be okay.' Polly sighed. It was the last race, and now they would have to wait until the stewards confirmed who'd won.

'I always intended to go back to Ashly one day and return the stone.' Her grandmother picked up the story again. 'Tell them what I went through and how I hadn't forgotten. I will never tell them now, but Beth, you could. You have to promise that one day, when Polly has left school, you'll go back.'

Polly frowned. What a stupid idea! Her mother could never confront this Lady Scawton person with Aggie's story. Lady Scawton would be long dead by now and Aggie's baby wasn't anything to do with them.

In the next breath, Nan turned on Polly. 'And Polly, as soon as you're 18, or whenever this law allows, you're to find your birth mother. You find out where you came from.'

Both Beth and Polly knew better than to argue with Nan. She could be pretty determined, and it was easier to acquiesce. Reluctantly, they both agreed.

They were still waiting for the result.

'You see there is more to the story,' said Aggie. Aggie's tone had changed. She had a steely look, a serious look.

Aggie looked around her as though to make sure no one else could hear. Then she began to speak and Polly and her mother had to lean down to hear.

They were the only ones left on the stands when the announcement came through on the loudspeaker. The winner had been disqualified. Nan's horse was now the winner.

'Just as well you didn't throw that ticket away, eh?' Aggie laughed as they climbed down the steps.

21

New Zealand & England 2013

It was mid-afternoon before the mince was ready to cook very slowly on the stovetop – at least an hour or longer to allow the flavours to develop. Pamela set the stove top to its lowest setting, then turned it up to the next mark, then decided no and turned it right down again.

Smoky was sitting expectantly by the door.

'Good idea, Smoky. Let's go for a walk. Can't do anything to this for an hour.'

She had just picked up her phone from the table and slipped it into her pocket when it rang. She opened it as she walked to the back door.

It was Charles. She glanced at her watch, thinking it must be night-time in England, but the dial was too small and the light not good enough. It didn't matter. Smoky was barking with excitement and she hurried through the back door with him so that he would stop. The door clicked behind her.

'Charles, what time is it? It's afternoon here. Surely it's the middle of the night with you?'

'We spent the day with the guys who want to run the house as a hotel and conference centre,' said Charles. 'They explained what they wanted to do. I thought I'd phone and tell you.'

'Oh, good. Go on.'

* * * * *

It was all happening so quickly with the house. Having listened to the consultants, using it for weddings and conferences was obvious. Charles now knew he had to resist any sentimentality over the changes, and since Joanna didn't flinch at the undoubted cost, he imagined the Thompson Truck money-pit must be deep enough to cover the cost.

After the long day, Joanna had fallen asleep almost as soon as she got into bed. Charles had slept fitfully, excited by the possibilities but worried about how it would happen and about making such massive changes. Mother, for instance, she was way behind.

Although the consultants assured him they would cope with her, the reality would be that she'd be living in the house while the builders were renovating. She'd come up with her own ideas, which would be old-fashioned and impractical, and she'd be horrified at the cost and would probably keep bleating on about money.

Even with the alterations complete, she really wasn't going to be the asset to the hotel he had once thought. She knew nothing of running a hotel but would still try and interfere. He remembered she had mentioned working for the Sheffords but she had no experience at doing anything useful. Joanna had suggested a cottage somewhere, but Charles could hardly ask his future father-in-law for money to buy her one.

His mind had wandered as he heard his mother on the other end of the phone. 'Godley did say the consultants were coming but I haven't spoken to him since. What do they think?' she was asking. At least she sounded accepting of the idea.

'We spent the day there today – no, yesterday now. We had a good look around. It's going to be just fantastic.' He outlined the consultants' ideas. Putting in more bathrooms upstairs was a priority. All the bedrooms would have en suite bathrooms and the old nursery could turn into a two-bedroom suite. Eventually the stables would be converted to apartments for staff.

'Ten rooms with bathrooms? Can they really do that? I suppose most of the rooms are enormous. It sounds very exciting. When are you planning on starting?'

'As soon as possible. The stables will take longer because they'll need planning permission. So you'll be able to keep your pigs a bit longer.'

'Won't it all need council permission?'

'They're checking on that.'

'Of course. Well, I'll just have to move to the Lodge – unless, of course, I work for Lizzie Shefford.'

'Lizzie wouldn't have been serious about you actually working for her and you've never worked a day in your life, Mother; she's just being kind. Moving to the Lodge may be a problem too. The two consultants are going to need the Lodge so they can supervise the alterations and probably put the manager in there later. They're planning a really good apartment for you in the stables and, in the meantime, they plan on you staying in the house. You may have to move to one end, but you really only live in the kitchen part anyway.'

'I don't think I'd want to stay while they are doing the alterations. It was bad enough when they redecorated the drawing room and dining room. Your father nearly went bananas.'

'Well, really, Mother, you don't have a choice. You were the one who suggested I do something with the house. Have a think and try and be reasonable. Where else could you go?'

'It sounds as though I'll be in the way and what about the dogs?' Oh, God yes, the dogs, thought Charles. There were so many damned dogs.

'We'll think of something, Mother. You could always come to London. Joanna would be delighted.'

He looked across at Joanna lying asleep beside him. Thank goodness she hadn't heard. She certainly would not be delighted.

*****

Pamela had barely swiped the phone shut when it rang again. She put it back to her ear, prepared to continue the conversation with Charles, but it was Margie.

'I'm so sorry, it looks as though I'm going to be needed to stay the night. They need to go out. Would you be all right staying there by yourself? Smoky's food is on the sideboard, and if you need anything there's the little shop on the corner.' Pamela was still thinking about Charles and answered automatically.

'No problem, I'll be fine. There's the telly if I get bored.'

'I feel really bad, but I'll be back first thing tomorrow.'

Pamela pocketed the phone and looked around for Smoky. He was still sitting at the top of the steps, which led down to the grass reserve at the edge of the lake. As she went down the steps, Smoky ran ahead towards the lake.

There was a concrete path all along the lakefront, laid by a considerate council. Pamela was wearing a light sleeveless jacket and walked with her hands in her pockets. A slight breeze blew at her hair. She realised she should have brought her navy coat, but the weather wasn't too chilly, and the lakefront was empty. She stood admiring some of the houses overlooking it. Some were built at lake level but most of the bigger houses were like Margie's and higher up with a steep path or steps up. From there, like Margie's, they would get a spectacular view towards the three magnificent snow-clad volcanoes at the far end of the lake.

She was still thinking about Charles' call as she began the walk along the lakeside. Charles made her feel like an old woman, a nuisance, just as CJ used to do. Once, CJ had told her bluntly that the only reason she gained any kind of respect was because she had a title. She supposed it was true, but she wished Charles didn't have to make it so obvious.

Everyone had been kind at CJ's funeral. Charles had been most considerate towards her then – when he'd finally agreed to come back from Sotogrande. She'd been unable to shed a tear for CJ, even when the coffin was being taken down the aisle to the waiting hearse. She'd held a handkerchief to her face but it was relief she felt, not sorrow. Sad relief, guilty relief, but relief nonetheless. For months afterwards, she just felt tired. Exhausted. It was over. She knew she should've grieved. Even the doctor offered her sleeping pills but sleeping was not a problem. All she felt was that relief. And guilt.

Lost in a reverie, she suddenly remembered she was at the other end of the world from Ashly and had walked a long way along the foreshore. She turned back the way she had come, with Smoky happily sniffing his way along the edge of the lake. They'd passed a few walkers and a man walking a retriever; the dogs ran around together before the man called his dog away.

Poor Charles. As a child he'd been terrified of CJ and, as an only child, he'd never had much of a home life. Now, at last, he was being sensible and trying to find a good use for the house. She rubbed the back of her hands and then pushed a hand through her hair as she walked along.

She was not excited by the thought of living in the stable block, the 'staff quarters' as Charles so tactfully put it. She was sure the consultants wouldn't want her there during the alterations either; she'd be in the way.

'You will need to get rid of her,' she could imagine them saying. Along with the chandelier in the ballroom and the stags' heads in the hall. And the dogs.

She would love to go to the Sheffords and work in the farm shop, but Charles was right. She really had no qualifications and would be hopelessly out of her depth. Being the pony club district commissioner ten years ago would hardly qualify her to run the Shefford House farm shop. No, it was out of the question.

Smoky had picked up a stick and brought it to her. Pamela threw it over the grass and the spaniel happily bounded after it.

It wasn't just the staff quarters she was worried about at Ashly. It was the house itself. She didn't want to feel the big house looming over her like a ghost but, as Charles had pointed out, she had no choice.

Smoky brought the stick back and Pamela threw it again.

'Last time, Smoky. We're nearly home'. This time it went askew and went sailing into the lake.

'Oh sorry, Smoky.' The dog had galloped off in a grey blur, his ears flapping up over his head. The dog splashed into the water and expertly swam to retrieve the stick.

'Good boy, well done. Bring it back.'

She idly watched Smoky, waiting for him to come out of the water. She could see him but he seemed to be swimming the other way.

'Smoky, come back. Where are you going?'

Pamela could see Smoky's ears floating outwards from his body as he swam confidently to an outcrop of rocks further along the beach. Surely it must be cold in that water.

'Smoky, back here boy, come on.'

Smoky obviously had his own agenda and certainly wasn't listening, let alone turning around and coming back. Pamela walked briskly along the beach to the rocks and began to climb carefully over the rocks towards him.

'Smoky,' she called desperately. The dog didn't even turn his head towards Pamela. He shook himself instead, the water flying in a spray around him and his ears flapping.

'Smoky,' she called again. With nothing more than an impudent glance in her direction, the spaniel took off up a small scrub-covered hill towards a gate in a paling fence, almost hidden among the bushes. Pamela couldn't see the house behind it but there was a man there who went through the gate. She scrambled off the rocks to follow.

The gate clanged shut before Smoky could reach it but, unperturbed, he wriggled under a gap at the bottom of the fence and disappeared.

'Oh, you wretched dog, where are you off to now?' Pamela climbed up the steep bank to the gate. The house would have a really prominent position over the bay, she thought. She tried the gate, found it locked. She looked over the top.

Yes, it was a big house and there was Smoky quite at home, rolling in a flowerbed, bare except for pruned roses. It was an open garden, much bigger that Margie's, with a lawn that was green and well mown. The man she had seen at the gate was just walking away, and she called out to him.

'Excuse me.' There was another person, sitting in a folding chair beside a lavender hedge, with his back to her. She called out louder, 'Excuse me.'

The man who had been walking away turned back and, with a surprised look on his face, started running towards her.

Pamela, thankful when he had turned, now didn't like the look of him. He was big, like a giant bodyguard, dressed in a tight black T-shirt and looking menacing.

'Where the hell did you come from?' the man asked in an American accent.

'I was just . . . that's my dog. Well, not mine, but . . . '

'This is private property.'

'I only want the dog. Smoky, Smoky,' she called out.

'What?' She saw the man feel in his pocket of loose-fitting trousers and for a minute wondered if he would bring out a gun or something. Pamela's chest tightened.

As though on cue, Smoky appeared from the far edge of the garden, still wet and now muddy but at least running towards her. The man turned his head and looked.

'Get it out! Quickly! He loathes dogs.' Pamela glanced at the man sitting down and saw he had headphones on and hadn't moved. As Smoky approached the gate, the big man pressed a button and opened it. Smoky rushed through.

'Don't come back.' His order held a threat.

Pamela was about to speak, when the gate clanged shut again. The man half turned as though she was dismissed. She just turned and scrambled down the bank after Smoky.

Obviously contrite, Smoky trotted obediently beside her, back along the waterfront to the steps up to Margie's house. She tried to breathe more normally but was still shaken and angry and was looking forward to getting back into the safety of the house. The meat sauce must be nearly ready.

She put her hands in her pocket as she climbed the steps to Margie's house. She felt her phone, but then realised she had slammed the door shut and didn't have a key. Sure enough, the house was locked and she and Smoky were outside.

✶ ✶ ✶ ✶ ✶

Smoky, after causing her so much trouble, just rushed into the house through a dog flap, no doubt happy to be home, while Pamela floundered outside wondering what to do. She remembered the keys were on the table. Pamela leaned down towards the flap which certainly wasn't big enough for her to get through. She walked around the house, hoping she had left a window open. Smoky came back out and followed, as though laughing at her, as she found there was no downstairs window open. There was a room upstairs with a window slightly ajar, but it was too high up. There had to be some way to get in; she walked around the house again but there was nothing. Nothing. Smoky disappeared back inside again.

She went and sat down on the garden chairs at the front of the house. She checked her watch. The mince would be done but the recipe did say *at least an hour*. Pamela was still smarting from the behaviour of the man down the road. She pursed her lips and huffed her breath through her nose as though it was the little man's fault she was locked out.

Within minutes she realised she was cold – she should have brought her coat. How stupid of her! She got up and, avoiding the dog kennel on the corner, wandered into the empty door-less garage, thinking that Margie might keep a spare key there. As she looked around, there was no obvious key hanging from a hook but there was a dirty old blanket, which Pamela took and threw round her shoulders. She went back to her chair.

She thought about the rude bodyguard along the road. It must be where the film star was staying – Stit something or other. Odd name, and he didn't like dogs. It wasn't her fault that Smoky had rushed into his garden. She shivered and took a large breath.

She looked up. The sky was clouding over and it was beginning to get dark. Through the window she could see Smoky inside. Sensible dog.

Oh Lord, she had no idea what to do now. It got dark so quickly in New Zealand. Wrapped in the dirty blanket and still shaking, although she wasn't really that cold, she stared up at the house. She felt in her pocket for the phone to call Margie, before she realised she didn't know her number. Ginny had lent her a New Zealand phone and she hadn't loaded any numbers into the contacts section.

Perhaps there was a next-door neighbour who might have a spare key. She brushed her hand through one side of her hair. The neighbours' houses looked closed up, and Margie had mentioned that most of the houses here were not occupied all the time. There were lights twinkling across the bay in town but not in the houses next door and she certainly wasn't going back to that nasty little upstart who couldn't live without his bodyguard.

She tried to remember Ginny's number, or even Bob and Anne's. They would have Margie's number but then Bob might answer and the 'She needs to bloody well go – she's had her holiday' comment came back. He certainly wouldn't want to hear from her.

She could hear the phone ringing in the house but there was nothing she could do, only listen until it stopped. Instead she sat, glowering as she looked out towards the lake. She could see a runner jogging along the path at the edge of the lake, but he was too far away to hear if she called out.

The mobile rang. Thank goodness.

'Lady "Scorn"?' Pamela didn't recognise the voice with the New Zealand accent. It was a woman's voice but a deep one.

'Yes, it is.'

'My name is Polly Wilson. Theodore Cook spoke to my uncle and he says I need to phone you because you had a note from Beth. I'm calling from his phone.' Pamela's breath caught in her throat. 'Beth was my mother.' Good, thought Pamela, Theodore has found them.

'Oh, how wonderful. I have been hoping you would phone. Dr Cook – Theodore – said and I was hoping . . . '

'I don't know what you were hoping,' the harsh voice interrupted.

Pamela tried to soften her own tone. 'Well, Professor Cook, who died, had a letter and a stone and we were wondering . . . '

'I know – from Diane, Mum's nurse – that Geoffrey had the stone and the letter, but I don't want anything to do with it. I was only phoning because . . . ' the voice hesitated a moment before continuing, 'my uncle said I should tell you myself. My grandmother never forgave your family. If my mother chose to send the stone back, that was her problem; perhaps it was more than a reminder, who knows? It's your family who are the guilty ones after all.'

'Er,' began Pamela, 'but what? . . . I'm not sure . . . I'm sorry if . . . '

'Goodbye.'

The phone went dead. Pamela frowned at it. Polly she said her name was . . . Polly Wilson. Dr Cook, Theodore, had contacted her. She was this Beth's daughter and obviously knew about the stone and the letter, but she sounded so vehement. Perhaps Beth had intended to blackmail them. Maybe Charles was right, but the voice sounded too angry and the woman didn't ask for anything.

Pamela really needed to get back into the house. She wished she had the stone in her hand now. She always felt comforted by its feel.

This was stupid, being locked out; she had to be more sensible. If Godley were here, he'd break a window or call the police. That wasn't so silly. She picked up the phone she had in front of her. She had never dialled 9-9-9. For an instant, she thought of that film star; the bodyguard would have taken no time to find a way into Margie's house. She dialled 9-9-9.

'You have been connected to 1-1-1, the emergency number for New Zealand.' Pamela glared at the screen, she was sure she dialled 9-9-9. The message continued. 'The penalties for dialling this number when it is not an emergency . . . ' Pamela snapped the phone shut. Of course this wasn't a matter of life or death; it wasn't an emergency.

She would just have to break a window, which she knew would really annoy Margie. She had already offended Bob, and Tim wasn't too keen on her either. Ginny was fed up too and had taken the opportunity to go home for a couple of days.

She bent down to the cat flap and called Smoky, but he didn't come. She glanced at the open upstairs window. As she straightened up she noticed a small sign beside the back door. It was old, but it read 'Taupō, all repairs, day or night, phone 0800 727544'. Thank goodness. She immediately dug her phone back out of her pocket again and dialled the number. A light was flicking at the top of the screen. It took a couple of attempts before she had the correct number on the screen and could press the green button.

'Good evening, how can we help?' What wonderful words!

'Yes, I have locked myself out of the house and need someone to come and open the door.'

'I'm sorry, this is an answering service. The number you dialled no longer has an after-hours service. You will have to call back tomorrow morning after 8.30am. I'm sorry.' The voice had an Indian accent and certainly didn't sound sorry.

'Oh, but you must be able to do something. Please don't hang up.'

'Perhaps you could contact your local police or information service.' Pamela had difficulty understanding the accent.

'Where are you?' she asked the girl on the phone.

'We are a national answering service based in Christchurch.'

'In Christchurch? But I am in Taupō.'

'One moment please.' A few seconds later another voice came on to the phone.

'May I help you? You seem to be having trouble.' This voice was also foreign, not Indian or Pakistani, but Pamela guessed Asian of some kind.

'Yes.' Pamela explained that she had locked herself out of her friend's house and could not get in. She was in Taupō. Could they give her a local number she could phone?

'It's not a very good line. Could I have your name, please?'

'Lady Scawton.'

'Laney? Well, Laney, I suggest you look up the *White Pages*, or Directory Service, to get a local phone number. You say the house belongs to your friend? Are you trying to break into someone else's house, Laney?'

Pamela was about to speak but there was beeping in her ear. She looked at the screen and noticed the blinking light at the top of the screen was now bright and solid. She could just make out *battery low* as the light on the phone died and the screen went black. The phone went back into her pocket. It had seemed a lifeline, a contact, the only one. Now that had gone.

She began to shiver and pulled up the dirty old blanket, which was still half around her shoulders. It didn't help much. She stood up and found the switch to the outside lights. One bulb didn't work and the other feebly tried to flood the small terrace. She really didn't want to break a window and couldn't decide which one she should break. She went to sit back on the iron chair with a cushion now damp with dew. The small round wrought iron table felt damp too. She sniffed in a big breath, but her breath began to stutter out. There seemed no one around. It was quite dark now but there must be someone. There was always someone.

She could hear a noisy car exhaust out on the main road. It was probably some hooligans about to burgle some of these empty houses.

She got up and walked to the edge of the terrace. The light shone out a little further. She stepped onto the lawn but slipped on the dew-covered grass and lost her footing. She landed with a thump, her feet on the grass and her bottom on the stone-flagged terrace. Christ, now she had hurt herself. What a fool she was!

'Is anyone there?' she called out, although she knew no one was. She was as bad as that film star man, having to rely on other people all the time.

She hoisted herself up, dusting herself down. The back of her trousers felt damp. She limped carefully back to the chair, putting the damp cushion on the table and sitting on the bare wrought iron. She felt bruised and her bad ankle really hurt.

Pamela wiped away the tears that were streaming down her face. Her stomach churned. No one wanted her here. She had no idea what she was even doing and now she was even more foolish and indecisive than ever. The tears continued.

The hooligan car was coming closer. The thieves would probably come here and there was absolutely nothing she could do against a couple of thugs. She was powerless.

The deafening exhaust was suddenly right outside, and she could see the beam of the headlights as it turned into the driveway. My God, they really were coming here.

22

New Zealand 2013

Pamela had to do something. She stood up and looked down at the uncomfortable wrought iron chair. She picked it up and held the chair to her like a shield as she walked around the corner of the house. She heard the car door open.

'Whoa there, Pamela, what are you going to do with that?' said a voice.

Pamela stopped. 'Tim? Is that you? What on earth are you doing here?' Pamela lowered the chair a little, her eyes dazzled by the headlights.

'Well, I'm glad you aren't going to clock me with that chair. You look pretty dangerous.' Pamela felt the breath go out of her and she tried to breathe normally.

'Oh, Tim, I'm so foolish. I've left the key inside. I took Smoky for a walk. He got in through the dog flap but I can't.' As though on cue, Smoky appeared at her side, barking and wagging his tail at the same time and then sniffing around the ute.

'You were going to use the chair to break a window? Wouldn't it be better to use the spare key?'

Relief flooded through Pamela as Tim explained that since Margie's nieces and nephews stayed with her from time to time they all knew where the spare key was kept. He went to Smoky's kennel. The lid of the kennel was hinged, and Tim lifted it and took the key off a hook.

It was a few seconds before Pamela could control her relief and wipe the tears from her cheek and then she began to gabble. 'Oh, thank you so much, Tim. Why are you here? And why is that car so noisy? Oh, thank goodness you came. I felt so stupid. I really didn't want to break a window.'

Tim didn't bother to say anything for a minute. Instead, he opened the door wide and turned on the lights. Smoky stayed beside the ute while Pamela, silent now, went into the warmth of the house.

'Had to bring the ute so a mate can change the exhaust. I was going to bring it up tomorrow then Margie suggested I come tonight and keep you company – and maybe stop you breaking windows by the look of it. Didn't she phone?'

As she followed Tim into the house, Pamela began to get her thoughts together. By some miracle, the meat sauce hadn't burnt dry. She turned it off and went to her room. She felt dishevelled and needed to put the mobile phone on the charger. How thoughtful of Margie to get Tim to come.

'Would you like a beer, Tim? I see there's some in the fridge,' she asked as she came back into the sitting room.

'Good one, Pamela. Would you like one?' He went over to the fridge, stopping at the stove and lifting the lid on the pot. 'This sauce smells really good. Ginny said I wasn't to expect too much because you have someone to cook and things. Would you prefer a wine?' Holding the fridge door open, he held up the half empty bottle of wine that she and Margie had shared.

'I would love one, Tim. And I can cook – not as well as your mother but I did a pretty good omelette for Ginny the other night.' She had never seen Tim so at ease. When she had seen him on the farm, he was either busy or more interested in talking to Ginny.

Tim helped Pamela cook the fettucine, and between them they polished off the meat sauce which Pamela had originally thought would feed about six. Tim finished his meal with a large bowl of ice cream as they sat in the warm room, watching the distant lights of the town twinkle through the window.

'You know, Pamela. I have to apologise to you.'

'Why on earth, Tim?'

'Ginny told me I was rude to you when you asked about the PTSD on the way down from home. I didn't mean to be rude, but I know sometimes I do just snap.' He paused. 'I just don't like people asking. Ginny said your husband had PTSD and he was difficult to live with. I didn't realise that.'

At first Pamela didn't say anything. She wasn't used to young men apologising to her, especially young men like Tim who seemed so masculine and physical but then happily helped her prepare the dinner and load the dishwasher. So unlike Charles.

'Tim, I shouldn't have been so tactless. I just wanted to know what treatment you had. You seem to be pretty well over it. I never knew that was why CJ was so difficult.' She stopped for a moment, embarrassed. 'That sounds awful, doesn't it? That I never even knew he had a problem. He did have some treatment but then gave it up and left the army. I always thought his problems were caused by . . . by something quite different and that it was my fault.'

Tim asked whether CJ had been in a war and Pamela told him what she knew; that he had been undercover on a mission which had gone horribly wrong.

Tim explained that, in his case, he had just finished university at Otago and had been celebrating. His friend was driving an old bomb of a car. He should have stopped his friend driving so recklessly.

'You know, I wasn't able to even talk about this until recently,' he admitted. 'The car crashed.' Even now Pamela could see it was difficult for Tim. When the car rolled Tim had managed to get out and crawl away, but his friend died, the car bursting into flames. Tim was sure he should have saved him, although when the police arrived they had assured him he couldn't have. Tim had a broken leg and was lucky to get out himself.

'Afterwards I just couldn't cope at all. I couldn't think straight. I couldn't get in a car without it all flooding back. I was a mess. I had a bit of counselling and then went home to the farm – fresh air and exercise.'

'And did the fresh air and exercise do the trick?'

'No, not at all. Dad and I clashed. Well, that was nothing new. I'd had my fair share of thrashings as a kid. Probably all deserved. It was Sal really, my sister. She insisted I get help. The doctors finally got on to it. A spell in a clinic and drugs. Cost a fortune, I gather, but it did begin to help.'

'What drugs?' Pamela wondered what drugs would help.

'Tranquillisers, antidepressants mainly. They talked about using more heavy duty, psychotropic ones; they change the chemical balance in the brain. They didn't give them to me, though. I just had a lot of counselling – cognitive therapy they call it. I'll always regret that night but at least I have a life now, except for lashing out like I did with you.'

For a second, Pamela wondered if the drugs would have worked on CJ. She would never know now.

'It must have been difficult for your mother,' she said.

Tim turned his head towards her for a second. They were still sitting at the table and neither of them thought to move. Pamela was fingering an empty wine glass but didn't want it refilled.

'Every time I lose my temper I curse afterwards because I know it upsets Mum or riles Dad. That's the trouble; you don't get cured. You just have to live with it.' Pamela looked down and was about to speak but Tim continued. 'Your husband must have coped with it somehow.'

Pamela looked out through the big window towards the twinkling lights of the town. 'Yes, I suppose he coped in his way. Drank a lot. Lived in his own world. As Ginny certainly did with her accident, but she never became angry or grumpy. She would just fall asleep.'

Tim laughed, perhaps happy to change the subject.

'Hers was a bit different. There was a physical injury. A TBI that the doctors say will get better over time as the cells repair. Did you know she went to the counsellor today? That was why she went up to Auckland. She didn't want to tell you before but he gave her the all clear and she said I could tell you. Back to 100 per cent, or nearly anyway.'

Pamela looked surprised. So Ginny wasn't just tired of her; she was on a mission.

Tim changed the subject. 'She's also arranged for the farm manager where she works to take an old dog we have – the one who could only work around the shed. The dog needs retiring and Dad's been grumbling about her holiday being over now shearing's finished. She'll suit them on flat land where they don't have many sheep.'

Pamela looked at Tim a moment. So Bob wasn't talking about her; no wonder he didn't look embarrassed.

'So, how's your mystery coming on, Pamela? Did Margie know about the stone?'

Pamela explained how a woman called Polly had phoned but had refused to tell her about the stone.

'It's now more frustrating than ever. She said she knows what it was about but just wouldn't tell me. She sounded most unpleasant.'

'Perhaps she doesn't realise you don't know. Can't you phone her back?'

'I don't have her number.'

'Didn't she phone your mobile? It'll be on there.'

'Will it?'

Pamela fetched her newly-charged phone and handed it to Tim. He pressed a few buttons.

Pamela noticed Smoky had got up from his place by the window and walked towards the dog flap. She wondered whether he would disappear again. Well, at least she had Tim to go and get him.

'You rang an 0800 number last.'

'Yes, I did. That was to try and get into the house. The phone ran out of battery halfway through.'

'Before that was . . . wait a minute. It went through to 1-1-1. God, Pamela, were you that desperate? I wonder how many calls they get from people who lock themselves out of their house. What did they say?'

'I never got that far. I panicked when they asked if it was a false alarm. It really wasn't an emergency.'

'Let's see the received calls. Here's one. Could this be it? It's a landline, not a mobile.'

'Oh, Tim, how clever!' Pamela looked at her watch. 'It's a bit late to call them now though. Let me think about it. She was so brusque on the phone. I'll have to pluck up the courage.'

Smoky reappeared back, and immediately went to his basket and jumped in.

Suddenly Pamela felt incredibly tired herself. She excused herself, leaving Tim as he turned on the television. There were fewer lights twinkling through the window now, and she was relieved that she wasn't alone in the house.

* * * * *

Ginny had hoped to get away from Auckland early but at the last minute she thought she had better tidy up the flat before she left. Pamela would be coming back with her and at least she should clean the shower which Pamela was so fussy about. As she cleaned and vacuumed, she thought about Tim. He was the first person she had really liked for ages – in fact, since her accident – since that bloody awful evening with Charles. She was well aware of Tim's problems, but she was sure, over the years, he wouldn't become a grump like CJ. She just couldn't imagine it; his flare-ups were so short lived.

She was later than expected getting to Taupō. The huge lake, right in the middle of the North Island, was nearly three hours from Auckland. Tim had texted, suggesting she go straight to his sister's shop. She found the place on a wide back street but close to the centre. It looked newly furbished, and it was strange to see the Scawton's name over a shop. Ginny was interested to meet Sally, Tim's sister. Tim said she was impressed to have Lady Scawton visit and was wondering how she could use her as a promotion. Ginny wasn't sure whether Pamela would like that but didn't say anything to Tim.

As Ginny walked up towards the shop, she could see Pamela and Tim inside talking to a girl who looked like Tim with long hair. The shop had a variety of produce – wine, wooden products, and some hand-made pickles – but Tim had said that the two main lines were the fantastic merino scarves and the skincare. The soft scarves were made from wool, which came from his brother's sheep station in the South Island.

Tim showed her around. The stuff all seemed expensive to Ginny, but she could see the scarves were high quality and just so light. Tim had tried to explain how good the skincare was, natural and environmentally friendly, no parabens and chemicals – whatever parabens were.

Ginny noticed that Pamela didn't look as English as when she had arrived. She seemed less formal, as she stood deep in conversation with Sal. They seemed to be talking about stock and how they tracked it, which surely wasn't Pamela's normal line of conversation.

'Ginny, I can buy all my presents to take home,' Pamela greeted Ginny. 'They're all here, with *Scawtons* written all over them.'

Ginny looked at Tim. He was smiling at her. Driving down, Ginny had been unsure about him; he was older, and maybe she was just dazzled by his looks or flattered by his attention, or just felt sorry for him with his temper problems. On the phone that morning, he said he and Pamela had a long chat about her; goodness knows what Pamela might have said but now Ginny saw him, his rugged looks and crooked smile were just as good as before and her doubts vanished.

Pamela, Sal and Tim had disappeared into a back room leaving her and Sal's assistant, Barb, in the shop. A small group of people appeared at the door. Ginny turned around as a burly man almost pushed past her. She was annoyed – until she came face to face with Stit Rennie. He was much smaller than Ginny expected but she recognised him at once and although he didn't speak, his smile was amazing. Automatically she moved so that he could pass. There were several people with him, all taller than he was but he looked so handsome. Ginny just stood there, awestruck.

She watched as he asked Barb about the skin care and handled some of the scarves, his voice so deep. Barb seemed dumbstruck too as he lifted up some of the products and chatted to the tall willowy girl beside him. In her tight trousers and high heels, the girl looked like a supermodel as she smiled at Barb and then whispered in his ear. Perhaps that was his girlfriend. Stit nodded and moved towards the door, thanking Barb in that wonderfully rich voice.

Ginny blinked. Sal was gawping from the backroom door as the group filed out and headed for the restaurant next door. The shop suddenly felt empty and Ginny was quite tempted to go and touch some of the things Stit had touched but Tim was there and didn't look that impressed. Sal was asking what he'd said, and Pamela looked quite annoyed.

They had regrouped in the room at the back, leaving just Barb in the shop. Ginny was talking about Stit to Tim when she heard Barb call to Sal from the door.

'I need your help.' Stit's girlfriend with the long legs had come back with another attractive girl who had been in the group. It seemed the girlfriend was French, and the other girl introduced herself to Sal as Stit's PA. They had a proposal. After some discussion beside the giftware, Sal returned, obviously thinking.

'She says Stit would like to take a whole lot of our stuff back to America with him, but he wants us to give them to him – gift boxes he could give to people. It'd be great promotion, but he likes the expensive box with a scarf as well as the moisturisers and he wants ten. We can't really afford to give away that many. Let me think.'

Ginny stopped herself from gasping. Stit Rennie taking their product! Then she remembered Tim saying that the family had stretched the finances pretty thin just to get this far. Sal surely couldn't afford to give away ten of their expensive gift boxes – even if it was for Stit Rennie. Before Sally could say anything more, they saw Pamela walking over to the two girls with a determined stride.

'Excuse me, I understand you are Mr Stit's personal assistant?'

Sal quickly followed and introduced her. 'This is Lady Scawton, from England. She's part of the original, very old family.' Sal emphasised the 'lady' so there was no doubt about the connection. The PA raised her eyebrows.

'A real lady? Like a title?' she said with an American drawl.

Sally nodded but Pamela answered instead. 'Yes, indeed. Lady Scawton of *Scawtons*. Now I understand you work for that Mr Stit.' Ginny noticed Pamela's accent seemed more English than ever compared to the girl's American accent.

'Yes, I do. I'm very lucky.'

'And does he pay you?' The girl frowned. Lordy, that was rude of Pamela, thought Ginny.

'Of course. He pays very well. I'm so lucky.' The girl gave Pamela an empty smile. Pamela was looking quite angry and her arms were stiff in front of her.

'Then I really don't see why he should expect to get these gifts for nothing. This company is trying to establish a top-quality market, not just give it away. Or perhaps Mr Stit will endorse all the products in exchange? So we could use him in our advertising,' Her English accent inevitably carried and there was a hush. Even Sal was silent.

Ginny took a deep breath and suddenly felt sorry for the girl. The PA hadn't had years of pony club instructions. 'There is no need to canter, a trot will do.'

The PA began to apologise. Silly girl. Wrong move. 'I am so sorry, Lady Scawton. I didn't mean to offend. Stit would be horrified to think he had offended a titled lady. We would be happy to pay.'

Sal stepped forward at once and gently touched the girl on the shoulder. 'Come and show me again which ones he would like. We can, of course, arrange a small discount. If you would like them duty free we can deliver them to the airport for you.' They began to move together towards the gift collections.

Just at that moment, the long-legged girl spoke to the PA in angry French. Ginny couldn't understand what she said but within minutes the voices were raised before, finally, the PA spoke in English. 'Of course. I'll ask her.'

Pamela was standing with her eyebrows raised and Sal frowning beside her, no doubt trying to understand the French spoken.

Then Ginny was surprised to hear Pamela speak.

'Lesquels voudriez-vous prendre comme échantillons?' Ginny was impressed. She didn't know Aunt P could speak French; she couldn't understand what she said but she sounded pretty fluent.

The voices quietened, and the French girl calmed down immediately and even laughed. Pamela then explained to Sal that the French woman was in fact representing a Paris department store. She had persuaded Stit to choose plenty of products so that she could take some back to Paris as samples.

Pamela continued to speak to them in French, translating for Sal as they went. 'I was saying that we only use the Scawton name on quality products,' Pamela explained to Sal, and Ginny wondered about the 'we'.

The two girls were quite relaxed now and seemed particularly impressed with the merino scarves, not at all put off by the price. It wasn't long before they had arranged to buy some gift boxes for Stit and for samples to be sent direct to a Paris store. Sal ushered them out of the door, promising delivery of the gift boxes to the gate security later in the day.

'Thank you so much, Pamela,' Sal gasped as they came into the back room. 'How lucky you were here. I suppose you don't want to stay and work for us?'

Ginny smiled to herself. She could actually see Pamela running a shop like this.

Tim was standing there beside Sal. 'She can't Sal. She's going back to run a top farm shop in England. She couldn't decide whether she was going to be able to. She doesn't need proof now. I reckon she'll make it rock!'

Ginny wondered what on earth Tim was talking about.

* * * * *

Uncle Pete had waited until Polly called in before he told her about the phone call from Lady Scawton and the visit they had arranged. Polly was furious. How could he!

'Uncle Pete, I have no desire to sit having afternoon tea with some fancy lady discussing the stone which should be in our family, not hers. I don't care if she has come halfway round the world to gloat. Anyway, why did she phone you? I'd already spoken to her.'

'If you remember you phoned her from here,' he continued before Polly could interrupt, 'and you were quite rude. I'm sure she won't gloat, as you say.'

Polly began to feel guilty. She knew she'd been abrupt on the phone but the lady on the other end had one of those up-herself accents. Polly knew Pete had been angry at her tone. She'd only spoken to the woman because Pete insisted, even dialling the number for her.

Maybe she had been too abrupt. 'Whatever. All Poms gloat. It's their natural arrogance. Probably because the Queen lives there.'

'She says she has no idea what the stone means. She says Beth's letter is only half a page and doesn't tell her anything and she never met Geoffrey.'

'Then how come she had the stone?'

'The police gave it to her.'

Polly frowned. She wished she had seen Geoffrey Cook when he came that last time, or Diane had told them earlier about sending him the stone. She supposed Geoffrey wasn't such a bad old codger. He had obviously been very fond of her mother and wasn't nearly as odd as his strange brother.

When her mother had died it had been early evening. Polly had been nervous of looking after her mother during the nights, which was why her mother had moved to the hospice. That morning, when she called in at the hospice, her mother was sleeping, and she was still the same when she got back from work. Diane had said she could probably still hear and so Polly just spoke about this and that – she couldn't remember what – and held her hand. She was sure that Beth had purposely waited until Polly had left the room to go and get a cup of coffee, because when she came back Diane was there and her mother had died.

Now Polly felt tears come into her eyes. She looked over at Pete who had a sad smile. Maybe he knew she was remembering; it was more than a year ago now, but it still felt like yesterday.

'Polly, Beth's letter evidently said nothing. It mentioned something about *now the adoption laws have changed*. I don't know what it was about, and so I can't tell her. The note from Diane, to Geoffrey, says that Beth expected him to tell them verbally about it.'

'He died in her garden. Geoffrey must have explained. She must know.'

'She didn't meet him. If Geoffrey had told them and given them the stone, the letters and the stone wouldn't have been on his body. The police, not Geoffrey gave them to her.'

Polly could feel herself frowning again. 'Don't frown,' her mother used to say. 'It'll give you wrinkles.' Probably too late now. 'So she never saw Geoffrey? Are you sure?'

Pete nodded.

'And she has our stone?'

Pete nodded again.

'But I don't want some English lady lording it over us about it. It's theirs now and she sounded so . . . so correct.'

'I know, she's English, but when she phoned back asking to speak to you, she sounded quite unsure of herself and very apologetic. You were rather abrupt.'

'I didn't want to speak to her at all.'

'I know, but when Theodore had taken the trouble to phone us . . . ' He stopped.

Polly could hear Beth in her head, telling her to meet this woman. In her mind she could see Aggie, sitting on the stands at Avondale wrapped in her old coat, glowering at her.

'This is your chance to set it all right. You're the only one who can.'

'I guess I could come on Tuesday. Simon plays sport till late.'

'She leaves to go back to England on Wednesday. I'll ask her for 4.30pm. Perhaps you could collect a cake from the bakery around the corner.'

★ ★ ★ ★ ★

As Ginny drove up to her barn, Pamela was relieved.

'It's like coming home, Ginny. We seem to have been away for much longer than just a few days. So much has happened. Fishing this morning was just wonderful.' The box on the back seat held a good-sized trout packed in ice.

'Yes, but you aren't much further on with the stone business.'

As she unpacked in her tiny room, Pamela silently agreed. She hoped the meeting with this Polly Wilson would at last give her some answers. She took out her phone and immediately Pamela realised that she had turned it off when she was fishing and hadn't turned it back on.

Now there were several messages: Charles, Godley, Charles, Charles.

'Where are you Mother? We really need to speak.' Charles kept repeating the message. She had only spoken to him two days ago. Something must have happened.

She needed to organise the trout first. Mike was coming to share it.

Catching it that morning had been a magical couple of hours. Margie had woken her soon after dawn and they had driven out to some spot she said never failed her. Margie had done all the work preparing the rods and flies. It was chilly as they stood on the banks of the clear stream, whispering quietly that the angler they could see standing in the middle of the river further down must be frozen to death. They began to tune in to the sounds of the birds, the rustle of the scraggy bush, as Margie called it, and the shiny transparent water as it splashed over low rocks. It was a world of its own.

The man down river had gone by the time Pamela had felt a tug on the line. Margie reeled her own line in and helped Pamela play what turned out to be a magnificent trout. Margie was sceptical that it was big enough to keep and even produced a tape measure. Pamela thought she was joking; it looked enormous.

Pamela took the cleaned fish from the ice it had travelled in and put in the herbs she'd picked from the vegetable patch behind the stables. Ginny was in charge of vegetables and started to peel potatoes. Once the fish was cooking, Pamela had time to make the phone calls.

She phoned Godley first. It was still too early to phone Charles.

'How are the dogs, Godley?'

'They are fine, Madam. But if you stay away much longer I will have to de-sofa Bentley. He takes up too much room and now sits on my side.'

'Oh dear. And what other news? I have several missed calls from Charles.'

'Oh, yes indeed. He was planning on you going to London the day you arrived back, for cocktails. I suggested that you might not be up to that, and so he's planning to bring Joanna's parents to meet you. I did suggest they come during the day as you might be tired by the evening.'

'Oh, yes. I don't see why that can't work. They could come for lunch. We can have Mrs Short, can't we? Presumably Jerry Thomson has a wife. What about the son, isn't there a brother?'

'Sir Charles didn't mention him. The son has just taken up polo too, I see. Sir Charles' low-goal polo team is called "Thomsons".'

'I'll be interested to meet them.'

'They do seem to be discussing a lot of changes to the house.'

'Well, that's fine as long as Thomson Trucks are paying.'

'And Lady Elizabeth phoned to ask when you return.'

'She offered me a job at Shefford House. In the farm shop. You know, Godley, if you retire, I just might take it.'

'She did mention it, Madam. It sounded as though it would suit you exactly.'

'I hope you gave me a good reference. Why don't you phone her back and arrange for me to go over there? Whenever it suits her. Now Charles' lunch . . . '

Mike arrived halfway through the conversation and inevitably heard the rest of the conversation. Ginny signalled that she was speaking to Godley.

'Have we any champagne left or has Charles finished it all? Yes, do. We better have really good stuff or Charles will complain. I'll bring some duty-free Glenfiddich. But I'll leave everything else to you . . . Warm all the house up if it needs it and we'll need to eat in the big dining room . . . salmon, I think, or coronation chicken . . . and salad. Tomato salad, too – my mother-in-law's recipe, Mrs S knows . . . Lemon mousse or caramel custard? Hmm, caramel is one of Charles' favourite, but I think the lemon would be better for this. Goes better with the champagne . . . '

Eventually she swiped the phone shut.

'That sounds a fine dinner,' Mike chuckled, 'in aid of Charles getting engaged to Jerry Thomson's daughter I take it.'

Pamela laughed as she greeted Mike. 'Oh yes, they're coming to lunch the day I get back. Thank God for Godley.'

'And Pamela has been offered the job to run the Shefford farm shop. Can't you see her doing that?' suggested Ginny.

'Absolutely, that's the shop by their big house which Lizzie Shefford started, isn't it?'

'I won't be running it – just helping Lizzie while she has the baby.'

'One titled lady to another,' laughed Mike.

'Well, I can't help that.' Pamela smiled. 'Can you cope a moment while I catch up with Charles?' Ginny and Mike took over monitoring the trout while Pamela punched in Charles' number.

'Mother, thank goodness. Where the hell have you been? I've left several messages.'

'Yes, I turned the phone off and forgot to turn it back on.'

'Oh, typical. Now I want to arrange for you to meet Jerry and Jill, Joanna's parents. And Joanna, of course.'

'Oh, lovely, yes. I'm looking forward to it. Godley just told me.'

'Jerry has to go away the day after you arrive home. Godley suggested we come down to Ashly. It'll be an opportunity for Jerry and Jill to see the house.'

'Good idea. I arrive home early as long as the plane isn't delayed.'

'We could have a late lunch in the pub or somewhere close and then come and look around the house.'

'Rubbish, you can have lunch at the house.'

'But you only get home that day.'

'That's not a problem. Mrs Short and Godley are there, and Godley says the garden is looking really good.' Pamela was surprised that Charles had even thought about lunching anywhere else. He wasn't usually that considerate.

'Well, okay then, but you'll have to shut the dogs up.' Oh, the pointers were the problem. She wouldn't have time to collect the terriers before lunch.

'Joanna will just have to get used to them,' she said. 'The pointers haven't eaten anything live for years.' Pamela looked down at her own feet for a second. Her shoes needed cleaning. 'Oh, I'm joking. The pointers can stay in the back passage. Godley says you have lots of plans for the house.'

'Yes, lots. You'll love the ideas they have for the staff quarters. Your apartment overlooks the vegetable garden.'

'That sounds interesting,' Pamela said, pretending to be enthusiastic.

'Joanna is a bit worried that you might interfere with the alterations, you know – not want things changed. If it all goes ahead of course. By the way, the gardeners weren't there this time even though it was a weekday. Moonlighting elsewhere at our expense no doubt.'

'Charles, what are you talking about? We have nothing to do with the vegetable garden.'

'No, the house garden. We'll discuss it when you get home,' he said. 'You leave soon?'

'Yes, and tomorrow I hope to catch up – at last – with the girl whose mother wrote the letter.'

'Oh, Lord. The blackmail bit. She'll think you're easy meat.' His voice hardened. 'Don't give them anything. Whatever it was about, it's nothing to do with us. If it was to do with Father, they're too late. And bring the stone back; we can get it cut. And also . . . '

Pamela could hear more instructions coming down the phone. She could see Mike and Ginny poking at the trout on the stove. 'Charles, I really have to go. The trout is ready. I'll see you at lunch on Friday.'

She swiped the phone shut and began to smile to herself. It sounded as though the house was going to get a new lease of life, hopefully without her. Except Charles didn't sound quite as enthusiastic as before, or perhaps that was her imagination.

23

New Zealand 2013

The meeting was to be at a house in Onehunga. Ginny had offered to come but Pamela thought it best she go by herself. She could set the GPS herself now. *One Hunga* only Ginny had insisted it was pronounced 'Onyhunga'. It didn't seem too far.

She turned off the motorway which had led past the airport. The streets here sloped upwards into wide tree-lined avenues. Most of the houses were smart wooden villas, set in their own gardens. When she found the right number, it was a much smaller, older house than the others. Pamela checked again that it was the correct number. A white cracked concrete wall ran along the roadside and a large magnolia tree shaded the garden which would make it cool in summer. She looked around. There was a small shop at the end of the road and a park in the distance. It was the other end of her world and in the middle of a city but, even though the magnolia had no leaves, the little house looked more private than living in staff quarters of a country hotel in England.

She turned back to face the house, taking a deep breath as she felt her stomach churn. She still felt so embarrassed at offending Theodore as she had and did not want a similar thing to happen. Pamela fingered the stone in her pocket, rustling the tissue paper around it. The stone had almost become a friend now, a loyal ally insisting 'you can do this'. She took another deep breath and huffed it out.

She walked through a creaky iron gate. A dog barked somewhere and so she shut it behind her carefully. The fractured concrete pathway led to three steps and a wooden porch. She pressed the rusty button beside the large wooden front door and could hear a vague ring within the house as she patted her pocket, looking for comfort from the stone. The barking was coming closer; it was a small dog by the sound of it.

'You must be Lady Scawton. Pleased to meet you. I'm Pete, Polly's uncle.' A wrinkled smiling face greeted Pamela, one which she could relate to immediately. The dog pushed out and Pamela automatically bent down to pat him before he disappeared into the garden.

'Come on in. Is the gate shut? Oh, yes, thank you. Excuse the stick. It just helps me get around without falling over.' He turned and led the way into a comfortable sitting room. A well-worn leather armchair sat beside modern sliding windows and there was a long sofa against the opposite wall. A cat was curled comfortably on top of an untidy pile of newspapers on the coffee table. Taking one look at Pamela, it gave an offended meow and hurried out towards the hall.

'Polly should be here in a minute. Do you want to take your coat off? I know it's warm in here.'

'I'm looking forward to meeting her.' Pamela slipped her navy coat off but then wasn't sure where to put it, so held it over her arm. Out of the sliding windows there was a small patio. A tall hedge and a large tree with hanging boughs beyond it meant there was no view of the neighbours.

'This has all been such a mystery,' she said.

Pete made his way to the leather chair and pointed to the sofa. Pamela went to sit down, then stopped and put the coat over a tall chair, and the bag she'd brought with her on the floor beside the sofa.

'Polly's a lovely girl. Done very well for herself. She is a bit . . . er . . . . independent sometimes but very kind to me.'

Pamela wondered what he meant. 'Is she married?'

'Married a dreadful feller. Glad when they split up. Didn't do her any good. It was years ago now, but she's coped ever since. They had two children only one died as a baby which was maybe why they split up. The other one, Simon, goes to school in Epsom. He's 13 now, and a great kid. Polly's very busy in her job and has plenty of friends. It's been hard since her mother died last year. She keeps an eye on me and we speak quite often. Ah, that will be her now.'

The gate squeaked, and the dog barked. Pete didn't move. As they heard the door open, Pete got up out of the chair and tried to hide his hobble as he walked towards the door. 'Come in, my dear.'

A tall angular woman walked confidently into the room and Pete introduced her to Pamela. Polly's almost black hair was pulled back into a severe pony tail; her skin looked clean and clear. She wore a thigh-length cardigan and boots which had clacked along the wooden hall floor. She had a thin smile on her face.

'Lady Scawton.' She pronounced it 'Scorn' as she had on the phone.

Pamela held out her hand, but Polly had already turned her head away to put a bulging bag on the table. 'No, no, I'm Pamela. I am delighted to meet you at last.'

'Yes,' was all that Polly said, turning and looking at her uncle.

Pamela estimated Polly was in her early 40s. Pamela deliberately kept what she hoped was a friendly smile on her face, but there was little reaction from Polly. Pamela shivered involuntarily, although she wasn't at all cold.

'I bought an apple cake, Pete. Shall I get the tea?' Her words were directed at her uncle as though Pamela wasn't there.

While she disappeared out the door, Pamela and Pete sat down again. The conversation became more stilted as they talked about how long Pete had lived here. Surely he wasn't intimidated by his own niece, Pamela wondered. Polly carried in a tray and placed it on the wooden dining table and went back out. Pete had expected her to put it on the coffee table and had moved a few magazines to a small table by his chair. Now he put the magazines back.

'My favourite cake.' He thanked Polly as she returned with a cake.

'I know,' Polly said but she didn't seem very forthcoming. Perhaps a woman of few words, thought Pamela.

Pamela moved further along the sofa. There was plenty of room and she assumed Polly would sit at the other end, but after handing her a cup of tea and a small plate with a piece of cake, Polly drew one of the upright dining chairs from the table.

'No, I'm fine here,' she answered when Pamela pointed to the sofa.

Pamela could feel her looming over them.

There was a moment's silence. The pleasantries were over, the tea served. Pamela looked to the uncle for help but he was looking down, not at her. Someone had to start and get this over. It had better be her.

'I don't know how much you all know about all this, but shall I tell you my side? About the stone and Professor Cook? The letter, which I think was from your mother, Beth, wasn't it? Ginny sent you a copy by email last night, didn't she?' Pamela realised she had picked up the New Zealand habit of ending sentences with a question.

Polly burst forth, stopping Pamela in her tracks. 'We didn't know she had given the stone to Geoffrey, and I can't believe he didn't say anything to us before he went off. Yes, the letter was from her.' Polly's voice suddenly faltered.

'I'm sorry about your mother. I gather from your uncle that she died.'

'Yes.'

Pamela was sitting still, her fingers clasped in front of her. She would have liked to finger the stone again, but it was in her coat pocket over the chair. The uncle was still looking down at his slippers. Pamela crossed her legs, trying to get more comfortable. Then she uncrossed them.

She began again. 'We just wanted to find out what it was about. It sounded very . . . or rather . . . threatening. Do you know what your mother was talking about?' Pamela leaned down to the canvas bag at her feet. She needed the clear plastic folder with the original letter.

'Oh yes,' came the answer. 'I know.'

Pamela straightened up, not wanting Polly to think she wasn't listening. There was an uncomfortable silence in the room. Pamela wondered how she had offended her, what she had done. She had tried to be polite.

Pamela glanced out of the window, looking for help. The boundary hedge shut out any view.

'The letter talks about adoption. I guess . . . ' Pamela spoke slowly and carefully. She bent down to her bag again. She pulled out some brochures of Scawton products by mistake and quickly stuffed them back in.

'I am adopted,' Polly burst out.

Pamela gasped involuntarily. 'So you're not Beth's . . . '

'Polly is Beth's daughter,' Pete interrupted with a loud voice, which almost echoed. 'Beth's only daughter. In fact my mother's only granddaughter. I have no children, and my brothers only have sons. Polly is the only girl in the family. She was christened Agatha after my mother, Aggie. Polly's her granddaughter,' he repeated.

Pamela was flustered. Now even the uncle was angry. She certainly picked up on his emphasis of granddaughter.

'I didn't mean to offend.' She paused. She was making things worse. She took a deep breath. 'You just took me by surprise. I was expecting the adoption part of the story to involve either my son or husband having fathered a child and the mother, um, wanting . . . I hadn't thought of it being the other way around, of a child wanting . . . The letter spoke of the adoption laws changing . . . ' Pamela was getting confused.

'The law was changed so that adopted children could find their birth parents. I assume that's what Mum meant.' Polly's clipped answers were not making the situation easier.

Pamela was floundering but still felt she should carry on. 'And do you know your . . . ? I am sorry; it sounds rather rude when I don't really know you.'

Now Polly stood up and was towering over Pamela, a scowl on her face. Pamela realised she'd already outstayed any welcome. Polly's face was telling her that she wanted her to leave. As Polly put her teacup on the table, Pamela bent down to her bag again, half thinking she would close it up and go. Then she straightened up in her seat; she had come a long way for all this and needed to see it through.

'Who were your parents?' Pamela asked, in a rush. 'Is that what this is about?'

'Beth was my mother and David my father. My father died a long time ago.'

'No, I meant . . . was any of our family involved in your adoption? I can't see how but if this letter was written by your mother . . . '

'I know my birth mother, if that's what you mean. I met her more than a year ago. She isn't anything to do with your family.'

For a moment, Pamela imagined what that might be like. 'Only last year? It must have been extraordinary to meet her.'

Polly's face clouded over before she turned to look at Pamela with a steady stare. 'Yes, it was. Uncle Pete was with me because it was when my mother was ill.'

Pamela put her hands on her lap and tried to relax as Polly continued in a calmer tone.

'I loved my mother, Beth. I didn't want things to change. It was my Nan, my grandmother, the Aggie who I was named after – even though I've always been called Polly. It was she who insisted I find out about my birth parents. You can find out when you're 18 but you have to have counselling before they give you the names. After she died my mother – Beth – kept reminding me that I'd promised. When Mum became ill, I couldn't really not try and find out . . . '

Now it was Polly's turn to hesitate and Pamela wanted to encourage her. 'It must be funny not knowing about your birth parents. I often notice I am doing things like my mother used to do. I don't know whether it's genetic or just habit.'

'I'm the same,' agreed Polly. Her tone had suddenly become

friendlier. 'Every time I put the washing on the line, I think of how my mother shook the clothes out, and I do the same. My mother, Beth, I mean. I suppose when she became ill – she had cancer – I did wonder whether I could expect any genetic illness from my birth mother. They talk about genes so much now. When the doctor asks, "Is your father still alive?" or "What did he die of?" I never know quite which father they mean.'

'What about your birth father?'

'My birth mother told me a bit. He was Māori or part Māori.'

'Māori?' repeated Pamela.

'Is that a problem?' came Polly's violent retort. Pamela had hoped Polly's anger had dissipated but it had suddenly flared again.

'Of course not,' persisted Pamela, keeping her voice intentionally quiet.

Uncle Pete's voice was insistent too. 'My father was part Māori too.'

In the ensuing silence, Pamela felt they were waiting for a reaction and answered, 'You can't come here to New Zealand without realising how important the Māori are to all New Zealanders. When the All Blacks do the haka, all New Zealanders are proud of it, not just Māori. I don't know much about Māori heritage except that it's very important. Only you don't call it heritage, do you?'

'Whakapapa.' The mood lifted as Pete spoke more quietly.

'Whakapapa,' Pamela stumbled over the word. 'It's so important, not just to Māori. So where do the Scawtons fit into your adoption? Why did your mother write the letter?'

'But it wasn't my adoption. The adoption involved your family. It involved my grandmother. My nan, Aggie.'

Pamela looked surprised.

'And it involved the stone.'

* * * * *

Polly began to speak, calmly now. When she relaxed, she had a rather pleasant, deep voice, and spoke well.

It was a strange story, going back to the First World War when Polly's grandmother was working at Ashly House as a scullery maid. Pamela wondered where the scullery would have been. Perhaps it was where the laundry was now. The house was big, but she still puzzled where on earth all those staff had slept. As the story unfolded, Pamela could imagine the predicament the young Aggie had been in.

Polly was a good storyteller. 'Do you know, in that nuns' home, back in 1920 or whenever, it was only by mistake that she had ever been told even the sex of the baby? She never saw him, let alone held him.'

'They probably would have had some cockeyed idea that it was better for the baby.'

'That might have been okay, if she hadn't realised later just how involved your family were. Nan said the usual thing in those days was for the maid to be sacked straight away if she was pregnant. She was told how kind Lady Scawton was to arrange everything and at the time she was grateful because she really didn't know what to do. Nan had expected that the baby would be adopted out and she realised that, even without a child, she probably wouldn't be welcome to work back at Ashly House. That wasn't the problem although she was forever sad that she'd never even seen the baby. She left England imagining him adopted out to a loving family who weren't so different to her own. Lady Scawton even gave her the stone as a parting gift. Aggie didn't know that was unusual.'

She paused again and Pamela, her mind back in Ashly nearly 100 years ago, waited.

'Years later, when Nan's brother told her about their father's funeral, and how Sir William had brought his 10-year-old son who had been born on 1 April – the same day as her own son – she realised that the Scawtons had taken her baby. The family had brought him up as their own, never telling anyone. He became the son and heir of Sir William Scawton and when Sir William died he became Sir James Scawton. Nan's son became Sir James.'

Pamela gave a gasp – she couldn't help it.

'Nan considered it stealing. Can you understand that?'

Pamela saw Polly looking directly at her but was too dumbfounded to say anything. She raised a hand towards her face but then dropped it back as she tried to breathe normally.

'She was never able to tell anyone here that she'd had a son before she arrived in New Zealand. It was her secret, but when she realised what had happened, she always wanted the Scawton family to know that she hadn't forgotten him. And that she knew.'

Pamela could say nothing. Suddenly the pieces all fell into place as Polly explained how Aggie had confided in Beth and Polly.

'She wanted Mum to go to England instead of her. Mum intended to, but then, when she became ill, she suggested I go, but I refused. We haven't got that kind of money. I have a son to bring up. It was a stupid fantasy.'

There was a guilty pause before she continued. 'So she gave the stone to Geoffrey and swore him to secrecy. I should've agreed to go. I knew how important it was to Mum. I should've agreed.'

Pamela could see Polly kept looking at her uncle, who was listening attentively from his chair and occasionally shaking his head. Pamela couldn't believe all this could be true; it meant her father-in-law was really Aggie's son and not the son of his baronet father.

Now Pete spoke, very quietly. 'So that was the real story behind the stone? We never ever knew. Our family always considered it a lucky stone, our taonga.'

Pamela turned toward him and realised the story was new to him too as Polly continued.

'After Mum's funeral, we found the stone was missing. Uncle Pete and I thought it was stolen. Just recently, we found out Diane knew what had happened to it. She was one of the nurses who had looked after Mum in the hospice. I didn't see Geoffrey when he visited Mum that last time, but she must have told him everything, maybe because he was planning to go to England anyway. Diane said Mum wrote a note to Geoffrey to take to England with him and return it to your family – which he did, sort of.'

Pamela stayed still. The story could have been Aggie's imagination although it did sound plausible. Too plausible. William's wife could easily have confined herself to Shefford House for a few months; in those days it was probably unseemly to be seen pregnant, in public. No one would have wondered. As soon as the baby was born, Henrietta could have removed the cushion from her stomach and announced the arrival of a baby son. It certainly was possible.

*****

There was silence in the room, except for a vague ticking of a clock somewhere. Darkness had fallen outside the window, and it was Pete who broke the spell and turned on the light beside his chair.

Polly knew tears were streaming down her face, but she had wanted to finish the story, for the sake of her mother and Nan. She kept looking at her uncle, but he didn't seem angry. He just seemed quiet. The woman sitting on the sofa looked mystified and maybe pale. Polly quickly wiped her face, trying to hide the tears.

Uncle Pete spoke first, his voice sounding especially kind. 'Poor Mum, having to carry that secret all that time. We certainly had no idea. She would tell us about Ashly House and about Lady Scawton giving her the stone when she left but never gave any hint that there was anything else.' Then he gave a brief laugh, bringing them all back to reality. 'Is there any proof? It wasn't just one of Aggie's stories?'

'Couldn't it just have been coincidence that both children were born at the same time?' asked Pamela, agreeing. 'And there must have been regulations for adopting children. Not even our family could have just taken someone else's child.'

Polly had got up and turned the main light on as Pete spoke. She picked up the bag she had brought with her when she came in. As she opened it, she explained, 'Laws did come in but not until 1926 in England. I looked all that up.' She found what she was looking for in the bag and now turned to her uncle. 'You know cousin Steve, Pete?'

'The tennis player? Well, he used to be a tennis player,' he said.

Polly produced a photograph and handed it to her uncle. It was a presentation of a tennis trophy to the winner.

Pete looked at the photograph and at Polly and asked, 'What's he got to do with it?'

Polly said nothing but handed Pamela a different photo, a cutting from a magazine. Written in handwriting across the top was *Woman's Weekly* and it featured Princes William and Harry in a polo team.

'I remember this,' Pamela said. 'This was a few seasons ago. It was a charity match at Beaufort. Charles had been pulled into the team at the last moment. I drove my husband down to watch. He was very proud of Charles playing with the Princes.'

Without a word, Polly took the photo back from her uncle and the magazine cutting from Polly and put them both on the coffee table in front of Pete. Pete moved forward to sit on the edge of his chair and Pamela stood to see Pete's photograph better, puckering her brow.

Polly watched as the Englishwoman picked up the photo of Steve. She obviously recognised the likeness, raising her eyebrows in surprise. Polly smiled to herself as they all compared the two images.

'They look so alike, don't they? Is that your son?' Pete asked pointing to the polo photo.

'Yes, it is,' said Pamela. 'Even I thought this tennis photo was of Charles for a moment. Though his hair isn't quite the same.'

'It's so obvious that Nan's story really was true,' Polly said. 'Mum and I never doubted about Nan having the baby but we did doubt about the baby becoming Sir James Scawton. It was after seeing this that even Mum thought it important that you Scawtons were reminded of it. That your family knew you hadn't got away with stealing Nan's son without her knowing.'

Polly didn't quite know how to go on. Both the lady and Pete seemed stunned but at least Pete didn't seem annoyed at her telling Nan's secret.

'I think we need a drink. How about a glass of wine?' Pete shuffled forward in his chair and reached for his stick.

'I can get it,' Polly said, pleased to have something to do. She stood up.

Pamela was still bent over the photos, comparing them. The scruffy dog appeared from the kitchen and wandered towards Uncle Pete's chair as he got up. Pete bent down to give him a pat before speaking. 'I'll help Polly. I need a bit of a walk around. Get too stiff. It's an interesting story, isn't it? They lived in different times then.' He paused, putting a hand out to steady himself against the table as Polly returned with three wine glasses and a bottle. Pamela saw him put his arm on Polly's instead. It was a sympathetic gesture not lost on Polly who had a look of relief on her face.

'A glass of wine, Pamela? You do drink? Red or white?' he asked.

'That would be lovely. White please.' She shook herself out of her reverie but her mind was still racing. Sir James Scawton. Her father-in-law, her loved father-in-law. That baby was Charles' grandfather. My God, the whole Scawton family was a sham. Surely not!

She was now thinking more clearly and began to dig in the canvas bag, coming out with a large piece of paper, the family tree. 'I really need my glasses. This thing has the birth dates on.' She peered at the paper. 'I want to see when my father-in-law, James, was born. It says here.' The other two turned to look at it.

'April 1, 1921,' said Polly.

'Yes, that was his birthday.' Pamela sighed. 'Of course it was. You know, no one has ever mentioned anything like this.' Pamela took the glass of chardonnay from Pete and continued to look at the family tree.

'I can't believe that no one ever, ever said anything.' She was still looking at the family tree. 'James, my husband's father, your relation, died in the early '70s in a car accident. He was a wonderful man.'

Pamela's thoughts were flying between time, between countries, between people, between all the baronets and between the two Aggies. How life had changed, how attitudes had changed!

Uncle Pete had made his way back to his chair. Pamela stood up and, turning towards Polly, was surprised at her height, or lack of it. Pamela had thought her very tall, but she now realised she was no taller than Pamela, just very slim. Pamela went over to her coat, took the tissue paper from the pocket and held it out to Polly.

Polly took it in her hand. Pamela could see Pete watching from his chair.

'People were cruel in those days, weren't they? Life was hard,' he said.

'As Polly told the story,' Pamela said, 'I tried to imagine what it would be like with all those servants. I can't imagine where they would have even fitted into the house. The attic rooms aren't that big. Your mother must have been very tough and resilient.'

'She was, wasn't she, Polly?' Pete encouraged.

'Nan? My goodness, yes. She was bossy as,' said Polly, looking down at the stone, now in the flat of her palm.

'Let me see it,' said her uncle.

Polly handed it over and turned to Pamela. 'Nan used to keep it in the box. I have the box at home.'

'It didn't always live in a box. My brother Bo made the box when he nearly lost it,' Pete explained, smiling as took the stone. 'I used to love looking at this. I don't know why. Why did the Scawtons have it in the first place? Why was it never made into a proper jewel?'

'It could be a proper jewel,' answered Pamela. 'It's called an alexandrite. In fact, it's very valuable. There are similar ones in the Russian crown jewels. You know, the Romanovs? Our family did have some family jewels and among them was a tiara with alexandrites. We sold it a while ago. The other side of the family, the Millers, have a Scawton necklace, which is their family heirloom and looks like it was made by the same jeweller. There are alexandrites in that as well. So we knew this stone probably did come from our family.'

'Where did they come from, these family jewels?' Pete asked.

'We just called it the Russian tiara. My husband assumed it was bought in Russia. He never knew any more than that.'

'Did you say it's called an alexandrite?' Polly asked.

'Yes, and the changing of colour is called the alexandrite effect. It changes from green to pink in the light – but you both know that already.' There was a pause. 'Polly, this jewel doesn't really belong to our family. We gave it to your family. I think it's best that you keep it.' As Pamela spoke she felt her heart give a lurch. The stone had become part of her; she didn't want to give it away.

'Mum sent it back to you. I didn't know she had done that,' said Polly, taking the stone from her uncle.

Pamela was resigned now. This had to be done. 'It was only to prove the story was genuine. You keep it. If I take it home, Charles will want it cut and turned into an engagement ring or something. I think it's best if you keep it. Your family own it and love it. You'd better insure it, though.'

She glanced wistfully at the stone while Polly turned it, trying to get it to change colour but the daylight had now gone.

It was Pete who spoke into the silence. 'Thank you for that. It's a strange stone and it's been part of our family for a long time. It belongs in both places really. My mother, Aggie, used to say it changes like people change.'

24

England 2014

Pamela walked out the back door and headed towards the gate to the vegetable garden. There was a wonderful smell in the air, of fresh summer air with a tinge of animal. She supposed that was from the pigs. The two pointers followed her, racing around the corner to the front garden. As she called them back, she could see old Batchelor coming towards her, his barrow full. The old boy must be in his 90s now and just came for something to do and to help his sons. He had been the assistant gardener when Pamela married CJ.

Pamela knew she must look ridiculous wearing Wellingtons with the new navy silk dress she had bought in Singapore during her trip but there had been a shower of rain and she didn't want to get her good shoes wet.

'Hello, Batchelor, how are you? The garden looks lovely.'

'Welcome 'ome, Lady S. The boys've been waiting for you to come and enjoy the garden. It looks the best at this time of year.'

Pamela agreed and asked if he and his sons were well.

'Oh, we're all good. I hear Sir Charles is getting engaged?' he said.

'Yes, we are about to meet his in-laws. Mrs Short needs some parsley for lunch.' She opened the wrought iron gate leading to the vegetable garden and held it while Batchelor pushed the wheelbarrow through. She followed him, telling the dogs to wait and shutting the gate behind her.

'I 'ear he's marrying the daughter of that truck man from the telly.'

'Yes, indeed. I'm sure the parents will be lovely. I have sort of met Joanna. She is beautiful.'

'Well, please wish 'im all the best, Ma'am. I'd best get this barrow out the way. The parsley's just in the next bed.' He nodded his head towards the green bushy Italian parsley, as he pushed the barrow off towards the potting shed at the far end.

As she turned to walk back towards the house, Pamela realised she still hadn't decided how she would tell Charles the secret.

For some reason even she could not fathom, after she had met Polly and Pete, she hadn't even told Ginny the full story. She had told her about Polly, and about how her grandmother had worked at Ashly and got pregnant. The father wasn't a Scawton – that had been Pamela's first thought when Polly had told the story – but Aggie had to adopt the baby out and leave the job. The Scawtons had given Aggie the stone when she left. Pamela just hadn't told Ginny who adopted the baby. Perhaps she'd felt Charles should know first.

She had phoned Professor Cook's brother before she left and thanked him for putting her in touch with Polly, assuring him the family would not sue. He seemed relieved.

With the bunch of parsley in her hand, she walked up the line of stables and looked over the doors to the snuffling pigs. My goodness, even in the short time she had been away, they had become shiny porkers. The dogs sniffed at the bottom of the stable doors.

She tried to remember how the transfer of the title worked when CJ had died. She remembered that when James had died, CJ had got an embossed certificate with seals everywhere from the Home Office or maybe the Justice Department. No, it was the Garter Principal King of Arms, that was it. Such an odd name. Now she remembered, about a month after CJ had died, Charles had received an official-looking letter saying that his claim to the baronetcy had to be approved. That hadn't been long ago. She had no idea what would happen now. The title could only be inherited by a legitimate natural-born son; Charles was CJ's son, CJ was James' son, but James was not his father's natural-born son. They would have to go back and take DNA samples – God knows who from – to ascertain who the rightful heir was. Or perhaps they would not be bothered.

The true line was Edward's line, which would end up with Bob Miller. On the plane home she had kept giggling to herself, imagining Bob Miller spluttering at the thought of becoming Sir Robert. She'd bet Bob would take the title in spite of all his blustering. 'Just for the sake of the family', he would say. On the other hand, Charles would overreact. He would deny the whole thing and want to contest it and that would cost money.

Pamela stopped to look at the house. It was ridiculously large and rather plain from this angle. Just a huge monstrosity really. She had spent most of her life under its spell. So much of what she did – committees, the pony club, the retirement home, even the possibility of being a local magistrate which CJ made sure came to nothing – so much of that was just because she lived in a big house and had a title. How ridiculous!

She checked her watch and, calling the dogs, marched off towards the back door. There she changed back into her new navy court shoes, gave the bunch of parsley to Mrs Short and directed the dogs to their beds in the corridor. She went through the door to the hall just in time to hear a car coming into the driveway.

She waited until the portly driver – that was Jerry Thomson, she recognised him from the adverts – got out of the shiny white Mercedes. He opened the back passenger door and Pamela watched as Joanna put her long legs, encased in white leather boots, out of the door first before carefully standing up. Pamela opened the heavy front door of the house. She heard Godley behind her and turned to see he had changed into his uniform and was smiling at her.

Charles rushed up the steps ahead of the others.

'Mother.' He stood back and looked at her with a surprised expression. 'You look well.' They kissed on the cheek.

'Thank you, Charles. I had a lovely holiday.'

Charles turned and introduced Joanna, her father, Jerry Thomson, and her mother, Jill.

'Jerry, how lovely to meet you at last. You look much slimmer than on the television.'

'You see, Jerry, I knew she'd have seen you on telly.'

'And you, Jill. Do come in.' Pamela smiled at Joanna, who gave a small reluctant smile back.

As Pamela led the way into the hall, she heard Charles saying that Joanna was dying to go to the toilet. 'Go on, darling, you know where it is,' he told her. Joanna disappeared towards the cloakroom.

Pamela stood by the table, beside the huge vase of greenery and white lilies, which were just coming into flower; she had finished the arrangement earlier in the morning. Joanna returned as Pamela was about to suggest a drink.

Joanna certainly was stunningly beautiful. Tall and willowy, she was massaging her hands as she spoke to Charles. 'Charles, where on earth did you get the soap with *Scawtons* on it. Gorgeous perfume. There's even hand cream as well.'

Charles looked perplexed.

'That's part of the range that our cousins in New Zealand make. They call their company *Scawtons*,' answered Pamela. 'It's nice, isn't it? I've a package to give to you to try. Shower gel and all sorts. It's over there.'

'Oh, that's lovely, thank you. You didn't have to bring me anything.'

'Lady Scawton,' Joanna's mother Jill began.

'Oh please. Forget the title.' Pamela interrupted. 'Please, just Pamela. Now I'm dying to know what you're planning for the house.'

'We're so late,' said Charles. 'Why don't we eat first and then look at the plans?' Joanna's parents looked at each other, and Pamela noted that they didn't react to Charles' suggestion with enthusiasm. Had there been some discussion or argument in the car?

'Are we in the nursery dining room?' Charles asked, heading for the door to the back corridor.

'Indeed not,' Pamela answered as she turned towards the main dining room. She had purposely set the table with the places down each side. No one at either end – neither Charles nor her. She sat next to Jerry while Charles sat between Joanna and Jill, looking out towards the French windows and the garden.

Pamela asked Jerry about his own childhood and how he had started his trucking business. He became more relaxed and began to tell her how he had started as a driver and now rarely drove a truck. She warmed to him as she was reminded of her own father, starting from almost nothing. She admired his fervour and energy.

Godley produced the champagne from the large ice bucket on the sideboard.

'Cristal,' exclaimed Jerry. 'Wonderful. Even better champagane than Dom Perignon.'

'Well, I thought we might have a toast to Joanna and Charles. You do it, Jerry.'

'Of course.' He waited until Godley had filled everyone's champagne flutes.

'To Sir Charles and the next Lady Scawton.'

Pamela smiled at Joanna. She really did look like one of those *Vogue* models. Her long blonde hair had a slight curl and hung to her shoulders. She was wearing a short dress of white net – lace, Pamela supposed it was, and probably Belgian lace at that – over a satin blouse and shorts. It looked very expensive. Even the fancy white over-the-knee boots with those ridiculous high heels looked expensive.

The salmon finished, Godley served the lemon mousse in small individual glasses – rather retro now but Mrs S had done very well.

Pamela again asked about the changes they were planning. 'You have got some drawings, haven't you? I'm dying to see them. Charles said he thought I could stay in the house while the alterations were being done but I've probably got other plans anyway.' She hadn't been able to tell Charles that she had decided to take up Lizzie's job in the farm shop.

Charles frowned at her and quickly changed the topic. He didn't seem to want to discuss the house. 'I can't get over how well you look, Mother. The holiday obviously did you good.'

'Oh, I had a lovely time, Charles. Our cousins in the Hawke's Bay were so hospitable.'

'And the alexandrite? You were off to see some woman who knew about it. Just before you left. Tell us what happened. Did they try and blackmail?'

'No, no, no, nothing like that.'

'Well, what was it about? Tell us.'

Pamela paused before answering. 'It was just something that happened generations ago. I'll tell you privately. I wouldn't want to bore our guests.'

'Don't be stupid, Mother. We're supposed to be all family now. You can tell Jerry and Jill anything. What was it about? What happened generations ago?'

'Oh, do, please,' said Jill. 'Charles did tell us about the alexandrite. I'd never even heard of one. It was all so mysterious.' Jill must have read her expression as she added, 'But Charles, you can't force her to tell us, you know.' She aimed a glance of rebuke at Charles and Pamela wondered whether Charles would take any notice.

'No, it can wait. It was nothing,' Pamela said. 'Now, where are those plans of the house?'

'We might as well look, I suppose,' said Joanna. 'I'll get them from the car.' She got up from her seat and walked towards the door. So there must have been some discussion over the house alterations, thought Pamela, or over the cost perhaps.

She could sense Charles' annoyance as he asked, 'Has Godley put the coffee in the study? We can go through there.'

She nodded and got up from the table. Jerry and Jill began to follow her into the hall. They began looking around at the portraits on the stairway, while Charles turned back to Pamela at the study door.

'Mother, for God's sake, you went all round the world. You might as well bore us with the story now as later,' he hissed. 'And anyway, where is the bloody stone?'

'I gave it back to the family.' She noticed Charles' scowling expression.

His shoulders were back and his arms tense as his words fired out. 'You left it there? But you said it was valuable. We were going to put it on show. It had better be a bloody good story, and you had better tell it.' Pamela stared at him. How he reminded her of his father!

'Charles,' she said, keeping her voice low, 'the story could have major ramifications for you. And Joanna.' Joanna was coming back through the front door.

'Blackmail was the only threat there could be and you say that's not the case.' Lowering his voice, he hissed at her. 'Mother, you make everything into such a pathetic drama. No wonder Father became so difficult. For Christ's sake, tell us the story and get it over with.'

Joanna had a roll of plans under her arm and peered at Charles with a quizzical expression. From the way Charles had reacted, Pamela thought that yes, there must have been an argument before the four of them had arrived, but she was not going to let him take it out on her; she was not going to let him turn into a CJ.

'Indeed, Charles. I will tell you. I will tell you all.'

'So I should hope,' Charles huffed as Jerry moved back towards them, perhaps pretending he had not heard the altercation.

'Did the story involve the guy up there with the spaniel at his heels?' Jerry asked innocently.

Pamela took a breath and gave Jerry a weak smile as she composed herself. She looked up to the Fuchs' portrait. It was one of the more valuable pictures and she always liked how he had included the dog.

'No, not really. He had died by then, but it did involve his wife and their son. That's his wife in the next portrait.'

'Ooh,' said Jill. 'She looks pretty stern, doesn't she? I wouldn't want to cross her.'

Jill was still standing on the first turn on the stairs, looking at the portraits, while Pamela remained by the study door.

'Her son was William and was CJ's – my husband's – grandfather.'

Charles had gone into the study and was standing by the mantelpiece. Joanna was putting the roll of papers down on the coffee table. They weren't speaking.

'Wasn't William the one who married a Shefford?' asked Charles as though to break a silence as the other three arrived.

'Yes, his wife Henrietta was Lord Shefford's daughter,' explained Pamela.

Charles marched towards the tray of coffee on a table by the window, asking Jerry if he would like some.

Pamela moved to the centre of the room and picked up the story again. 'The story goes back to just after the First World War. It seemed there was a young maid working in the house at the time. Her name was Aggie . . . '

As his mother finished the story, Charles tried not to panic at the implications of it all. Joanna's family were so besotted with the bloody title. Surely his mother realised that. Joanna was standing stiffly beside him and Jerry had a slight frown on his face.

Charles tried to make light of it. 'I bet ours isn't the only family to have dodgy ancestors. That kind of thing must have gone on quite a lot.' Damn his mother for telling them.

'What happens if the descendants of Edward's lot contest?' Joanna asked.

'I don't know, Joanna,' Pamela replied.

'We would fight it obviously,' Charles insisted. 'I have it confirmed that I'm the baronet.'

'But there's DNA and things now, which could make a difference,' said Joanna. 'I don't see it being that hard to find out. What do you think, Daddy?'

Jerry had said nothing, but he seemed to come to life now. 'I say we don't bother about it at the moment but I've an idea. We've come here to see the house and I know Jill is still keen. Let's see what those plans are about before we have to leave.'

'Good idea.' Charles immediately acquiesced. At least it got them all off this topic.

The conversation in the car on the way down had become quite heated. It seemed there were problems. Jerry now realised that English titles were not automatically accompanied by great wealth and was seeing himself as being 'taken for a mug'. He had produced a pre-nup document about which even Patrick – normally quite reserved – had some succinct derogatory comments on Charles' behalf. Who was taking whom for a ride was questionable.

Now, as they climbed the stairs towards the empty guest wing and Joanna began to describe the consultants' ambitious plans for top-of-the-range communication systems in each suite, Charles could imagine Jerry counting the cost, and Jill, glancing back up at the portraits up the stairs, would be panicking that her daughter would have the title snatched from her at any moment.

＊＊＊＊＊

It was a few days before Pamela began to make sense of everything. On that first day home, almost as soon as the Mercedes had disappeared, Ally Williams arrived with the two terriers. Pamela was in bed by seven o'clock that night and had slept soundly but over the following days the jet lag had kicked in and she found herself awake at three o'clock in the morning, feeling bright and ready to pack for another journey.

She thought back to the lunch. It was obvious Charles was having problems with Joanna's parents. The body language had not been good.

It didn't take much to see that the alterations were going to cost an enormous figure and that was probably the problem. Before she had gone away, Pamela had flinched at hearing Patrick's quote to repair the roof and now the consultants were talking about re-wiring and re-plumbing the whole house. Let alone those glamorous renovations.

Joanna's taste was certainly good although Pamela didn't like a lot of the consultants' ideas. She had been right to imagine the velvet sofas and glass topped tables in the hall. She smiled at Joanna describing how the larger suites would each have 'bespoke staircases to access a mezzanine sleeping area', which meant a hole would be knocked through the ceiling into the attic floor. It was a good idea, though. The kitchen area was going to be enormous, using all the downstairs area she lived in now. No pokey little butler's pantry for this lot. She wondered if they'd have to employ a scullery maid!

Even if the hotel was full all year round, it wasn't clear that it would make money with only eight guest rooms. They planned on the stable block being extra accommodation for staff but getting planning permission for that could take years.

Pamela wriggled up in her bed to lean against the bedhead. The dogs looked up from their mats expectantly even though there was barely a sliver of dawn light through the curtains. She'd had several phone calls with Lizzie Shefford and was due to go over there tomorrow. Lizzie still seemed keen to employ her and Pamela was looking forward to it. Lizzie was talking about a more permanent position.

Charles, of course, had reacted quite predictably: 'You have no qualifications'; 'They've only offered out of kindness'; and 'You'd make a fool of yourself'. She was surprised he didn't categorically say she shouldn't take it but then it was obvious she would be in the way during the alterations to the house and it would solve that problem.

She was excited at the thought of being totally independent and moving out from under the shadow of this big house or the demands of the family. She snuggled down into the bed sheets again.

* * * * *

Charles cursed as he moved around the flat. Joanna had moved out. It was over. The flat felt empty now, big.

It was not unexpected. They had been arguing for weeks and it was a relief not to have to listen to Joanna's next demands, and he could stop discussing bathrooms designs and kitchen layouts.

Money was at the heart of it, of course. It usually was. It didn't take a mind-reader to know that the costs of the alterations would be high. The cosy partnership of Jerry's money, Charles' house and the consultants' expertise had fallen into an imbalanced heap of capital, security and viability. It seemed Jerry blamed him for such expensive alterations. His daughter, of course, was faultless.

Jill had stopped fawning over him – that was a relief – but he wasn't sure whether her disparaging looks were because she thought he was taking advantage of Jerry's money or because of his mother's story of his grandfather. She could probably see newspaper articles about the _stolen title_ and fingers pointing at her precious daughter.

He turned on the coffee machine, wondering what the hell he was going to do now. Several other polo players were talking of going to Argentina for a month in the autumn. Visions of endless expanses of polo fields, horses, and offers to practice with high-goal players were tempting but he doubted he could get the bus man to pay.

He thought about his house – Ashly House – the long sweeping drive, the stately look, the clean lines as it towered above the huge front door. He was surprised that his mother seemed so excited about moving out of it. Then he remembered the potholes in the drive, the hole in the roof, the pigs in the stables. Perhaps Patrick's suggestion of letting it out didn't sound so bad after all. He looked around for his phone.

* * * * *

'Charles, how are you? It's a lovely morning, and I'm sleeping much better now. That jet lag took nearly a week to get over.'

'Mother, the engagement is off. Joanna has moved out.'

There was a pause.

'Oh, Charles, I am sorry. She seemed a lovely person and you had such great plans.'

'Well, Joanna did. She was very demanding. So was Jerry. Patrick wouldn't have a bar of what his lawyers wanted.'

Pamela had spoken to Patrick the day before and had already heard that Jerry's suggestions were impractical.

'I suppose there would have been a problem for Jerry using his money on property he didn't own. He would have needed security.'

'Your story was the final straw, Mother. Making it sound as though the title was in jeopardy. We really didn't need that.'

Oh, so the breakup was going to be her fault? 'I did suggest . . . ' She stopped. She was not going to take the blame and changed her tone. 'If she was only marrying you for the title, it sounds as though it might be a good thing.'

For once Charles did not come back with a retort. 'Patrick's just phoned back to say the people who wanted to lease the house are still keen and want to come down tomorrow. Patrick is coming with them. Look, Mother, I've got a game this afternoon, but I'll drive there tonight.'

'What time are they coming tomorrow?'

'Two o'clock.'

'I was going over to the Sheffords again tomorrow but I suppose I can put that off.'

'This is more important. I'll be late tonight, though. Don't wait up. I'll see you tomorrow morning.'

✶ ✶ ✶ ✶ ✶

The dogs barked when Charles' car came up the drive in the dark but soon settled back as he went up to his room.

Pamela had been up for some time the next morning before Charles appeared. Godley had a hospital appointment and she had refused to allow him to cancel it.

She felt sorry for Charles. She had warmed to Joanna and liked her father. Besides, Charles had never thought to marry any of his previous girlfriends. Rejection hurt.

'Breakfast?' she asked, when he finally appeared.

'Just coffee will do but not that instant stuff, Mother. Where's Godley?'

Pamela explained that Godley wasn't there today. The 'humph' of Charles' reply inferred he was not in a good temper.

She found a small coffee plunger in the larder and a bag of coffee. She brought them out.

'Do you have any plans for after the polo season? Were you thinking of going to Argentina?' she asked.

'I need to do something that brings in income. Although I wouldn't want a regular job would I?'

'Why not?' she asked.

'Because of my position, Mother.' His tone made him sound like an eight-year-old. 'Would you have your son working as a maître d' in a restaurant? Father would turn over in his grave. You'll have me being a truck driver next.'

'A truck driver isn't a bad idea.'

'Mother, it wouldn't be a good look.' He sounded more petulant than ever. 'I shouldn't need to earn an income. Father never did.'

'He had a job in the army.'

'It's all your fault. And Father's. You brought me up to inherit all this. Not to work.'

Pamela had put the coffee pot on the side of the Aga and reached for the boiling water. Suddenly she stopped. She stared at Charles. He was reading yesterday's paper and waiting for her to make his coffee.

'If you make the coffee, then you can make it how you like. There's milk in the fridge. No cream, I'm afraid.'

She paused. Charles looked up from his paper at her change in tone.

'Can't you do it?'

'No. And Charles, if there is one thing I've learnt since I've been away, it is how unimportant all that is. The title, the importance your father put on it. Yes, he had plenty of money to enjoy the position. Until he lost it. And what have I done with the title? Opened fêtes in the old days, given speeches at school functions. It's all so antiquated.'

For once, Charles was silent, listening to her.

'Because some ancestor donated money to the king doesn't mean we can sit back in luxury while the serfs wait upon us. Not now.' She walked towards the sink and looked out of the window. 'Even helping with the hospice was only because I had a title and a big house. Although I suppose it did help the community.'

Charles looked taken aback by her outburst. 'Having a title is an honour. Even having all this,' he said, waving his arms around.

'But it wasn't you that earned it.' She went on quickly. 'I'm not saying give it all away. I'm just saying that a little more humility on your part would not go astray, Charles. You have to earn that honour.'

'I was born in the wrong generation,' complained Charles.

'You mean you weren't of a generation who thought nothing of taking a maid's illegitimate baby without her knowing and bringing it up as their heir.'

For once, Charles had no reply.

'It's time we both moved on. You are perfectly capable, and you know I'd always help. Lizzie – whose family have a far better title than us – offered me the job because I asked the right questions, not because I had a title too. Every time I walk into their shop, I get excited. Here, every time I open the door to the hall, I wonder what needs cleaning.'

She picked up the wide basket sitting on the bench beside her and walked towards the back door, the dogs running on ahead. 'I'm just going to get some more flowers for the hall,' she said.

Charles stood. The kettle was boiling. He spooned out some ground coffee and poured the water on top. He started to go towards the fridge but then stopped and stood where Pamela had been standing by the sink. Why did it have to be him who changed, dammit?

He watched his mother as she headed across the garden towards the path in the beech trees. It seemed a long time ago that she had found that body up there. A lot had happened since. Was he really living in the past? Could he change?

He looked down. A shaft of sunlight played on the flag-stone floor. It didn't quite reach him.

Acknowledgements and Author's note

The Alexandrite is a work of fiction. There is no village of Ashly in England and no Ashly House. I was brought up in the Home Counties and I have based Ashly in a corner of Hertfordshire I knew well as a child. I have not named the village because, like so many, it has changed over the years and the village I describe is not the village in 2013, at the time the book is set. In New Zealand, I have used existing towns and areas with fictitious, but plausible, farms and homes.

There is a rare mineral called an alexandrite with the properties described here and I am grateful to Terry and Di Seward for telling me about it.

The quote at the start of the book is from Debretts online guide to the peerage. *New Peerage* was first published in 1769 and they have been publishing up-to-date guides ever since.

This story involves the adoption of children. There are nine adoptees in our extended family and I thank them all for the fullness they have given our family and the inspiration they have given in writing about adoption.

None of the main characters are based on real people. There is no titled Scawton family as far as I can find out but I thank John and Jane Boardman for suggesting the name. Inevitably, some characters may have opinions or mannerisms which friends may recognize but I have tried to maintain all the characters with their own unique personalities. Although I have known a few baronets, I have never known any of them, or any of their families to have a similar mystery to the one described here.

If I were to thank all those who have helped me get this far my writing life – there are just too many. So I will mention some of those without whom this book would not have come into being.

First of all my husband Chris, my family and friends, both in New Zealand and England, have been encouraging throughout, with much more faith than I!

Many people have read, suggested, assessed, critiqued, edited and proofed the drafts of the manuscript. Kathy Gibson and Sue Taylor gave helpful comments on earlier drafts, our critique group of AUT alumni were essential in helping with later drafts. The Literary Consultancy, Lesley Marshal, Nicky Crutchley and especially Nina Seja have all edited the book at one stage or another. I was very fortunate to have James George, AUT's inspiring teacher of creative writing, as a mentor for my master's degree and as the literary adviser for Cloud Ink Press. All the members of Cloud Ink Press – Alana Cooke, Annabelle Grierson, Thalia Henry, Helen McNeil and former member Mark Johnson – have been very supportive and worked to bring the publication to the market. Warwick Russell and Paul Dowie both contributed to the cover design which Craig Voilich brought to life.

And lastly you, the reader. I hope you have enjoyed *The Alexandrite.*

Thank you all, so much.

About the Author

Dione Jones attempted to write her first book at aged 10. She was born and brought up in England, in a village similar to Ashly, where she could ride her pony to explore the surrounding National Trust common land. She achieved a B.A. at Trinity College, Dublin and then worked for an aeroplane salesman and learnt to fly, before venturing to New Zealand to help set up a laboratory to collect animal blood.

Once married to Chris, she followed his involvement in farming, polo and property. They have two adult children and three grandchildren and live in south Auckland. Apart from her family, dogs and horses, she is interested in the environment we live in, the social changes of the twentieth century – and, of course, good books and writing. Dione Jones has a Master of Creative Writing.

www.dionejones.com